Dear Reader,

Double Your Reading Pleasure (the unofficial Duets motto) can only begin to describe the fantastic books we have for you this month.

Kristin Gabriel, popular with Love & Laughter readers, will charm you with a woman who has too many fiancés in *Annie, Get Your Groom*. Then Jennifer Drew writes a You Tarzan, Me Jane story set in the corporate wilderness! Readers of Yours Truly books will recognize the fresh and exciting talent that is Jennifer Drew and we welcome her into Harlequin Duets with *Taming Luke*.

Jacqueline Diamond returns with the hilarious *The Bride Wore Gym Shoes*. Need I really say more?— except the heroine's friend predicts she is going to marry the most unsuitable, although delectable, man.

We're thrilled that Tracy South is back with her second book, *Maddie's Millionaire*. If you like eccentric characters and a story filled with charm, this is the novel for you.

I hope you're enjoying our books. Feel free to write to us!

Malle Vallik

Malle Vallik
Senior Editor
    Harlequin Duets
    Harlequin Books
    225 Duncan Mill Road
    Don Mills, Ontario
    M3B 3K9 Canada

The Bride Wore Gym Shoes

Flashbulbs blinded Krista, and then Connor pulled her into a swooping embrace.

He uttered a low growl, an instinctive response. Or maybe that sound came from her own throat, Krista thought distractedly.

For a moment she forgot that others were watching, indeed, capturing this embrace on film. She knew only that a torrent of hot lava was flooding her previously tranquil circulatory system.

His lips trailed down her throat to the collar of the sequined gown. She felt her breasts strain upward, waiting for his tongue to dart down into the bared circle of cleavage.

She wished they were alone. She wished the dress would peel away and let them get on with an indescribably delicious experience.

Instead, he righted her. "Okay, fellas," he told the photographers. "I think you've got enough."

Never, thought Krista.

Maddie's Millionaire

Maddie Randall's car was parked by his house, but where was she?

She wasn't on the porch, but the wooden front door was wide open, providing an invitation to every flying, biting insect known to man.

From inside the house, he heard the unmistakable lyrics of "Blue Christmas." It was definitely June. The song was definitely "Blue Christmas." It was a good thing the words were familiar, since the voice singing it was trying to make up in enthusiasm what it lacked in skill.

Keller stepped into his home. Maddie's back was to him as she nosed through his bookshelves.

He meant to ask, "What are you doing here?" or "Did you break into my house?" Instead, he heard himself say, "You really can't sing, can you?"

Maddie jumped slightly and whirled around. "Oh, it's you." Sport barked and ran to her. She crouched down to hug him, cooing in his ear.

For a split second Keller wondered what he would have to do to get that kind of welcome from her. Besides be born a dog, of course.

HARLEQUIN DUETS

ISBN 0-373-44074-X

THE BRIDE WORE GYM SHOES
Copyright © 1999 by Jackie Hyman

MADDIE'S MILLIONAIRE
Copyright © 1999 by Tracy Jones

This edition published by arrangement with Harlequin Books S.A.

® and TM are trademarks of the publisher. Trademarks indicated with ® are registered in the United States Patent and Trademark Office, the Canadian Trade Marks Office and in other countries.

Look us up on-line at: http://www.romance.net

Printed in U.S.A.

JACQUELINE DIAMOND

The Bride Wore Gym Shoes

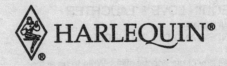

HARLEQUIN®

TORONTO • NEW YORK • LONDON
AMSTERDAM • PARIS • SYDNEY • HAMBURG
STOCKHOLM • ATHENS • TOKYO • MILAN • MADRID
PRAGUE • WARSAW • BUDAPEST • AUCKLAND

When **Jacqueline Diamond** got married, she wanted to elope. Her husband preferred a big wedding, so she told him, "Fine, if you do the work."

He became the lone male poking through wedding supply stores, photography studios and catering menus. He had to reassure confused clerks, who feared the bride might pop in to reverse his decisions.

The wedding came off perfectly. The one thing Jacqueline contributed was her white dress, which she sewed herself. It is, she says, the only thing she ever made that fit her. As for what shoes she wore, well, she swears she can't remember.

She did own a pair of red gym shoes. But she can't seem to find them....

Next month, look for *Assignment: Groom!* by Jacqueline (Harlequin American Romance #790) and *Mistletoe Daddy* on sale at Christmas (Harlequin American Romance #804).

Books by Jacqueline Diamond

HARLEQUIN DUETS
2—KIDNAPPED?

HARLEQUIN LOVE & LAUGHTER
11—PUNCHLINE
32—SANDRA AND THE SCOUNDREL

1

On Friday morning, Krista Lund was perfectly organized and only fifteen minutes late to the office. Everything would have been fine if only she hadn't tripped over the kitten.

It was all Connor Fallon's fault, of course.

She couldn't blame him for the fact that the first two pairs of panty hose she put on had holes in them, or for running out of coffee and having to stop at the convenience store for takeout. No real harm done; her first session wasn't scheduled for another half an hour.

She lived only a few miles from work, and, while some February gusts had littered the streets with palm fronds, traffic was light for Southern California. By her highly accurate watch, the drive had taken less than fifteen minutes, including the stop for coffee.

Krista had no trouble parking at the two-story white stucco office building. She slid her silver Taurus into her space in front of the sign that read: Krista Lund, Marriage and Family Counselor.

Before getting out, she checked the notepad clipped to her dashboard. Yes, she'd brought the files she'd taken home last night to review. Yes, lunch was in the bag.

If Krista didn't write things down, she got distracted. That's what had happened when she forgot to remind herself to buy more coffee yesterday. Organization was the key to overcoming life's chaos, she'd learned. Besides, checking things off a list gave her a warm buzz.

The problem, she discovered as she crossed the sidewalk toward her office, was the kitten. Sometimes Krista thought Connor collected animals as a hobby just so he could set them into her path or let them shed on the carpet in the office he rented from her.

Connor Fallon, private investigator, oozed animal magnetism. It drew women, a different one every time Krista looked, although she considered herself strictly an objective observer. As for stray dogs and cats, the minute they hit La Habra, California, they seemed to sense exactly where they could come to mooch.

Krista had never seen this particular gray-striped kitten before. Unfortunately, she didn't see it this time, either, because she was balancing her briefcase, a cup of coffee, her lunch, her purse and an oversize key ring.

She wasn't sure which came first: the screech of outrage from below, the dizzying sense of her long legs flying out from under her, or the sound of Connor's baritone voice calling, "Here, kitty— What the heck?"

Krista's knee hit the step with a jolt, and hot liquid splashed all over her green silk blouse. The words that immediately sprang to her lips were inappropriate for a twenty-nine-year-old woman who advised others on how to handle relationships in a mature manner, so all she said was, "Oh, shoot!"

"Are you hurt? Are you okay?" came his caressing

tones. A boyish lock of black hair fell across Connor's forehead and his eyes melted like chocolate as he knelt to scoop up the kitten.

The little creature spat toward Krista, baring a row of miniature barracuda teeth. Then it whimpered ingratiatingly, nestled against Connor's oxford-cloth shirt and began batting at his tie.

"Oh, I'm fine, thank you very much for asking." The sarcasm was lost on the man, Krista could see, but it made her feel better. Only a little, though, as she brushed herself off and discovered she had torn out the knee of her last pair of panty hose.

"What's going on? Is everyone okay?" From the other side of the building popped Ruth Roth, resident psychic. An imposing lady in her forties, she wore her champagne-beige hair brushed back, revealing a strong, sympathetic face. "Oh, Krista, did you hurt yourself again?"

"It's been days. More like a week." Last Wednesday, Krista had mashed her fingers grabbing for her car door as it swung shut with her keys inside.

"You shouldn't let yourself get so distracted." Ruth began collecting dropped items. "You need to focus on one thing at a time."

"I try to." Skirting a puddle of coffee, Krista picked up her keys. "It's just that I sometimes forget which thing I'm focusing on."

"Oh, by the way, I know I'm a little late with the rent," Connor said. He still hadn't apologized for the kitten and didn't look like he was going to. "I'll give you a check on Monday."

Only a week overdue. At least he always paid, or

had so far during the year he'd rented one of the three downstairs units.

Stroking the kitten, he swung back into his office. Krista didn't want to look, but she couldn't resist watching the masculine length of his stride and the slim-hipped tautness of his retreating butt.

"He's definitely an improvement over that accountant you used to rent to," Ruth noted as she helped Krista inside her office. "Do you need a change of clothing? I have a smock you could borrow."

"Thanks, but I've got a spare blouse." Krista kept one on hand, knowing she was inclined to spill things on herself. "I guess I can let my legs go bare. They're tan enough that no one should notice."

The outer office boasted a vacant receptionist's desk; Krista hadn't found a replacement since her secretary left to have a baby. On the right-hand wall, clear plastic racks offered pamphlets on parenting and communication.

The rest of the office projected an inviting warmth. She'd chosen the flowered couch and two stuffed chairs for their coziness, while balloons brightened the wallpaper. At the windows hung cheerful striped curtains, and, since some clients brought their children, one corner was furnished with toys.

"I'll straighten up your stuff." Ruth began mopping off Krista's purse with a wad of tissue. "You go change."

"Thanks." Ruth might be engaged in a dubious profession by Krista's standards, but she was a good-hearted soul. Her customers swore by her predictions, which she animated for them via a computer program so they could personally witness what the future might hold for them.

It was Ruth's contention that people remembered better when they experienced something visually. It was also possible, in Krista's opinion, that seeing was believing, and that Ruth instilled such faith in her clients that they turned her visions into self-fulfilling prophecies.

Anyway, Krista reflected as she went into the bathroom, she already knew what the future held for her: more stubbed toes and spilled coffee.

It was possible, she supposed, that her frequent stumbles and bumbles were due to some underlying psychological need to punish herself. She was reluctant to explore that subject, however, because the last time she tried, she'd become so preoccupied that she'd run her cart into a display of gefilte fish at Ralph's and disrupted the entire supermarket.

Thanks to stacks of lists and iron discipline, she'd managed to get a degree in counseling and save enough for a down payment on this building and on the bungalow where she lived. Now she needed to get her overactive thought processes under control and she'd be home free.

A dearth of stray kittens would help, too. Or maybe a less devil-may-care tenant.

Upstairs, the students at the Jon Lu School of Martial Arts began rampaging across the floor. Any day now, Krista expected to get a call from Caltech announcing that her second-floor tenants had scored a 6.0 on the Richter scale. Thank goodness the early morning class was ending soon and the students would be scattering to their day jobs.

She put on a tan blouse, mopped a stray splatter off her beige jacket, and emerged. Ruth held out a videotape.

"What's this?" Krista asked.

"Could you take a look?" the psychic asked. "I was on my way to bring it over when I saw the commotion."

"It's one of your visions?" Krista didn't care to get involved with such nonsense and besides, her first appointment was in ten minutes.

"It's about Melissa and Bret Graves." Last month, the couple had come to Ruth for a reading and had quarreled so much that she'd referred them to Krista. They'd gone through three counseling sessions, none very productive, and were returning this morning. "I thought you might want to warn her."

"Warn her?" It sounded ominous but this was, after all, some hokum Ruth had dreamed up. However, from what Krista knew of her tenant, it would take more time to argue than it would to screen the video, so she said, "I have to hurry."

"Then let's get on with it." Ruth led the way into Krista's private office.

Except for a desk against one wall, it resembled a family den right down to the toys on a low table and the VCR in one corner. On one wall hung a black-and-white dartboard, which allowed the more aggressive patients to vent their hostility.

Krista used it, too. When her frustrations spilled over, she would picture Connor's grinning face right in the middle, and score a bull's-eye.

After slipping in her video, Ruth turned on the TV.

A moment later, Krista found herself looking at a bird's-eye view of the white building and parking lot.

The animated graphics had a realistic, almost photographic quality. She recognized the Graves' blue Honda, parked next to Krista's silver sedan.

On the screen, a cartoon Melissa, complete with Brillo-pad red hair, stepped out of the office. "How did you get it to look so much like her?"

"I drew her from a photograph," said Ruth. "I shoot my clients at the first session—front and side views—and make sketches from the prints. Then I scan them into my computer, and the program fills in the rest."

"Amazing." Before Krista could stop herself, she asked, "Did you ever try to draw Connor's rear end?"

"One of my favorite subjects," said Ruth.

On the screen, a pickup truck zoomed into the lot. Out jumped a thin, pale man identifiable as Bret Graves. As his wife tried to wave him away, he aimed a spray can at the car.

The TV went dark. "That's all I saw," Ruth admitted. "I thought she should be alerted in case they break up. He might decide to damage her car out of spite."

"I see what you mean. Literally." Actually, the video gave Krista the willies. She didn't like the sense that she'd witnessed a real scene instead of make-believe.

More than ever, she understood why so many of Ruth's visions came true. Even a scientist knew how profoundly the mind influenced the body.

The psychic had predicted, a month before it happened, that Krista's secretary would fulfill her goal of becoming pregnant. No doubt the secretary's renewed confidence had been a factor in her success.

Which meant Krista had better not show the tape to Melissa and Bret when they arrived. It might give the guy ideas.

"Thanks." She removed the tape from the VCR and handed it to her neighbor. "But as far as I know, he'll be accompanying her today, not arriving in a pickup. Besides, I've seen their other car, and it's a white Olds."

Ruth hopped to her feet as the front chimes rang. "Sounds like they're here."

Sure enough, there was Melissa Graves in the outer office, her hair even wirier and, if possible, redder than ever. After greeting them, she paced over to the window and peered through the curtains.

"Gotta go." Ruth folded her hand a couple of times as if waving goodbye or, possibly, trying to catch a fly in midair, and scooted out.

After the psychic departed, Krista said, "Will your husband be joining us?"

Melissa hugged herself. "We had a fight yesterday and I threw him out. Would you mind if we talk in this room rather than your office? I want to keep an eye on my car."

Krista got a twitchy feeling. *It was just Ruth's fantasy on that videotape.* "What do you mean?"

"It would be like him to get back at me by letting the air out of my tires," Melissa said.

Letting air out of tires wasn't the same as spray painting, Krista told herself. It wasn't even in the ballpark. To further settle her edginess, she added, "He's driving the Olds, right?"

"No, it's in the shop. He borrowed a pickup truck from work," Melissa said. "Have you seen one around?"

"No. Not…really." She struggled to maintain her composure. The world operated in an orderly fashion; it always had and it always would. She refused to accept, just because of a few minor coincidences, that anyone could see the future. "Why don't you tell me about your fight?"

"The man's impossible. Selfish and…" Melissa launched into a series of scathing adjectives.

As she listened, Krista hoped Bret wasn't going to show up and make the rest of Ruth's prediction come true.

Well, of course he wouldn't. The very idea was preposterous.

CONNOR FALLON needed a woman. Ordinarily, that wouldn't pose a problem, but he needed a woman who looked like his uncoordinated neighbor.

Not for himself, but for an assignment. A very lucrative one. If only she would spare him one weekend!

It was hopeless, of course. In addition to being his landlady, which was never a good omen, Krista had shown no remorse about practically obliterating poor Futz-Paws, who was even now drowning her sorrow in Cheez-Its.

Worse, Krista had almost as quick a brain as he did, and didn't hesitate to use it. He'd caught the sharp edge of her tongue often enough to have scars.

Usually he enjoyed their battles of wits. Today, however, he could use a reprieve, but she wasn't likely to take pity on him. Especially when he was three days late with the rent.

He glanced again at the fax. The photo of Ellen Hardison showed a young woman with short blond hair and expressive eyes that were, according to the description, blue. She wasn't as pretty as Krista Lund, in his opinion, and might be a couple of inches shorter, but still, they could pass for sisters.

With most women, a bit of charm and the promise of a romantic Las Vegas vacation would have done the trick. The only thing that might work with Krista was pointing out that helping him with this assignment would enable Connor to pay his rent for the next few months.

Not that he was broke. During his ten years on the LAPD, he'd saved a fair amount and invested it well. However, he'd sworn never to touch his nest egg for day-to-day living and, besides, his investments weren't liquid.

The world was full of tall blondes, Connor supposed, but he doubted he could find a suitable one with two days' notice. So how was he going to talk his klutzy landlady into this?

He allowed himself, in a moment's self-indulgence, to picture the lady counselor in a luxurious suite with its own heated whirlpool. Lounging in a swimsuit…make that a bikini. Naked would be better, but he had to keep a grip on himself or he wouldn't be able to function for the rest of the day.

It wasn't Connor's habit to fantasize about landladies, especially his. Krista, though, had a sweet sensual quality that put him off guard, usually right before she skewered him with some acid remark.

He hated to admit it, but he liked the way she never bought into his snow jobs. Underneath the soft exterior, she could be tough, a quality he admired, though in moderation. Last month she'd dared to tack a late charge onto the rent, and he'd even momentarily considered paying it.

Stretching his legs and plopping his feet on top of the clutter on his desk, Connor recalled how angrily those blue eyes had flashed this morning. Tumbling over a kitten had ruffled her short blond hair, almost as if he'd run his hands through it. He wondered what she would say if he tried it.

Krista's intensity hinted at a passionate nature that could use some awakening. Connor wouldn't mind volunteering for the job, which brought him back to the Las Vegas spa and his landlady in a bikini.

Okay, now just suppose he talked her into the trip and the pool and the fantasy. Those firm, round breasts would form tantalizing mounds above the scooped edge of the bra. The steam would leave strands of hair sticking to her forehead and temples, and her lips would part hungrily as she watched him swim lazily toward her across the pool....

Next door, a woman began shouting. Connor tried to ignore it, but then he heard a tenor response from the parking lot and realized these quarrelsome intruders, whoever they might be, weren't going to disappear.

Besides, someone might be messing with the cars. Specifically, with *his* car, a green 1968 Firebird with a new paint job and a restored black hardtop.

Annoyed, Connor quickly swung his feet off the desk. Standing up proved more awkward than expected, due to the effects of a seductive image of Krista on his fully functioning male hormones. With a groan, he put on his jacket and went outside.

A thin young man stood with legs braced, spraying whipped cream over a blue Honda. The bad news was that the car taking a frosting sat right next to Connor's, and flecks of white foam were blowing onto it.

The Honda must belong to that plumpish woman with the red porcupine hair. In addition to hopping up and down on the sidewalk, she was, Connor noticed, waving a container of pepper spray.

This situation could easily get out of hand. There was no telling what damage pepper spray might do to his paint.

And here came Krista, calling, "Bret, please, let's talk about this!"

Ignoring her, the young man striped the Honda's windshield with whipped cream. Connor went back into his office. He came out armed.

Nobody paid any attention as he strolled across the parking lot, until he got close to the Honda. Then Bret turned toward him with a snarl.

"Spoon?" said Connor, and held out a plastic one.

"What?" the man said.

"You going to waste all that whipped cream?" he asked. "Got any cherries?"

"Connor, I think you should go inside." Krista spoke in the soothing yet authoritarian tones that Connor might use to dissuade stray dogs from eating his shoes.

He turned toward the round lady. "Pepper tastes

lousy on sundaes. You wouldn't happen to have any chocolate sauce, would you?''

Her face displayed surprise, then dismay. ''Actually, I do.''

''You have chocolate sauce in your car?'' said the man named Bret.

''It's in the trunk,'' she snapped. ''With the melted ice cream I bought for your birthday. If you hadn't started yelling at me the moment I got home, I wouldn't have forgotten them!''

''You were at the supermarket? I was ticked that I got home on my birthday and you weren't there.''

''Well, I see you've been celebrating without me.'' She pointed at the whipped cream.

''I swiped it from my mom's fridge,'' he admitted.

''You're staying at your mother's?''

''Where did you think I was staying?''

''Well, you're always talking about that new woman at work.''

''You're jealous?'' said her astonished husband.

''Here.'' Connor handed them each a spoon. ''Clean up, will you? Krista, care for some?''

The corners of her mouth quirked. ''No, thanks. Bret, Melissa, why don't we go inside? I think we're finally making progress here.''

''I never thought—you were buying ice cream for me?'' The man couldn't take his eyes off his wife.

''I figured you picked a fight so you'd have an excuse to spend your birthday with someone else,'' she said.

''I wouldn't do that!''

Krista took their arms and led them inside. Connor went around the building and came back with a hose.

He was spraying off the cream from his car when he noticed Ruth watching him from the walkway.

"So it did happen," she said. "Maybe now Krista will realize I'm not a kook."

"You foresaw this?" Connor didn't believe in psychics; most of them were outright frauds. However, he knew of some who consulted for police departments, so he tried to give his neighbor the benefit of the doubt.

"I have visions all the time," the older woman said. "About you, even."

"Such as?"

"You're going to find that kitten a home this afternoon," she said. "You'll meet a nice lady and two kids at the gas station."

It wasn't a bad idea. If he hung around a gas station long enough with the kitten mewing, someone might fall in love with it. "Get any tidbits about our landlady?"

"Sure."

"It wouldn't be her giving me a break on the rent, would it?" Stepping over a rivulet of water, he went to turn off the hose.

When he came back, Ruth said, "She's going to have a fender bender today or tomorrow. I've been debating whether I should tell her. Some people don't want to know about the future, even about minor things."

That was when Connor got his idea. It would solve a lot of problems. For him, anyway.

"You think you could persuade her that you can really see the future?" he asked.

"I *can* see the future," Ruth said.

"Yeah, yeah." He tried in vain to suppress his sarcasm. "I mean, great. So you go ahead and prove it to her, and then I've thought of a way that you could help Krista loosen up and live a little. You agree she needs to get out more, don't you?"

"She does seem rather isolated," Ruth agreed cautiously.

"Well, why don't you picture her going to Las Vegas and soaking in a whirlpool?" Connor asked. "With me. And then I'll figure out a way to make it come true. I mean, once you've broken the ice."

The psychic eyed him sternly. "You're asking me to fake a video? I would never..." She paused with a strange expression on her face. "Wait a minute."

Her eyes glazed over. For an alarmed moment, Connor wondered if she were having an attack of some kind, until she started to laugh.

"What?" he demanded.

Ruth tried to speak, and doubled over, hooting. When she finally righted herself, she shook her head.

"I wouldn't touch this one," she said. "It's too preposterous even for me." She started for her office, but swung around halfway there. "It would serve you right!" she called.

Psychics. Anybody who believed in them ought to have his brains dry-cleaned, Connor reflected grumpily.

Now where was he going to find a tall blonde to go to Las Vegas with him for the weekend?

2

AFTER SENDING Melissa and Bret home for a late birthday celebration, Krista took a Connor break.

Ever since the rangy, dark-haired man with the bedroom eyes had rented the office next door, she'd found herself unable to resist fantasizing about him. Not often. Not more than three or four times a day.

Knowing that her next client wasn't due for half an hour, she tried to busy herself updating records in the computer.

It didn't work.

Images of Connor kept creeping in. That melting gaze, turned not toward the kitten but on Krista herself.

That spectacular butt, tightening as he—well, she wasn't sure how she could exactly see his rear end when he was poised over her, but, in a fantasy, it worked.

Those corded thighs. That teasing grin, hovering halfway between sarcasm and seduction. The grin wasn't anywhere near the corded thighs, but that didn't seem to matter, either.

It was a good thing, she told herself, that not all visions came true. Because Connor Fallon was the wrong man for her in every way.

He blew through life and relationships—judging by

the series of girlfriends she'd observed—like a cyclone. She was cautious and sensible, as well as old-fashioned enough to have preserved her virginity until the age of twenty-nine.

Before she went to bed with a man, he would have to be Mr. Right. Someone she could count on. In fact, she had a list at home of all the qualities she required in a man, none of which Connor remotely possessed. So why couldn't she stop thinking about him?

It was a relief when Ruth sauntered into the office. "How did it turn out with Melissa and Bret?" she asked. "Remember, I have a vested interest in that pair. They were my clients first."

Sitting behind her neatly arranged desk, Krista folded her hands. "Once they started talking, they opened up to each other for the first time. A real breakthrough. Sorry, but I can't tell you any more."

"Professional ethics. I know." Ruth smoothed her embroidered green caftan. Red and amber stones set into the fabric glowed beneath the overhead light.

"How did you do that?" Krista asked.

"Do what?" Ruth frowned.

"How did you predict the scene in the parking lot? You must have known Bret had borrowed a pickup. Was the rest guesswork?"

The older woman paced across the pile carpet. "You refuse to accept that my visions are real. Well, that isn't unusual. But it makes certain things difficult."

"What things?" Krista asked.

"I hardly know where to begin," her tenant said. "You've been on my mind a lot."

Krista got a funny feeling. "Don't tell me you've

had a vision about *me*. Ruth, I don't believe in that stuff."

The psychic thought for a moment. "I'll tell you what. I've seen two different things, but one is so peculiar, it may be some kind of aberration. The other one, however, is small, but you should be warned."

"Warned? I'm in some kind of danger?"

"Not necessarily," Ruth said. "Not if you take evasive action."

Krista wasn't sure whether to be concerned about what Ruth might have foreseen, or to indulge her curiosity. She chose the latter. "You mean the visions don't have to come true?"

"Not if people take precautions," Ruth said. "It's my belief that I was given this gift so I can help people."

"If you wanted to warn me, that kitten would have been a good place to start," Krista grumbled. "Don't tell me this has anything to do with Connor."

Ruth peered at her with a guilty expression. "Well, not the vision I'm going to tell you about."

That meant that the other prediction, the bizarre one, did, Krista realized. Despite her skepticism, she felt her throat tighten.

What exactly did Ruth see Connor doing? What if there were such a thing as thought transference, and scandalous images of those powerful thighs and that pumping rear end had thrust themselves right into the adjacent office? Heaven help Krista if Ruth started reading her mind!

"You didn't make a tape, did you?" she asked, holding her breath.

"Oh, it was too routine to bother." Ruth tapped

her fingers on the desk. "I saw you backing your car into a pole or a narrow pillar of some kind. I suggest you take extra care driving for the next day or so."

"Is that all?"

"What were you expecting?"

"You mentioned Connor," she said.

"No, you mentioned Connor. Besides, that was the second vision." Her neighbor eyed her speculatively. "Of course, if you'd really like to know…"

"Never mind. A pillar or a post?" Krista hurried on. "They have those in the parking garage at the Brea Mall, but I wasn't planning to go shopping this weekend, so I'm safe."

"I hope so." Ruth sighed. "You'll never be a believer, will you?"

"If a pole materializes in the middle of the parking lot, I might be."

"I'm glad I didn't tell you the other one," Ruth said. "It's the first time I've had a vision I couldn't believe."

"The one with Connor in it?" Krista probed, despite her best intentions. "So what was he doing, paying his rent on time? That *would* be a surprise."

"I wouldn't want to strain your credulity any further," was all Ruth said before she left.

"She could have at least given me a hint," Krista groused aloud to the empty office.

The Connor in her mind grinned knowingly and shrugged his outrageously broad shoulders. Then he pinned Krista to the bed and resumed doing what he'd been doing before they were interrupted.

AT LUNCHTIME, Connor decided to take the kitten home before it knocked the papers off his desk for the third time. He tried to stuff it into a box, but it mewed piteously and its tail kept getting caught when he attempted to close the lid.

Giving up, he let it curl happily on the seat beside him. They would be traveling less than two miles, anyway.

En route, he stopped at a drive-in convenience mart to get cat food. As he waited in his car for the window clerk to ring up the purchase, he hoped Futz-Paws wouldn't be lonely. The Moochers Club, also known as Connor's back yard, was temporarily empty of other strays.

He found homes for most of his four-legged friends. However, the most recent arrival, a tomcat, had decamped following an abortive attempt to put it in a cat carrier so it could be taken to be neutered. Its reservations were completely understandable, in Connor's opinion.

"Look!" A childish squeal drew his attention to the passenger window, through which peered a little boy. "Mommy, it looks like Whiskers!"

"It's a Baby Whiskers!" piped the little girl beside him.

Their mother shifted her daughter's position on her hip. "Honey, Whiskers was old and he went to heaven, remember?"

"Me wuv him!" wailed the toddler.

"Look how cute it is," added the boy. "Maybe they're related."

Their mother glanced inside with an apologetic expression. "I'm sorry, mister. We had a gray-striped cat that died recently." Her weary expression softened as the kitten mewed at her. ''It is awfully sweet.''

This was an opportunity not to be missed, especially since Baby Whiskers, formerly Futz-Paws, had begun sharpening its claws on Connor's new black upholstery. Rolling down the window, he said, ''This kitten is free to a good home, ma'am.''

''Really?''

''I'm serious. It's a stray.''

''How can I resist?'' she said. ''Thank you very much.''

As if to show its assent, the kitten propped its paws on the bottom of the open window, leaned out and began to purr. Amid the delighted cries of the children, the woman hoisted it to her shoulder, and off they went.

Ruth had more or less predicted this scene, Connor recalled, although she'd been wrong about the gas station. Then he saw the family getting into their car in front of a pump. When had the convenience store owner added gas service?

He wasn't sure how Ruth had done it, but what a great gimmick! She even had Connor halfway convinced she was psychic.

He paid for the cat food, which he would need sooner or later anyway, and headed back to the office. A dozen phone calls failed to turn up a tall blonde for hire, however.

Now more than ever, he believed Ruth offered his best chance at persuading their mutual landlady to help him. Connor didn't have a plan yet, but he figured he would come up with one any minute now.

"I NEVER MISUSE my gift," Ruth sniffed as Connor stood in her doorway, laying his most boyish grin on her.

"I'm only asking you to tweak it a little."

"Tweak what?" she demanded. "If there's any tweaking to be done around here, I must ask you to leave Krista and me out of it."

"There's nothing immoral about what I'm asking!"

"You want me to pretend I see her spending a weekend with you in a hotel?" she snapped.

"I told you, it's a job. Strictly business." Although he struggled to maintain his air of nonchalance, Connor felt his face coloring. What was it about the two women in this building that made him feel like an overgrown adolescent?

Ruth aroused his long-suppressed sense of embarrassment. Krista aroused something entirely different: a set of male hormones that had mercifully subsided after his midtwenties but were now raging so furiously, they deserved a nap. Preferably in the same bed as her hormones.

Connor was on the verge of leaving when the image on Ruth's computer screen caught his eye. "Wait a minute! That's me in that picture!"

She glanced over her shoulder. "Oh, that," she muttered, and waved one hand helplessly. It was the first time he'd seen his neighbor at a loss for words.

He must have caught her in the act, Connor thought, although he wasn't yet sure what act that might be. "Come on. What's your vision this time?" *And how can I use it to persuade Krista to go to Las Vegas with me?*

Before she could block his path, he strode into the center of the room. He'd forgotten about the wind chimes and macramé decorations strategically hung from the ceiling, and got bonked in the forehead twice on his way to the computer.

It was worth it. On the screen, Connor stared open-mouthed at the cartoonish picture of himself and Krista, and what they were doing. The corners of his mouth sneaked into a disbelieving smile.

"Well, well, Ruth," he drawled. "I didn't know you were branching into fiction."

"I know it's hard to believe, but..."

From outside, came a crash. More of a crunch, really. Followed by the sound of an engine gunning and tires screeching.

"Krista!" Ruth hurried toward the door. "I knew this would happen! Oh, dear, I hope she's all right!"

An unfamiliar fear twisted Connor's gut. Had something happened to that sweet-faced, ditzy blonde with the wide blue eyes? He didn't know why the prospect filled him with such gut-wrenching alarm, and he didn't give himself time to dwell on it.

Ducking past Ruth, he raced outside, and scanned the scene. A dazed Krista sat behind the wheel of the silver Taurus she'd backed partway from its space. On the other side of the cramped lot, a small flatbed truck was madly trying to turn around.

"Are you all right?" he shouted.

Stiffly, she nodded.

"Are you sure?"

"Yes. I think so."

A metal rod rolled off the back of her car and clanged to the pavement. One of the truck's load of poles must have come loose and crashed into the Taurus.

Sheer rage shot through Connor as the driver tried to straighten his wheels and escape. He wasn't sure where this protective fury came from, but the sight of Krista's stunned expression galvanized him.

Without giving a thought to the danger, he leapt across the blacktop. Seeing him coming, the ashen-faced driver stomped on the gas pedal, but in his panic he must have put the truck into neutral, because the motor roared impotently.

Reaching through the open window, Connor yanked the keys from the ignition. He barely restrained the urge to grab the hit-and-run driver and shake him.

"What did you think you were doing?" he demanded. "You could have killed somebody! Let me see your license!"

"Don't hit me!" At close range, the guy looked young and scared as he fished his wallet from his pocket. "I didn't mean any harm. It's my first day on the job and I got lost. Please don't call the police!"

"Get out," Connor roared, although his anger began to subside when he saw Krista walking toward them, a bit shaky but unharmed. A glance at the young man's license revealed that the kid's name was Benjamin and that he would celebrate his eighteenth birthday next week. "You're new on the job, eh, Ben?"

"Please don't turn me in." The young man's lips trembled. "My parents will kill me if I lose this job. I panicked. It was wrong. I'll never do it again."

Connor still wasn't inclined to cut the guy any

slack, until Ruth said, "He's telling the truth. He *won't* do it again."

He supposed he ought to believe her. Besides, the decision belonged to Krista, who said, "The last time I reported a minor incident like this, it proved more trouble than it was worth."

"You need to secure that load," Ruth added from the sidewalk. "Who tied it that way?"

"I did," said Ben. "They seemed to expect me to know how, so I fixed it myself."

"Next time you don't know how to do something, ask!" Connor said sharply.

"Yes, sir."

Grumbling under his breath, he helped the young man reload the fallen pole and secure his cargo. They checked the Taurus, which had sustained a few scratches.

"I've got matching paint," Krista said. "I can touch it up."

Connor provided directions to Ben's destination. The young man thanked them profusely and left.

Krista sagged against her car, her vulnerable expression reminding Connor of a frightened kitten. It made him want to wrap his arms around her and take care of her.

Fiercely, he reined in his sympathy. Collecting lost animals was one thing. Women were another.

Connor had been married once, early in his police career. He'd learned the kind of lesson a man never forgets: that the daily grind takes the joy out of a relationship, for both the man and the woman.

He and Lydia had started out as enthusiastic lovers. After their wedding, though, the day-by-day pressures had gradually robbed them of their spontaneity and turned them into crabby roommates.

Lydia had been the one who called it off, saying she couldn't handle the stress of being married to a cop. Connor believed, however, that it was marriage itself that had destroyed their relationship.

Freedom was a great aphrodisiac. Routine killed all the fun.

Still, gazing at Krista's full, slightly parted lips, he couldn't resist saying, "You wouldn't happen to need mouth-to-mouth resuscitation, by any chance?"

"Stuff it." Ruth steered Krista toward her own office. "She needs coffee, loverboy, not you."

"You never know," said Connor, and tagged along.

MOUTH-TO-MOUTH resuscitation, Krista mused, still in a fog from the shock of her accident. Would it really have been such a bad idea?

She felt giddy, as if her brain had been pickled in a brine of endorphins. It kept replaying the sight of Connor pounding across the parking lot in pursuit of the fleeing truck.

He'd sprung to her defense. Despite her confusion, she hadn't missed the fierce protectiveness in his face when he ran outside. And she'd felt, for a precious moment, some of the security she'd known as a child, before her father virtually abandoned his family.

What was wrong with her? She wasn't a child, or some princess in a tower waiting for a knight to rescue her. Especially not a knight who was nearly a week late with his rent, she reminded herself.

Ruth escorted her into the last office on the left, a

large room decorated with sixties-style macramé hangings and overstuffed velour couches. On the walls hung poster-size framed photographs of a Buddhist temple and the ruins at Delphi.

The psychic clucked about like a mother hen, fixing coffee and tucking a couple of vanilla wafers onto a plate. "You've had a shock. You need sugar and caffeine to jump-start your system."

"I'm fine. Really." A memory came to Krista, floating at the edge of her consciousness. Something about Ruth and a parking lot. "Oh, my gosh!"

"What?" came Connor's worried baritone. "Is something broken?"

"No. It's that she predicted this." Krista's throat got so thick, she had to cough before continuing. "Ruth said I would back into a rod or a narrow pillar. I didn't believe her. It was as if the pole came out of nowhere."

"I don't enjoy being right when something bad happens." Ruth handed her the coffee and cookies.

"Are you ever wrong?" Connor asked. It surprised Krista that he wasn't more skeptical.

"I've been wrong a few times," Ruth said. "Fate can be circumvented, although it has a stubborn way of reasserting itself."

The psychic positioned herself in front of her computer, blocking the screen. How odd, Krista thought as she sipped the hot liquid. Could Ruth be hiding something?

She was munching a cookie when she remembered that there'd been a second vision, one involving Connor. Could that be what Ruth didn't want her to see?

A preposterous scenario, she'd said. Except that

Krista was now ninety-nine percent convinced that Ruth really could foretell the future.

She needed to see that computer. Her intense reaction to Connor a few minutes ago had emphasized her vulnerability. She had to armor herself against him, and forewarned was forearmed.

"You've animated your other prediction, haven't you?" she said.

Reluctantly, Ruth nodded.

"I want to see it." Behind her, Connor cleared his throat. Intuition told Krista that he'd already viewed it. Now she *had* to know what it was. "Show me!"

The psychic wavered, then stepped aside. "I have no right to keep you in the dark. But it's so outrageous, I'm ashamed for anyone to see it."

"I won't tell." Krista moved toward the screen.

She stared at the animated sequence for several seconds before its meaning penetrated, and then she felt a wave of dismay. This wasn't merely wild, it was unthinkable. A nightmare.

According to Ruth's vision, Krista was going to marry Connor Fallon.

3

KRISTA FELT as if she were falling. Through the rabbit hole, perhaps, or into Connor's bed, which amounted to the same thing.

It would be one thing if the man were capable of love, and faithfulness, and reliability. But he was dangerous, in more ways than one.

Around Connor, Krista felt stirrings of the impulsive person she'd once been, the one she'd struggled to suppress since her father left. If she weren't careful, she could easily succumb to a vibrant primitive male who would sweep her off her feet—and drop her with a thud when he moved on to something new.

There he was, onscreen, perfectly realized. It was obvious Ruth hadn't been joking about appreciating his rear end, because she'd caught muscular inlets practically invisible through his slacks to any but the keenest observer.

When he changed position on the screen, Krista saw that the artist had also captured the knowing tilt of his chin, the half-scornful curve of his mouth, and a dirt smear on his cheek. But what on earth was he wearing?

Over his rumpled tuxedo lay a sash of white fabric and atop his head sat a turban. The getup reminded Krista of an old film she'd seen, set in India.

"What's that costume for?" she blurted. "And why does he have a smudge on his face?"

"I don't think it's a formal wedding...the dirty face is optional," Connor said. "But hey, you don't look bad yourself."

According to the vision, Krista was going to get married wearing a monstrously fluffy white wedding gown with pink bows stuck all over it. From her hair sprouted huge fake daisies.

Instead of a bouquet, she clutched a whisk broom. And from beneath the stiff hem of her gown peeped a pair of bright red gym shoes.

Krista had never gone so far as to make a list of what she planned to wear to her wedding. She felt certain that when she did, however, those items would not be on it.

Under a rose-garlanded trellis stood a minister in a dark suit. Beside him, the best man wore ill-fitting plaid clothes and had a camera dangling around his neck.

"Do you recognize that guy?" she asked.

Connor shook his head. "No, but I think it's very efficient of me to have my best man double as the photographer. Think of the savings!"

"Is that all you can think of?" she demanded.

"Not by a long shot." He leveled her a probing look.

Did he mean the wedding night? Or something more? But Connor Fallon would never want more, she was certain of that.

A shift on the screen caught her attention. Suddenly the bridesmaids came into view.

One young woman resembled Krista so strongly

they might have been sisters. Even more oddly, the woman also wore a wedding dress, although her shoes weren't nearly as colorful.

The other bridesmaid resembled Krista's Aunt Bea. An energetic woman who had retired last year from her job as a legal secretary in Philadelphia, Bea— whom Krista had never seen wear anything undignified, even on vacation—was garbed in a short, shiny black cocktail-waitress dress, complete with mesh stockings and a small tray of drinks.

"Ruth, I didn't know you'd met my Aunt Bea." She couldn't tear her eyes from the screen.

"Is that who that is?" said her tenant.

"Then you haven't met her?" Indeed, it would scarcely have been possible. Until last year, Bea had never traveled further west than Chicago in her sixty-six years.

Last fall, she'd taken off in a motor home and was, at last report, somewhere in Canada, enjoying the splendors of nature. According to Bea's last Christmas letter, she was tired of her restricting life-style and planned to turn over a new leaf. Literally.

"The woman simply appeared in my vision," Ruth said.

"You made her up?"

"Believe me, I couldn't have invented something this weird," the psychic said. "The fact that she's your aunt is a sign that this is a true vision. I'm afraid it confirms that this wedding, crazy as it looks, is going to take place."

Krista couldn't accept that. "Surely there was something different about this vision from your other ones?'' she probed. ''Maybe it isn't a prediction, but a symbol.''

''I doubt it.'' Deep lines creased Ruth's forehead. ''My having two previous visions that more or less involved you, well, those were signs, too. They were preparing us for this—revelation, if you will.''

At one time, Krista would have laughed off the whole situation. But Bret *had* arrived in a pickup and sprayed his wife's car. A pole *had* appeared behind Krista's bumper, too. Still... ''Me marry Connor? It's ludicrous.''

''Oh, come now. Ludicrous?'' rumbled the topic of conversation. ''If I had feelings, you might have hurt them.''

He moved closer, until his breath whispered across Krista's cheek. It made her skin prickle, her breasts tighten and her brain begin replaying the fantasy about the bed and the corded thighs.

This was insanity, or as close to it as she ever cared to come. Few things are given to man, or woman, to know absolutely, but this much came clear to Krista: Connor was not the kind of man she should ever consider marrying.

Not only did he date a variety of women, but he kept no pets except strays, for which he quickly found new homes. He even chose plastic office plants so he wouldn't have to remember to water them. This was not a man who would stick around for a lifetime.

Yet her long-suppressed instincts yearned for one shot at him. To see those eyes shine for her, and touch his cheek, and hold him through the night.

Krista shuddered. Never would she put herself in such a vulnerable position.

Still, she couldn't simply ignore Ruth's vision. She needed to reassure herself she would never be foolish or deluded enough to walk down the aisle with Connor.

"Could this be something other than an actual wedding?" she ventured. "Like a costume party?"

Ruth sighed. "It would be a rather odd setup, don't you think? Besides, who gives costume parties in February?"

"No one I know." Not to mention the fact that Aunt Bea wouldn't be caught dead in a getup like that. Furthermore, as far as Krista knew, her aunt was somewhere north of Manitoba, communing with beavers.

"I've got an idea," Connor said.

His voice resonated into Krista's ear. She discovered the previously unsuspected medical fact that the bones of the inner ear are connected directly to the hips and pelvis.

Of its own accord, her body swayed rhythmically. This brought her derriere into riveting contact with the same muscular thighs that had been dominating her imagination in spare moments.

It was a musical sequence, a torrid tango and a shock, because when her buttocks brushed Connor's midsection, she discovered that his libido had also joined the act. To put it plainly, another rod had materialized out of nowhere.

Krista decided there and then that she would never back up again as long as she lived.

"You have an idea?" she said shakily.

"Mmm-hmm." He brought his cheek down against her hair. "I sure do."

"Not in my office, you don't!" said Ruth.

"It isn't that kind of idea." Connor ambled away and propped himself against the wall. "I have an idea about how to keep this wedding nonsense from coming to pass."

"What would that be?" asked the psychic, much to Krista's relief, because she didn't trust her own vocal cords.

"If what you've seen comes true once," he said, "it can't come true twice, can it?"

"It's never happened as far as I know," the psychic conceded.

"Aha!" Connor dusted his hands as if he'd proved a point.

"Aha what?" Krista steadied herself against the desk. The computer, which had run out of animation, began showing a screen-saver scene of the *Titanic* sinking. It seemed apt.

"We stage the whole thing," he said. "There's a costume shop in Fullerton that I use when I have to disguise myself on assignments. We could find people who resemble those guys and walk through it."

"A woman who's practically my twin?" Krista demanded. "Do you know someone like that?"

"We could put Ruth in a blond wig," he offered. "Some of the details might not be perfect, but didn't she say you would back into either a rod or a narrow pillar? The visions aren't exact."

"That's true," Ruth conceded.

"We stage the whole thing, and then we're safe!" he said.

Ruth folded and unfolded her arms. "No one's ever tried to stage one of my visions before. I'll wear a wig if you like, but I can't promise it will keep what I saw from occurring.''

''There's a first time for everything,'' said Connor.

Why would he offer to put on a turban and smudge his face, let alone stage this entire charade? He had to have an ulterior motive.

''In return for your cooperation, you expect me to waive a month's rent?'' Krista guessed.

''I beg your pardon!'' He drew himself up, the picture of affronted dignity, and grazed a macramé hanging. ''I always pay my debts.''

''Eventually,'' she conceded. ''Come on, what's the catch?''

''I need your help with an assignment in Las Vegas this weekend.'' Connor brushed the hanging aside. ''One that will pay my rent for several months to come. That's all I ask. A little help.''

''In Las Vegas? What kind of help?''

''I'll explain as we go.''

If the vision were real, Krista must find a way to circumvent it. On the other hand, she couldn't possibly put herself in Connor's power for a weekend. Not only didn't she trust him, she didn't trust herself.

His assignment must be a tough one, or he'd have found a female to assist him already. Still, she didn't need the details to know it was wrong, wrong, wrong.

''No,'' she said.

''I suggest you reconsider.'' He quirked an eyebrow.

Anxiety nibbled at Krista's resolve, but she forced herself to remember that she was a trained counselor, an objective observer and a social scientist. ''I'm sorry, Ruth, but despite everything, I can't take this prediction seriously.''

''Maybe that's for the best,'' said the psychic.

''It's not for my best.'' Connor looked so rueful, with a shock of black hair falling over one corner of his forehead, that Krista could barely restrain herself from mussing it. ''I need you.''

His words hung in the air. ''You need me,'' Krista said quietly, ''the way you need a full tank of gas or a sack of groceries. That's not very flattering, Mr. Fallon.''

An unfamiliar expression flickered across his face. Was it regret, or simply embarrassment? ''Maybe you should give me a chance,'' he said. ''Maybe we'd find out...''

''What? That you had something in mind in taking me to Las Vegas besides making a buck and having a little fun?'' She was surprised to feel tears stinging behind her eyes. What on earth was wrong with her?

''Do you want more?'' he asked.

It was a scary question, and an unfair one. ''You only want an answer so you can use it to manipulate me,'' she said. ''Sorry, I'm not playing this game.''

''You tell me the rules,'' he said. ''I'll play if I can.''

''I'm not playing, period.'' She straightened. ''I don't have any more appointments, so I'm going home for a long, quiet weekend. Alone.''

Connor pulled out a business card. ''Here's my pager number.''

''I have your pager number.''

''You have it at your office, but you need to take it home with you. Call at any hour. We could stage this thing in a hurry and be on our way tomorrow morning.''

Krista was tempted to throw the card in the trash, but there was no point in being rude. Irritably, she stuck it into her coat pocket.

"Sorry about this situation," said Ruth. "I wish I knew what it meant. Maybe it's the psychic's equivalent of hot flashes.''

"Let's hope so," said Krista.

"I WISH SHE would quit fighting her instincts," Connor confided after the silver Taurus pulled out of the lot. "There's so much bottled up inside that woman, I'm surprised she doesn't explode.''

"Whereas in your case, a little restraint might not be a bad thing," Ruth said.

"I tried that for a long time." His gut tightened, just thinking about the rigid schedule he'd followed as a police officer. "Never again.''

"Never?" she said. Connor didn't want to admit how serious he'd been when he asked what Krista meant by "more." The prospect of cozy evenings by the fire, someone to cook dinner for and bicker with over the remote control, had a seductive appeal.

This past Christmas eve, he'd lost his appetite in the middle of a freezer pizza, even though he'd decorated it with green parsley and red pimientos. He'd sat there, alone in his house, listening to the silence echo inside him. Well, he'd tried marriage, and it had ended in pain and recriminations, but that hadn't provided him with much consolation on that very lonely Christmas eve.

"You'd think she'd leap at the chance to spend a

weekend in Vegas and have an experience she'll never forget,'' he blustered.

"Can we spell 'male ego?' " Ruth asked.

"The truth is the truth,'' he said, which was more or less a quote from Gandhi, although taken out of context. "By the way, I owe you.''

"For what?''

"I'm not sure how you figured this would persuade Krista to help me, but it had to be something like that.'' Connor moved toward the door. "You aren't serious about this wedding nonsense, are you?''

"I suggest you line up a tuxedo and a turban, because one way or another, you're going to need it.'' With her hands on her hips, the woman resembled someone Connor had once known. His mother, that was who.

A tall, proud woman who ran her Montana ranch with an iron hand and a bullwhip, she'd dominated him, his father and his two brothers. Connor liked to joke that his visits to the ranch had gone a lot more smoothly since he joined the police force and started carrying a gun.

"Well, don't worry,'' he said. "I'm sure Krista will agree to my idea once she gives it some thought.''

She had to spend the weekend with him. Connor believed strongly in fate, and fate had sent him both a lucrative assignment and an empty checking account at the same time. It couldn't be a coincidence.

KRISTA WAS GLAD she lived near the office, because she had trouble focusing on her driving. She kept seeing that smug grin on the screen and on Connor's face.

She refused to become one of his playmates, a toy to be discarded. Well, maybe that was unfair.

She'd run into some of his former dates around town, women she'd met when they dropped by his office. They'd inquired after him with no sign of hard feelings.

Apparently the man picked girlfriends who shared his footloose attitude. So why was he so dead set on getting Krista alone for a weekend?

She might understand better if she knew the nature of his assignment, but asking for details would imply she was considering going. She was not interested, period.

Maybe it wouldn't be such a tragedy if he never paid the rent. Covering the mortgage would dent her bank account, but at least she could boot him out. Then maybe she'd stop mooning over him and find a man who had all the qualities on her list.

No more kittens underfoot. No more sly teasing grin. No more melting chocolate eyes.

The sparkle went out of Krista's afternoon. She was glad to turn onto her street, a curving tree-shaded lane near the La Habra Civic Center. The modest houses dated back forty or fifty years, to the days when people knew their neighbors and kids grew up with stability.

Her own upbringing had been stable, at least for the first thirteen years. Although her father, a surgeon, had worked long hours, their home in San Francisco was never lonely.

She'd loved the color-daubed studio where her

mother painted. Krista's brother Devon, now a biologist, had maintained a snake and lizard collection in his large bedroom, while she herself had hosted slumber parties and homework sessions for her girlfriends.

When she was thirteen, Dad had decided to pursue his lifelong dream of moving to a rural African village and providing medical care. After studying the matter, her mother had concluded that the move would expose the children to unacceptable risks. When she had refused to pack up and accompany him, he'd left anyway.

Eventually, they'd divorced. Mom had to resume teaching, and the three of them had moved into a small apartment. Krista's world had fallen apart.

The lizard collection had faded away, and a lot of the friends had, too. Most painful of all, she and her brother hadn't seen Dad for years at a time.

His goal had been noble. Krista wondered, though, if he appreciated how much his kids had suffered in the process.

She believed that once people had a family, their first obligation was to their children. She wouldn't marry until she found a husband who would never let her down.

As for Connor Fallon, she'd never seen a more unlikely prospect for fatherhood. Marry the man? No way!

Rounding a curve, Krista spotted a motor home in her driveway. It had a Pennsylvania license plate, and window stickers from Montreal, Toronto and Winnipeg.

Aunt Bea had arrived unexpectedly. Was this the

first step toward Ruth's loopy vision becoming a hor-
rifying reality?

Okay, it was a coincidence, but hardly a reason to
panic. And what a treat to have her sensible aunt to
talk things over with.

As Krista parked behind the RV, she noticed a light
in the living room. Since she, like other members of
her family, always hid a house key near the back
door, she wasn't surprised her aunt had found her way
inside.

Krista let herself in through the front. She'd enjoyed furnishing her own little house yet, today, the
pink-and-blue flowered sofa, ruffled draperies and fig-
urine-filled glass hutch struck her as too feminine for
a living room. This place needed an armchair solid
enough for a man.

Which man? What was she thinking?

"Krista? I'm in the kitchen!" The swinging door
opened, wafting out the heady scent of lasagne and
garlic bread, along with her tall, white-haired aunt.

"I'm so glad you're here!" Krista cried as she ran
into Bea's arms.

Only when she straightened did she notice her
aunt's clothing, a brightly colored cotton shift.
"What? No more shirtwaist dresses?"

"It's my new look, the second one this winter. I
started out with that fringed, fake-leather Pocahontas
stuff." Bea chuckled. "I guess I'm trying to find myself. Isn't that ridiculous, at my age?"

"Not at all. It flatters you." Indeed, the soft fabric
emphasized her aunt's vibrancy and trim figure.

The square-jawed face and soldier-straight shoulders had relaxed, giving Bea a more womanly ap-

pearance. Krista wondered why her father's sister had
never married. She would never be impolite enough
to ask, though.

"I brought a dress for you, too. It's in your room,"
Bea said. "Why don't you try it on while I put dinner
on the table?"

"Thanks! I'd love to."

Krista found the dress on the bed. It was a short,
scoop-necked shift in shades of blue and tan.

When she put it on, she saw in the full-length mirror that the low neck bared the tops of her breasts,
and the colors gave her skin a sensual glow. As if she
were ready for a man to hold her.

The man who came to mind had dark, sleepy eyes
and a flashing sense of humor. In her imagination, he
leaned against a wall and studied her approvingly.

Quickly, Krista hurried into the kitchen. "It's beautiful."

Bea stopped rattling around in a cabinet and swung
toward her. "Splendid! Just as I hoped."

"As you hoped?" Krista repeated.

Two spice bottles crashed to the counter. "Oh,
dear! Thank goodness they didn't spill," Bea said,
returning them to the shelf. "Don't you have any
more Parmesan cheese? I ran out."

"It's in the pantry. I suppose it would make sense
to keep it on the spice shelf," Krista said. "I had
everything perfectly organized when I moved in, but
things got out of control."

"That's what I mean," Bea said, with a vague gesture.

"Excuse me?"

"Cabinets take on a life of their own," her aunt

said. "So do wardrobes. How long have you been wearing those business suits?"

"I like tailored clothes," Krista said.

"So did I. For years and years." Her aunt closed the cabinet. "Oh, never mind. I'm glad you like the dress. We don't really need Parmesan on the garlic bread, do we? Come on, let's eat!"

As they dined, Bea regaled her niece with tales of the friendly Canadians she'd met. Nevertheless, Krista got the impression that, whatever her aunt was searching for, she hadn't found it in the frozen north.

In turn, she recounted the events of her own day, from the accident in the parking lot to the oddball scene on Ruth's computer. "To Connor, it's a big joke. But to me, it's a mockery of everything I stand for."

"Exactly what do you stand for?" her aunt asked as she reached for a second slice of bread.

"Steadiness. Reliability. I've got a list of what I want in a husband, if you'd like to see it," Krista offered.

"Sounds like you ought to check *Consumer Reports,*" her aunt joked. "They rate cars that way. Why not men?"

"I wish they could," Krista said. "I hate taking unnecessary chances."

"You know, I thought that way until… " The older woman stopped. "No, that was my life, not yours, and I'm not going to burden you with my mistakes. But this man is on your mind for a reason. I think you ought to find out about his assignment in Las Vegas."

"Why?" Krista shifted position. When had the

cushions in her dainty chairs gone flat? Maybe they'd been flat to begin with, and she'd never noticed.

Her aunt took a forkful of lasagne. "Because I'm dying to know more about it! Oh, Krista, you could have an adventure. Don't throw it away!"

Krista squirmed again. These chairs were much too delicate, almost better suited to a dollhouse than a real one. If Connor tried to sit in one, he'd squash it like a bug. "I don't want to have an adventure."

"What do you want to do?"

Her aunt's question caught her off guard. Without thinking, she blurted, "Reorganize my cabinets. You made me realize what a mess they are."

"After you've reorganized your cabinets, what are you going to do with the rest of the weekend?"

"Catch up on psychology magazines. Browse through some furniture stores." To look for an armchair big enough for Connor?

Oh, heavens, Krista did want to find out more about his plans, see where he lived, and hear his voice. The notion of sorting through canned goods and spices bored her senseless.

"It isn't like you to drift off in midsentence," said her aunt. "Go see this man. Satisfy your curiosity and mine. I'll redo your cabinets. I'm very good at it, you know."

"Of course you are," Krista said. "Your condo is the most organized place I've ever seen."

"So was our law office, and who cares?" Bea said. "I'm dying for a madcap experience, and here you have opportunity fall in your lap. Besides, you're too restless to stay here all evening."

"I'm not restless."

"You haven't stopped twitching for more than two minutes during this whole meal."

"It's these chairs!" Krista stood up. "Let me do the dishes, and we can catch a movie."

"So you can thrash around in those seats?" Her aunt took a second helping of salad. "Besides, I'm not done."

Krista couldn't stand here another minute, in this stuffy house cluttered with delicate objects. Maybe she would go see Connor, just to please her aunt.

"Okay," she said, "I'll see if he's home," and went to the phone before her better judgment intervened.

4

CONNOR STAGGERED into his house through the back door, his arms loaded with costumes. At least he had plenty of closet space, since he never owned more clothes than fit into a couple of suitcases.

Krista would be arriving any minute. He was glad he'd returned her page promptly, although he wasn't sure from their somewhat disjointed telephone conversation why she was now willing to listen to him. Maybe her aunt's arrival had convinced her niece that fate was at work.

She'd never visited his house before. The fact gave Connor a strange impulse to spruce the place up.

It was too late to plant anything in the weed-infested front bed, where rose hips dotted an old bush and a wilted batch of pansies testified to the broken-down condition of the sprinkler system. Thank goodness darkness fell early in February.

He couldn't even blame his landlord for the poor condition of the lawn since he owned the place. His financial adviser had recommended buying it as an investment, pointing out that Connor could rent it out if he chose to relocate.

Striding into the living room, he tried to see it from Krista's viewpoint. It looked a bit stark, with the lumpy thrift-shop furniture.

At an estate sale, he'd paid practically nothing for the brass pole lamp. Its light was so weak, you could hardly tell it had warped in a house fire.

He should buy a new couch, and maybe some chairs, he supposed. But before filling the room with new furniture, he ought to replace the worn-out carpet, which testified in splotches to the poor bathroom habits of stray animals. He'd been meaning to touch up the paint, too, and buy a couple of paintings.

The lack of decor had never bothered Connor until now. What was wrong with him?

He went into the kitchen to brew coffee. He figured Krista would need it, once she saw his house.

They could sit at the dark-green plastic resin table with its matching cheapo chairs. What kind of furniture did she have in her kitchen? he wondered. Probably an antique-style oak dinette set, polished to a high sheen.

He heated water on the stove, since the drip coffeemaker didn't work properly. He would have taken it back, but it only cost fifty cents and, besides, he'd never seen the same vendor at the swap meet again.

With Connor's investments, he could afford to live well, but possessions tied you down. Junk like this, he could leave behind any time he felt like it.

He'd moved three times in the past four years, never paying much note to his surroundings until this past, lonely Christmas. That was the day he'd begun contemplating the merits of wallpaper and new appliances, fresh-baked turkey and a pretty lady taking it out of the oven with flowered, Martha Stewart-type pot holders. Only on holidays and occasional week-ends, of course.

The doorbell rang. His heart gave a skip. Krista was here.

EVEN IN THE early darkness, she could see that Connor's front yard sprouted an amazing variety of weeds. One pod-covered stalk that reached to shoulder-height might have been growing since the Jurassic period.

As she reached for the doorbell, a tingle ran along Krista's arm. At first, she suspected a short circuit, but the tingle affected her other arm, too. Also, her stomach and knees. Besides, she hadn't quite touched the button yet.

This was Connor's home, the place where he stripped off his clothes at night and showered. His den, his lair.

She had come here of her own free will, although possibly in a fit of insanity. Trying to ignore the uneasy sense of stepping onto quicksand, Krista pushed the bell.

Firm footsteps sounded within. The door creaked, shifted on its hinges, stuck, and finally was yanked open so hard she half expected to see the knob break off.

"Well, hi." Connor's rugged shape filled the entrance. He gave no sign of having just done battle with the door. "Welcome to my humble etcetera, etcetera."

She was itching to make some sarcastic remark about the botanical marvels in his yard. She couldn't think of anything to say, though, except, "Well, I'm here."

It occurred to her, too late, that she should have

changed back into her suit. Connor's gaze trailed across the short dress, taking in the way it dipped low across her chest.

She wondered how it would feel if he ran his finger along the neckline of this dress and touched her breasts, bringing them to life. The thought filled her with a burning ache.

Why had she believed that coming here would relieve her restlessness? Instead, it was rapidly intensifying into a fever.

Determined not to let him see her confusion, she marched inside, accidentally brushing Connor as she went. Darn the man! Did he have to smell of aftershave lotion and pure masculine oomph?

"Have a seat." He gestured toward what passed for furniture in his living room.

Krista spared a glance at the dilapidated furniture. Was that a spring struggling to break through the fabric of the couch? "Thanks, but I'd rather stand."

"We could talk in the kitchen." He prowled toward her.

She took a step backward. Then another. "Okay."

"Not that way. Although if you insist…" He left the sentence unfinished.

Obviously, she must have been heading for the bedroom. The prospect was enough to make Krista break out in cold sweat. "I insist, all right. On the kitchen."

Once again, she was forced to scoot by him. In the evening air, his body radiated warmth.

Mentally, she stripped off his sport jacket. Unknotted his perpetually crooked tie. Undid the buttons on his oxford-cloth shirt.

Just once, Krista reflected as she averted her eyes and hurried into the next room, she would like to see those fascinating muscles bulging uncovered along his chest and stomach and thighs. Connor was like one of those subliminal advertisements that flashed a message too fast to be perceived at the conscious level. In his case, the message was: Make love to me.

"Coffee?" he said as she perched on a dark-green resin chair.

"No, thanks." She'd tasted his coffee at the office, and found it too thick and bitter.

He slung a chair backward and sat, leaning toward her across the table. It was a very small table, Krista thought. If she were to angle forward a few inches, their mouths would meet.

"So you've accepted that Ruth can foretell the future?" He favored her with his trademark lopsided grin. "That we really are going to march down the aisle together unless we head her off at the pass?"

"Not at all. I'm merely curious," Krista said. "My aunt suggested that I gather some more information."

Connor rested his arms on the table, his hands close to hers. "I stopped by the costume store, just in case. They rented me a tuxedo and two wedding gowns, although we'd have to fake the pink bows. I got a cocktail-waitress dress with mesh stockings, too."

"I suppose you already own a camera," she said.

"Sure. I use it in my work."

There was a jagged scar on the back of his hand, she noticed. It ran from the knuckle of his forefinger almost to his wrist. "Did you get that in your work, too?"

"This?" He turned his hand to give her a better

view. "It was a gift from a tomcat. He was protecting that which a tomcat values most."

"I guess you'd know about that," she said before she could stop herself. Immediately, Krista wished a hole would open in the floor and drop her out of sight, until she considered that, if Connor had a basement, it was undoubtedly full of spiders.

His mouth worked as if he wanted to pursue the topic, but he reined himself in. "I can pick up a whisk broom at any supermarket. I'm a little stumped on the red gym shoes, though."

"I used to have a pair," Krista admitted, "but I lost them. I probably gave them away the last time I cleaned out my closets."

"You clean your closets?"

"Once a year," she said. "What do you do when stuff accumulates?"

"I move," he said.

They stared at each other in mutual recognition of the abyss that stretched between them. He was a loin-cloth-clad hunter of ten thousand years B.C., the type who might drag home a slain mastodon and plop it in the middle of the cave; she was a twenty-first-century woman who would take one look at the huge hairy carcass and send for a Molly Maid crew.

Never the twain shall meet, Krista thought with a twinge of regret. Still, she might as well get the information she'd come for.

"Are you going to describe this job you want my help with? That is the point of my being here, isn't it?"

His tongue traced his upper lip. "All right. Ever heard of Ellen Hardison?"

"The college student who won the lottery?" She sat up straighter. "Sure, who hasn't?"

"Well, she's in love and she needs our help," he said.

CONNOR TRIED not to keep sneaking peeks at the front of his landlady's dress. Why had she chosen to wear that scoop-necked, clingy outfit to his house?

It only made the situation more painful. Since his divorce, he had avoided any woman who gave out nesting signals. Especially Krista.

Yet his attraction to her, which had begun as a mere itch a year ago when he first rented his office, had grown into a raging rash. Was it because she aroused his protective male instinct? Or was the pain of the divorce starting to wear off, leaving him vulnerable?

Connor fought down the urge to cup that firm little chin in his palm and forced himself to concentrate on the tale. He enjoyed watching Krista's blue eyes widen as she listened with growing sympathy to the story of Ellen Hardison, even though some of it was obviously familiar.

Three years ago, Ellen, who was working her way through college, had risked her life to pull a toddler from the path of a car. As a reward, the child's grateful mother gave the shy young blonde the only thing she had: a lottery ticket. It paid off to the tune of forty million dollars.

Other young women might have showered themselves with designer clothes and yachts. Ellen signed half her winnings over to the mother of the toddler, and began endowing scholarships with her own share.

The young woman's generosity fascinated the public. Talk show hosts clamored for her presence, but she declined. Soon her friends, and friends of friends, and former neighbors were being interviewed instead.

The tabloids and TV gossip shows trumpeted her every move. Would-be suitors camped outside her small apartment, forcing her to move, reluctantly, into a housing tract with a guard at the gate.

Overwhelmed by attention, Ellen had withdrawn into solitude, and taken refuge in the Internet. Via Cyberspace and, later, the telephone, she had found the man of her dreams.

He was Myford Ames, heir to a computer fortune and, despite being only thirty-three, also a recluse. The two of them wanted to meet in person, but Ellen's fear of flying prevented her from traveling to Ames's private island off the North Carolina coast.

Instead, they planned to meet at a hotel that Myford was part owner of. They needed to find some way to distract the paparazzi.

"Wait a minute." Krista cocked her head. "I'm beginning to follow your drift. Ellen Hardison looks a little like me, doesn't she?"

"Yup. And Myford's been so protected all his life that the only press photographs of him are blurry and taken from a sharp angle. Aside from the fact that he's tall and has dark hair, he could be anybody."

Connor could see her mind working as she weighed his comments. Every reaction showed on her expressive face.

"We're supposed to pose as them?" she guessed.

"Bingo." She was quick. Connor only wished that mental agility didn't also apply to puncturing his weak excuses when he was late with the rent. "He's sending a limo to drive her from California to his hotel in Las Vegas. The Taj Mahal-O-Rama."

"You'd think they'd pick a place closer to her house."

He shrugged. "Myford likes to frequent places he can control, and he doesn't own any hotels out here. Besides, Vegas is the wedding capital of the world. If they hit it off in person, they can get married on the spot."

She had halfway guessed the assignment already, so he filled in the rest: rumors of the meeting had reached the press, and a couple of tabloids were sniffing around.

Rather than scramble for another place to meet, Ames had hit on the idea of hiring a pair of lookalikes to draw off the reporters. He'd contacted a security service, and the owner, an old friend of Connor's, decided to hire him for the specialized job.

"He figured you'd be perfect to play a rich Romeo?" Krista's eyes narrowed, or maybe she was squinting against the glare of the naked overhead bulb.

"He wanted someone who could outthink a bunch of reporters. Someone suave." Laying it on thick, Connor added, "A James Bond type," and buffed his fingernails against his jacket. The effect was spoiled when he got one of his hangnails caught in the tweedy fabric.

"In a cheap suit?" she asked.

"I've got one Armani that I bought secondhand, and I can keep the rented tuxedo until Monday,"

Connor said. "The pay is triple my usual rate, and you'd get the same."

Krista frowned. "I wouldn't do this for the money."

"It also means I can pay you what I owe," he reminded her.

"There's a weak link in your plan."

"And that would be—?"

"Me." She shook her head. "I can't act my way out of a paper bag. If reporters asked me questions, I wouldn't know what to say."

"That's fine. Ellen's so shy she can hardly put two words together in public." Connor caught her hands in his. A shimmer of exhilaration ran through him at the contact. "If we get cornered, I'll handle the talking."

"People have seen Ellen Hardison on TV." For some reason, Krista didn't yank her hands away. "They'll be able to tell that I'm not her."

"In sunglasses and a scarf? You'll do fine."

She shivered. Connor didn't think she was cold; it must be fear. "I'll be there to protect you." He ran his thumbs across her palms, to reassure her. "Besides, we'll spend most of the time in our room."

"Our room?" she repeated. "Surely you don't expect me to share a—"

"Suite, I meant."

"How big a suite?"

"Big enough for an Indian rajah. The best the Taj Mahal has to offer," he said. At least, he hoped it would be. Sam Rush, the head of the security service, had made the arrangements.

"Will there be two bedrooms?"

Connor didn't know, and rather hoped not. "Whatever. I'm sure we'll cope."

She pulled her hands away. "No."

"Why not?"

"It's too intimate." She swallowed hard. "I couldn't. Not even to prevent—you know."

"That silly wedding business," he said. "Listen, you seem awfully tense. Are you sure you wouldn't enjoy getting away for the weekend? We could take in a show, and the food will be terrific. Krista, it wouldn't hurt us to spend some time together, and it might be good for you."

He didn't mean anything sexual by it, not that Connor would object if matters evolved in that direction. But Krista scraped her chair back and jumped to her feet as if she'd been burned.

"I can't believe I came here! I can't believe I nearly agreed to this madness!"

"Wait a minute!" As she raced through the living room, Connor wanted to catch her and make her hear him out. That, however, would only frighten her more.

At the door, she grabbed the knob and pulled. Nothing happened.

He ambled toward her, wondering why she looked so alarmed. Did he really have that unpleasant an effect on her? "I'm not going to pounce, you know."

"Did you lock me in?" she demanded.

"It sticks. Remember?"

"Oh, that's right." She balanced on the balls of her feet. "Well, let me out."

"You're blocking the door."

"I am?" She hesitated.

Lord, that dress was appealing. Connor didn't want to stare, and yet there was something magnetic about Krista tonight, all inviting curves and enticing movement. "Are you afraid of me?"

"No!" She backed against the wooden panel. "I know you wouldn't hurt me."

"Not that kind of fear."

"What kind, then?"

"This kind," he murmured, and touched one of her shoulders. His hand rested on bare skin as his mouth came down on hers.

Their lips met. He felt a flick of her tongue, and a trace of moisture.

When her chest heaved, a tight nub of a nipple brushed his forearm through the fabric of her dress. Connor's body came erect, hard desire warring with the need to proceed with caution.

He wanted to lift her in his arms and carry her to his bed. To bring to life all the lovely colors and eager passions bottled inside her.

A harshly indrawn breath drew him back to reality. "Let me out," Krista said.

With rigid self-control, he shifted her to one side and jerked on the door. As soon as it opened, she darted out.

She'd enjoyed the kiss, he felt certain. He was equally certain that, after this encounter, she would never, under any circumstances, go with him to Las Vegas.

KRISTA'S BODY THROBBED. It might have been the cool evening air or perhaps the narrowness of her escape that raised goose bumps along her arms. Mostly, it was the memory of Connor's strong hands and the invitation in his teasing mouth.

Why had she yielded to him? Why hadn't she fled sooner?

Krista's hands got slippery on the steering wheel. She knew why. She just hated to admit it.

Keeping her virginity hadn't been difficult all these years because she'd never met a man who had tempted her. Until now, she'd believed that her biggest problem was finding a man to love and build a home with.

Only now did she recognize the threat hidden within her nature. She had a powerful urge to share herself with this stalking creature named Connor Fallon, to let him run his hands not only across her shoulders but over her breasts. To let him take what she should never even consider giving him.

She wasn't sure how she made it to her street without crashing into the curb or running a red light. In her present mood, she was prepared to run a lot of red lights, symbolically speaking.

No. All she had to do to cool her longing was to picture the aftermath of surrender.

Connor would return to his bargain-basement living room, and she would curl alone in her canopied bed with its Laura Ashley sheets. In the mornings, arriving at the office, she would hear his low words of encouragement as he took in another stray. To Krista, he would offer only more excuses about the rent.

Maybe he would move away altogether. Or, worse, stick around. New girlfriends would drop by and life would go on unchanged, except inside Krista.

She must never open her heart to Connor Fallon. If she did, she might not get it back again.

By the time she halted in her driveway behind Aunt Bea's RV, Krista had regained her grip on herself. A long breath escaped as she relinquished forever the possibility of adventure. Of danger. Of Indiana Jones and the Hotel Suite of Doom.

Krista killed the motor. Hooked to an extension cord that stretched across the front yard, the RV's lights glowed through its cheery yellow curtains. Apparently Bea preferred to sleep in the motor home rather than the guest room, which was a good thing, because Krista was in no mood to talk to anyone.

Inside, she stalked through the too fussy living room, which improved only marginally in comparison to Connor's. Remembering her aunt's promise to go through the cabinets, she went into the kitchen and flicked on the light.

The place sparkled, neat as a pin. There was only one thing out of place, and it had a note attached.

"I found these under the sink," it read. "You don't suppose it's an omen, do you?"

It was her missing pair of red gym shoes.

Into Krista's shocked mind popped a conversation she'd had that morning. *"You'll never be a believer, will you?"* Ruth had said.

If a pole materializes in the middle of the parking lot, I might.

A lot more than a pole had materialized. Like Aunt Bea. And these shoes.

It was only a matter of time until Krista walked down the aisle with a whisk broom in her hand, to marry a smudge-faced Connor Fallon. Unthinkable.

They had to stage the wedding, to validate the vision and make sure it never came true on its own. Because if it did, if Connor were her husband, she would give him everything. And all she'd get back in return would be a few nights or weeks of pleasure followed inevitably by a lifetime of emptiness.

In Las Vegas, on the other hand, she would have shows to attend, food to eat, paparazzi to distract. A gym where she could work out in her red tennis shoes. And, most importantly, her own separate room.

Maybe Aunt Bea would come along. She'd said she wanted an adventure, hadn't she? Maybe they could have one together.

Krista felt better already. All she had to do was get this silly wedding over with.

It would be a piece of cake.

5

KRISTA LEANED BACK against the seat cushion and listened to the drone of the airplane. She wished an alien would zap them into another dimension before they landed in Vegas.

She must have been insane last night, to call Connor and promise to go through with this deal. Once she'd set the wheels in motion, though, he'd made arrangements at a lightning pace.

By 8:00 a.m., he'd rounded up the appropriate personnel, assembled them in the kung fu school upstairs from their offices, and even swiped a trellis some homeowner had left for trash pickup.

With a flourish, he'd produced a fistful of plastic daisies for Krista's hair. She recalled seeing them months earlier, sitting in a cracked vase in Connor's office.

She had walked through the ceremony with her cheeks flaming to match her shoes. She hadn't been this embarrassed since high school graduation, when her panty hose elastic died beneath the long dark robe, and she had to march up to receive her diploma with little geisha-size steps.

At least Connor had behaved like a gentleman. After they muttered their vows—something like "until

Sunday night do us part"—he'd given her only the briefest of kisses.

Yet it had set her on fire, worse than last night. She could still feel the heat beneath her tailored white suit.

"Krista?" he murmured, close to her ear.

It took her a moment to catch her breath. "Yes?"

"Did your aunt have to wear the cocktail-waitress dress on the airplane?"

She glanced across the aisle at Bea, who was happily showing off her shapely legs. In less than an hour, three elderly men had walked by for a total of at least eight trips to the bathroom. Either they were randy as all get-out or there was an unusually high incidence of enlarged prostates on this flight.

Not only had Bea been delighted to help with the wedding, but she'd jumped at the chance to accompany them. The waitress dress made her feel sexy, so she'd decided to wear it.

"I can help you confuse the paparazzi," she'd said with a wink. "Wouldn't that be a kick?"

Myford Ames hadn't requested a loose cannon to trot around his hotel making trouble, and under normal circumstances, Krista would have suggested that her aunt cool it. But normal circumstances no longer existed, not as long as she was pledged to spend the weekend with Connor.

She'd slept fitfully last night, awakening sweat-soaked from dreams of tangling bodies and hard, probing lips.

She'd scarcely been able to concentrate this morning as she packed her suits and nightgown. At first, she'd absentmindedly tried to stuff everything into her briefcase. Only when it overflowed did she remember to fetch the beige suitcase with diagonal green-red-and-brown stripes that her father had given her on one of his rare visits home.

The new low-cut shift had been left behind as too fantasy-inducing. Bea, however, being Connor-proof, was entitled to wear anything she liked, even if it was a short, shiny black dress with fishnet stockings.

"Don't you think she looks nice in it?" Krista asked.

"Charming." Connor called up some financial information on his laptop computer.

"Why are you reading that?"

"I want to see how my stocks are doing."

"Stocks?"

He froze. It was the first time she'd ever seen him taken aback. Then he gave a shrug of resignation. "Uh, yes. Stocks. And a few bonds. Mutual funds, too. I like to hedge my bets."

"You're habitually late with the rent, while you own stocks and bonds?" she asked.

"If I keep cashing in my assets to pay you, how will my retirement fund grow?"

"I don't believe it!" She ground her teeth, until she caught herself doing it. All she needed to add to her problems were dental bills. "You—you—"

"I'd be happy to advise you on your portfolio," Connor said.

"In case you missed it, I own an office building," Krista growled. "My only problem is deadbeat tenants. Know any?"

"You'll get your money next week." His mouth quirking, he returned to his financial pages.

To keep her temper in check, Krista reached into

her purse and fished out the photos of this morning's mock ceremony. The kung fu student who posed as best man and took the pictures had raced to a one-hour service, and brought back his masterpieces with a flourish.

She'd been touched by his thoughtfulness, until he announced that he'd had two sets made. One for the bride, and one to entertain his friends.

There was Jon Lu, the Kung Fu master, posing as a minister. She hoped the karate-style black belt tied around his dark suit wasn't too much of a deviation from Ruth's vision.

Ruth herself photographed rather well, with her strong bone structure. The blond wig sat askew, giving her a rakish air.

As for Bea, she'd played her role to the hilt. The camera had captured her flirtatious approach down the aisle, one mesh-covered leg raised as she executed an impromptu cancan. She'd avoided dropping the tray of champagne glasses, so maybe she wouldn't make a bad waitress, after all.

Krista tilted the next photo to catch the light. "Now, you," Connor said over her shoulder, "make a scenic bride in that getup."

"Do you have any idea what a pain it was, cutting those pink bows out of construction paper and pinning them on?" she asked.

"Is that why you're wearing such a sour expression?" He pointed at the photo for emphasis.

"I was humiliated! Are you saying you weren't?"

He flipped to the next shot, of himself in a tuxedo and a makeshift turban. "I had to wind toilet paper around my head. Are we taking bets about who was the most embarrassed?''

Krista conceded the point. Besides, she felt surprisingly at ease, sitting here with their heads together, going over the pictures like old friends.

Then Connor lifted out the last one, which showed them as a pair right after their you-may-kiss-the-bride embrace. His turban was coming loose, and she looked as if she'd just fallen out of a tornado and couldn't figure out why she wasn't in Kansas any more.

"I hope this isn't some sick joke," she said. "Does Ruth have a reason to hate either of us?"

"Did you raise her rent?"

"Why would I raise hers and not yours?"

"Because she pays hers. Raising mine wouldn't do you any good." He planted a kiss on the tip of her nose. "Have I told you that I'm glad you're along for the weekend? We're going to have fun."

"Not that much fun," she muttered, and, stuffing the photos into her purse, pulled a magazine from her tote bag.

Peripherally, she was aware of him studying her as if he wanted to reply. After a moment, though, he returned his attention to the laptop.

CONNOR HAD BEEN about to argue that his motives were pure. Except, that wasn't entirely true.

When two people responded to each other physically the way he and Krista did, and enjoyed their verbal sparring as much, he didn't see the point in holding back. Life, as he'd learned when his best buddy on the police force died in a gunbattle, was too short to take anything for granted.

He treasured having a friend like Krista. Come to think of it, Connor reflected as the plane descended toward McCarran International Airport, he'd never exactly been friends with his wife, Lydia. Passionate lovers, at first, but after the wedding they'd slipped into roles.

She became a wife who expected to find fulfillment through her husband and wanted to be the center of his world. He was a man who took his financial obligations seriously and had nothing left to give after working long hours in a dangerous profession.

He would never get caught up in that kind of crushing pressure again. After the divorce, Lydia had found someone else and Connor had regained his freedom. He knew better than to make the same mistake twice.

If something did happen between him and Krista, they would stay together as long as the good times lasted. Then he'd make sure they ended their affair amicably before deadly routine and unrealistic expectations turned them, day by day, into enemies.

On the runway, the plane jounced to earth, then roared its way to a halt. With Bea's eye-catching figure leading the way, the three of them made their way into the bustling terminal.

Despite the moderate size of the city, its airport had a cosmopolitan feel. The throng ranged from middle-American tourists and statuesque showgirls to visitors chattering in foreign languages.

"Look!" Bea cried as they passed a row of one-armed bandits. "Slot machines in the airport! Isn't that a hoot?"

Connor noticed one group of model-sleek young men among a pile of film equipment. They were shepherded by an older man with a goatee, who gave them orders in French. He wondered if they were here to shoot a commercial or a movie.

A couple of the younger men turned to smile at Bea as she passed. One of them applauded, as if delighted by the audacity of her costume, and she dipped a curtsey in return.

Krista, wearing a scarf and cheap sunglasses in her role as Ellen, peered around as if she couldn't see very well. Which she probably couldn't.

En route to the baggage claim, he adjusted the lapels of his Armani suit. Although a trifle dusty from hanging in the closet, it retained its elegance.

Like Krista, he was already assuming his role, but he hoped no one from the press would spot them yet. It would raise too many questions, since Myford Ames would have flown on a private jet, not a commercial carrier.

Sam Rush had promised to send a car for them. Some distance away, a limousine driver in a gray uniform caught Connor's eye. The man held a hand-lettered sign that read, "Mr. and Mrs. X."

Connor waved. "I'm afraid this is where we part company," he told Aunt Bea. "Would you like me to find you a cab?"

"The hotel has a shuttle service." She adjusted her short skirt. "I'm going to have such fun mingling with everyone! Maybe I'll even serve a few drinks."

"You're actually going to pose as a waitress?" Krista asked. "The hotel might object."

"Why should they? I'm sure the staff can use some

help,'' her aunt teased. ''You know, when I was younger, I would never walk on the grass or use the men's room if the ladies' room was full. Well, I'm too old to be a goody-goody any more. To use a little casino terminology, let the chips fall where they may.''

The limousine driver was making his way toward them. ''I hardly think you'll get arrested for impersonating a waitress,'' Connor said.

''I'll also keep an eye out for Ellen,'' her aunt added. ''That millionaire better treat her properly or he'll have me to answer to!'' Then off she went, her silver hair bobbing through the crowd.

''She certainly knows her own mind.''

''Even if she does keep changing it,'' Krista said.

The driver reached them. Yes, he was expecting ''Mr. and Mrs. Ames,'' he confirmed, and whisked the two of them to his limo at the curb.

He unlocked it, then realized he'd forgotten to collect their luggage. With an apology, the man hurried off.

As he helped Krista into the ultralong black limousine, Connor noticed passersby staring at her, no doubt wondering who the celebrity was. With blond bangs peeping from beneath the scarf and the sunglasses emphasizing her well-shaped nose and full mouth, she could easily pass for a movie star.

Inside the spacious vehicle, Connor let his gaze roam over her suit. The tailored lines couldn't disguise the lovely curves of Krista's breasts and nipped-in waistline.

It took all his self-control not to reach for her right then. He wished she could experience the world as a man did, even for a moment, and feel that overriding need, that ache to consummate the connection between them.

WHEN HIS THIGH accidentally nudged Krista's, her body sparkled right to the core. Oh, heavens, and they hadn't even reached the hotel yet.

It had been years since she visited Las Vegas, and in the meantime new hotels had sprung up, palatial amusement parks swarming with tourists. She scarcely noticed.

In his usual cheap suits, Connor reminded Krista of Tarzan uneasily stuffed into civilized clothing. The artfully cut silk fabric of this designer outfit, however, emphasized the power and grace of his build. It made her want to run her hand along his chest and feel the man beneath the veneer.

She must come up with a way to keep herself in line, but she wasn't sure how to proceed. She needed a sign, as Ruth might call it, to point the way. Please let fate send her one, soon.

The clink of champagne glasses drew her from her reverie. Connor was helping himself to a bottle from the bar along one side of the car.

"We'll be at the hotel any minute," she protested. "Besides, alcohol doesn't agree with me."

"It's carbonated white grape juice." Expertly, he extracted the cork and poured them each a bubbly serving. "To my new bride and to new horizons."

"To new horizons." *Please don't let me view them horizontally.*

The limousine glided into the long, curving driveway of the Taj Mahal-O-Rama, past a giant reflecting pool. The exotic, dome-studded structure gleamed like marble in the desert sunshine, although Krista doubted its Indian namesake had an eighteen-story hotel structure in the back.

The limousine halted among a knot of cars and tour buses at the curb. Among the other new arrivals, she recognized the group of stylishly dressed young men accompanied by a bearded man and assorted camera equipment.

They must have ridden the shuttle with Bea, because she was standing near them. Krista nearly waved to her aunt, until she remembered that she was supposed to be Ellen Hardison.

"Is something going on here?" she asked the driver. "Are they shooting a movie?"

"Could be. That happens a lot here."

"Let's move. Myford Ames would never risk getting cornered by the press in a public place." Connor steered Krista out of the limo and into the revolving door.

Whether by misjudgment or out of mischief, he stuffed himself into the same wedge-shaped space. They compressed like two sardines in a can.

In the few seconds before they stumbled into the lobby, his lean hips and his belt buckle made a semipermanent impression on Krista's rear end. She was regaining her balance and considering whether to retaliate when she spotted a rumpled-looking man stationed at one side of the lobby.

Standing with two cameras slung around his neck, he watched the crowd with keen interest. He hadn't noticed them, but at any moment he might. In her role as Ellen, she couldn't risk giving her beloved

Myford a swift kick in the shins, no matter how well-deserved.

When they walked through the lobby, he still didn't spot them, thanks to the large number of people surging past. Some dispersed toward the reception and concierge desks to the left; others into an enormous casino to the right.

Krista couldn't see far into the cavernous space, but she could hear one-armed bandits spinning, coins clanking into buckets, and dealers calling for bets. Waitresses, whose short costumes reminded her somewhat of Aunt Bea's, were circulating with drinks.

She checked her watch. Even before noon, the Las Vegas high life was in full swing.

"Your kind of scene?" she asked Connor.

"I never gamble with money," he said.

"With what, then?"

"Almost anything else." He tugged her around a small potted palm that she could have sworn hadn't been there a moment ago. "The biggest gamble in life is to always play it safe. You sit there and wait for the walls to close in."

"Is that what you think I do?" Krista asked.

"Not this weekend." Placing one hand on the small of her back, Connor propelled her forward.

Adjusting the suitcases in his grasp, the driver led them past two life-size white elephants that shone like ivory. The only other hint of an Indian theme were a couple of hotel employees wearing turbans.

At the back of the lobby, directional signs pointed toward meeting rooms. Krista tried in vain to figure out what all the initials stood for. "What kind of convention is this, anyway?"

"There's a trade exhibit in the main ballroom," the driver said, stopping at a bank of elevators. "It's the annual wedding show."

She detected a slight tremor in Connor's hand, which still rested against her back. As if he felt the walls closing in already.

"Weddings?" Krista said. "In February? I thought most people got married in June."

"It's for the trade," the man explained. "They work several months in advance. Magazines do layouts, store buyers pick out new gowns, that sort of thing."

"It isn't open to the public?" Viewing a ballroom full of elegant wedding clothes and decorations might help erase the memory of this morning's travesty.

"After 1:00 p.m., I believe." Their elevator arrived.

"Oh, good! We can come down later," she said.

"No hurry," Connor said, as the driver pushed the button for the tenth floor.

When they emerged, Krista struggled to keep track of the twists and turns that led to their suite. She wanted to be able to come and go as she pleased.

"You're already checked in." The limo driver opened their door and handed them a pair of card keys. After placing their luggage inside, he accepted Connor's tip with thanks. "Sorry to rush but I've got another plane to meet."

"No problem," said Connor. The man hurried away.

Krista stepped over the threshold. She intended to hurry into her own bedroom and lock it as quickly as possible.

She stopped abruptly. Something was wrong.

At first she entertained the wild hope that they might be in the wrong room. But this was too big and luxurious to be an ordinary chamber.

It was a suite, all right. But the Taj Mahal-O-Rama's idea of a suite was not what she'd had in mind. Not even remotely.

6

THERE WAS NO living room with two bedrooms, or even one separate bedroom. Instead, the suite featured a central open area and, on a curving platform three steps above, a bed covered in kingly purple velvet.

The furnishings were sumptuous and the draperies lush. A giant vase of flowers perched atop the bar, and a miniature refrigerator adjoined the whirlpool spa. The only thing lacking was privacy.

She would have to sleep in the bathroom, Krista thought grimly. Or not sleep at all.

She had hoped for a sign. Could this be it? If so, she hated to think what it might indicate.

Maybe she ought to phone Ruth and ask her help. Then she remembered that Ruth's advice had gotten her into this mess in the first place.

"Hey, this isn't bad," said Connor.

"In whose opinion?"

He ducked his head, conceding the point. "Sorry about the sleeping arrangements. I'll take the sofa."

"We could splurge and get another room." Immediately, Krista saw the flaw in her own reasoning. "But Myford and Ellen wouldn't do that, right?"

"'Fraid not."

Krista wanted to stay mad at him, because anger would help her keep him at bay, but she couldn't. For one thing, she didn't believe he had known about this in advance.

For another thing, the desert light filtering through the curtains brought out the mellowness in Connor's expression. The man seemed happy to be here, and it was flattering to think that she might be the reason for it.

In his silk suit, he looked so rakish and jaunty, he reminded her of the hero of a thirties screwball comedy. And this setting fitted him perfectly.

Why not relax, as he'd suggested, and make the best of things? Was she so eager to go home to her frilly living room and to another lonely night in front of the TV?

Connor wasn't the right man for her, yet her skin got all tingly and the air brightened whenever he came around. They could, as he'd said, have fun. If necessary, she would indeed sleep in the bathroom.

"Let's unpack." He carried her suitcase up the three steps and laid it on a luggage rack next to the bed.

"Sure." Krista started after him, then remembered what was in the suitcase. Beneath the suits lay pale pink bras and panties. "Surely you don't expect me to take out my personal things in front of you!"

"Why not? We're married, aren't we?" Connor regarded her with cheerful anticipation, as if she were a box of chocolates.

"No, we're not!"

"Well, not technically," he agreed. "Sorry. You unpack, and I'll pour us something to drink."

"I don't want anything."

"How about cranberry juice? Every woman I know

drinks the stuff by the gallon.'' The man poked through the refrigerator and pulled out a tulip-shaped bottle. ''Hey, and it's carbonated! Viva Las Vegas.'' Without waiting for a response, he unscrewed the lid.

''What's with you pouring me drinks all the time?''

He hesitated with a glass in one hand and the bottle in the other. ''It's the hospitable thing to do.''

''Good hosts don't press refreshments on reluctant guests. You're trying to loosen me up, aren't you?''

''This has medicinal qualities.''

''I'm already healthy.''

''And I intend to keep you that way!''

Deciding that the best argument was a rapid retreat, Krista mounted the platform toward her suitcase. A ray of sunlight showed previously unnoticed fading along the tan-red-and-green-diagonal stripes, she noted with a twist of regret.

The bag had been a gift from her father, who'd bought it overseas a couple of years ago. On his tight budget, it had represented a sacrifice.

Her father had never been good with words. In a way, this suitcase said what he couldn't, that he cared about Krista even when he was far away, helping people in Africa.

She hated to see it wearing out. She hadn't even used it many times, she reflected as she inserted her key into the built-in lock.

For a puzzling moment, it failed to catch. Was the lock wearing out, too?

''Here you go,'' Connor mumbled as he angled a glass of cranberry juice into her hand. He was mumbling, she saw, because he had a rose clamped between his teeth.

"What are you doing?" With no flat surfaces nearby, she couldn't readily dispose of the glass. Darn him!

Deftly, he removed the flower and tucked it behind her ear. "Adding the finishing touch. Welcome to Sin City."

"Go away."

"I'll bet that's not what Ellen is saying to Myford."

"I'll bet Myford doesn't owe Ellen a month's rent."

That set him back, although she suspected the respite was temporary. He was in such high spirits, nothing could faze him for long.

Krista was relieved when he withdrew down the steps. His playful attitude was having an effect on her. Every time his dark gaze raked her, her pulse speeded and her clothes felt too tight.

Where had this lascivious other self been all her life? And why did it have to emerge now?

Grumpily, she yanked on the key, and this time it clicked. Being careful not to tip the glass of juice, she flipped open the suitcase and reached for the top garment.

It didn't feel right. Too heavy, too crinkly, too sequinned.

Sequinned?

Clutching the stem of the glass, she stared at the dress. Its form-fitting length twinkled with sea-green sequins that flashed deep aqua on the reverse. Two playful cutouts belied the conservative neckline: one was positioned to reveal cleavage, the other to bare the navel.

An outrageous design like this would make heads turn and male instincts stand at attention. Who could have played such a trick on her? Krista might have suspected Connor, except that this gown had surely cost a fortune.

"Wow," he said from across the room. "I didn't know you wore that sort of thing."

"It isn't mine." The rose dropped from Krista's hair into the case and landed atop a silver high-heeled shoe. "The limo driver got the wrong suitcase."

She hadn't been able to find her luggage receipt in a hurry, but she'd described the bag. Since she'd never seen another one like it before, she hadn't worried about him making a mistake.

Now she checked the flight tag. Air France. That might explain the similarity, since her father had bought her suitcase in Europe. "Some French lady must be very upset. I doubt whoever owns this dress will appreciate my conservative suits."

"Why don't you try it on?" Connor shifted position to get a better view. "It would look smashing."

The newly discovered minx inside Krista seconded the motion. *Go ahead, try it. You'll never get another chance like this.*

There were, however, ethical considerations. "I couldn't wear someone else's clothes. What if I got it dirty?"

What happened next might have been a symptom of incipient carpal tunnel syndrome. Or, perhaps, her evil twin was asserting herself from behind the veil of the subconscious.

Whatever the reason, Krista's wrist flicked. Juice

dripped. Near the hemline of the fabulous dress appeared a tiny spot.

"Oh, no!" she cried.

"You'll have to have it cleaned." Connor came to stand beside her. "Might as well wear it once before you do."

"Thank you, Mephistopheles." She frowned at the forbidden fruit, but she couldn't resist.

The swapped suitcases, the dress that appeared to be her size, the spilled drink. It was too much for mere coincidence.

This was almost certainly the sign she'd been seeking. What did it mean?

"I could get arrested for misappropriating someone else's property," she said. "Couldn't I?"

"I promise not to turn you in," said Connor. "Besides, no one else is going to see it."

He assumed she was going to model the dress exclusively for him? And then, perhaps, let him strip it off, inch by pulsating inch?

Resistance hardening inside her, Krista fixed him with a disdainful stare. "If I'm going to wear this dress at all, you think I'm going to waste it hanging around this suite? I'm tired of—how did you put it— waiting for the walls to close in. I'm going out!"

If she could have bottled the dismay on Connor's face, Krista would have made a fortune selling it to the wives and girlfriends of arrogant men. It was the look of a wolf that bites into a tasty treat only to have it bite back.

"Wait a minute," he said. "You're planning to march around in public wearing that?"

On the heels of her declaration of independence,

doubts rushed in. What if she ran into the owner of the dress? What if she caused some further harm to it? What if…?

What if she stayed here with Connor and got her heart broken?

"I'm in a city where anything can happen, and a fairy godmother in the guise of a limo driver has delivered my magic gown! I'm going to try it on right now." Shoving her glass into his hand, Krista whisked the dress away.

"Don't forget about midnight!" Connor called. "What if your dress turns into a pumpkin?"

"I'll make pumpkin pie!"

The suite's bathroom fell short of Krista's expectations, she discovered as she locked the door behind her. Maybe the designer had figured that, with a Jacuzzi in the suite, only a modest-size retreat was needed.

It offered the regulation-size plumbing fixtures and a postage stamp of a floor. If she intended to spend the night here, she'd have to stuff cushions into the tub.

Which gave her even more reason to party all night, Krista decided as she shrugged off her suit jacket. Now all she had to do was find the right party, and enough nerve to let a bunch of strangers ogle her cleavage.

CONNOR PACED around the whirlpool bath. He started to pour more juice, couldn't remember which glass was his, and filled them both. Then he set them on the bar, untasted.

The purpose of inviting Krista to Las Vegas hadn't

exactly been seduction. But that kiss last night had broken a barrier between them.

He wanted to spend time in her company, in or out of the suite. What he hadn't expected was that the fates would send her this flamboyant dress.

For some time, he'd toyed with the notion that she was overripe for a sexual awakening. He'd imagined himself drawing her out with slow caresses and romantic dinners for two.

Instead, she was planning to take her show on the road. His masculine instincts weren't the least bit pleased at the prospect of sharing her, even at a distance, with other men.

Of course, as Ellen and Myford, the two of them needed to trot around in public. Which reminded him of something.

"Hey!" he called, tapping at the bathroom door.

"What?"

"When we go out, don't forget your sunglasses and scarf." He smiled. That ought to put a crimp in her Marilyn Monroe-ing merrily down the stream.

"We?" she called through the door.

"Ellen would never strut her stuff for anyone but Myford."

"I suppose not."

Score one for him. It annoyed him to have to make the point, however.

Connor wanted Krista to enjoy being in his presence, to respond to him the way he responded to her. Sometimes he thought she did, but then she would push him away.

He stepped back as the door opened. Hesitantly, Krista emerged. "Well?"

Usually, compliments came easily to him. He genuinely enjoyed women and found plenty to admire.

Now he didn't know what to say. He recognized those full lips and clear blue eyes from day after day of Krista-gazing at the office. In this shimmering blue-green dress, however, a new creature had sprung to life.

Her blond hair haloed a perfect oval face; her skin shone; and below...

If he dared, Connor would have swept her into a kiss and then moved his mouth down to that cutout. It begged to be traced around the edges with his tongue. Then he would thrust it into the sweet naked valley of her cleavage.

"Thanks for the compliments," she snapped, breaking the silence.

"You look...great." The words were inadequate, but he couldn't find any others. Not without revealing how fiercely he wanted her.

"I hope other men will be more appreciative." She slid her feet into the silver sandals. "A little loose, but I'll manage. Well, come along, Myford."

Sidestepping Connor, she snatched the sunglasses and scarf from the coffee table. He lengthened his stride to catch up as she hurried from the suite.

AROUND KRISTA, people streamed into the trade show. She paused at the entrance to the ballroom, nearly overwhelmed by the noisy scene and suddenly gripped by intense self-consciousness.

The slinky dress clung to her curves like a hungry man. It didn't help that she'd had to forgo wearing a bra, due to the diamond-shaped cutout that revealed way too much cleavage.

She didn't even want to think about her navel, making its public debut down below. Krista never even wore a two-piece on the beach, and she was parading around like this?

It was in a good cause, though. The cause of staying out of Connor's bed.

Perversely, she'd yearned to stir a reaction when he saw her in this outfit. At first, the way his eyes widened, she'd believed she was making an impression, but he hadn't said much. Maybe he'd been too overwhelmed but, given his presumably vast experience with women, she doubted it.

Did he have to keep moving in front of her? She was tall, but he was considerably taller. "Connor, I can't see!"

"There's nothing to see. Just some trade show." His smoky gaze blew over her.

"Well, nobody can see me!"

"That's the general idea," he muttered.

Krista couldn't believe it. "You're protecting my virtue?"

"I'm saving you from some crazed French lady who's likely to fly at you with a hat pin when she sees you in her gown."

"There could be two gowns like this. She can't be sure it's hers." Despite her defiant words, guilt zinged through Krista.

She really ought to go take this off and return the suitcase. Unfortunately, that would mean being alone with Connor again.

Determinedly, she moved around him. Trying to

ignore the gazes aimed in her direction, Krista took the lay of the land.

Circling the room were booths displaying wedding-related paraphernalia. Signs were advertising everything from gloves to jewelry.

The enormous center space had been given over to individual settings, some featuring mannequins dressed and arranged in bridal parties. There was a garden filled with potted plants; a rose-entwined chapel; a fern-bedecked grotto where water trickled between fake rocks; even a heavenly chamber where stuffed angels strummed their harps above cloudlike mounds.

She blinked at a Hollywood-style marquee rimmed by sequentially flashing lights that spelled out *La Grande Noce Satirique.* Dredging up her high school French, Krista translated that as "The Great Satiric Wedding." Was it the title of a movie?

Below the marquee, a cameraman measured the light levels with a handheld device, while a goateed man argued with a rather pretty male model. She'd seen them both arrive from the airport earlier.

The young man glanced at Krista. His startled expression mutated into a slow smile, as if he were admiring her dress.

Connor tapped her arm and pointed toward another part of the room. "It looks like somebody's getting married over there."

Krista followed his gaze to a mockup of the prow of the *Titanic.* Beside a captain in full dress uniform waited a tuxedoed young man, scuffing his feet impatiently.

Rows of folding chairs held an assortment of guests

who were craning their necks watching for the bride. A flower girl skipped down the aisle, but instead of petals she was scattering little rolls of candy.

"I don't believe it," Krista said. "She's giving out Life Savers."

"It *is* the *Titanic*," Connor noted. The music segued into "Here Comes the Bride," but no one appeared. "I'll bet she's got cold feet. You suppose that's from the iceberg?"

"There she is." Krista indicated a gowned woman half-hidden behind a large cardboard lifeboat. The bouquet trembled in her hands as she talked earnestly with someone out of sight.

That someone moved, and Krista glimpsed white hair, a clingy black waitress costume and a finger waggling in the air. "Don't tell me Aunt Bea's giving marital advice!"

"Why shouldn't she?" Connor stepped closer, still trying to keep people from eyeing her. Could the man be jealous, or was he playing the role of the devoted Myford?

"Because my aunt's never been married or even had a long-term relationship with a man, as far as I know." She dug her high heel into his instep hard enough to make him yelp, then pushed past him. "Heaven knows what she'll say!"

Across the room stalked Krista, matched with fierce strides by her would-be guardian. She arrived to hear her aunt advise, "The bottom line is, do you love him?"

"Of—of course!" stammered the young bride. "But marriage is so permanent. What if it doesn't work?"

Bea, who hadn't noticed Krista, responded after a slight hesitation. "A long time ago, before you were born, I was afraid to take a risk, and I lost the man I loved. I never found another one."

"How sad." Then the bride's expression cleared. "You're right. I do love him! In fact, I'd better hurry. I'm keeping Hank waiting."

As she scurried off, Bea spotted them. Her regard blazed a trail down Krista's dress, and up, and down again. "Goodness."

"It's a long story." She hoped her aunt wouldn't disapprove.

Bea, who'd been full of surprises this weekend already, didn't fail her now. "You're a knockout. Good for you!"

"Don't you find it too revealing?" Connor said.

"Do you?" asked her aunt.

"Not in private. Out here, however, it's—"

"—smashing. Where did you get it, anyway?" Bea listened intently as Krista explained about the switched suitcases. "Oh, you do have a gift for stumbling into adventures! I'll ask around and see if I can find this French lady. I'd love to see the rest of her wardrobe!"

"Please tell her I want my suits back," Krista said.

"You know my philosophy. Trying out new clothes helps broaden your perspective," said her aunt. "Give it a chance!"

Connor stiffened as a couple of young men stopped to give Krista the once-over two or three times. He leaned over her protectively.

Against her will, she found it a relief to have him guarding her. He felt so safe, so strong, so...

She brushed his midsection and mentally added, *so aroused.* Definitely unsafe at any speed.

His glare finally intimidated the young men, who beat a reluctant retreat. Connor's nearness, combined with the pressure of the heavy dress against her skin, gave Krista an itchy sensation. Without thinking, she wriggled.

A low groan tore from his throat. He wasn't the only one affected, either. Across the room, male faces came into focus. Grinning in appreciation. Whistling soundlessly.

"You're definitely a head-turner in that outfit," Bea said. "You should dress that way more often."

"She should not!" Connor roared over Krista's head.

"She could pass for a movie star," Bea continued, unfazed. "Especially in those sunglasses. Have you ever considered modeling?"

"No. And I don't plan to." Krista didn't feel like herself with so many people staring at her.

Connor was right; the dress ought to be worn in private. Sheltered against him, she could barely remember why she'd been so anxious to leave the suite.

Something about not getting her heart broken. But when he protected her like this, it was hard to believe he wasn't the safe harbor she'd sought since childhood.

"Could I have your autograph?" asked a girl, holding out a souvenir booklet and a pen. Her boyfriend lifted a disposable camera and snapped away, too close to Krista's navel for her peace of mind.

"I'm not an actress or anything," she protested.

"You're so beautiful!" the girl said. "You must be famous."

"That's right." Taking the booklet, Connor held it in front of Krista's belly button. "Go ahead and sign it, Ellen."

That reminded her of their assumed identities. She scribbled the name Ellen, then tried to recall whether it was Hardison or Hardeson. With an *i*, she decided.

More people approached. A plump woman fingered the sequins on Krista's shoulder. "I've never seen anything like this! Is it from Paris?"

"Well, yes."

"We live in a little town in Utah, and I was hoping to meet a celebrity!"

"Would you like her autograph?" asked Connor. "Ladies only, please."

"Myford!" she protested.

"I'd love to have it!" said the woman. "Who are you, anyway?"

"Just call me Ellen," Krista said as she signed a parking ticket the woman held out.

People didn't try to keep their voices down as rumors swept the ballroom. "That's Ellen Hardison, the lottery winner!" "I had no idea she was so striking." "His name is Myford something. Who do you suppose he is?"

"You're a hit," said Aunt Bea.

"I'm a fraud," sighed Krista.

"Can I have my picture taken with you?" A man sidled up too close and breathed down her cutout. His wife eyed them dubiously.

"Why don't you both get in the frame?" Connor snatched the woman's camera and steered her between Krista and her husband. "One, two, three, say 'sleaze!' Thank you very much." He handed it back and reclaimed his position beside Krista.

"Thanks," she whispered.

"My pleasure."

This business of fulfilling herself, or flaunting herself, or whatever she was doing, wasn't the fun that she'd expected. The best part was Connor's reaction.

Krista didn't believe in deliberately making a man jealous. It was hurtful and destructive to a relationship. The one positive thing about the man's response, however, was that it indicated that on some level he cared for her.

She liked having him here as her guardian angel. If only she could trust that he would always be there, maybe she would dare to let herself go. However, she wasn't a child, or a fool, either.

"I don't feel right, signing someone else's name," she said when they got a break between autograph hounds. "Having all these men stare at me makes me feel unclean, too."

"You're right," said Connor. "Let's go back to our room."

"No!"

"I didn't mean we had to stay there," he amended. "We could go out later."

"How much later?"

"As much later as you like."

"Five minutes would be fine," she said.

"Much as I hate to interrupt," said Bea, "there's a couple of men heading this way that you might want to take note of."

Krista spotted them at once. There was the rumpled

man she'd noticed earlier in the lobby, with two cameras slung around his neck, and a gawky young fellow in an orangy-brown polyester suit. He, too, carried a camera.

The paparazzi had arrived.

7

"CALL ME 'MYFORD,'" Connor murmured. "Note how easy it is to smile as you say it."

"I can't." Panic was making Krista jumpy. She hadn't expected to wind up with her face, let alone glimpses of the rest of her anatomy, in some tabloid. Despite the sunglasses, suppose one of her professional colleagues recognized her? She'd never live it down.

With one finger, Connor traced a curl on her cheek. "Act infatuated. Remember, you're in love with Myford."

"I can't lie to the press!"

"Does either of those men look like Tom Brokaw to you?"

The paparazzi were elbowing people aside as they raised their cameras. Krista was trying to figure out how best to discourage them when, at the edge of her vision, she observed a couple trying on rings at a jewelry booth.

Beneath a floppy hat, the blond woman beamed at the brown-haired man. He gazed back at her through thick horn-rimmed glasses as if the rest of the world didn't exist.

Nothing about the pair's modest clothes and quiet

manner drew anyone's notice. But, to Krista, their happiness filled the ballroom.

The real Ellen and Myford. She couldn't let them down.

Squaring her shoulders, she faced the cameras. Flashbulbs blinded her and then Connor pulled her off balance into a swooping embrace.

He uttered a low growl, an instinctive response. Or maybe that sound came from her own throat, Krista thought distractedly.

For a moment, she forgot that others were watching, indeed, capturing this embrace on film. She knew only that a torrent of hot lava was flooding her previously quiescent circulatory system.

His lips trailed down her throat to the collar of the sequinned gown. She felt her breasts strain upward, waiting for his tongue to dart down into the bared circle of cleavage.

She wished they were alone. She wished the dress would peel away and let them get on with an indescribably delicious experience.

Instead, with a dizzying motion, he righted her. "Okay, fellas," he told the photographers. "I think you've got enough."

Was that what he'd been doing, putting on a show? Krista's body echoed with unfamiliar sensations. How could he treat her so cavalierly? But no doubt these weren't unfamiliar sensations to him.

"Are you Myford Ames?" asked the portlier of the two men as he switched to his second camera. His younger rival was frantically trying to change film.

"Let's just say I'm a man in love," Connor said.

In love? What did he know about that? And he had

a lot of nerve, saying it as if he were, well, at least half serious. The man was a better actor than she'd given him credit for.

"How about taking off the sunglasses, Ellen?" asked the heavier man. "Let's make sure you are who you say you are."

"I haven't said I'm anybody!"

"In fact," Connor intervened smoothly, "these photographs might be worthless. You don't know for sure, do you?"

"I can find out." The photographer stepped forward as if to snatch off her disguise. Before anyone else could react, Aunt Bea blocked him with her tray.

"Care for a cocktail?" she asked. "Vodka martini? Gin and tonic? They're on the house."

"Beat it, lady," the man snarled.

"Hey!" said the gawky fellow in the orange suit. "There's no need to be rude."

"Who do you work for, *The Ladies' Home Companion*?" mocked his rival.

"I may be new, but I was raised to have good manners."

"Well, you're in the wrong profession!"

While they quarreled, Connor led Krista away through the onlookers. "I think we've made our presence known enough for one afternoon," he said under his breath.

She yearned to yell at him, or stomp on his foot, until it occurred to her that doing so would only reveal how strongly his kiss had affected her. She lifted her chin. "What about that show you promised me?"

"It's a bit early," he said. "I'm sure we can find other things to do."

Krista halted. "Connor, we need to get straight about this. I am not going to bed with you."

He glanced around. "I don't think this is the best place to have this conversation."

Other people were watching with open interest. Reluctantly, Krista conceded the point. "Let's go."

They came abreast of the couple trying on rings. As they went by, the real Ellen gave Krista a small, appreciative wave and mouthed the word, "Thanks."

Her mood lightened. This whole charade had been worthwhile, after all.

CIVIL WAR was tearing Connor apart. His mind declared that he should honor Krista's wishes and leave her alone. His body had other ideas.

Once again, the North was battling the South. And this time, the South might win.

Connor wasn't the kind of man who sought sex for its own sake. There had to be mutual liking and respect. His attraction to Krista confused him, however. Sexual hunger kept getting tangled with a deep-seated need he didn't care to identify.

When they entered their suite, the bed seemed unreasonably empty. When Krista brushed by him, soft and scented, he felt the South rise again.

It was a relief to hear the door to the bathroom slam shut behind her. Yet Connor's brain insisted on conjuring images of Krista in there slipping off the slinky dress.

What he needed was a workout to vent his frustrations. That gave him an idea.

"Hey!" He banged on the bathroom door. "Did you bring exercise clothes?"

"I don't have my suitcase. Remember?" A pause, then, "I do have the red shoes in my tote bag. Why?"

"The hotel offers exercise facilities, and I need a workout. I'll ask the concierge to send you some shorts and a T-shirt."

"What about the photographers?"

"I doubt we'll run into them," he responded. "Those guys looked to me like they get their exercise at the corner bar."

"Good point."

Connor phoned the concierge. Of course, the man said, he would send up a pair of shorts and a Taj Mahal-O-Rama T-shirt, compliments of the house.

Since the limo driver had brought the wrong luggage, he assured Connor that the hotel would have the dress cleaned at its own expense. He would also expend every effort to find the correct bag.

A churning in his stomach made Connor check his watch. They'd missed lunch, not an unusual occurrence in his line of work, but he saw no reason to suffer when Myford was paying. "What's the fastest way to get some food?"

"I'll connect you with room service right away, sir," said the concierge.

Since he wasn't sure what Krista liked, Connor ordered a buffet. While he was on the phone, she emerged wearing the hotel's complimentary white bathrobe. It might lack the suggestiveness of the glittery dress, which she carried over one arm, but he liked her this way. At ease and approachable.

Except that he wasn't going to approach. Not unless she wanted him to.

"The hotel staff's coming to collect the dress," Connor said. "They'll have it cleaned, free."

"Maybe I should pay anyway," Krista said.

"Why? It was their driver who made the mistake."

"It's not his fault I spilled juice on it."

"Obviously, you were startled at seeing someone else's clothes in what you presumed was your suitcase," Connor pointed out. "In fact, that dress startled a lot of people."

"I suppose you could view it that way." Krista reached down and pulled the red gym shoes from her tote bag. "I may get sentimental about these. What a day they've had!"

"It's not over yet." Seeing her fiery blush, Connor realized he'd made another double entendre. "I didn't mean that the way it sounded."

"I don't understand you," she said. "You're not usually this nice."

"Nice?" he said.

"As opposed to obnoxious."

"Thank you for the clarification."

"You're welcome." She climbed the steps and folded the dress gently into the suitcase. "I wish I didn't feel so guilty."

"Guilty about what?" He fished through his own luggage and retrieved his jogging clothes.

"I had no business wearing another woman's gown."

"She'll never know." Where had he put his own exercise shoes? All he had to do, he realized, was follow his nose, and there they were, tucked along the edges.

"That isn't the point."

On the verge of arguing, Connor halted. Krista's strict sense of honor was a trait he admired. She could be maddeningly stuffy, but she could also shine like a beacon. Even a buccaneer's ship sometimes needed a light to bring it home.

Home. Christmas with roasting chestnuts instead of microwave popcorn for one. The notion made Connor's world buzz pleasantly. No, wait, that wasn't the world; it was the doorbell.

He admitted the bellhop. In keeping with the Taj Mahal theme, the man's dark blue uniform came with a white sash fixed diagonally across the front. Atop his head rode a matching turban.

From a cart, the man removed a large platter of fruit, vegetables and cheeses, and set it on the coffee table. Then he brought another tray of shrimp, canapés and cold cuts, and a third filled with breads and muffins.

"Wow!" Krista said. "Can we eat all that?"

"We can try," Connor said.

The bellhop presented them with the shorts, a T-shirt and socks. He collected the suitcase, and promised to return later with Krista's.

"Well, that's that." Krista gazed wistfully after the vanished bag.

"Are you telling me you miss the gown?" he asked. "You could probably buy one like it."

"Where would I go dressed like that?" she asked.

"Good point. Forget I mentioned it."

While she donned her new clothes, Connor tucked into the food. Krista joined him a few minutes later. "I'm overwhelmed by this abundance."

"Don't be. Myford can afford it." He resisted the

impulse to hand-feed her a plump red strawberry. "Have whatever you like."

Sitting cross-legged on the floor, she helped herself to some shrimp. In the shorts and T-shirt, she reminded him of a teenager. How could one woman appear so glamorous one minute and so fresh and innocent the next?

"You're allowed to use the furniture, you know," Connor said.

"My house is full of furniture. I miss my college days when I used to sit on the floor," she said.

"I don't."

"No, but then, you only have furniture in the loosest sense of the word," she returned.

He decided to return to a safer subject. "Where did you go to college?"

"Cal State Fullerton." The campus wasn't far from La Habra. "How about you?"

"Community college, then UCLA."

"I know you used to be a police detective, and that you were divorced, although that personal stuff is none of my business." She was, he gathered, hoping he'd provide some details anyway.

He had no intention of reopening barely healed wounds. "It's old news."

She took the hint. "Where did you grow up?"

"On a ranch in Montana."

"Did you like rural life? I should think it would suit you." Krista tried a blueberry muffin. "I get the idea you don't like being fenced in."

"I don't, but whatever glorified claptrap you've heard about cowboys, forget it." A muscle tightened in Connor's jaw. "It's hard, grinding work. Lots of dirt and sweat and taking orders."

"Your dad was a taskmaster?"

"My mom." He began building a sandwich, layer by layer. Provolone, corned beef, ham, a tomato slice. "She ran the ranch with an iron fist. When she was in a bad mood, Dad would sleep in the bunkhouse with my two brothers and me."

"Sounds like he went to great lengths to avoid conflict." Across the table, Krista's blue eyes fixed on him. "It's possible your mom had to take charge in order to keep the ranch operating."

"She did seem relieved when my brothers took over, after Dad died." He added lettuce and pickles to his concoction. "She spent a year baking pies and knitting scarves, then signed on as a foster parent. Now she whips mixed-up kids into shape. I have to say, she does a good job."

"She certainly did with you."

Connor hesitated with his sandwich in midair. "I must be missing something. Was there a barb buried in that remark?"

"No, it's a compliment," Krista said.

"I kind of suspected it might be, but I thought the age of miracles had passed."

She laughed. "Am I that bad?"

"We both are," he admitted.

"By the way, are we really going to exercise right after this meal?"

Connor stared down at the remaining half of his immense sandwich. "We do need to take a break. Would you mind if I did a little work on the Internet?"

"Fine with me."

When they finished eating, he set up his laptop computer. He'd been hired to find a runaway husband, and he hoped to track him down by monitoring his credit card purchases.

Krista settled into an armchair with a magazine. The minutes passed in comfortable silence.

Each time he came up for air, Connor enjoyed seeing her there. It was a long time since he'd shared companionable silence with a woman. He'd never been able to concentrate when Lydia was around. She'd been an active person, always wanting him to accompany her shopping or take her to the movies.

Half an hour later, Krista stretched. "I can't remember when I've spent a day doing so little."

"Little?" Having searched in vain for some clue to the man's whereabouts, he logged off. "You got married, flew to Las Vegas, and put on a show for a bunch of tourists. Not bad for a day's work."

She winced. "Did I really put on a show?"

"It was great entertainment." Before she could reply, he grabbed his gym clothes and vamoosed.

THE WOOD-FLOORED GYM echoed with the rhythmic thump of a rowing machine which a well-buffed, balding fellow in his sixties was doggedly exercising on. Every now and then the sauna room would open, and a blast of hot air hit the back of Krista's neck as people came and went.

Otherwise, she and Connor had the place to themselves. Although her arm muscles ached from their earlier upper-body workout, she was determined to keep up with him on the exercise bikes.

Connor hadn't said much since they arrived at the spa here in the hotel's basement. He'd simply attacked the equipment with intense concentration.

A dark sweatband held his hair off his face, emphasizing his sculpted forehead and his well-defined cheeks and nose. His eyes formed pools of darkness and he pedaled as if plunging into some unseen danger.

Across his shoulders, sweat formed a dark V on the T-shirt. His arm muscles bulged, and his forward-leaning position gave Krista her best glimpse yet of those tightly shaped buttocks.

Her fantasy returned with full force. Those hips poised over her. She couldn't hold him off, and didn't want to.

She sighed, pushing away once again her surge of longing for Connor. So far, this weekend, he seemed so different. She wished she knew why, and when it would end.

Despite her training as a counselor, Krista wasn't egotistical enough to consider herself an expert on men. Besides, she felt certain that, in the known universe, there existed no experts on the masculine beast known as Connor Fallon.

She herself was finding it hard to resist the temptation to reach over and run her hands across that corded back and those taut thighs. To check out those straining hindquarters, too.

"I think I've had enough." She stopped pedaling.

He continued pumping away, faster and faster, as if he hadn't heard. Riding into some male adventure, no doubt.

At last he eased up. "You're right. There's no point in overdoing it."

"Where were you?" she asked. "Back on the ranch?"

His gaze seared her like a blast from a furnace. "I was a lot closer than that."

"Closer to me?"

"Very, very close." He wiped his forehead with one arm. "Forget I said that."

"I guess we could both use a cold shower."

"Cold? Not on your life!" He grinned. "Let's do something crazy."

"Like what?"

Without waiting for a reply, he swung off his machine and helped her down from hers. "Come on." Grabbing her hand, he yanked her out of the room.

"Aren't we going to wash up?" she asked.

"Sure. Later." He tugged her along the hallway, past a snack bar where a couple of patrons turned to stare at the sweaty couple.

"Connor! We're making a spectacle of ourselves!"

"No, we're not." He punched the button on the elevator. "Ellen and Myford are making a spectacle of themselves."

"But I don't have my sunglasses on!"

"Keep your face covered." As the empty elevator arrived, he swept her inside and pressed her face into his shoulder. "Now nobody can tell who you are."

"I can't breathe."

"If you can talk, you can breathe."

The truth was, she could breathe fine, but every time she did, she inhaled his musky, sensuous odor. The texture of his T-shirt and the pressure of his ribs against her breasts carried her into a heady world where nothing existed but the two of them.

They stopped to pick up passengers. Krista could feel eyes burning a hole in her back, but as long as she couldn't see them, she didn't care. When Connor's arm tightened around her waist, she burrowed deeper into him.

The doors slid open and he eased her into the corridor, still clutched against him. "Keep breathing," he said as he steered her around a corner.

"I'm trying."

"Kiss me."

"Not here."

"No one's looking."

"We can't—" She made the mistake of lifting her head as she spoke.

His mouth covered hers and his tongue anchored itself. At the same time, he reached out and waved the key card at the entrance to their suite.

The mechanism clicked, admitting them. They stopped in the doorway, locked together like amorous teenagers. Krista felt the imprint of Connor's aroused self on her, from the inside of her mouth to the yielding readiness of her abdomen, yet she couldn't seem to tear herself away.

At last, he spun her inside. The door swung shut behind them and he piloted her across the room. "Kick off your shoes."

"What?"

"Better hurry."

Puzzled, she obeyed. The next moment, he swooped her through the air. Krista clutched his shoulders as they dropped into hot, churning water.

"Connor! What are you—we can't—" She spluttered as a spray of water hit her in the face.

When she came up, his muffled voice said, "Take a bath and wash your gym clothes, two accomplishments for the price of one."

"You're insane!"

"And proud of it." His arms tightened, gathering her to him. While his hardness stirred an almost unbearable yearning in her core, his tongue licked fire along the inner edges of her lips.

Krista ran one hand along the back of Connor's neck, feathering the edges of his hair. Free at last to touch him, she clutched his shoulders, relishing the intimate feel of his contours beneath the thin fabric.

He groaned as if the pleasure were almost too great to bear. It gave her a sense of power that she could draw this response from Connor.

Words had always been her tools for exploring relationships, for finding truths, for healing rifts. Now they stuck in her throat. In the heart of the volcano, words melted and the soul spoke a language of its own.

When the buzzer sounded, Krista almost didn't register it. It sounded a second time, then a third.

"Damn the doorbell," Connor muttered. "Ignore it."

"Absolutely." It might be the bellhop with her suitcase, but who needed clothes at a time like this?

A light tapping replaced the buzzing. "Hello?" said a young woman. "Oh, please be home! It's Ellen and Myford and we've got to talk to you!"

8

_____

"I wish I hadn't heard that." Glumly, Connor released Krista.

"Duty calls." She sounded as bereft as he felt.

He braced himself against the edge of the pool and lifted his body straight out of the water. His muscles tingled, reminding him of his workout at the spa. The rest of his body sizzled, reminding him of… "Can I get you a towel?"

"Yes, please."

He called "Coming!" toward the door, and fetched the towels. At the same time, his mind raced over what had just happened between the two of them.

Desire had seared away his judgment and his caution. He knew Krista wasn't the kind of woman to be satisfied with an affair, and he was no longer sure that was all he sought from her, in any case.

What _did_ he want? Certainly not the long, slow slide into antagonism that inevitably came with marriage.

He'd have to resolve the issue later. Right now, there were more pressing demands on his attention.

As soon as he and Krista were suitably robed, he opened the door. There stood a dark-haired young man in thick glasses, and a beaming Ellen Hardison.

The shy lottery winner, who on TV answered reporters in monosyllables, was bubbling with happiness. "You're Detective Fallon, right? Thank you so much for letting us have a day to spend as normal people!"

Although she bore a slight similarity to Krista, this blonde wasn't nearly as stunning. She was pretty in a sweet way, and seemed very likeable. "My pleasure. Please come in."

Myford, who was a few inches shorter than Connor, shook his hand. "This is a nice suite. Not as nice as ours, of course."

Scooting inside, Ellen said, "We're getting married tomorrow! Isn't that wonderful?" She exchanged smiles with her fiancé.

"Congratulations." Obviously, this would not be a brief interruption, so Connor had to resign himself to playing host instead of lover. "Help yourselves to some food," he offered.

Myford loaded up on shrimp and stuffed mushrooms. Ellen scooped a handful of radishes from the vegetable tray. "Isn't this the most wonderful coincidence, that they're having a wedding show right at our hotel?"

"Not entirely a coincidence," Myford said.

"Really? You knew about it?" Her eyes widened. "Of course you did! You planned everything." She turned to Krista who was toweling her hair dry. "Isn't he wonderful?"

Myford smiled rather smugly. Through a mouthful of shrimp, he said, "She's wonderful, too," and began picking out the best strawberries.

"I'm glad we could help." Her hair curling damply around her face, Krista set the towel aside and perched on the edge of the pool. To Connor, she resembled a mermaid regarding the human world with sunny curiosity. If her cheeks were a bit flushed and her eyes brighter than usual, neither of the others appeared to notice.

"I just had to tell someone, and the only people I could think of is you!" Ellen continued, her face filled with joy. "I'd love for you to attend, since I don't have any family."

"Darling, we need them to distract the paparazzi." To Connor, Myford added, "I've arranged to have a minister and Ellen's wedding gown ready at nine o'clock tomorrow, at tableau number twelve in the ballroom. We expect you to keep those vultures busy while we tie the knot."

"I'm sure we can arrange it," Connor drawled.

"See that you do," said Myford.

How could two people get married on such a short acquaintance? he wondered. If not for a quirk of the lottery, Ellen would never even have entered Myford's rarified world. And although he was politely offering her a plate of strawberries, it was hard to believe his gallantry ran very deep.

Well, Connor didn't pretend to be an expert on marriages. No doubt Krista could offer more insight. At the moment, her sphinxlike expression revealed nothing.

"Do you mind if I check the fridge for champagne?" Ellen asked. "I'd love to make a toast."

"Don't be ridiculous, sweetheart," Myford said. "These people work for us. Let them pour the champagne."

The hackles, or whatever passed for hackles in a

human, rose along Connor's back. Being born rich didn't excuse this kind of arrogance.

"I'll get it." Krista hurried to find the bottle. She must have noticed his tension and decided to head off a confrontation.

She needn't have worried. Connor often had to deal with clients who were under stress, and knew better than to overreact.

When the champagne appeared, he found four glasses and poured a round. "To true love," Myford said.

"To happiness," said Ellen.

"To luck," said Krista. She took one sip before setting hers aside.

Connor's watch was edging toward seven o'clock before the visitors made their farewells. At last, peace settled over the suite.

"I don't much care for that man," he said.

"He might make a good husband for her, though." Krista sounded as if she were trying to convince herself.

"With that snobbish personality?"

"People compartmentalize," she said. "They can behave one way toward employees and quite differently toward their family."

"Let's hope so."

"He does seem kind of hung up on power, doesn't he?" She untied her robe and glanced ruefully at the wet gym clothes underneath. "I do hope they can work things out once they get past the honeymoon period."

"The honeymoon period? You think they'll break up after two weeks?"

"I didn't mean literally the honeymoon. Marriages go through stages," she said. "The early part, the 'honeymoon,' is followed by a period of adjustment. That's when the couple has to work at resolving their differences."

"Work at being married?" Connor said. "I thought things either happened or they didn't."

"If that were true, I'd be out of a job." Their eyes met, and she appeared to lose her train of thought. "Connor, about what, um, what we were doing…"

He didn't need reminding. His skin hummed and he could still taste her mouth. "Let me help you out of those wet things."

"No!"

"You're scared. That's natural, but it isn't healthy." He couldn't believe she'd changed her mind. Her response had been as vigorous as his. "I know you analyze emotions for a living, Krista, but it's time to let go."

"People need to go into relationships with their eyes wide open, Connor."

"Do they?" he parried. "I've always thought the best way was with your eyes shut. But if you prefer, we could try both ways."

She glared at him. His attempt at humor had been a misstep, Connor realized.

The wise course would be to let her retreat. He hated wisdom.

"You can't expect to get the future gift-wrapped and tied with a ribbon," he said. "Life is about seizing the moment. Corpus Christi."

"I think you mean *carpe diem*," she said. "Seize the day."

"Whatever. Krista, there's something special between us. If we analyze it, we could kill it."

She moved away, wrapping her robe tighter. "I don't believe that. It goes against everything I've dedicated my life to."

"There's a time for everything," he said. "That includes throwing caution to the wind."

She turned and paced across the carpet. "I need a sign. Something to show me the right thing to do."

"How about one that says 'Yield'?" The doorbell buzzed. "Not again!"

Krista beat him to it, admitting the turban-topped bellman with her suitcase.

The fellow launched into an explanation of how much trouble the staff had gone to, locating the owner of the other suitcase. He didn't shut up until Connor tipped him double.

When they were alone, he turned to see Krista frowning at the suitcase. "Oh, dear, it picked up a nasty scuff mark. I wonder if that can be cleaned?"

"Could we forget the suitcase?" he said.

"You promised to take me somewhere. Like a show."

The last thing he wanted to do was watch some dancers or a trained tiger act. Maybe he could discourage her. "There's a sitar-playing fakir in the Himalayan Lounge, and a hands-on seminar on finding your chakra points in the Dervish Room. Either of those appeal to you?" he improvised.

"Maybe Aunt Bea's come up with something." She fiddled with the lock on the suitcase, opened it and stood frowning at the contents.

A flash of red caught Connor's eye, and he peered

over her shoulder. He doubted Krista owned this slinky carmine dress sprouting feathers from one shoulder.

"I don't believe it." She lifted a note on hotel stationery from atop the gown. In slanted, foreign-looking lettering, it said, "Come to the party! Tonight, Suite 893B. Love, René."

This must be a joke. "Don't tell me somebody put another fancy dress in the same suitcase and sent it back."

Krista lifted out the red garment and examined it. "No, the other suitcase was faded."

"Is this your bag?"

"I don't think so." She blew on the feathers, ruffling them. "There's the scuff mark, and I had trouble getting the key in the lock."

He tried to make sense of the situation. "You think there are three suitcases in the same design?"

Krista held the dress against her body. A perfect fit, if he were any judge. "It's not surprising that this René would own two matching bags, is it? Look, she sent me a pair of strappy black sandals, too. And a velvet choker and crystal earrings!"

"Something's fishy." It didn't take a detective to detect that much.

"You're right," she said. "I smell Aunt Bea."

"Excuse me?"

"She was going to try to find the Frenchwoman. See, she's got this notion that changing the way you dress will change your frame of mind."

"I have to admit, she has a point," he said.

"And she's very persuasive."

"In French?"

"I wouldn't put it past her," Krista said. "She worked for an international law firm all these years. Anyway, I asked for a sign, and she sent me one. We're invited to a party! Doesn't that sound like fun?"

"I don't buy it. No normal woman would send an expensive dress like this to a stranger, regardless of how convincing your aunt is. Besides, what about this honeymoon period we're having? Maybe it won't withstand all these interruptions."

"Then it wasn't meant to last. Excuse me." Dodging his outstretched hand, she whisked away with the red dress.

For the first time since leaving Montana, Connor wished he possessed a lariat and a trained roping horse. Nothing less was going to prevent this woman from disappearing into the bathroom and locking the door with a—

Click.

CONNOR HAD A POINT, Krista admitted silently as she faced the full-length mirror.

Red feathers on the shoulder and hip, shimmering, clingy fabric, a slanting off-the-shoulder cut and a high-slit skirt—no ordinary woman would even own such an outfit, let alone send it to a stranger.

The overall impression was sexy and bold. She definitely did not resemble your garden-variety marriage counselor on holiday.

In fact, she hardly knew herself. But then, she didn't know the wildly inflamed woman she'd become in the pool with Connor, either.

She could still feel his hands stroking her hips, and

the pressure of his intense masculinity against her. If she let him hold her again, if she spent the evening alone with him, she would never be able to resist.

The desire for him was so strong, it took on a personality of its own. Alluring, tantalizing, whispering to her. *Seize the moment. Don't let it leave you behind.*

It wasn't the moment that would leave her behind, it was Connor. She couldn't allow herself to become that vulnerable to him.

She had to get out of the suite. And the only place she could think of going was to the party.

Maybe they would meet René. At least then she'd get an answer to her questions, possibly even reclaim her suitcase.

When she came out, Connor was tidying up the food trays. He couldn't have been standing there the whole time, however, because he'd changed into his rental tuxedo.

Without the silly turban, the dashing suit gave him an air of dangerous intensity. Taking in his raffish black hair and dark, burning eyes, Krista had to fight the urge to touch him.

No touching. She couldn't take the risk. "You're coming with me?"

"I'm not letting you go out dressed like that alone." He studied the form-fitting gown. "Krista, you may be illegal in a couple of dozen states."

"Lucky we're in Nevada, then," she said. "I don't think anything's illegal here."

"By the way, did you notice this?" He tossed her a lady's bejeweled half mask. "It was in the luggage."

Krista stared at it until the meaning dawned. "You mean it's a costume party?"

"Apparently." He held up a black Zorro-style mask. "This, I presume, is mine."

"How would René know about you?"

"Maybe a little Bea told her."

He was accepting her change of plans with good spirit, Krista had to admit. "Thanks for going along with this."

"I'm ready when you are. For whatever." Reaching her side, he cupped his hand beneath her elbow.

The slight contact stirred her ever-ready imagination. She could almost feel his fingers skimming across her throat and easing down her strap.

Maybe her instincts were wrong. Could an experience so wonderfully enticing, so natural and universal as making love, really hurt her?

Her mother's favorite song, after Dad left, had been that old melody, *"Plaisir d'Amour."* The pleasure of love, the lyrics said, lasts a moment. The pain of love lasts your whole life long.

This entire weekend seemed calculated to strip away the mental armor she'd worn since her teen years. For a short time, holding Connor in the whirlpool, she'd almost dropped her guard.

If she went too far, she would sacrifice her resolve to wait for a steady, reliable mate. In exchange for what? A pleasure that would scorch her as it burned itself out?

"Let's go," she said.

Connor's hand felt solid against her arm as they stepped forward. He had such a firm, reassuring presence, that she might almost have believed he was a man she could lean on.

The sooner they got out of this suite, the better.

ANNOYED AS HE WAS at being dragged to a party, Connor enjoyed watching Krista undulate down the corridor. The red feathered gown, like its sparkly predecessor, drew out her natural sensuality.

She was a feast for the eyes. Of course, once they reached René's suite, a lot of other men's eyes might be feasting as well, but he felt confident of his ability to keep the hordes at bay.

The more time they spent together, the more he was discovering unsuspected facets of her personality. And a new susceptibility in his own.

He didn't want a few nights or weeks of passion. He wanted to wake up with Krista morning after morning, to fix her banana pancakes on Sundays and enjoy coffee from a coffeemaker—hers—that functioned properly.

He would enjoy surprising her with a serenade on her birthday, and a yardful of rose bushes for Valentine's Day. It would be a challenge, hunting for fresh and creative ways to make those blue eyes shine.

Was it indeed possible to keep the excitement in a relationship, year after year? Krista had mentioned working at it. He hoped that meant working as in perfecting one's tennis serve, rather than as in fifty years of hard labor.

While they waited for the elevator, Connor shot a sideways glance at her. In that outfit, with her hair brushed back, she had the serene air of a goddess.

He knew her other side: bumbling, key-losing and cup-spilling. And the impatient way her mouth would twist on a rainy day when she came marching damply into Connor's office to retrieve the umbrella he'd borrowed without asking.

Nobody else knew her that intimately. They had a bond that was too precious to break.

When they entered the elevator, two businessmen stared at Krista so hard their facial muscles must hurt. Connor didn't mind; in fact, he felt proud.

My wife. True, she'd gone through with the ridiculous ceremony this morning precisely because she didn't want to marry him in real life. But minds and hearts could change.

In shock, he realized what he'd been thinking. He was actually considering matrimony.

The elevator glided downward. Connor's stomach remained above.

Marriage, to a woman who hung color-coordinated pictures on her office walls and cleaned her closets? To a person who made an actual commitment to furniture?

"What?" Krista said.

"Excuse me?"

"You look as if someone just stepped on your foot."

"Do I?"

"There must be a serious problem," she said. "You've got a befuddled expression, like one of your strays."

He waited until the businessmen exited. "Actually, there is no problem. I'm proud to be escorting you this evening. You look lovely."

"Oh?" She regarded him suspiciously. "You don't mind going out, after all?"

"I wouldn't miss it," he said. "Besides, as we saw this afternoon, you need a bodyguard."

"I do feel safer around you." Not exactly an overwhelming testimony of devotion, but at least she wasn't giving him the cold shoulder.

For the evening, he would hang loose and show Krista what a good sport he could be. Sooner or later, she'd be going back to her room, and she'd be going there with him.

After that, the future would have to take care of itself.

9

KRISTA HADN'T EXPECTED to find the suite packed wall-to-wall with people, the air reeking of cigarette smoke, and conversation flying thick and fast in several languages. Maybe coming to a party given by strangers wasn't such a good idea, after all.

Connor shouldered a path for her through the throng. Once they got away from the door, at least they found room to breathe. She was glad he'd come, although she didn't entirely trust this change in his treatment of her.

Until today, she could have listed Connor's character traits without a moment's hesitation. Now she wasn't sure she knew him. Or herself.

As they drifted between groups of people, she became aware of the notice she was attracting. It was hard to say why, because there were plenty of well-dressed women in the room, and some striking men, although none as appealing as Connor.

Nevertheless, men's heads swiveled as she went by. She was glad when she and Connor found a place to stand at one side, where they could watch the others instead of being the focus of attention.

Through the slits in her mask, Krista observed the assortment of costumes. One statuesque lady had come garbed as the Statue of Liberty, complete with crown and torch. Another tall, slim woman wore a Jacqueline Kennedy bouffant wig and strapless, sixties-style evening gown.

Almost all the women were tall. They must be models, she decided.

Few of the men, on the other hand, were as tall as Connor. Maybe it was their masks and costumes that was making them appear so glossy and a bit affected; she supposed they must be models, too.

The exception was the rotund, bearded man she'd seen several times before. He'd garbed himself in a leopard-print Tarzan suit that exposed plump legs and a hairy chest.

"Why is he studying at me that way?" she asked Connor.

"What way?" He squinted through the smoke in the direction she was pointing.

"As if he can't figure out what I'm doing here." The man's expression was a mixture of hostility and confusion.

"It's because you look like a real, down-to-earth woman." Leaning close, Connor added, "The other females around here seem kind of brittle, don't you think?"

"I think they're models," Krista said. "It's probably a defense mechanism."

Then she spotted a familiar figure heading their way. Aunt Bea paused to serve a couple of drinks before coming abreast of them.

"Glad you could make it," she said. "Krista, I love your outfit! It's even more spectacular than the last one."

"Did you have something to do with this?" She

raised her mask and fixed it atop her head, out of the way. "You said you were going to look for the Frenchwoman."

"Well..." A guilty expression flitted across Bea's face. "I did, er, meet René. Charming person."

"And she happily agreed to send me this expensive, flashy gown?"

"It wasn't my idea, believe me," Bea said. "Maybe I nudged a little, but—"

"She's a generous woman," muttered Connor. "Too generous. She ought to keep her clothes to herself."

"That isn't clothes!" Bea protested.

"I know, it's a new personality, right?" Krista said.

"No, it's a costume," said her aunt. "These people are shooting a satiric television show. They're in Las Vegas to burlesque our American excesses."

"Are they the ones throwing this party?" Connor asked.

She nodded. "They're very outgoing."

"Talk about excesses!" Krista said as a couple went by in elaborate cat costumes. "Every outfit here is custom-made. They didn't buy these off the rack."

"I told you, they're costumes. The show parodies all kinds of situations," Bea said. "Last month they went to Asia and posed as endangered species being wiped out by emissions from pocket calculators."

"René certainly told you a lot." Krista could hardly believed this was the staid aunt she'd known all her life. Maybe there was some magic about that waitress costume.

"Oh, everybody tells me stuff. I've made a lot of friends, wandering around the hotel."

"Meet any worthwhile men?"

Her aunt sighed. "Just lounge lizards. I don't suppose I'm likely to meet anyone with long-term potential in a casino, but hope springs eternal."

Connor didn't seem ready to leave the subject of the French people. "Bea, you've met René. Do you see her around?"

"Not yet."

He studied the chubby bearded man. "Maybe they sent the costumes to Krista as a kind of lure. They might be fishing for local models. Once the suitcases got mixed up and they saw her in the blue dress, it might have given them an idea. What do you think, Bea?"

"I think my niece would make a splendid model," she said.

"On French TV?" Krista asked. "Isn't that more risqué than in America? I hope they wouldn't expect me to pose—well, you know—"

"Naked," said Aunt Bea.

"Over my dead body!" Connor bristled. "That pudgy guy must be a director or a producer, the way everybody seems to be arguing with him. I'm going to have a talk with him." Without waiting for a reply, he battled his way through the throng toward Tarzan.

"Did anyone ever mention that that man has a terrific butt?" Bea remarked as she watched him go.

"Practically everyone," said Krista.

Even from the back, Connor looked fierce as he marched to her defense. Or, at least, she assumed that was his purpose. Maybe he simply wanted to negotiate her fee.

In his wake, people closed in. Men ogled Krista as they swirled by and the women fixed her with assessing gazes. Did they consider her competition for modeling jobs?

Bea noticed her unease. "Don't start huddling back into your shell," she said. "You've got it, so flaunt it."

"You're a bad influence," Krista said.

Her aunt beamed. "Thank you!"

"You don't mean that!"

"Only a little." Her aunt sighed. "I would like to meet a nice, reliable sort of man. But flexible enough to act crazy once in a while."

"Why didn't you show this side of yourself when you were younger?"

"I suppose I'm like your father," the older woman said. "He bottled everything up, then he exploded. Only in his case, he left a wife and children behind, which was wrong. You have to know when and what to gamble, and you shouldn't gamble more than you can afford to lose."

"What did you mean when you told that bride this afternoon that you loved a man once?" Krista asked. "I never knew about that."

Moisture darkened Bea's gray-flecked lashes. "It's something I didn't choose to talk about."

"I'm sorry."

"It's all right," said her aunt. "I said 'didn't,' past tense. His name was Ralph and he's the son of one of our law firm's partners. His family wanted him to marry someone in their social class."

"He didn't love you enough to stand up for you?" Krista asked.

"It was a long time ago, back when people felt obliged to follow their parents' wishes," she said. "I knew I should confront him and force him to face the fact that he was betraying his own feelings. I told myself it would be unladylike. In reality, I was afraid he might reject me anyway."

"So he married this other woman?"

Her aunt nodded sadly. "They've made each other miserable for thirty years. And I made myself miserable. Isn't that pathetic? Don't you be afraid to take a chance, Krista, or you might lose that man."

"Lose him? Until five minutes ago, I couldn't get rid of him." She peered around. Among so many tall people, she couldn't spot Connor. She missed him more than she would have expected. "That's just like him. Here one minute and gone the next."

"He'll be back," said her aunt. "When he does, have a good time together. Don't let the years get away from you, like I did. Enjoy the moment."

"I know." She smiled. "Corpus Christi."

"NO, NO, NO," said the man in the Tarzan suit. "We seek no models. We bring our own, as you see." He gestured vaguely around the room.

"Do you know a lady named René?" Connor pressed.

"A lady? No." The bearded man waved at someone. *"Comment ça va, Jean?"*

His friend replied in a stream of French from which Connor could extract only the name Pierre. It apparently belonged to this fellow in the fake leopard skin.

"So you wouldn't know where the red dress came from? The one with the feathers?"

Pierre glanced at Krista. "That one, do you mean, monsieur?"

"That's it."

The man responded with a Gallic sigh. "Ah, Milan, possibly. Their designers are doing a great deal with feathers this year. In Paris, things have become much simpler. Classic, they call it. I call it boring."

High fashion held no interest for Connor. "I don't mean where the dress was made, I meant, is it René's costume? Why would she send it to my girlfriend?"

Girlfriend seemed the easiest way to characterize Krista. If Pierre could chatter at such length about feathers, who could tell how long he might spend discussing the terms *landlady* or *temporary bride?*

The rotund fellow adjusted his furry over-the-shoulder strap. "The important question, monsieur, is where are her own clothes?"

Connor frowned. Until now, it hadn't occurred to him that this foreign woman might have retained the suitcase because she liked Krista's conservative taste. "You think someone is parading around in her clothes?"

"Such as that one, for example." Pierre waved toward the center of the room.

In the crush, it took Connor a moment to pinpoint his target, a woman about Krista's height with a stiff-looking honey-blond pageboy. She was pretty but angular, and gave an impression of cool calculation.

What riveted him was that the woman was, indeed, wearing a suit that could be Krista's. Come to think of it, he recalled seeing that tweedy jacket with the dark-brown velveteen lapels and that high-necked cream blouse only last week.

There was no doubt about it. She must be René.

Trying to rein in his irritation, he plowed his way toward the center of the room. He was prepared to negotiate a discreet compromise to get this mess straightened out.

Mostly, he wanted these French people out of his hair so he and Krista could spend time alone—without costumes, bellhops or missing suitcases to distract them.

"Excuse me. I believe this is yours." Removing his mask, he handed it to René.

She took one look at him and nearly jumped out of her low-heeled brown pumps. Or, rather, out of Krista's low-heeled brown pumps.

Not a bad-looking woman, on closer inspection. Her high cheekbones and gray eyes would have been more attractive, however, if she wasn't wearing so much makeup.

"Oui?" The word gasped out of her.

"You sent that red dress, right?" He pointed toward Krista.

"Je ne comprends pas. I do...not...speak... English."

"Is there someone who can translate?" Judging by her blank expression, she didn't understand the question. "Pierre. Let's get Pierre."

"Au revoir, monsieur." She sidled hurriedly away.

"No! Wait!" He couldn't exactly tackle her and pin her to the floor. Then, as she disappeared into the throng, he remembered a key point. The note that came with the feathered gown was written in English.

"Liar! Fraud!" he yelled, and would have barreled after her, except that in front of him stepped a woman dressed as a peacock. With the help of a male companion, she began fussily spreading her tail.

Connor weighed the possibility of stepping on it or diving underneath, but he wasn't sure he wanted to take the consequences. Besides, he'd lost sight of René.

What the devil was she up to? He swung around, trying to spot Pierre again, but Tarzan had also beaten a strategic retreat.

Why would a woman wear Krista's business suit to a costume party? And why would she pretend not to understand English when she knew it well enough to write a party invitation?

"Something stinks here," he muttered. Nearby, a man in a cowboy suit took a surreptitious sniff under his armpit.

Experience had taught him that a well-timed withdrawal was the next best thing to victory. So, reluctantly, Connor abandoned the hunt.

When he reached Krista, her face lit up. If he didn't know her better, he might think she was glad to see him. Bea had departed, no doubt to meet some more oddball friends.

"I found René," he said. "She's wearing your suit with the brown lapels."

"I hope the tag doesn't scratch her neck," Krista said. "I keep meaning to cut it off."

"Too bad it doesn't have a homing device sewn into the seam so we could track her down," Connor said. "She pretended she didn't speak English."

From an adjoining room boomed the mesmerizing

rhythms of Caribbean steel drum music. He slipped one arm around Krista's waist, and she swayed against him. The contact drove René and the suitcases right out of his mind.

"Let's go," he murmured.

"Why not?" said Krista. "Party on!"

As SHE MOVED to the music, Krista had never felt so light or so free. Her self-consciousness drifted away along with the occasional scarlet feather.

On the dance floor, the music's sensuality claimed her. She and Connor seemed to be floating on the same cloud.

The heat and sizzle of the Caribbean blended with his vitality as he twirled her and caught her smoothly. She had never been more keenly aware of his potent masculinity.

Don't let the years get away. Enjoy the moment.

A delicious longing spread through her. When the music shifted to a slower beat and Connor drew her tight against him, she lifted her arms to encircle his neck, leaving herself vulnerable to the pressure of his chest and the rocking of his pelvis. Points of fire flared along her skin.

Her eyelids drifted downward. Paradise had become distilled into a few square feet of dance floor, and she never wanted to leave it.

"Krista?" Connor murmured.

"Mmmm?"

"Are you falling asleep?"

"Try me," she said, and raised her mouth to be kissed.

Instead, he bent and scooped her into his arms.

Held securely in midair, Krista relaxed against his chest. "This works, too," she said, nuzzling his cheek.

"I'm carrying you back to the suite," Connor said. "Before you collapse of exhaustion."

"I'm not tired." Once they got there, she hoped he would kiss her senseless. Then they could seize the moment for all it was worth.

CONNOR WAS SUFFERING from an ethical dilemma. Not to mention a strain on his back. It would hardly be romantic to throw Krista over his shoulder in a fireman's carry, however.

It would hardly be romantic to take advantage of her present exhausted condition, either. He could see that she was unusually vulnerable. Although he ached for Krista in parts of his body that had only recently awakened from standby status, he refused to take advantage of her.

Not that he usually worried about acting like a gentleman. Opening doors for ladies was an act he performed solely when it was convenient. Nor had he offered to carry anyone's packages since an old lady had jabbed him with her umbrella, accusing him of trying to steal her groceries.

However, there were some things a decent human being did not do to another. Making love to someone who wasn't fully possessed of her wits was one of them.

He reached the suite and unlocked it with one hand only to discover that entering was far from a foregone conclusion. No matter which way he angled Krista, some part protruded too far.

At last she settled the matter by snuggling into a ball against him, and they went straight through. Across the living room. Up the steps.

Gently, he rolled her onto the bed. She smiled at him alluringly. "Teach me everything you know."

With her blond hair wisping against the pillow and her curves outlined beneath the sheath dress, Krista presented an almost irresistible temptation. "No, no, no," Connor said aloud. "Now, put on your nightgown."

"I haven't got one."

"You didn't bring one?"

"René must have it."

He'd forgotten that her suitcase was still missing. "Well, maybe she sent you one of hers." He stepped to the luggage rack and poked through the bag. It didn't contain much: a pair of glittery stockings that Krista had had the good taste not to wear, and some fuzzy mule-type slippers.

From beneath them, he lifted the sheerest negligée he'd ever seen, a black lace confection cut so high and so low that there was practically nothing in between. It was not what he'd had in mind.

"Don't forget this," Krista giddily called out. The red dress sailed through the air, landing across the suitcase in a shimmer of scarlet feathers.

Connor stared down at it in disbelief. Great. She'd taken it off. And was wearing what?

He battled the urge to turn his head. One peek was all it would take to unravel his best intentions.

"Almost done!" she teased. A second later, her choker landed on top of his head.

"Great." Connor fished it from his rumpled hair.

"Don't try it with the—" two glittery objects in rapid succession plopped into the suitcase "—earrings. Never mind."

Her mask followed. Keeping his face averted, Connor did his best to fold the red gown neatly. He tucked the jewelry and both masks alongside it.

The doorbell buzzed. "I'll get it," said Krista.

"No, you won't!"

Swinging toward her, he was greeted by a sight beyond his wildest fantasies. Krista Lund, sultry and sumptuous and wearing a sweetly innocent smile, teetered down the steps in high-heeled sandals, tiny bikini underpants and a lacy bra.

In her off-kilter state, she showed not the least sign of self-consciousness. In fact, if he didn't get a move on, she was going to open the door that way.

"Krista! Get in the bathroom!" He charged down the steps.

"I don't need to go."

With a mind like a steel trap, Connor could see it would take far too long to wrestle her out of sight. Choosing a more practical route, he leapt onto the platform for the purple bedspread and pitched it over her, covering her from head to toe. "And stay there!"

"It's dark under here." Krista's voice came out muffled. "Hot, too."

"Don't move!" Connor yanked open the door.

The bellhop regarded him blearily. "I think this time I got the right one," he said, and held out a suitcase.

Despite the urgent need for haste, Connor took the time to inspect the flight tag. It bore the name of their airline from California.

"Okay. Hold on." Shoving the bag aside, he raced to get René's case, skirting the confused mass of bedspread that was wandering around the center of the room.

On the way back, he realized what he'd missed. "The shoes!"

"Shoes?" said the bellhop.

"Lift your feet!" he ordered Krista. She gave a little hop. "One at a time."

"I can't hear you," she complained, and began shrugging off the spread.

"No!" He pushed her onto the couch, where she collapsed in a fit of giggles.

"Who's under there?" asked the bellhop. "Is she all right?"

"She's fine." Connor removed the sandals, transferred them to the suitcase, and gave it back. Fishing a generous tip from his wallet, he handed that over, too.

"Thank you, sir!" The bellhop all but saluted before making his departure.

Hoping they were at last finished with this suitcase nonsense, he knelt to open the case. It wasn't locked, thank goodness.

Unfortunately, it was nearly empty. The contents consisted of a flowered nightgown, a pair of bunny slippers, underwear and a swimsuit. Plus a note.

"Dear beautiful lady," it said in the same distinctive handwriting as before. "I apologize for borrowing your clothes but it is in a very good cause. All will be explained tomorrow. René."

"This lady has a lot of nerve," he said.

Krista trailed toward him, the bedspread wrapped

around her shoulders like a mantle. "You shouldn't sit on the floor in a tuxedo."

He handed her the flowered nightgown. "Would you please put this on?"

Instead, she settled onto the carpet beside him. "I'd rather not. I really do want to be with you tonight, Connor."

Her mood had shifted from silly to serene, he saw, but it was still hard to tell how much was Krista and how much was fatigue-inspired light-headedness. Her waiflike air as she huddled inside the velvet bedcovering prompted him to put one arm around her, and she rested her cheek on his shoulder.

A light fragrance invaded his senses, her usual floral scent plus a new note that was very, very womanly. "You should go to sleep," he forced himself to say.

"Don't push me away," she said. "I want to do this, Connor. I know I'm a little giddy, but I mean it."

He was being offered what he'd desired for months, but he maintained a tight, if ragged, grip on himself. "You might hate me in the morning. I want us to stay friends."

"I'm twenty-nine years old. If I deny myself much longer, I might explode."

"Krista, sex isn't merely a form of physical release." Even in his wildest entanglements, he'd never sunk that low. "It goes much deeper."

"I fantasize about you all the time," she said.

Connor couldn't believe what he'd heard. "You do?"

He felt rather than saw her nod. "Sometimes between clients, when I'm sitting in my office, I imagine you making love to me.''

She wouldn't have invented this, exhausted or not. "I didn't know women did that sort of thing."

"Oh, yes." Although breathless, she sounded steadier than before. "Of course, I lack experience, so what I fantasize might not be technically accurate."

"My technique is accurate enough for both of us," Connor assured her.

"Sometimes I picture your rear end," she continued earnestly. "It's very nice, you know, although I've only seen it clothed."

"Thank goodness." He waited, amazed.

"You poise over me—I'm lying down, you understand—and your rear end is in the air, and it starts pumping," she said.

"You've got this down pretty well."

"I've seen it in movies," Krista explained. "In my fantasy, you're kind of grinning, the way you do when you're teasing me, but I don't know if men really do that while they make love."

"Next time, I'll bring a mirror and find out," Connor promised.

"The muscles stand out in your thighs," she said, not at all embarrassed. "Those are the things I notice, your rear end and your thighs, and of course your mouth. I suppose not every part of the anatomy is equally important, or at least, not at the same time."

"That's one way of putting it." He'd never had a conversation like this before. He doubted there was another woman in the universe with whom he could have it.

And he didn't want there to be. The only woman for him was this crazy, endearing, unbelievably sexy creature sitting next to him on the carpet, the purple velvet cloth slipping from her shoulders to reveal the tender rounded tops of her breasts above the bra.

It came to him that his feelings for Krista had been growing for a long time. She was offering herself to him, and, from what she'd indicated, it was her first time. Once they made love, she would be his forever.

It was exactly what he wanted.

10

How often in life does a woman's fantasy come true? Krista wondered.

Not a ridiculous vision like Ruth's, but a daydream she'd been nursing through coffee breaks and slow rainy afternoons. A fantasy involving the handsomest man she's ever met, in a wonderfully romantic setting?

One of the lovely things about her relaxed state was that she'd scarcely registered the transition from sitting on the floor to lying on the bed. Or how Connor had managed to remove his tuxedo. Or what had happened to her bedspread for that matter.

Somewhere in the back of her mind lurked a pesky frump who kept trying to warn that actions have consequences and particularly this kind of action. Gleefully, Krista ignored her.

She was here, now, in real life, running her hands across Connor's bare chest and feeling the rapid thump of his heart. He had turned off the lights except for one lamp, which gleamed across his golden skin exactly as she had pictured it.

"You're beautiful," she said.

"Hey, that's my line." Lying beside her, he favored her with an expression of mingled mischief and delight.

She ran her hands lower, along his flat stomach and solid hipbones. "You took everything off."

"You mean you weren't watching my striptease?"

"I was watching your face," she admitted. "You look so happy."

"Want to make me a whole lot happier?" He raised himself on one forearm.

"Sure."

"Tilt your head back a little—like that—mmm. I've never seen your lips this full." He brushed a kiss across them, then went on murmuring hypnotically and, at the same time, positioning her. "Arch your back, this way. Is that comfortable?"

Not the word she would have chosen, exactly, but Krista had no name for the sensations rushing through her as he slipped the bra straps from her shoulders. Her breasts felt heavy and lush.

The whisper of his breath made patterns on her skin. Other perceptions, sight and hearing and taste, that normally shaped her experience, faded before the hypnotic power of touch.

The air changed pressure as his lips lowered toward the straining peaks of her breasts. He nibbled one, then the other. Licked them lightly. Held her steady, awaiting his claim, and then made a lightning raid with his mouth.

His black hair filled the valley of her cleavage. Krista gasped, wanting to rock rhythmically against him but reluctant to do anything that might dislodge this gloriously fierce pressure on her nipples.

With a naughty sense of venturing into forbidden territory, she ran her palms along his powerful, naked shoulders and down his back to the tapering waistline. Her change in position brought her breasts deeper into his mouth, and she rested her cheek against the top of his head.

She wanted to stay here forever, letting rivulets of molten longing flow through her veins. But she also wanted to grasp Connor's fabled butt of which she kept catching glimpses. Who knew when she might get the chance again?

Krista stretched, which had the effect of dislodging Connor and sending his tongue trailing down her stomach. Good heavens, she hadn't expected him to actually—such a shockingly intimate act—explore her navel!

Until now, she'd been unaware of holding anything back. But this unexpected penetration unleashed an overwhelming urge to surrender everything.

Her knees parted, and she knew then what she wanted him to explore. She couldn't imagine letting any other man hold her this way, but it was Connor, and he knew her so well that before she could quite formulate the desire, he was tasting her there.

Hot waves lashed Krista, and she fell back against the pillow. His hands cupped her tender core as his mouth ignited a firestorm.

Wave after wave of passion rolled through her. It was almost more than she could bear. "Connor?"

The marvelous pressure eased, and she heard him draw a strained breath. "Do you want me to stop?"

"No, no." How could anyone stop now? "I want the rest of it."

He gave a deep, sexy laugh. "You and me both, sweetheart." Instead of rising over her, however, he drew away.

She watched him roll out of bed and fumble in the wallet he'd left on the end table. "What are you doing?"

"Protecting you." A moment later, the bed dipped as he returned.

"Thank you." She hadn't even thought about it, and doubted she could ever summon such self-control, although perhaps that came with experience. This was, after all, her first time.

Then Krista remembered that she hadn't yet achieved her objective. She wanted to study and fondle that fabulous male bottom, the one other women could only admire from a distance.

"Would you turn over?" she asked.

"Excuse me?"

"There's part of you I haven't seen yet."

One of his dark eyebrows quirked. "Why don't you turn me over?"

He was, she saw, inviting her to wrestle. The man was twice her size, or almost. On the other hand, he appeared to offer no resistance.

"Okay." Tentatively, Krista caught him by the hips. A couple of tugs failed to dislodge him, so she decided to take a more scientific approach.

She laid one arm over his chest and, with her other hand, gripped his shoulder. Giving it her full strength, she pulled.

He rolled toward her, slowly and smoothly. Instead of continuing until he lay facedown on the bed, however, he managed to land facedown on Krista.

It was, no doubt, what he'd intended in the first place. She didn't mind. How could she, with his mouth tenderly kissing hers, and his chest rubbing her breasts, and the hard male part of him inflaming her most private self?

She didn't want to struggle, not when she could much more easily yield. In a surge of pure joy, she opened herself to Connor.

When he pushed into her, there was a moment's pain, gone so quickly she scarcely minded. The way he filled her seemed strange and marvelous and the most natural thing in the world.

To her disappointment, he withdrew. "Why—"

The inward plunge startled her. She gripped his shoulders, surprised at the wildness that throbbed through her. She wanted him to do that again, and again.

Connor's face was suffused with tenderness. With great deliberation, he again removed himself, then entered. It was maddening, delirious, perfect.

She loved the way his eyelids drifted down and his lips tightened, as if he were experiencing a joy almost too great to endure. Why had she fought him for so long, when they might both have been giving each other this gift?

He thrust harder. She renewed her grip on him, anchoring herself.

Suddenly she realized that she had it. His butt. Her

hands clutched that tight portion of his anatomy as he propelled himself into her with raging abandon.

She could detect every muscle, inlet, contour, as in her fantasy. Now she understood how she could experience him so many ways at once, inside her and atop her.

All sensation came together in a rush of searing lava. The world melted away, leaving only Krista and Connor and this triumphant burst of ecstasy.

She couldn't believe she was capable of experiencing such intense pleasure, or that the flames would ever abate. But, gradually, they did.

In the embers, they lay side by side. It was a good thing, Krista reflected, that she hadn't tried to repress her instincts much longer. This had been explosion enough.

"I love you," Connor whispered.

She didn't know what he meant. Did men always say that to women, afterward?

"It was—terrific," she replied cautiously.

Propping himself on one elbow, he gave her a typical Connor look of strained patience. "You're supposed to say the same thing back to me. Let's try it. 'I love you.'"

"What does it mean?" she asked.

"We're not exactly speaking Swahili here," he said.

Krista struggled to clarify her confusion. "I mean, do you always say that?"

"Of course not!"

"It's just for me?"

"Absolutely." He didn't appear to be joking.

"Krista, that was your first time with a man. I'm not mistaken about that, am I?"

"No." She wanted to cuddle against him and forget about talking. "It was great."

"You didn't save yourself for a one-night stand," he pointed out.

"You don't owe me anything."

"I'm aware of that! But I'm serious. I love you. I want more. A whole lot more."

Krista tried to absorb this turn of events. If there was anything she hadn't expected from Connor, it was a commitment. "This is new to me. I'm not sure what I want."

"That's a fine way for a virgin to respond when a rake offers to mend his ways for her!" His voice, as always, contained a note of teasing. Beneath it, she could tell, he was in deadly earnest.

"Is that what you're doing? Offering to mend your ways?"

"Well, what were you doing? Performing a science experiment?"

"Growing as a human being," she said. "Releasing my inhibitions. Making my dreams come true."

"So your dreams have been fulfilled. But don't you feel anything for me?"

The man was being unreasonable. "What do you expect—a declaration of undying devotion?"

"That would do for starters."

"Connor, give me a break! Until today, I couldn't stand you," she pointed out.

"You only wanted my body?" Those dark eyes wore a hurt expression.

"I said until today," Krista reminded him. Would the man never let her sleep? An unusually long day and an overabundance of stimuli were dulling what remained of her wits. "The way things are progressing, by tomorrow I may be madly in love with you. Who can tell?"

"Where do I stand tonight?"

"Well, I...I like you...." She couldn't keep her eyelids open, and her lips refused to operate, which might have been because her brain had already drifted into a sea of tranquility.

Sleep came so swiftly and deeply that she didn't hear the phone ring.

SHE LIKED HIM? That was all?

Connor Fallon, who had spent the eleven years since his divorce vowing to avoid entanglements, had fallen hopelessly in love with a virgin and introduced her to the thrills of intimacy, an experience that she had enjoyed to the point of delirium.

And she liked him?

He wanted to punch the pillow. Stalk around the room. Maybe fix himself a sandwich, when he got near the food trays. He hadn't, come to think of it, eaten dinner.

The phone rang. If it was René, Connor intended to give her a piece of his mind.

"Yes?" he snapped.

"Connor! Thank goodness you're in!" said a familiar male voice. "Sam Rush here." It was the head of the bodyguard service who'd hired him for this assignment.

Concern pushed Connor's personal problems to the back burner. "What's wrong?"

"That man staying with Ellen Hardison. He isn't Myford Ames."

He swallowed this news in a gulp. It was almost a pleasure to learn that the snotty fellow in the thick eyeglasses wasn't a millionaire. Unfortunately, it might mean that Ellen was in danger. "Who is he?"

"I don't know. You've got to find her and make sure she's safe."

Connor swung into a sitting position on the edge of the bed. Krista stirred in her sleep, mumbled and then burrowed deeper into the covers.

"Do you know her room number?" he asked.

"No. They must have registered under pseudonyms, and there are hundreds of rooms in that hotel." Sam's voice was thick with worry. "Whoever did this, he's clever, and he's spent a lot of money. He even took me in, and I'm not usually gullible."

"How did you find out?"

"Myford Ames' personal assistant called me. This time, I confirmed his identity via a source, which is what I should have done the first time."

"I presume you've already tried to track the man who hired you?"

"The phone number he left me is a pay phone. He gave me Myford's real address, but I never double-checked to make sure he was there."

How happy Ellen had been this afternoon. Connor realized that his presence and Krista's, as the hired doubles, had helped assure her that "Myford" was indeed the man he claimed to be.

This wasn't merely a job. He felt a personal responsibility to the woman. "How did Myford's people find out what's going on?"

"Apparently you did a good job of persuading the tabloid reporters and a lot of other people that *you* were Myford, because word got back to him through the hotel staff." Who, Connor recalled, indirectly worked for the millionaire.

"Why didn't he have them oust this imposter?" Then he recalled that, as far as Myford was concerned, he himself was the fake. "It gets complicated, I see."

"Fortunately, I'd made the reservation for you myself and left my phone number. Myford's assistant had the brains to check out the situation before sending someone to confront you in person. That's how he and I connected."

"I'll go hunt down the night manager to help me figure out which room they're in. I presume he's aware of the problem?"

"If Myford Ames is concerned enough to call me in the middle of the night, he'd better be," said Sam.

With a groan, Connor signed off. What a mess!

He didn't waste time speculating about who the fake Myford might be or what his purpose was. The key was to locate Ellen as quickly as possible.

She planned to marry this imposter tomorrow morning. Or rather, this morning, he saw when he checked the clock and discovered that it was after midnight.

Trying not to wake Krista, Connor hurried about the room, grabbing the first clothes that came to hand.

He wasn't sure he got all the tuxedo parts on straight, but it hardly mattered.

After leaving a note atop the coffee table, he hurried out.

KRISTA FLUTTERED to near-consciousness in what must be the early morning hours, but she didn't open her eyes. Something magnificent had happened to her, and she was afraid it might be a dream.

Better not to wake up. Better not to risk finding herself alone in her cold bed.

She wanted to savor the memories of Connor imprinted all over her body and her heart. The way he'd looked at her, and held her, and aroused her.

Had he meant it when he said he loved her? She hoped he would confirm it in plain daylight. Her answer would be...would be...?

Too weary and too contented to finish the thought, she fell into the golden depths of a blissful sleep.

NEARLY 7:30 a.m., and what had he accomplished? Connor's hands were bone-dry from handling paperwork and, even without looking in a mirror, he knew his eyes must be red.

Neither the computer records nor the guests' sign-in sheets were any help in finding Ellen and the fake Myford. Any of several dozen clients might fill the bill.

Connor's only hope was that Ellen and "Myford" would show up as scheduled at tableau number twelve in an hour and a half. He didn't relish the task of waylaying a merry bride at the altar and breaking her heart, but what choice did he have?

"Sorry about this," said the night manager, a pleasant middle-aged man who'd done his best to help but had been interrupted repeatedly by hotel business. "I've got some last minute details to take care of before the daytime manager arrives. I'm sure he'll be helpful."

"Thanks." Idly, Connor rubbed his cheek, and realized he'd probably smudged it.

Well, given his current disheveled state, he doubted anyone would notice. He'd better head back to his suite to clean up and fill Krista in on the details.

These were not the most promising circumstances under which to launch their new relationship. What he really wanted was to spend the whole day making love with her, until she stopped denying her feelings.

His mind was crowded with memories of last night, of Krista unveiled and glorious. As he left the manager's office to return to the lobby, Connor scarcely noticed the twists and turns of the staff-only corridor.

He chuckled, recalling Krista's description of daydreams that featured none other than himself. Especially his posterior, to which he had never given more than a passing thought except when he sat on something sharp.

He would like to hear more about those fantasies to make sure all of them came true.

A final turn brought him to a vast kitchen gleaming with steel tables and perfumed with the scents of maple syrup and scrambled eggs. Connor stopped, annoyed. Obviously, he'd taken a wrong turn.

From behind him came a rattling sound. "Excuse me! I need to get through!" called a youthful male voice.

Connor turned to see a bellhop with a cart full of dirty dishes. The young man looked preposterous in his white turban and sash. "How do I get out of here?"

Accommodatingly, the bellhop backed up his cart. "Can you squeeze by, sir? Go to the first corner and turn left."

"Connor!" Down the hallway behind the man came Aunt Bea, disgustingly bright-faced for such an early hour. She'd exchanged her rented costume for a similar one with a shorter skirt.

"Do you work here now?" he asked, puzzled.

"I'm covering a shift for one of the girls who got sick. Personal favor," the white-haired lady said. "What's up?"

"Take me to the lobby and I'll explain everything."

OKAY, SO THE MAN had deflowered her and left before she regained consciousness the next morning. That didn't mean he'd abandoned her, Krista reflected, trying hard to fight down a deep pang that lay somewhere between disappointment and homicidal wrath.

She didn't think it unreasonable to expect her hero to stick around long enough to yawn, stretch, and ask how she'd slept. He could even offer to let her use the bathroom first.

Or he might ravish her again. Either would be fine. Anything but this silence, this Connorlessness.

When she swung out of bed, the rush of cool air reminded her that she'd slept naked. Trying to bat down the goose bumps on her arms, Krista scooted over to her suitcase.

Well, darn. What was she going to put on, the flannel nightgown or the wrinkled white suit she'd worn yesterday on the plane?

This time, René hadn't even sent her anything enticing. Come to think of it, that woman had a lot to answer for.

Deciding on the suit, Krista grabbed it and her blouse from the closet and carted them into the bathroom. She hoped that by the time she finished showering, Connor would return from wherever he'd gone.

"I SAW THEM heading up to their room last night," Bea said when Connor finished his account. "A pretty blond woman and a man wearing thick glasses, right? They got off the elevator on the eighth floor, but I don't know their suite number."

Only a small part of each floor was occupied by suites, so this information limited the search considerably. "If you're willing to help, you could pretend to be delivering a room service tray and knock on doors until we get the right one."

"Whoa!" Bea raised her hands. "I'm covering for another waitress, remember? My shift doesn't end for an hour. *You* could deliver a tray."

Connor wouldn't mind doing the job; in fact, he preferred being on the front line in case anything went wrong. "Can I pass as a bellboy in this tuxedo?"

"It needs a little doctoring," Bea said. "Wait here."

He agreed, although every instinct in Connor's soul urged him to surge into motion. Sometimes, though, the most effective action was to bide his time.

Besides, Krista must have awakened by now. He needed to make contact.

Leaving her alone after their first night together went against the grain. Connor wished he could have been there to watch the sleep-softened innocence of her face, and the dawning warmth when she opened her eyes and saw him.

Locating a house phone nearby, he dialed the suite. He counted ten rings before hanging up.

She might be taking a shower or have gone out to eat. By nature, Connor didn't chew over things that might or might not happen. He controlled what he could, and put the rest out of his mind.

Yet now he felt a prick of worry. What if she'd gone out? What if she'd run into the fake Myford, without knowing he was a fraud?

Normally, Connor dismissed this type of speculation as useless, but last night had changed something essential in him. With a jolt, he realized that love means often having to say you worry.

Because he cared about Krista. More than he even cared about himself.

If not for his obligation to protect Ellen and the knowledge that her danger was immediate, he would have gone to check on Krista. He was weighing his options when he saw Bea heading back toward him.

"Here." She was pushing a metal cart with two

small metal domes covering plates. From a lower shelf, she fetched a turban and a sash. ''Put these on. They ought to convince a casual observer that you're one of the staff.''

Connor felt like an idiot as he plopped the turban onto his head and shrugged into the sash. ''How do I look?''

''Disreputable,'' said Bea.

''Great.'' With a grimace, he headed for the elevators.

11

KRISTA HEARD the phone ring while she was in the shower, but by the time she dried off, it had stopped.

Had that been Connor? she wondered, almost ready to forgive him. Maybe he'd gone downstairs to get a newspaper and wanted her to join him for breakfast. Or, more importantly, for Ellen and Myford's wedding.

She glanced at her watch. There was nearly an hour to go before the big event.

In hopes that he'd left a message, she wrapped a towel around herself and went to check the red message bulb on the phone. It was dim, not flashing. Then she spotted the note on the coffee table.

"Ellen's in danger. Gone to help."

He hadn't indicated the time, or what kind of danger. Had he rescued Ellen by now? Where was he?

Krista tapped her fingers on the table. Something needed to be done and she wanted to be a part of it. Yet she had no idea what to do.

Should she try to phone Ellen's suite? It was unlikely Ellen had registered under her own name. And even if she reached her, without knowing the details, Krista might make matters worse.

Darn Connor's arrogance! He should have awakened her and told her everything. Didn't he realize she would want to help?

Frustrated at her inability to take action, she sank down onto the couch. Had Ellen become a fixation for some deranged fan? Were kidnappers chasing Myford?

Then another implication of the note hit her. If Ellen was in danger, then, as her would-be rescuer, Connor was, too.

Until now, Krista had never given much thought to the risks involved in his line of work. Detectives, he'd once explained, spent most of their time spying on cheating spouses and on employees who claimed to be disabled when they were actually training to run marathons.

Now a host of terrifying images sprang to mind.

When the phone rang, she grabbed it. "Connor?"

"No, it's Ruth." The psychic's voice sounded early-morning hoarse.

"Are you in Vegas?"

"No, I'm home," she said. "Why isn't Connor with you?"

"He's working." In a case like this, Krista supposed it was best not to reveal too much, even to a friend.

"I'm concerned about him." That statement made her nervous, coming from a psychic.

"Is something wrong?" If she pressed the phone any more tightly to her ear, she would cut off the blood supply. "Don't tell me you've had another vision!"

"More of a revised vision." Ruth cleared her throat. "This has never happened before."

Krista caught the towel as it tried to unwind itself. "Which vision? The wedding?"

"I'm afraid so," Ruth said. "There were some significant changes."

"Such as?"

"For one thing, you and the other blonde got your roles reversed. This time, she was the real bride and you were a bridesmaid. Or standing around watching, anyway."

"He's going to marry someone else?" Krista couldn't believe it.

"There's more," said the psychic. "I saw a man pointing a gun at the groom."

"A gun?" She felt foolish, repeating the words, but they took time to sink in. "A real gun?"

"There's no way to tell," Ruth said. "I couldn't have failed to notice these things before, so circumstances must have changed."

"Does this have anything to do with the fact that we staged the wedding?" Krista asked. "Could we have changed the future?"

"It's possible," Ruth said. "My visions are only a likelihood, not a certainty."

"Does this mean it's going to happen the way you see it now, not the way you saw it before?"

"I'm afraid so."

This was even worse, because fate had added a gunman, and Connor was taking the wrong bride. The whole point of walking through that nonsense had been to save herself from marrying the man, but Krista was no longer sure she didn't want to marry him.

"I've got to talk to him," she said. "We can't let this happen."

"Be careful." Ruth clicked her tongue worriedly. "I hope I haven't caused any serious trouble. If it weren't for my showing you the vision, you wouldn't even be in Las Vegas."

"Connor would be here, with or without me," she noted. "The point is that he's in danger. Ruth, I've got to go find him."

"Let me know how it comes out."

"You bet."

Krista raced to get her clothes. Where the heck had she put her pumps? She couldn't find them near the bed or in the closet.

There was no time to hunt. Pulling out the red tennis shoes, she laced them on.

She would check the lobby for some sign of Connor. If he weren't there, she would tear the hotel apart until she found him.

CONNOR HAD GAINED the impression, probably from old comic books, that the people of India were a mild-mannered, dignified people. He now understood why. If they moved too fast, their turbans fell off.

At least, his did.

It fell off when the tall, bulb-nosed man in suite 817 slammed the door in his face. It fell off when a naked two-hundred-pound lady answered the door of suite 818 and gave a shrill whistle at the sight of him.

At suite 819, half a dozen people jammed the doorway and chattered to him in a foreign language. Connor sighed. "Sorry, guys, wrong room."

They all bowed. When he bowed in return, his turban fell off.

This was not the toughest assignment Connor had ever had, nor the first time he'd worn a disguise, but it was the most outlandish one. Thank goodness there were only three suites left.

He was about to knock on 820 when the next door opened and a woman tiptoed out. All he glimpsed was a mass of disheveled blond hair above a T-shirt and jeans.

Then she brushed back the hair and he saw that she was crying. "Ellen?"

"Oh!" She stared at him in alarm. Even when recognition dawned, she remained tensed for flight. "What are you doing here?"

"Looking for you." He positioned the cart out of the way against a wall. "I guess you found out that Myford's a fake."

She nodded, still not trusting him.

"Believe me, Krista and I were tricked, too." Connor pulled out his wallet. "Here's my detective license. Early this morning, I got a call from the man who hired me. He's the head of a security service. We don't know who this guy is, but he's not Myford Ames."

Ellen scanned the license. "All right. Please, please, get me out of here, and I'll never do anything this foolish again."

"Falling in love isn't foolish. It's not your fault you were tricked." He started to reach for her arm, but she flinched, so Connor gestured her ahead of him toward the elevators. "Did he hurt you?"

She swallowed hard. "Not physically. Thank goodness I didn't—we didn't—you know."

Connor knew, all too well.

"I can't believe anyone would do this," she continued, the emotions spilling out. "Then this morning, while he thought I was asleep, he started taking pictures of me in my bed. I played possum. I didn't know what else to do."

"Sounds like he's a reporter," he said. "Not a legitimate one, obviously."

"When he went to take a shower, I looked in his wallet," she said. "That isn't illegal, is it?"

"Not under the circumstances," he said.

"His name is Horace Flipperson. He works for some computer company," she said. "He has a company badge that says he's an engineer."

"If he works with computers, he might have been able to figure out who you are over the Internet before you identified yourself," Connor said. "Once he hacked into your identity, he must have decided to find some way to rip you off."

More tears slid down her cheeks. In her misery, Ellen resembled a distraught child, and Connor barely restrained the impulse to put his arm around her.

At the bank of elevators, he punched the down button. "We can send someone to retrieve your belongings."

"Thank you." She hesitated, then added, "I looked in his pants pocket. Isn't that awful?"

"Under the circumstances, I hardly think you need to worry about ethics," Connor said. "What did you find?"

"A phone number." She shivered as they stepped into the elevator. "I called it. I just had to know!"

"Did you reach anyone?"

"Voice mail at *Round the World Insider*. You know, the tabloid. Then I saw the back of the note." She gulped.

The doors closed, isolating them. Connor's heart went out to this lost kitten. "Ellen, don't torture yourself. The details don't matter."

She squared her shoulders. "It said: 'Weekend together, $20,000. Marriage, $50,000.' They were paying him to marry me! Why, Mr. Fallon?"

"Probably so he could tell all the gory details for their readers," Connor said grimly.

"Why would he do it? I know people do terrible things for money, but he's got a good job, or at least, I think he does. I didn't even care whether he was Myford Ames! He was so tender and kind, I would have married him for himself! If he wanted money, he could have had mine."

The kid was a true innocent which made this betrayal all the worse. "He may have acted nice, but the way he was puffing himself up yesterday, I'd say he's got an ego problem. Maybe he saw you as a way to make himself look more important."

"I wish I'd never won that lottery," Ellen said miserably. "It's messed up my whole life."

"It's also let you help a lot of people," Connor reminded her.

She didn't seem to hear. "This whole thing is going to be in the newspapers, one way or another. Everybody will know that the only reason Horace wanted to marry me is for money."

"And for his ego," Connor finished.

She burst into a fresh round of weeping.

"Please, Ellen," he said. "I hate seeing a woman cry."

"I'm sorry!" she blubbered.

At the lobby, the elevator doors parted. Connor was not pleased to see, turning toward them with a look of dawning recognition, the young man in the plaid suit who'd been fighting to photograph him and Krista yesterday.

The man started to lift his camera into position, until he saw Ellen's tears. "Hey, are you all right?"

"No pictures!" Connor moved forward protectively. "Which rag do you work for?"

"Gossip Incorporated," he said. "Why?"

"Because if you worked for *Round the World Insider,* I'd teach you a few lessons in manners!" he snapped. "Now beat it."

"Please, mister," the man said. "I'm new at this job and that other guy, the one from *Round the World,* has whipped my tail at every turn. Please let me get the picture."

"It's all right," Ellen sniffled. "Poor guy."

"Poor guy like a snake in the grass!" Connor grumbled.

The young man frowned at him. "Wait a minute, you were with a different woman yesterday. Aren't you Myford Ames?"

"There is no Myford Ames," he said. "That is, not locally."

"Who was that other woman?"

"She works for Ellen," he said. "Okay? Now, does the word *amscray* mean anything to you?"

"Connor?" Ellen tapped his arm. "Could I, uh, talk to you?"

As she stepped from behind Connor, the young man whipped his camera into position. At that instant, he could have taken a great shot of Ellen's tear-stained face, but he hesitated. "I can't do it."

"Oh, for Pete's sake." Connor couldn't believe the guy was such a soft touch. "It's your job!" Then, remembering his position, he added, "And thank goodness you didn't do it or I'd be grinding your camera into little pieces!"

Ellen's tug on his sleeve drew him away. "I have this idea. It's really important to me. Please, I don't have time to explain right now. Just go along, will you? I'll make it worth your while, honestly."

At least she'd stopped crying. Poor little stray, Connor thought, how could he say no? "Sure."

She gave him a quavery smile. "Thanks!" Turning to the photographer, she said, "Want a scoop?"

He blinked in surprise. "Well, sure."

"First, let's introduce ourselves. I don't like treating each other like some kind of objects." She held out her hand. "I'm Ellen Hardison."

He extended his own and shook, firmly. "My name's Mack Harris."

"This is Connor Fallon." She rested one hand on his arm, prompting Connor to shake hands, too. "You can take our picture, now." Linking her arm through his, she posed for the camera.

The lens clicked obediently. "What's going on?" Mack asked. "Who is this guy, anyway?"

Ellen chewed on her lip as if in desperate need of breakfast. Her painfully tight grip on Connor's arm revealed her tension as she replied, "He's my fiancé. We're getting married in half an hour, and we want you to photograph the whole thing."

IT WAS TWENTY MINUTES to nine when Krista reached the lobby and made a rapid scan. The first person she saw was, unfortunately, the young photographer who'd pestered them yesterday.

Despite her efforts to ignore him, the man kept throwing himself into her path until she realized he was trying to talk to her, not take her picture. "Weren't you the one who was with Mr. Fallon in the ballroom? In what capacity do you work for Ellen Hardison?"

He knew Connor's real name. That fact was enough to give her pause. "I'm a public relations assistant," she improvised.

"So you know about this wedding business?"

Which wedding? More importantly, *whose* wedding? Krista had an urge to shake the man to find out what he knew, but that wouldn't look good. "I'm supposed to be discreet. How much did they tell you?"

The young man blew a speck of dust off his lens cap. "They agreed to let me take pictures at their wedding. I'm supposed to meet them inside in twenty minutes."

"Meet who?"

"Mr. Fallon and Miss Hardison, of course."

Her breath caught in her throat. In a way, it made sense: Ruth had foreseen a second bride who resembled Krista, and Ellen filled the bill.

Yet it made no sense at all. Why would Connor be

marrying the heiress? And why invite a tabloid photographer?

Perhaps, in some convoluted way, Connor was protecting Ellen from danger, as he'd said in his note. Or had he seen his chance to marry a rich woman, and jumped at it?

Krista didn't believe he was capable of such duplicity. Correction: She didn't *want* to believe it.

Yet until this weekend, her impression of the man had been anything but flattering. Had her original skeptical instincts been correct?

If this marriage was for real, Krista had a moral obligation to warn Ellen what kind of man she was getting. Her own feelings could wait. She refused to break down and cry, or curse, or throw red gym shoes at him until she'd saved Ellen.

If this was a trick or a trap for some third party, he should have warned her. Leaving Krista ignorant and therefore vulnerable to danger was almost as bad as abandoning her for another woman.

"I can't add anything to what they've told you," she admitted to the photographer. "Have they already gone into the ballroom?"

He nodded. "Miss Hardison said there was a wedding dress waiting for her."

Barely remembering to thank him, Krista hurried off. She had to reach Ellen and Connor before they did something stupid.

Then there was the matter of the mystery man with the gun. In spite of everything, she didn't want Connor to get shot.

At the entrance to the ballroom, a guard stopped

her, politely but firmly. "Sorry, miss. The trade show doesn't open until one."

"I have to go in!"

"Do you have an invitation to a wedding?" he asked. "Only members of wedding parties and fashion shoots are allowed inside."

"No, but—"

"Sorry, miss." Folding his arms, he regarded her coldly.

Krista pressed her lips together so he wouldn't see how upset she was. She had to reach Ellen, but how?

As for Connor, if she ever saw him again, she was going to make his life miserable. But probably not half as miserable as he'd just made hers.

"LOOK, I want to help you out, but marriage?" Connor said when he got Ellen away from the photographer.

"We won't get married in the legal sense," she informed him in a low voice as she waved a pass at the guard outside the ballroom. "It's just for show."

At this early hour, workmen dotted the ballroom, nailing up floral displays, adjusting lights and scraping open one folding chair after another. Tableaux were being transformed for weddings, real and staged.

Connor sidestepped an electrician fixing a floor outlet and nearly ran into a cleaning cart. "I can understand you wanting to get revenge on *Round the World,* but this is carrying things too far."

"Revenge?" She looked shocked. "That's not it!"

"Do you think this will safeguard your reputation?" he asked. "Faking an annulment or a divorce isn't going to look good, either."

"Oh, no!" she said. "I'm trying to help that young man keep his job."

His jaw wouldn't work. Connor simply stared at her. Finally, he managed to say, "You want me to pretend to marry you to do that bloodhound a favor?"

"He has such a sweet face," Ellen said. "Don't you think? He could have taken my picture and he didn't. How many reporters would do that?"

"So he acted like a decent human being!" Connor said. "You're carrying gratitude too far."

She wrapped her arms around herself. "That Horace—what he tried to do—he tried to make love to me! Can you imagine? I feel so hurt and so lost. Doing something kind for someone else makes me feel clean again. Is that ridiculous?"

The worst part this time was that she'd run out of tears. Her shoulders shook in dry sobs.

"I'm sorry." Connor struggled against his own sympathy, but he was weakening. "It won't work anyway. The truth will come out, and then what happens to Mack's job?"

"The truth doesn't have to come out right away," Ellen sniffled. "Are you and Miss Lund more than friends?"

He nodded.

"This would create problems for you?"

He nodded again, harder.

"Is there something I could do for you both?" she asked. "Buy your dream house? A honeymoon in Hawaii? I'll make all this up to you, I promise!"

"Save your money," he said. "If it means this much to you, I'm sure she'll understand."

"Oh, thank you!" Ellen flung her arms around

him. "Thank you, thank you! I'll run and put on my wedding dress! Please don't change your mind. Please don't go away." She gazed at him as if the fate of the world hung in the balance.

"I'll be here." After she departed, he surveyed the ballroom in case the evil Horace Flipperson put in an appearance.

A familiar rotund figure with a goatee, but mercifully sans Tarzan costume, caught his eye. Pierre was waving a clipboard and snapping orders at a man replacing bulbs in the "La Grande Noce Satirique" marquee.

The rest of the French TV crew couldn't be far behind. Connor still didn't understand what, if anything, the mixed-up suitcases had to do with their filming a satire of American excesses. Once this wedding was concluded, however, he'd confront them and get Krista's clothes back.

Thank goodness she'd slept late. With luck, he'd make it back in time to explain the whole thing, and they could share a good laugh.

12

It took Krista a while to locate a corridor leading into the ballroom. When she tried to sneak into the ballroom through an inner door she was turned away once again. Even more irritating was the way the guard let several women in business suits breeze right inside.

"They aren't brides!" she pointed out.

"They're in costume," he said.

"Costume? I've got suits exactly like those!"

"They have models' passes," he said.

She hadn't seen the women show any passes, but Krista could tell he wasn't amenable to argument. Furious, she made a couple of wrong turns in the corridor, and then arrived, with the luck of the lost, at a dressing room.

Here, at least, no guards stopped her, and she walked right in.

A bulb-topped mirror ran along one wall and a rack of frothy clothing lined the opposite one. At the counter, two models were applying makeup.

"Excuse me," she said. "Does either of you know how I can lease or borrow a gown?"

One of the women blinked at her. The model's long black hair was arranged in such a perfect French twist that Krista suspected it might be a wig. "Why? Are you getting married?'' With her throaty voice and heavy accent, she sounded almost like a man.

"No, I've got to stop a marriage,'' Krista said. "It's going to be a disaster.''

Then she noticed the woman's suit. A light-green tweed with braid trimming and frog-style closures, it was an exact duplicate of one that Krista had purchased on sale at the Brea Mall.

She'd brought it to Vegas with her, too. Coincidence? Not likely. "Hey!'' she said. "That's my suit!''

The other woman paused with her mascara wand in midair. Huge blue eyes and rouged cheekbones made an odd contrast to her hairless head, which, at second glance, Krista could see was covered by a flat skullcap. On the counter, atop a styrofoam dummy head, sat a honey-blond wig fixed with a daisy-studded bandeau.

"*Mon dieu,*'' the woman muttered. "It seems the cat has fled the bag.''

Krista stared at her in shock. Or rather, at him, because despite the makeup and the silk dressing wrap, this was unquestionably a man. "Who are you?''

"Allow me to introduce myself,'' he said thickly. "My name is René.''

CONNOR WONDERED WHY, across the ballroom, Pierre was shouting at several women models, gesturing at their suits and trying to shoo them back toward the dressing rooms. He seemed to be objecting to their choice of clothing.

Come to think of it, those looked like Krista's suits.

He wondered, for a moment, if staying up all night had addled his brain. Could he be hallucinating?

A movement near one of the side doors caught Connor's attention. He turned to see Ellen sailing toward him, radiant in a white gown.

Beside her strolled a sixtyish man in a dark suit, with a Bible tucked under one arm. Now Connor hoped that he *was* hallucinating.

When the pair reached the rose-covered trellis, Ellen said, "Connor, this is the Reverend Marlow."

Maybe this was merely a stand-in for their mock ceremony. "Exactly what church are you affiliated with?" he asked. "The Church of the Taj Mahal Everlasting?"

"Don't worry, I'm fully qualified to perform marriages in the state of Nevada," the silver-haired man assured him. From inside his jacket, he pulled out a pen and a sheaf of papers. "Here are a few things you need to sign."

"Excuse me?" Connor turned to Ellen.

She flinched. "Please."

"Wait a minute!" Seizing her arm, he steered her behind a cardboard Cupid. "I am not really going to marry you." He pronounced the words slowly and clearly. "I thought we were clear on that. It's only pretend."

"I know," she said, "but Myford—I mean, Horace—arranged for this minister, and we need someone to play that role, don't we?"

"Am I missing something here?" he said. "This man wants me to sign papers."

"Look at him!" Ellen said. "He's an honest-to-goodness preacher! I can't ask him to perpetuate a fraud even to help out that nice photographer.''

Connor ran his hand through his hair, and knocked off the turban. He caught it a foot from the floor, and jammed it back onto his head. ''You expect me to marry you to spare this minister's feelings and help some scandalmonger land a scoop? Get real!''

''We can have it annulled!''

''Have you lost your mind?''

As Ellen stared at him, her face crumpled. ''Yes! I'm so upset I can't think straight!''

Connor gathered her against his sash, patting her shoulder awkwardly. ''There, there.''

From nowhere, a strobe light nearly blinded him. ''Hi!'' Through the spots before his eyes, he perceived the plaid-clad form of Mack Harris. ''What a great picture! Are you ready to start the wedding now?''

How, Connor wondered frantically, was he going to explain this to Krista?

IN CHARMINGLY accented English, René explained that the men were performers on a satiric TV show that used male actors to play both male and female roles. They'd come to Las Vegas, the world capital of kitsch, to tape a program, of which the climax would be an outlandish wedding.

''You people in America seem to us to be sometimes clever, sometimes tasteless,'' he explained. ''We admire you. Also, we see your flaws. So we come here to make a little friendly parody.''

''And you brought all these costumes?'' Krista indicated the rack, which overflowed with feathers and sequins, gold lamé and mirrored beads. Among the outfits, she glimpsed familiar bits of sea-green slinkiness and heart-stopping scarlet. "Why did you send me those gowns?"

"They looked so lovely on you!" René murmured. "It is too bad you are not a man so you could be in our show."

"Yeah, too bad," Krista said. "But you haven't answered my question."

"When we arrive, we see that everyone in Las Vegas is outrageous!" said the other "woman," whose name was Michel. "That white-haired lady in the short dress—"

"Aunt Bea."

"Yes, yes," Michel said. "With that white hair and that short dress, those stockings, she puts us to shame! Also the wedding on the *Titanic*. That is better than what we have planned."

"Still, our director, Pierre, wants us to wear these froufrou dresses." Peering into the mirror, René outlined his lips in a darker color. "When I opened your mistaken suitcase, it has given me such an idea! Something entirely different and surprising!"

"René should be a director," Michel added. "He is brilliant!"

Krista wasn't sure she agreed. "You consider my suits different and surprising?"

"For a wedding, yes!" said René. "Business suits at the altar—it is perfect. A satire on the American obsession with making money!"

"What's wrong with making money?" asked

Krista.

"Voilà," said Michel, who apparently thought he'd just proved some point or other. "You are the American female of the millennium. Pierre should realize that we are right on target!"

"Even now, he is no doubt having a fit as his models appear in your suits. Meanwhile, I am stuck with…" René stopped. He eyed Krista. He smiled. "This white outfit! Ideal for today's bride, with a little ironing. Could I borrow it?"

She glanced down at her wrinkled skirt and jacket. "Sure, if you can find me a wedding gown. I've got to get into the ballroom."

Still bald but otherwise completely made up, René uncoiled from his seat. "I have the perfect item. Perfectly ugly, of course. It is my own costume, and I am heartily glad to be rid of it."

From the rack, he lifted a monstrosity of white organza and leg-of-mutton sleeves. Pink rosettes dotted the bodice and the skirt, giving the impression that the dress had come down with the measles.

Krista stared at it numbly. On the wall, the clock's hands shifted. Two minutes to nine.

She couldn't let poor innocent Ellen walk down the aisle. Or Connor get shot, even if he did deserve it. Why couldn't he simply have come and explained why he was acting this way? It was all his fault that she found herself confused and angry and desperate enough to relinquish the only decent garment she had left.

"Let's do it," she said, and reached for the hideous dress.

"COULD WE SIGN the papers afterward?" Ellen asked the minister. "I mean, could we walk through a rehearsal first? That is—Connor, tell him!"

Connor cleared his throat. He had no better idea what to say than Ellen did.

Mack backed up a step, snapping away. Then he paused. "Say, Ellen, you look upset. Are you sure you want to marry this fellow?"

"Wait a minute. Who's marrying whom?" Bea scooted toward them with her ever-present tray of drinks. "What's going on here?"

"This may be Las Vegas, but perhaps we shouldn't rush into the ceremony," said the minister. "I'd say the two of you could use a marriage counselor."

"And here comes one now," said Bea. "It's about time she showed up."

With a gulp, Connor spotted his landlady-turned-lover hurrying past the guard with an expression of hurt and fury on her lovely face. Ellen sagged against him. "I'm sorry," she said. "This is my fault, isn't it?"

Instinctively, his arm clamped onto her waist to hold her steady. The friendly gesture didn't go unnoticed; across the room, Krista glared at him.

Connor tried to signal her. Ignoring him, she glanced wildly around, no doubt for a weapon.

She found one: a whisk broom on a cleaning cart. Snatching it, she advanced toward tableau number twelve.

Sometimes women just needed to get things out of their system, Connor reflected. And winced, in advance.

WAS THIS REALLY HER, prim and proper family counselor Krista Lund, storming across a ballroom in full
view of dozens of people, waving a whisk broom like
a madwoman?

She'd never felt such rage. She didn't understand
it, or herself.

From the corner of her eye, she caught a shocked
look on the face of René's director, Pierre. He was
eyeing her gown as if contemplating wrenching it off
her body. Well, he could have it back as soon as she
was done with it.

And with Connor.

"Get away from him!" she shouted at Ellen, who
rocked backward. "You can't marry that man!"

"You call this a marriage counselor?" asked an
older man in a dark suit.

"I suppose sometimes the direct approach works
best," said Aunt Bea.

The photographer, frowning, snapped Krista's picture. Portrait of a lunatic, she thought, and planted
herself in front of the happy couple.

Up close, she could see that Ellen's eyes were red
and her cheeks damp from crying. It didn't gibe with
the image of a joyful bride.

As for Connor, he was gazing at Krista with in-
dulgent humor and a trace of concern. Not alarm. Not
guilt. Not even disapproval. She gripped the whisk
broom so hard, she could hear the straw crunching.

At the French tableau across the room arose a collective gasp. At first, she thought the actors were reacting to the soap-opera scenario playing out in real
life.

Then she heard cries of alarm. And saw a man in thick glasses racing toward them from the door, his face contorted with fury. It was Myford Ames. From his hand jutted the cold metallic snout of a gun.

13

ELLEN YELLED, "Horace, don't!" A couple of security guards dashed in from either side, but stopped at the sight of the pistol.

The photographer frowned at the man. "Who is this clown?"

"Don't let him have the story!" screamed Myford, or Horace, or whoever he was. What story? Krista wondered.

His arm was swinging so crazily, a shot might have hit any of them. That was the last thing she noticed before Connor thrust himself in front of her.

"Stay back!" he commanded. "I don't want you hurt!"

A minute ago, he'd stood with his arm around Ellen, yet she wasn't the one he chose to protect in this moment of danger. His willingness to risk his life for Krista spoke louder than words.

Her anger vanished. How could she have doubted him?

Right now, though, a villain in Coke-bottle glasses was waving a lethal weapon in their direction. She might lose Connor before she even got a chance to tell him that she loved him.

"I hired you two fakes to make my job easier, not get in my way!" the man yelled.

"You tricked us into going along with your con game," replied Connor in a cool baritone. "Come on, Horace, you work for a computer company. You're not Myford, and you're not a killer, either. Put down the gun."

"I'm not giving up my story!" the man shouted. "For once in my life, I want to be the face on the newsstand!"

"They're not going to put your face on the cover," snorted the photographer. "It's Ellen's face they care about. You'd still be just some clown who spent the night with a celebrity."

At last Krista grasped what was happening, or part of it, anyway. Fake Myford. Grieving Ellen. But why had she and Connor told the photographer they were getting married?

Ellen spoke next. The young man in plaid tried to shield her, but she waved him away.

"Did you ever think about me, even once, Horace?" Her voice quavered. "You hurt me and humiliated me."

"This isn't about you, Ellen," he said.

Her shoulders trembled. "Do you think because I'm famous, I don't have feelings?"

"You'll get over it," he snarled, renewing his grip on the gun. "You're rich and important. I'm a nobody. A programmer. A nerd. I want my five minutes of fame and I'm going to get it any way I can!"

Apparently, that included shooting anyone who got in his way, Krista realized. In that moment while Horace was still snarling at Ellen, she leaned around Connor and flung the whisk broom as hard as she could.

Direct hit, right in the schnozz! Thank goodness for her practice on the office dartboard.

Startled, Horace grabbed the brush. Connor dived for the gun, while Aunt Bea threw a drink in the man's face. When the photographer and the guards pounced, he went down sputtering and cursing.

"Très magnifique!" cried the French TV director. Beside him, René, looking chic in Krista's white suit, raised his hands in a victory salute.

"Wow!" said Ellen. "Mack, you were wonderful!" She hugged the photographer as he withdrew from the fray.

"Aw, anybody would have done the same," he said, and happily accepted a kiss.

By the time matters got sorted out, Krista learned that the gun was a realistic fake and that "Myford" was a computer programmer named Horace Flipperson who'd been trying to rip off Ellen to get a story for a tabloid. He was dragged away growling and grumbling, his wrath cooling as he realized that he could face assault charges despite having used a toy gun.

"He's so pathetic," Ellen said. "I kind of feel sorry for that creep,"

"It's because you have a kind heart," murmured Mack.

"Don't feel too sorry," said Bea. "He caught the bride's bouquet. No doubt he'll be finding true love in the slammer."

"You weren't really going to marry Ellen, were you?" Krista asked Connor. "I feel like an idiot."

He tucked one of her daisies back into the headband. "Why would I marry her when I'm in love with *you?*"

"You are?"

"One hundred percent," he said. "You can tell it's for real—I'm not even asking for a break on the rent."

"You mean you weren't going through with the wedding?" The photographer raised one fist; the other arm was holding Ellen. "You're as big a double-crosser as that other guy!"

"No, Mack, I asked him to pretend he was marrying me," Ellen said. "To help you out. You know, to give you the scoop."

"What?" the man said. "Why would you do that?"

"Because you're so sweet," she sniffed. "I don't want you to lose your job."

"I hate my job!" he said. "I'm only doing this till I can find a position with a real paper."

Krista clutched Connor, grateful for his strength and still basking in the revelation that he loved her. Now they could go back to California and talk at leisure. She felt certain they could get their differences resolved before the wedding.

Mentally, she began making a list. It started with their taste in decorating and ended with where to put the stray animals.

Connor was studying her with a warmth that mirrored her own. "Mr. Marlow?" he asked. "Could we have those legal papers to sign?"

Krista scratched her neck beneath the itchy organza fabric. "Surely you're not suggesting we go through with a wedding now!"

"It was foretold." With a flourish, Connor indicated their costumes.

He had a point. They looked exactly as the psychic had foretold: The dirty-faced groom in a tuxedo, a turban and a sash; Bea, wearing the waitress uniform and holding a tray of drinks; the dark-suited minister beneath a rose-covered trellis; the photographer in plaid; blond Ellen in a white gown; and Krista herself floating in a cloud of pink-spotted white froth.

With her red gym shoes peeping out from under the skirt.

"Well?" said Connor.

She blushed. "Are you asking me to marry you?"

"Did I forget that part?"

"You did."

"Just a minute." He walked over to the French marquee and spoke earnestly with Pierre. Heads bobbed, and then a whole group of men and women—or rather, men and men—headed their way.

"What on earth are they doing?" Bea asked.

"Connor's so impulsive." For once, Krista didn't mean it as an insult.

She needed a husband she could count on, deep down. That didn't mean he had to be convention-bound on the surface.

Love blossomed inside her, full and free. Unpredictable Connor was exactly the man she wanted to share it with, now and forever. As soon as she got home, she was going to throw all her stupid lists away.

Suddenly she found herself surrounded by French actors, humming "Here Comes the Bride" while tossing bits of confetti into the air. In their midst, Connor fell dramatically to one knee.

"Krista," he said. "Wanna get hitched?"

"Yes," she said.

He cupped his ear, as if he hadn't heard.

"Yes!" she shouted. "I love you, you maniac!"

He grinned. "Thank goodness. Now let's go make an honest woman out of Ruth."

THE STRANGEST THING about the wedding, to Connor, wasn't the French actors humming on the sidelines, or Aunt Bea handing drinks around, or the way his turban fell off when he kissed the bride.

It was how natural the whole thing felt. As if he'd always been headed toward marrying Krista, and doing so in precisely this manner.

True, if Ruth hadn't envisioned the scenario, Krista would never have consented to accompany him this weekend. But he had the strangest feeling that fate had been lurking offstage, with a dozen variations and machinations, to bring them one way or another to this point.

He picked up his turban. Standing on tiptoe in her red gym shoes, Krista kissed him again.

Their guests cheered. His bride's eyes twinkled like sparklers on the Fourth of July.

Mack took one more picture and handed Connor the roll of film. "No charge. It feels good to be doing honest work for a change."

Ellen slipped her hand shyly into his. "Maybe I could help. I've come to know some reporters for the legitimate papers. I'll bet they could persuade their editors to look at your portfolio."

"You don't have to do anything for me," the photographer said. "I'd like for us to be friends with no strings attached."

The two regarded each other with dawning affection. Connor wished them well. Maybe this escapade with Horace would turn out to be as lucky for Ellen as it had been for him and Krista.

"Too bad Ruth couldn't be here," he said.

"We'll give a party when we get home and make her the guest of honor." His bride traced one finger along his cheekbone. "Won't that be fun?"

He could think of something that would be even more fun, and they wouldn't have to wait until they got home, either. To his relief, no one else appeared eager to stick around.

Not even Bea. "You'll have to excuse us," she said.

"Us?" said Krista.

Connor noticed the minister waiting with his arms wrapped around the Bible. "Such a delightful woman," he said. "So youthful in spite of her years. I rarely meet her like in this city."

"We're going to have coffee," Bea said. "I think I'll change into something more conservative first, though. I wouldn't want to hurt his reputation."

As they were leaving, Connor saw the camera rolling at the French tableau. He and Krista joined other onlookers on the sidelines.

To the beat of "The Stars and Stripes Forever" blaring from a tape recorder, bridesmaids and ushers marched down the aisle. The men wore pin-striped suits; the women wore prim expressions and Krista's clothes. Everyone carried a briefcase.

They fanned out at the altar. The music segued into Mendelssohn's wedding march, and here came honey-blond René, simpering in Krista's white suit and carrying a bouquet of dollar bills. She hung on the arm of a man in an Uncle Sam suit.

When they reached the altar, the others reached into their briefcases and began pelting the bridal couple with coins. After trying to shield their faces, the pair turned and ran, with the others on their heels.

"Cut!" Pierre came toward Krista and Connor. "You know, I did not like the idea at first, but it is not bad, with these suits." He kissed Krista on both cheeks. "Do not tell anyone I said so, or René will crow about it all the way to Paris, and it is a very long flight."

"All I want is my clothes back," said Krista.

Pierre stopped in front of Connor. From the anticipation on his face, it was obvious he intended to kiss *his* cheeks, too.

"You do it and I'll tell René everything!" Connor said.

Pierre sighed. "You Americans. So inhibited!" He went to summon his actors back for a retake.

Time to depart. Time to begin the honeymoon.

Connor felt an urge to sweep Krista into his arms and carry her through the lobby, except that he'd tried something like that last night with painful results. "From the elevator," he said aloud.

"What?"

"Let's go to the tenth floor and I'll show you."

KRISTA SUPPOSED the fault was hers, that they didn't consummate their marriage in a slow and tender fashion. The minute Connor finished carrying her over the threshold, she ripped off his turban and started kissing him madly.

The big white dress, the red tennis shoes and the tuxedo left a trail across the floor. The two of them barely landed on the edge of the bed before Connor finished undressing her and they fell back together, laughing and moaning.

How had she kept him at bay for so long? Krista wondered. And why?

The old images of Connor had been replaced by new ones: Connor standing protectively in front of her; Connor kneeling in public, asking her to marry him.

Why had she believed she wanted dullness in a husband? With this man, she could have trust, along with something equally precious: passion that painted the world with fresh, bright colors.

This time when they made love, everything had changed. Instead of reaching tentatively for Connor, she indulged herself in grasping his back and kneading the powerful, bunched muscles.

Her bridegroom, no longer concerned about her inexperience, cupped her face in his hands and kissed her deeply. Then he thrust into her down below, long and hard.

The rhythms of their bodies formed a perfect counterpoint, rising toward a crescendo. Two souls merged and they became in every way husband and wife.

Afterward, they nestled there for a long time, then showered together. Krista laughed as she soaped Connor's sculpted body, and he teased her in return with a lingering, slippery rub.

She wished they didn't have to check out of their suite by noon. On the other hand, she couldn't wait to turn her cozy four-poster into a marriage bed.

They'd really gone through with the wedding. She could hardly believe, as she gazed at this black-haired, dark-eyed charmer, that they belonged to each other.

"What are you going to do for clothes?" Connor asked as they ventured out, towel-wrapped.

Krista stared around in dismay. "That's right! I don't have anything to wear except this wedding dress. I can't see myself flying home in that, can you?"

"Stranger things have happened," Connor deadpanned.

"I suppose they have, haven't they?"

The buzzer sounded. "Wait!" Quickly, Krista shrugged into her nightgown, which was the only other garment she had available to cover herself.

When Connor opened the door, the same bellhop stood waiting. This time, he held not a suitcase but an armload of Krista's suits, wrapped in clear plastic marked with the logo of the hotel's one-hour dry-cleaning service.

He also handed her a shopping bag filled with her shoes, and a brand-new pair of Ferragamo pumps in the same size. "That's a gift from—from—some French people. Satiric something-or-other."

"Thanks." With Connor's help, she transferred everything to the couch and returned with the wedding gown. "I expect they'll be wanting this."

The young man took the fluffy thing gingerly. "They did mention it, yes."

Clutching his towel around his midsection, Connor searched for his wallet. "Hang on and I'll tip you."

"That isn't necessary," the bellhop said. "René took care of it. He's a very generous guy."

"He?" Connor stopped in bafflement. "What do you mean *he?*"

"Thanks for everything." Krista shooed the bellhop outside and closed the door. She would prefer to keep this conversation private.

"What did he mean, *he?*" Connor said.

"Didn't you think those Frenchwomen were a little odd?" Krista asked.

"I suppose so." To her husband's credit, he didn't take long to get the point. "So all this time, those people wearing your suits—and the, er, *person* who was sending those fancy dresses—was, er—"

"Yes," Krista said.

Connor released a long, slow breath. "Well, I wasn't born yesterday, but I'm from Montana, and men in Montana don't do that sort of thing."

She chuckled. "No, but men from Montana do all sorts of other, wonderful things."

"Like for instance?" he teased.

"I'll show you," she said, and gave his towel a tug.

TRACY
SOUTH

Maddie's
Millionaire

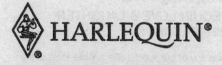

HARLEQUIN®

TORONTO • NEW YORK • LONDON
AMSTERDAM • PARIS • SYDNEY • HAMBURG
STOCKHOLM • ATHENS • TOKYO • MILAN • MADRID
PRAGUE • WARSAW • BUDAPEST • AUCKLAND

After living in the mountains for all of my thirty-odd years, I recently moved to the beaches of Southwest Florida. *Maddie's Millionaire,* then, is my swan song to the Appalachian region. The world Maddie finds—nosy neighbors, garden-variety eccentrics and an unspoiled landscape—is the world of my childhood.

—Tracy South

Books by Tracy South
HARLEQUIN LOVE & LAUGHTER
12—THE FIANCÉ THIEF

I owe special thanks to two great friends:
Thea Lane, who let me borrow her dog,
and Marcia Simonetta, who let me borrow her brain.
This book is for Bob, my real-life hero and husband.

1

SHE WOULD HAVE KNOWN him anywhere.

High, fine cheekbones and merry black eyes, eyes that contradicted the stern set of his lips. Thick black hair that his aunts and sisters must have considered wasted on a boy. Full eyelashes that probably pained them for the same reason. A bearing that said he was a man in charge of his own destiny.

"Lucas Keller," Maddie whispered.

"Do you recognize the old coot?"

Startled, Maddie looked away from the framed photograph and around the cluttered and dusty store. She hadn't seen anyone when she walked in, but the craggy voice seemed to be coming from behind a bin of irregularly sized work shirts and a crate of mismatched Mason jars. Craning her head around the boxes, Maddie watched as a man of about seventy rose from a chair and walked toward her. Rocking back a little on the balls of his feet, his hands shoved into the pockets of his khaki work pants, he whistled as he studied the picture with Maddie.

"Do you recognize him?" he repeated after a few seconds.

Maddie nodded. "That's Lucas Keller. He died about thirty years before I was born," she said.

He snorted. "I'd call that a close call."

Ouch. Obviously he wasn't going to launch into a

respectful tribute to the deceased author, but she hadn't really expected such contempt, either.

"You didn't like his fiction?" It was hard to believe there were still people who held a grudge about the relatively tame town secrets revealed in Lucas Keller's novels, but this person definitely was one of them.

"His fiction?" He raised one eyebrow at her, a trick she had always wanted to master but never had. "It has nothing to do with his books. I didn't like the way he chased me all over town with his cane whenever he found me cutting school."

She folded her arms across her chest and cocked her head toward the photo. "Then why do you have his picture on your wall?"

"It scares the shoplifters."

She had to give in and smile. She extended her hand to the man.

"I'm Maddie Randall, from Knoxville."

"You say that like you mean to stay a while," the man said, returning her handshake.

"For the summer." She willed him to leave it at that, since she still hadn't come up with a story about why she was in Ravens Gap. Not a convincing one anyway. She'd had a moment of pure panic earlier, when her new landlady asked her point-blank what had brought her from a sizable east Tennessee city to a tiny one across the mountains in North Carolina, but she'd been saved by a phone call from someone in the woman's bingo group.

"If you were a weekender, I was going to give you a fake name," the man said. "But since you're staying, I'm Connie Turner."

"Oh," she said. "I thought…"

"You thought the Connie Turner of Connie Turner's store was going to be some sweet little old lady in pin curls and a housedress and fuzzy slippers, not some mean old man."

Even someone who was as usually blunt as she was could see there was no safe way to reply to that remark. Instead, she did her best to dance around it. "I don't know why I assumed you were a woman just because Mrs. Martin said Connie. My grandfather was a Carol, and his brother was a Shirley," she went on. "You must feel—"

Thankfully, he interrupted her before she could say, "Like the last of a dying breed."

"Harriet Martin? Is that who you're staying with?" He pointed toward the back of the store. "You'd better stock up on some food then."

"But she said breakfast and dinner were included in the rent," Maddie said, confused.

"That's what I mean. As skinny as you are, you can't afford to be eating her cooking."

She hadn't come into the store to buy anything other than a Coke. Really, she'd just come to look at the bulletin board Mrs. Martin had told her of when she'd asked her about how to find some sort of part-time job in town. But now that Connie had mentioned her in the same sentence with the word *skinny*, she felt honor-bound to reward him by shopping a little more. Especially considering that she probably had a good ten or fifteen pounds on the wiry older man.

"I guess I might pick up some peanut butter," she said, getting a plastic basket and moving toward the back of the store.

"You do that."

Idly picking up one jar of peanut butter after another, not sure what she was looking for since they all looked the same, Maddie was struck by just how long it had been since she'd shopped for herself. All her grocery trips had been made on behalf of the restaurant where she'd worked, so that instead of shopping for one tiny jar of banana peppers or artichokes, she'd lug back jugs of them. As for peanut butter, unless Meredith, the owner, was making her famous Thai peanut sauce over pasta, it just wasn't part of her diet. Since leaving graduate school, she'd lived, breathed, and slept the Good Enough Gourmet and its funky, uptown fare.

As if to remind her of what she was missing, her stomach rumbled. She chose what seemed to be the least dusty jar of peanut butter and added a box of saltines to her basket. It's okay, she reassured her stomach. *Remember, cooking and waitressing at someone else's restaurant was getting us nowhere. It was time to think about a real Career.*

Trouble was, all her life she'd been interested in so many different things that she couldn't shake the idea that a career was one of those things she still meant to think about on some faraway, unlikely someday, right up there with death and marriage. She'd tried grad school, but hadn't taken it very seriously either. Finding her purpose in life hadn't really concerned her, at least until people stopped asking her when she was going back to school and started assuming that at twenty-six years old, she must be doing what she wanted to be doing for the rest of her life. Even then, although it nagged at her, the nagging wasn't strong enough to fight the appeal of a job that fit her like her favorite old cotton sweater, a job that gave her free meals, enough money for books and music, and the feeling that the restaurant and its customers really needed her.

But then came the day that Dr. Jeff Alvin, respected literary scholar and onetime love, had let it be known in front of the whole lunchtime crowd that he didn't think she had it in her to be anything more than glorified counter help. And since she didn't plan on doing anything with her research on Lucas Keller, he'd said in a voice that had managed to be both sweet and slimy, he was sure she wouldn't mind that he had incorporated her hard work into a book he was writing himself. After all, wasn't her only concern that Lucas Keller get the rediscovery he deserved? He said all this knowing that she was at the height of the lunch rush, betting that she wouldn't embarrass him in a public place. But mind? Hell, yes, she minded. For one thing, she knew that Jeff didn't really *get* the author. He could joke all he wanted to about Maddie's obsession with Lucas Keller, tease her about being half in love with a novelist who'd been dead for decades, but Jeff had no emotional attachment to the work, no clue about who Lucas Keller was as a person.

She had tried to explain that, calmly at first, even though her mouth had gone dry and her knees were getting weak and Brink, one of the cooks, was yelling at her to pick up her orders. And as for what Jeff was doing with her work, true, you couldn't own facts or ideas, true, she didn't have a formal, legal case against him—he had made sure of that—but didn't he see the wrong in what he was doing, in using her this way?

No, he hadn't. When he'd finished his portobello mushroom sandwich and started walking away, she'd noticed that he had tipped her with a ten-dollar bill on a five-dollar check, as if to prove what a great guy he was. She had been flooded with a rage that she had never felt before.

Tossing aside her oversize apron, she had hurried over to the cash register, where, still calm, she had urged Jeff to rethink what he was doing. When he had looked at her as though she were nothing more to him than one of the ill-prepared freshmen he was always flunking in introductory composition, she had gotten a little louder. Then she had threatened to call the dean, to tell him everything. And she'd meant everything. He had simply responded with a simpering smile, then said to call him when she'd calmed down. That's when she'd grabbed the key lime pie.

The world hadn't fallen apart because of what she'd done, but there had been a definite crack in it after that. With every plate she carried, every drop of iced tea she poured, she saw herself as Jeff Alvin had seen her—a flake, a dilettante, someone who didn't deserve to be taken seriously. She knew that unless she did something about it, she would see those mocking eyes everywhere. It was time to ask herself some tough questions. If she didn't think Jeff Alvin was good enough to write about her beloved Lucas Keller, then why wasn't she doing it herself?

That incident had nudged her into her own career as a scholar and, she hoped, as Lucas Keller's primary biographer. As for the other biggies, marriage and death, Jeff had been her closest brush with marriage. Or so she had thought. Now she knew that he had no intention of ever marrying her—he just wanted her around to grade his papers, take his cat to the vet, and marvel at how intelligent he was. And as for death, well, she never gave her own any thought, but she would admit to more than a few fantasies about Jeff Alvin's. Just thinking about him now, her hand closed tightly on a bag of chips, and a loud "crunch" echoed through the store.

"You break it, you buy it," she heard Connie say.

"Sorry," she said meekly, adding the chips to her basket. She couldn't remember whether she'd packed everything she needed and, deciding to play it safe, walked over to an aisle jammed with health and beauty aids. She had just decided on a marked-down *Beauty and the Beast* toothbrush when she was startled by a commotion at the front of the store. A deep "woof" was followed by a piercing shriek. Whether it was from a cat, a bird or one really colicky infant, she couldn't tell. The evidence for cat mounted when a mangy ball of fur barely big enough to be a rat streaked by her legs and into a room at the back.

"I told you to keep that dog out of here," Connie yelled. "Miss Kitty is already losing her fur, worrying about that dog. My daughter's threatening to take her to the pet psychologist in Asheville."

"Sport tricked me into letting him in," a deep voice replied.

"Tricked you?" She heard Connie scoff. "I don't know how it is in the big city, but around here we like to think we're smarter than our animals."

Maddie had to see whom Connie was tormenting. Despite the bass voice, he sounded young. She pictured some scrawny college student, blushing madly at Connie's scolding.

"Was that a cat or a rat that went by me earlier? Because I'm really phobic about rodents," she said as she rounded the aisle to where the two men were arguing.

"You'd be more afraid of the cat if you met her," the stranger said. He was bent down, tugging on the collar of a huge dog that seemed to be half Akita, half Abominable Snowman. She saw that her guess about him being scrawny had been way off track. He easily filled out his tight, faded blue jeans and navy polo shirt. Since his head was down, she couldn't tell if her guess about his being a college boy was correct. When he finally looked up at her, she stepped back in shock. She was staring straight into the face of Lucas Keller.

"Sport!" she heard as at least one hundred pounds of dog barreled toward her, jumping up onto her shoulders and giving her a sloppy canine tongue in the face. Caught off guard, she sat down hard on the wooden floor. Judging from the dog's ensuing slobbers and wiggles, this made him very happy.

"Cats weren't enough. Now he's trying to terrorize young women, too," she heard Connie say. The other man extended one hand toward her while pulling the dog off with the other.

"I'm really sorry," Sport's owner said. "He's not usually like this." She took the hand he offered, half expecting her own to disappear through it. Instead, she felt a decided tingle as the strong, warm hand gripped her own. She dropped his hold as soon as she regained her balance, still feeling the imprint of his touch.

But if he were flesh and blood, how was it possible for him to look as though he'd just stepped out of the photograph on the wall? He had the same shock of dark hair, the same full mouth, identical cheekbones.

He even looked to be the same age as the Lucas Keller in the photograph, in his early thirties. As for his eyes, there was no mistaking them, dark and sharp and sly all at once.

"Are you all right?" the man asked.

"What do you mean he's not usually like this?" Connie asked. "He's always like this."

"Well, okay, so he is," the man admitted to Maddie. She didn't say anything, just kept gaping at his appearance. "I've tried everything," he continued. "I don't know what to do." When she didn't respond, he looked at her with what seemed to her like undue concern. "Are you all right? Do you need to sit down somewhere?"

"She thinks she's seeing a ghost," Connie said, just as Maddie said, her voice shaking a little, "I feel like I've seen a ghost."

The stranger blinked, frowned, then said, "I must be the only one who doesn't get it." He bent down to pat Sport, who seemed permanently lodged at Maddie's feet. The closeness of the look-alike made Maddie back up a little, and when she did so, Sport scooted, too, settling back down on top of her sandaled feet.

"The old coot, you idiot," Connie said.

"Oh." He turned and looked at the picture of Lucas Keller. Clearly, he and Connie shared this nickname for Maddie's hero. But that still didn't explain who he was.

"I know there's a resemblance," he said. "Although I have to say that most people aren't as overcome by it as you seem to be."

"She was staring at his picture right before you came in," Connie said. Hearing herself talked about in the third person, and realizing what she must look like, standing in front of this man with her mouth hanging open, Maddie tried to get a grip on the situation.

"So if you aren't Lucas Keller, come back from the grave, who are you?" Oh, great. Now she sounded like some kind of crazed ghost buster.

It wouldn't have surprised her if those thoughts had crossed his mind, too. But rather than question her sanity, he smiled politely and said, "As far as I know, I'm the one who lives in this town, not you. I should be asking you who you are."

Connie interrupted. "Where are my manners? My wife always said I thought tact was something you left in the stable. Maddie Randall, Keller Lowry. Keller, Maddie's here for the summer. And Maddie, Keller hasn't been here that long, either."

"Keller?" She said it before she could stop herself. All right, so she seemed to have a one-track mind. But still, he couldn't be....

"His great-grandson," Keller Lowry said. "But he was out of the picture long before I got here."

"But that's not possible," Maddie said, frowning. "Lucas's three children died before adulthood."

"No," Keller said. "My grandfather—he was the youngest—ran away from home after they had a fight. The old man just told everybody he was dead."

"But acting as though someone is dead and that person actually being dead are two very different things," Maddie said. They looked at each other, then looked at her as if to say, "Hello, Einstein." She blushed, not able to tell them that she had only been thinking out loud.

A living, breathing descendant of Lucas Keller. If

Jeff Alvin had known that, she would have heard about it, thanks to a friend who worked in the English department. She wanted to run to the phone and taunt Jeff with her discovery, but she knew that would bring his smarmy self here. Her friend seemed to think that he hadn't found a very welcome reception when he was in Ravens Gap a few months ago. The last thing she ever wanted to do was be confused with Jeff, or associated with him, but if he came back to town, there would be no way to keep people from linking them together. This was not a war in which Jeff Alvin would fight fairly. Just in case he had built some connections or sources, she'd rather that people not know she was here to write a book about Lucas Keller. If she acted too excited about this knowledge, she risked having everyone find out the truth. For now, it was best if she didn't arouse anyone's suspicions.

That wasn't as easy as it sounded. Connie gave her a sharp look and said, "So how do you know so much about Lucas anyway? I didn't know they still taught him in school."

"Oh, they don't," she said, trying to think of a semi-plausible story about why she knew who he was. "Um, my grandmother was a big fan. She had a few newspaper articles about him, and she had those pasted in his books." This sounded okay to her, since she was always finding old books where people had done this. "These articles had his picture, of course, so that's how I knew what he looked like." Ooh, even better. "And of course I loved his books when I read them, and I read them all, since what else is there to do when you're at your grandmother's house but find a good book and go off somewhere by yourself?"

Conscious that she was moving out of plausible and into overkill, she shut up.

Connie was looking at her skeptically. "Play outside in the fresh air?"

She'd rather be trapped inside a preschool with twenty children who'd eaten nothing but cake and Kool-Aid all day. She'd rather be the lunch shift's only waitress with half the tables full of notorious non-tippers and the rest packed with people with special diets. Anything was better than going outside, where some element of nature was always waiting to make you itch, burn or sweat.

She blinked, then said, "I meant on rainy days, of course."

"Of course," Connie said.

"Woof." Sport's voice echoed through the building. Grateful to him for changing the subject, Maddie crouched down to his level. "What's the matter? Not getting enough attention?"

"He thinks he never gets enough attention," Keller said.

"It's because his name's Sport," Maddie said without thinking.

"What do you mean?"

"Well, it's such an ordinary name for such a big and beautiful dog. He feels like he has to do something to differentiate himself from all the other Sports out there. I mean, when you walk him, people stop and stare, don't they?"

"Yeah," Keller said.

"They snatch their small children up, too," Connie chimed in.

"Well, when people see him, and then ask you, what's his name, and you say Sport, the dog is con-

scious of the letdown that his name represents. Why
do you think there are so few supermodels named
Mary or Sue?'' She thought for a second. ''Well,
there's Cindy, but then she's working that whole all-
American-girl persona, so the name Cindy's a delib-
erate—'' She might have gone on, except Keller interrupted her.

''What are you suggesting I do? Rename him?'' In
her eagerness to help, she barely registered his skeptical tone.

''I think that's a great idea,'' she said. ''We need
something that fits his personality. Something that he
won't hear a thousand times in the park.'' She studied
Sport eye to eye, and he took that opportunity to get
in another good face lick.

''I like the idea of some kind of literary reference,
since his family has such a great literary figure in it.''

''His family?'' Keller said.

''You. You and your ancestors are his pack,'' she
explained. ''The trouble with literary, of course, is
that we don't want anything too sensitive. We want
something rough and rugged. But no Hemingway—
that's going to be too much of a burden. Same with
Faulkner. Something from Mark Twain would be perfect, but I have this feeling that everybody names
their dogs after Twain, don't you?'' She looked at
Keller, and when he merely shrugged, she went on.
''Something to go with his devil-may-care personality,'' she mused, as the dog yawned, then conspicuously rolled over on his back to have his stomach
rubbed. ''Devil. *The Devil's Dictionary.* Ambrose
Bierce. That's perfect. Ambrose.''

''Ambrose?'' Keller and Connie said together. The
dog jumped up and woofed, and Maddie saw the ro-

dentlike cat streak through the store again, this time from her hideout in the back to the top of a cabinet behind the store's front counter.

"I should get you to analyze Miss Kitty," Connie said, pointing to the huddled piece of fur atop the furniture. "Don't you think so, Keller?"

Keller was staring at her with what was probably the same expression she'd worn when she saw him— a mixture of horror and fascination. "Did you just rename my dog?"

"I thought you wanted me to," she said. As he continued to stare at her, she realized how she must look, squatted on the wooden floor, her shorts and blouse covered in dog hair. She stood slowly, one hand on the dog to steady herself.

"It's just a suggestion, of course. If you're happy with Sport, then by all means it's important that I not interfere. You're his alpha, his leader, after all. I'm just some strange lady." She addressed the dog. "Isn't that right, Sport?"

He pretended not to hear her.

"Sport?" she said again. Nothing. Uh-oh, she thought. "Why don't you try talking to him?" she stage-whispered to Keller.

"Sport, let's go." He gave a tug on the leash. No response.

Her stomach sinking, Maddie tentatively said, "Ambrose." The dog gave a woof of assent, then jerked his head toward the door as if to indicate that she should follow.

"Well, this is just a phase," she said. "He's just testing you while I'm here," she continued, while Keller stared a hole through her. "In fact, the sooner

I leave, the sooner you all can get back to a normal relationship."

"How considerate of you. Unless you want to take this time to become Sport's new alpha," he said.

"No, that's all right," she said. At least Lucas Keller's sardonic sense of humor hadn't died out over the generations.

As she handed her basket of goods to Connie, she could see a barely concealed grin on his face. She knew that as soon as she left, Keller Lowry would be in for no end of teasing from the older man. Maybe by the time she got around to asking him for family stories about Lucas Keller, his dog would be back to answering to Sport and all would be forgiven. She could only hope.

"Done enough damage?" Connie asked.

"What?" Maddie said.

"To your pocketbook, I mean. Did you find everything you needed?"

"Oh, yeah, thanks." She was conscious of Keller behind her. She turned to see him with a bag of chocolate chip cookies. Before she could stop herself, she said, "I hope you don't give those to him. Chocolate works like cocaine on dogs."

"I knew that, thanks. He's got his own treats at home." As Maddie blushed once again at her forwardness, he said, "He's already forgotten his name. The last thing I want him to do is start wandering the streets as a drug addict."

She turned back to Connie, who was whistling as he put her groceries in a paper sack. "Anything else we can do for you today?" he asked.

Now that you've let me humiliate myself, alienate the only living descendant of the man who'll make my career, and generally let me behave like I Love Lucy *goes to the general store, no, there's nothing else you can do,* she thought. "Actually, I came here to check out any help wanted ads on your bulletin board. I guess I'll do that next time."

She knew the chances of finding a job in town were slim. She'd gathered that no one, with the apparent exceptions of herself and Keller Lowry, ever moved into or left Ravens Gap. She got the feeling that people had been settled into their jobs for years. Well, she wouldn't starve. Ever since she had started working as a teenager, she'd shoveled money into savings in case she ever figured out what she really wanted to do. If she had to, she would live on that, but she didn't want to.

"Lucy's hiring across the street," Connie said. "Her great-niece was supposed to come in for the summer, but she got a better job in Asheville. Can you wait tables?"

"Better than I ever wanted to," she said.

"Can you cook?"

"I'm a great cook," she admitted.

"That'll be a Lucy's first. Get on over there," Connie said, handing her her bag.

"Mrs. Martin's expecting me back for supper, but I'll go first thing in the morning," she said. *When I'm not wearing the latest in canine fuzz,* she added silently. "I really appreciate you telling me about it. I'll be seeing you soon."

"Can't wait," Connie said. If there was any sarcasm in his voice, she tried to ignore it.

She gathered her package, considered telling Ambrose/Sport goodbye, thought better of it, then gave his owner a weak little wave. She had almost gotten to the door when Connie said, "You didn't come to Ravens Gap just to wait tables, did you? I forgot to ask you what brought you here."

She wished that the question had stayed forgotten. She'd gone through a variety of possibilities. She was a writer and had come to the mountains to finish a piece of work. Unfortunately, that story was true. She was in the throes of a nervous breakdown and had come to Ravens Gap for rest. But considering that she'd charged in here like a lunatic and proceeded to become best buddies with some sort of overgrown fur rug, that one might hit a little too close to home. She could always say that she had a horrible respiratory illness and had come to Ravens Gap to take some sort of cure. But the air here wasn't exactly that clear, thanks to a nearby pulp mill. Plus, her busty figure gave the lie to the idea that she was suffering from any sort of wasting disease.

Frantically, her eyes darted around the store, searching for any sort of inspiration. They lit on a crooked and amateurish mountain scene hanging behind the counter.

"To paint," she said. "I'm here to paint."

"Really? We've had a few painters. They come mostly in the fall and spring, though."

"Right, exactly," she said. "Summer is the overlooked season. Which is an advantage, to me, because that means it suffers less from its own set of clichés." She talked to both Connie and Keller, then, for moral support, addressed some of her remarks to the dog, who listened intently. "I say fall, you see red and gold. Winter, you see snow. Spring, you see the pink blossoms blossoming. But summer, you feel rather than see. I'm here to capture that feeling in pictures."

Not bad, she thought to herself. Especially not so bad for someone who had only the vaguest idea of the differences between oil and acrylic, watercolor and pastel. She'd learn a little, she guessed, just to keep up the facade. She figured she didn't need to worry about actually producing a canvas—she had lots of friends who were artists and she'd never seen a thing any of them had done.

She looked to see how Keller and Connie were taking her impromptu speech on art. They were simply staring at her.

"I'll see you guys later," she said, her hand on the door.

"Maddie," Connie called after her.

"Yeah?"

"Mrs. Martin's a busy woman. When you go into one of your theories about art or animals, keep it short and snappy."

"Gotcha," she said, conscious of the heat rising to her cheeks and of Keller Lowry's impassive stare following her as she fled down the street with her groceries.

KELLER PAID for his bag of cookies as Sport whined by the door.

"Don't worry," Keller said. "It's a small town—I'm sure you two will see each other again." Not if I can help it, he added silently. He'd only known the woman ten minutes and she'd already given him a headache to rival any he'd experienced in all his stressed-out years in Manhattan. Even though she was out of his sight, he could still see her—with those big green eyes, made even bigger by her dark red hair being piled up in some ridiculous knot on top of her head. Her skin was as white as it could be, but he, who had always thought a woman looked better with a tan, couldn't get those pale features out of his mind.

"If she's an artist, I'm a good-hearted old country shopkeeper," Connie said.

"But you are a good-hearted old country shopkeeper," Keller said.

"So what are you worried about?" Connie asked, handing him back his change.

"I'm not worried." He put a hand to his temple. Now Connie was doing it, too. "We've got to go, Sport." Keller had told himself he'd work in his garden today. Not that working in the garden had made him happy yet, but he was confident that someday it would. It was just a matter of getting the hang of it first. And of course it would help if, someday, something he had planted actually grew.

His dog hadn't moved from the door. Keller said goodbye to Connie, then walked out, expecting Sport to follow. Instead, he stretched out fully in the doorway and yawned.

"Sport. Get out of Connie's way so his cat can come down." The dog didn't move.

"Sport, I'm warning you." Another yawn.

"You're going to have to try it," Connie said.

Keller knew what he was talking about. "No, I'm not."

"Do what you like, but I bet the dog's not coming out."

"Sport." It was the harshest tone he'd ever used with his pet, but the dog didn't even seem to hear him.

He gritted his teeth, took a deep breath and reached

for Sport's collar. Going completely limp, the dog let it be known he'd rather choke than get up.

"See what happens," Connie said. "What could it hurt?"

My dignity, Keller thought. An asset he found slipping away faster and faster since his move to Ravens Gap.

"Ambrose?" he mumbled.

The dog stood up and walked out the door, shaking his head as he always did for Keller to follow.

"It's a phase," Keller heard Connie say as they left.

A phase, all right. A tall, goofy, chatty, inexplicably attractive phase, one that threatened to last all summer long. Keller vowed that the next time he came to town, he'd try to buy enough supplies to make leaving his land as rare an event as possible. After all those years dreaming of sleepy little Ravens Gap, he suspected that, thanks to Maddie Randall, it wouldn't be so sleepy anymore.

2

MADDIE KNEW there were people who considered eight o'clock a reasonable, even a late hour at which to begin the day, but it was the earliest she'd been up in years. She wanted to get to Lucy's as soon as possible, on the off chance that the job she already considered hers would be taken by some other vagabond former waitress with nothing to do but hang out in Ravens Gap all summer. After that, she was going to track down the land where Lucas Keller had lived, even though she had steeled herself for the likely prospect that his Shangri-La was now the site of a gas station, video store or factory.

Or was it where Keller Lowry lived? she asked herself as she made her way down the boarding house's creaky and unlit staircase. Unless you counted the "one hour motel" Maddie had seen near the county line, Mrs. Martin's was the only housing she had been able to find. She wondered if Keller Lowry had actually reclaimed the old homestead or was living elsewhere. But if Keller's grandfather hadn't been in touch with Lucas Keller, what would possess Keller to move here? It couldn't be for sentimental reasons, since he'd shown exactly how sentimental he was about "the old coot."

But where else would he live? In a double-wide with a wife and kids, or in a VW bus by the side of the road? No, scratch that last one. It was a stretch even for her overworked imagination. And besides the fact that he didn't *seem* married, she knew she hadn't noticed a ring, not that she was consciously checking out whether he wore one or not. What business was it of hers?

Still, last night alone in her cramped room, she hadn't been able to get him out of her mind. Not even when she tried to distract herself with her notes on Lucas Keller and how to get to the old Keller place. She knew only a few things about Keller Lowry—he had lived in "the big city," which could be anywhere from Asheville to Los Angeles, he looked good in jeans, he loved his dog, although he didn't understand him, and he thought she was stark raving nuts. It wasn't much to go on.

What she didn't know was what he was doing in Ravens Gap. Had he inherited Lucas Keller's place? Was he getting the land ready to sell off to some developer? Face it—with a face and a body like that, he should have some tan blonde hanging off his arm in some trendy bar somewhere, not living with a dog in some out-of-the-way country town. He was only here long enough to get what he wanted, and then he'd leave. What else besides money from the land could bring him here? And if he did live at the old homesite, would she find him there today?

Her heart gave a funny little jump at the thought, and she straightened the collar of the white rayon blouse she wore. She reminded herself to take extra care with her coffee. For the job interview, not in case she ran into Keller. Within minutes of seeing him, anyway, she'd be wearing Ambrose, so what did it

matter? Better for her dry-cleaning bill not to encounter the pair at all.

Had there been coffee, she would have been careful
not to spill it on herself, but the sludgy stuff in the
pot no longer resembled a beverage. The smell of the
cabbage soup Mrs. Martin had served last night still
hung in the air. She had explained that it was the only
vegetarian thing she could find in her cookbooks, but
Maddie knew it as the tomato juice concoction that
was the staple of her mother's thousand and one diets.
You could eat all you wanted of it, but the trick was
that no one who wasn't about to drop dead from star-
vation would ever willingly swallow so much as a
teaspoon.

Mrs. Martin had hightailed it out last night after
ladling out the soup and pointing out the Chips Ahoy
for dessert, leaving Maddie to sneak back to her room
for potato chips and peanut butter. From the unopened
package of icing-covered cinnamon buns left on the
table, Maddie gathered that breakfast was going to be
solo as well. Noting that the outside wrap bore several
stickers, indicating where the buns had been marked
down several times during their stint on the shelf, she
grabbed a couple of cookies to eat on the way to
Lucy's.

As she got out of her car in front of the restaurant,
she glanced over at Connie's, but he was nowhere in
sight. She didn't know what she had expected the
inside of Lucy's to look like, but she was delighted
by the sparkle of vintage steel and pastel-colored appliances and the polished chrome on the retro-looking
bar stools. Well, on second glance, it didn't seem that
much polishing had been done in this place in a while.
And the bar stools weren't retro-look—they were the

genuine aged article, with the rips in the saucy red imitation leather to prove it. Still, Maddie had already fallen in love with the stained Formica counter, the cracking black and white tiles, and the overstuffed booths lining the walls of the diner.

Two older men in baseball caps sat at the counter, one eating what looked like a very runny omelette, the other munching on toasted white bread with patches of black. Both were watching a television mounted overhead. Lucy had to be the woman behind the counter, sitting on a stool and watching the show with her customers.

She looked so serious that Maddie immediately thought there'd been some kind of nationwide or international disaster.

"What's going on?" she asked as she sat down on one of the stools.

Lucy shook her head, her lips tight. "She oughtn't to have cut her hair that short."

Glancing at the screen, Maddie saw that the anchorwoman on one of the morning news programs now had about a half inch of hair all over her head.

"I don't think it looks bad," Maddie said. "But whenever she gets it cut that short, she seems to lose confidence in herself. You can't talk to a world leader when you're worried that your scalp is showing."

"Exactly," Lucy said, beaming at her. "She's not wearing that hairstyle. It's wearing her."

They watched in companionable silence for a few moments, then Lucy said, "Did you want something to eat, honey?"

"Oh, no." She stood up. "I'm Maddie Randall. I'd like to apply for the waitress position you have open."

"Be here at four today for the dinner shift," Lucy said, her eyes back on the television. "Tomorrow we'll start you on lunch. Let me get you a cup of coffee to go, honey." She stood up and reached under the cabinet, then filled a travel mug. "Are you sure you don't want anything else? I know Harriet Martin and her idea of breakfast."

"How did you...? I guess you talked to Connie," Maddie said, accepting the coffee with thanks. She remembered that he hadn't spoken any more highly of Lucy's cooking than Mrs. Martin's, but she decided to keep that to herself. There was such a thing as tact, after all. "What exactly did Connie tell you about me?"

"That you'd waited tables in Knoxville. That I ought to let you cook."

"Is that all he said?"

Lucy smiled a slow, mischievous smile. "And that you renamed Keller Lowry's dog Ambrose." The two men at the counter, who had seemed to be ignoring Maddie in favor of the television, looked over at her with interest.

"There are a lot of ways to catch a rich man's heart, but I never heard of that one," Lucy said.

"I didn't know he was rich," Maddie said, surprised. Rich from what? From selling the family land in Ravens Gap? "I mean, not that it matters to me whether he's rich or not. I'm not interested in him in *that* way. Or in any way," she added hastily. "I was trying to help Ambrose, um, Sport."

There was real potential here for getting into some heavy-duty explaining, if she didn't escape right away. She thanked Lucy again and headed for the door.

"If you see Ambrose, give him a pat on the head from old George," said one of the men.

She closed the door on their laughter and walked the few steps to her car.

"Don't tell me you drove four blocks. You are a city girl," she heard Connie shout from across the street. She looked up to see that he'd dragged his chair onto the front porch of his store, where he sat whittling.

"City girls do walk," she shouted back. "I walked a half mile from the parking lot to work everyday."

"It doesn't beat walking to school in the snow uphill both ways," Connie countered.

"I know," she muttered to herself. "With Lucas Keller chasing you with his cane all the way."

"What did you say?" he asked.

"I said I'll see you later," she yelled.

Taking a sip of her coffee, which erred on the side of weakness, Maddie started the car and got a few yards down the road before rolling down her window and driving back to where Connie sat.

"I forgot to say thank you," she told him.

"Now you're driving across the street. People like you are the reason we had a gas crisis in the seventies, not that you remember it."

"What exactly did you tell Lucy about me?"

"That it would be a refreshing change to see Lucy's staffed by somebody who'd actually carried a tray before. And that I didn't think you were making up the story about being a waitress."

"Which story did you think I was making up?" she asked before she could stop herself.

"I don't know. Were you making up one?"

"No," she said, putting the car back into drive and

taking off. Really. She had a feeling that Connie was going to be one of her best sources of information about Lucas Keller. But how was she going to worm information out of him if he kept getting information out of her? And what right did he have to tell that story about poor Ambrose, knowing that it made Keller look as goofy as she did? Something about Keller Lowry, something about the way he stood and the way he talked, made her think he wasn't used to being a figure of fun. Now that Lucy said he was rich, well, that added a whole new layer of uptightness to him. Maddie could only hope that the next ridiculous thing she did in front of Connie Taylor would make everyone forget about this supposed link between her and Keller.

Somehow, that thought wasn't as comforting as she wanted it to be.

"YOU DIG A HOLE. You put seeds in the hole. You cover the hole with dirt. Plants come out. What is so damn hard about that?" Keller looked over at Sport, who studied the landscape through the car window. The dog had let it be known in many, many ways that gardening, and talk about gardening, bored him. Unfortunately, Keller had no one else to talk to.

Back when he worked for the brokerage, if he went more than a few minutes without a call, he buzzed the department's sales assistant to make sure the line wasn't dead. Now, except for the Sunday updates from his parents, his phone stayed silent. Well, there was the occasional weekend call from some of his old buddies in New York. They'd thought it was hilarious that he had abandoned Wall Street for North Carolina and the land his grandfather had talked about so fondly. They called him when a few of them were drinking beer and watching a football game and asking themselves how old Keller was doing and how high the corn was growing.

"The corn would be growing high," he told Sport. "If the crows weren't eating the kernels first."

Sport looked at him, making no attempt to feign interest, then looked back out the window again.

"It's not as if I were raised on a farm. Those guys in New York assumed I was a farm boy anyway, just because they'd never met anyone from North Carolina. But you know, you're not born knowing this stuff. Just because someone was raised in Manhattan wouldn't mean that you could slap him down on Wall Street and expect him to make money."

Keller was thankful for a moment that Sport couldn't talk. He'd let the conversation drift dangerously into the "So what the hell am I doing here?" territory. If it were his mother, father, or ex-boss sitting across from him, instead of a relatively mute canine, he'd be in the middle of a great big argument by now. He'd had a job he was good at, one he liked, more or less. So if he could make that kind of money doing something that came easily to him, why trade it for something that made no money and was clearly out of his aptitude?

"Because I'm a stubborn bastard," he told Sport and got a woof in response. Finally, a topic the two of them agreed upon.

He turned his eyes away from Sport and back to the road, just in time to see a car identical to his speeding in the opposite direction. Identical to his, that is, except for a few dings and dents in the hood, and a paint scrape along the door. It was also in great need of a wash.

As the car flew past him, he saw that the driver was singing at the top of her lungs. He caught a glimpse of her red hair flying out of its bun as she sped away.

"Where do you think she's going?" he asked.

Sport turned and growled low in his throat.

"I didn't say she was going someplace she shouldn't be. I just asked a question. You're awfully protective of her."

This from a dog who, upon seeing his first deer in the garden, had scurried inside and under Keller's bed, leaving Keller to scare off the stupid thing himself. And although he couldn't expect an answer from Sport, he did wonder where Maddie was headed. There were only two things out that way: his house and the liquor store over the county line. There was no reason for her to come to his house, so it had to be the liquor store. Maybe that explained some of her spaciness yesterday, but he doubted her behavior had such a rational cause. Wherever she was going, what was she doing out at the crack of almost nine? He had been up for a good three hours, but she had struck him as the type who wallowed about in a T-shirt until noon. As soon as he thought it, he couldn't get the picture of her in that T-shirt out of his mind. A short T-shirt, one that didn't quite cover her curvy legs.

I've got to get out of town more, he thought. *This is ridiculous.* He'd dated plenty of women in Manhattan, and none of them had ever looked or acted anything like Maddie Randall. She wasn't his type. He was simply reacting to the fact that she was the only unmarried woman under sixty and over sixteen that he'd seen in a while. A night out in a club in Asheville would remind him that there were lots of women in the world, not a single other one of whom would constantly compare him to his great-grandfather or rename his dog.

He doubted he was her type, either. She seemed as if she would be hanging out at the coffeehouse with some sensitive long-haired poet, listening to him prattle on as she bought him another espresso. Certainly, they were two different kinds of people, similar only in that they were both outsiders in Ravens Gap.

He got out in front of Morrell's Feed and Seed, nodding hello to the men sitting on the store's front porch.

"What's going on?" Little Tom asked, nodding back at Keller and Sport. If Tom Morrell, Jr., had ever been little, Keller thought, that person had long ago been swallowed inside someone who was large even by ex-linebacker standards. Even more confusing, his father, who was Big Tom, was about five feet nine and less than half his son's weight. Keller raised a hand in greeting to Big Tom, positively lost inside an oversize rocker.

"My beans aren't coming up," Keller said. "I wondered if anyone else was having that problem."

"You get the rocks out of your soil?"

Keller nodded.

"You check to see if it needed lime?"

He said yes again.

"You buy fresh seeds?"

"This time, yeah," he said, still smarting from Little Tom having sold him dud broccoli seeds two weeks ago.

"Sorry about that. The expiration date got a little

smudged," Little Tom said, not sounding very sorry. "I don't know what to tell you about your beans, then."

"I saw some shoots last week," a man said.

"The spring was colder than usual. You may just need to wait a while," said someone else.

"Yes, but the winter was warm," said another man.

A warm winter, a cold winter, a rainy spring, a dry spring. He didn't know what the hell difference it made, and they knew it. They could tell him his beans wouldn't grow until he walked out with a tambourine under a full moon and recited the Pledge of Allegiance backward, and it would make as much sense as anything else they had told him.

"How deep did you plant them?" Keller was always surprised when Big Tom spoke, his voice a deep bass trapped inside that tiny body.

"About seven inches."

Big Tom shook his head. "They don't need to be more than two or three, four at the most. Where'd you hear seven?"

Keller pointed to a man sitting on a bench toward the back of the porch.

"Mel," Big Tom scolded.

"I must have been thinking about the metric system," Mel said. "Ever since we tried to switch, it's got me all confused."

Keller raked a hand across his hair in frustration as everyone chuckled. He knew that out of all the men in the town, he was the most open to teasing, and not just because he was a newcomer, or a city boy, or the descendant of someone generally agreed to be the meanest man who ever lived. It had to do with being, at thirty-three, one of the youngest, and also with knowing nothing about what he was trying to do. When he'd started his career as a broker right after college, he'd been truly young, twenty-one, but he'd quickly learned the ins and outs of what he was doing, just by watching the others. Unless someone was going to invite him into his garden for a free tutorial or toss him some straight answers soon, he didn't know how he was going to get the hang of this.

He left with bags of mulch, some mild pesticides, more bean seeds, a trowel to replace the one Sport had buried somewhere, and another batch of corn kernels.

Loaded down with bags, he opened the trunk and shoved everything in.

"If you need anything else, let us know," Little Tom said.

"Next time I'll just open my wallet as soon as I walk up and let you help yourself. It will save us both some time," Keller said.

Little Tom put his hand to his heart. "You hurt me, my friend. Come back soon," he said, as Keller opened the passenger side for Sport. "Don't you and Ambrose be strangers."

Keller's head shot around toward the men as Sport went into enthusiastic woofs, his tail wagging ninety miles an hour. Keller could do no more than nod goodbye, jump in his car and peel off to the sound of the men's laughter.

"That one ought to be an old reliable for a while," Keller told Sport. "Especially since you so willingly agreed to play the straight man." Sport wagged his tail again. "But look at it this way. They might get so much mileage out of it that they stop selling me stuff I don't need.''

He'd hung on to a lot of the money he'd made in New York. Not just to have money for the sake of having money—he wasn't a miser—but to have enough money to support this crazy dream he had about living in Ravens Gap. It was so much cheaper to live in western North Carolina than in New York that he'd figured he'd have a good seven to ten years to establish his farm before he had to even consider adding to his savings in some way. So far, though, he could have dined out nightly at a four-star restaurant in New York for what he was paying here for vegetables that hadn't even grown yet. As for the house— hell, with the work he was going to have to do to it, he could have had a penthouse overlooking Central Park. Maybe that would have been enough to satisfy this bizarre urge he'd had to see some greenery around him.

Having worked himself into an all-out, full-blown, kick-a-few-tires kind of bad mood, Keller had no illusions that digging in the garden was going to turn him into a ray of sunshine. Forget all those granola types he'd seen in *Mother Earth News,* swearing that there was nothing like a little yard work to help a person relax. Sadder and wiser, he now knew there was nothing like a little yard work to make you want to go to the nearest hardware store and buy enough cement to pave over the whole damn thing.

When he pulled into his gravel driveway, he was trying to decide whether a walk across his acreage with Sport would cheer him up or send him to the phone to call his real estate agent. The odds were still fifty-fifty when he saw a car at the top of the drive, next to the house. A blue sedan, exactly like his, except for the extra dings and scrapes and a fairly thick layer of dirt across the whole thing. There was no mistaking it. It was Maddie Randall's car.

So she had been on her way to his house. But what was she doing there? And where was she, anyway? He didn't see her in the backyard glider, or in the scraggly garden. He couldn't see the front porch from the driveway, but that was the most likely place for her to be. The most likely place considering that there was no likely reason for her to be here at all. Keller let Sport out on the passenger side, and, together, they walked around to the front of the house.

She wasn't on the porch, but the wooden front door was wide open, the hole-ridden screen door providing an open invitation to every flying, biting insect known to man. There was a pair of sandals heaped next to the door. Keller expected Sport to bark, but instead he stood frozen in front of the house, his ears standing straight up. Keller strained to hear whatever it was Sport was hearing, then caught the unmistakable lyrics of "Blue Christmas."

He looked around at his wide yard, covered in green grass, with patches of Queen Anne's lace and other wildflowers just blooming. It was definitely June. He listened again. It was definitely "Blue Christmas." It was a good thing the words were familiar, since the voice singing it was trying to make up for in enthusiasm what it lacked in skill.

The singer was just delivering a strained rendition of the chorus when Keller opened the screen door and stepped into the house. Her back was to him as she looked through his bookshelves, although she already held in her hand what looked like one of his paperback Tony Hillerman mysteries.

He knew that he meant to ask, "What are you doing here?" or "Did you just break into my house?" Instead, he heard himself say, "You really can't sing, can you?"

Maddie jumped slightly and whirled around, the hand that wasn't holding the mystery grabbing one of the *New York Times'* heftier business best-sellers. She seemed fully prepared to hurl it at him, presumably for daring to walk into his own home unannounced, but then she seemed to think better of the action. "Oh, it's you," she said, her flushed face vying in color with the auburn tints of her hair. Sport barked and ran to her, and she put both books down on the floor as she crouched down to hug him, cooing in his ear. For a split second Keller wondered what he would have to do to get that kind of welcome from her. Besides be born a dog, of course.

She looked up at Keller with such a winning smile that he was prepared to wave away the apology he thought she was going to give. But instead of explaining or excusing herself, she said, "I can't dance either."

"We have something in common then." Now where did that come from? He ought to be asking her what she was doing in his house, not acting like some goofy sixth grader trying to find ways in which they were alike. "I'm sure Elvis is spinning in his grave at what you've done to his song."

"Oh, no, I saw him yesterday, and he said, 'Little lady, you go right ahead and sing.'"

It took him a beat to figure out that she wasn't serious. And even then, he thought it wouldn't hurt to double-check. Just as he opened his mouth, she stood up, one hand on her hip in what he guessed was meant to be outrage, although her bare feet and the strands of golden dog hair clinging to her white blouse undermined her posture.

"You think I'm serious." She looked down at the dog. "He thinks I'm serious."

The dog looked at him accusingly and gave a stern bark.

"Now, wait a minute," Keller said, wondering why she'd made him feel that he was out of line to doubt her. He didn't know how she managed to turn everything upside down when she spoke. Desperately trying to reclaim the high ground in this conversation, he said, "Look at it from my point of view. The first time I see you, you stare at me like I'm the latest addition to some circus freak show—people who resemble dead authors no one's ever heard of. Then you tell me you can see into my dog's soul and that he wants to be called Ambrose." He raised his voice a little. "A name, by the way, that no self-respecting dog would have, but a name I'm going to have to get used to, since everyone in town already calls him that." The dog formerly known as Sport woofed ecstatically, while Maddie, at least, had the decency to blush. "Then I come home to find your shoes on my porch and you playing Little Red Riding Hood in my living room."

"Goldilocks," she interrupted. "You're thinking of Goldilocks."

"Whatever," he said. "Don't try to throw me off track."

"I wasn't. But they're two very different stories,

with two very different morals. Although I'm not sure what the moral of Goldilocks is.''

"How about, don't break into other people's houses?''

She stared at him, a very serious expression on her face. "No, I don't think that's it. But I can't think of what else it is.'' She looked down at Ambrose again. "That's so annoying when that happens, isn't it?'' He wagged his tail in agreement. "I'll have to go to the library tomorrow and figure it out.'' She turned to Keller again. "Have you been to the library yet? I just poked my head in for a second, but I was very impressed. Not that you don't have some good books here. I'm surprised you don't have any gardening books, though. I stopped by your garden on the way in, and, of course, you probably know a lot more about it than I do, but it looked kind of rough to me. Is it going okay for you?''

She had to bring up the garden. In all the excitement over having his home invaded, he'd forgotten his morning humiliation at the Feed and Seed. A fresh wave of irritation washed over him, and his voice was sharper than he meant it to be when he said, "Don't you have anything to say for yourself?''

"About what?'' she asked.

He waved his hands around. "About this.''

She paused, then said in a small voice, "How about, if you're explaining, you're losing?''

Only the sight of Lucas Keller walking down the staircase would have surprised Keller more than what Maddie had just said. He was immediately back in a sales meeting in New York, his tie choking him and his blood racing while his boss berated the whole team. Keller had had only a few encounters with the legendary tempers in his firm, and those were just because he'd been the first underling they'd stumbled into in the hallway, but he'd watched plenty of others get chewed up and spat out for honest mistakes. If You're Explaining, You're Losing was one of the bigwigs' favorite pieces of corporate jargon, and hearing it now made him feel suddenly grateful to be standing in a house in Ravens Gap, hearing the distinctive whine of a mosquito somewhere around his ear and arguing with a beautiful lunatic.

He smiled, feeling the tension seep from his shoulders. "Where did you hear that phrase?"

"Oh, I collected a lot of those phrases, eavesdropping on my customers when I waited tables. I like to try them out sometimes." She stood straight, her posture uncannily like one of his former bosses. "Let's get on the same page with this. I wanted to give you a heads up on the Acme deal. It's easier to ask forgiveness than permission." He joined in with her as she said the last, "There is no I in team."

"Of course, I know a lot of academic jargon, too, but that's not nearly as much fun to use," she said.

"You waited on a lot of rude professors?" he asked.

Something that looked like a mixture of guilt and confusion washed over her face. "Oh no, I dated someone who spoke it," she said. He waited for her to elaborate, as she had elaborated on everything else she'd ever said to him, but she didn't. It must have been a fairly painful breakup, he thought, if it could render even Maddie silent.

There was an awkward pause, and Maddie gathered up the two books she'd taken from the shelves.

"Did you want to borrow one of those? The one you weren't going to throw at me?" he added.

"Oh, I couldn't. I've already made enough of a disruption in your day." She smiled. "I'm sorry about all this. I wasn't going to come into your house, really, but I was sitting on the porch and these awful little bugs kept flying into my mouth and eyes. I came in to get a book because I thought reading would help me ignore them. I'm sorry. I need to get going, don't I?"

She looked so contrite, so sincere, that Keller felt like a heel for even questioning her right to poke around his house. Sport, or Ambrose—was he ever going to get used to that name?—seemed to share Keller's low opinion of himself, as he turned his back to his master and extended a paw to Maddie. Watching her bend down to take the dog's paw, her face lighting up in a smile as she whispered to him again, Keller thought he'd never sunk so low. He might as well be raiding the pension funds of widows and orphans, instead of throwing this woman out, and before he'd even found out why she was here. Although he knew he should seize the chance to have his peace and quiet back, he said instead, "Can you stay for lunch?"

"I break into your home, I snoop around your shelves. I can't start eating you out of house and home now."

He was off the hook. He could just say goodbye and send her off, especially considering that lunch should have been a good couple of hours away. "Come on, stay."

Now she favored him with that bright smile. "It

really does sound like Goldilocks now. But I promise I won't mind if anything's too hot or too cold.''

"Well, only one eye of the stove works, and it doesn't get above medium. So there's never any danger of anything being too hot.'' Great, blabber was catching. He doubted it suited him the way it suited her. And what exactly was he going to feed her? "Um, I have peanut butter or pimiento cheese.''

"Do you still have some of those chocolate chip cookies you bought yesterday?''

"I do.''

"It sounds wonderful,'' she said. She moved toward the kitchen, Ambrose at her heels. "And no cookies for you,'' she said to the dog. "But I did stick some animal crackers in my purse, just in case I saw you again.'' She turned to Keller. "You can have some, too, if you want. I don't want you to think I like him better than I like you.'' She blushed again. "I mean, not that it matters to you whether I like you. I just don't want you to think I have ulterior motives in befriending your dog. Not that you were thinking that—''

He was greatly tempted to watch her squirm, but the gentleman in him outweighed the tease. "Why don't you talk to Ambrose while I make lunch?''

"You mean because the sooner I get some peanut butter in my mouth, the less likely I am to stick my foot in it?''

"I didn't say it. You did,'' he said, moving toward the refrigerator, handing her the bag of cookies as he went.

3

So she'd been caught waltzing into Keller's house and making herself right at home—something she was pretty sure people didn't do even in places where they didn't lock their doors—and instead of trying to come up with some reasonable explanation for her actions, all she could think of was that Keller had heard her sing. How mortifying! Not since the first grade Christmas pageant, when she had been the only child expressly directed to simply move her lips during the program, had anyone else heard her indulge in this private vice. And "Blue Christmas"? What could he think?

"Why 'Blue Christmas'?" Keller asked.

Could he read her thoughts? She looked at Keller, unwrapping the loaf of bread, his strong hands laying out the slices. His dark hair looked freshly cut, and his handsome face was wrapped in a concentration probably more serious than peanut butter and pimiento cheese deserved. In his jeans and sports shirt, in this comfy old farmhouse, he looked like some kind of Madison Avenue prototype for the good life, certainly not someone she was likely to have any kind of connection with, psychic or otherwise. No, he was asking about "Blue Christmas" because, face it, it wasn't every bright June day that you came across someone singing seasonal Elvis in your living room. Certainly it was more than Keller Lowry was used to.

"What did you do before you came to Ravens Gap?"

He gave her a sharp glance, then shook his head. "Uh-uh. I asked first."

"Okay," she said, exhaling. "'Blue Christmas.' While I was driving, I passed a blue balloon stuck in a tree, and the balloon made me think of the child who lost it, and child and tree together made me think of Christmas, and suddenly there was the song." She accepted the sandwich he handed her, and continued. "Well, I think the only way to get a song out of your head is to sing it until it's gone."

"Does that work?" he asked, sitting down across from her at the table as Ambrose scooted closer to her feet.

"Not really," she confessed. "I thought it worked once, when I had 'Yellow Submarine' going around, but now I think it must have been a coincidence."

"Let me guess what made you think of 'Yellow Submarine.' A yellow…"

"Yellow sign on a sandwich shop."

"Of course. Why couldn't I figure that out?"

"Your turn," she said, taking a bite of pimiento cheese.

"You mean, what did I do? I was a stockbroker."

A stockbroker? He might as well be wearing a sign that said, I've Come to Sell the Ancestral Land. She swallowed, then crinkled her nose as she said, "Ooh."

He looked at her for a beat. "Ooh? Ooh? Thanks for not insulting me with your mouth full, at least."

"Oh, I didn't mean to insult you. It's just that it's

so…so…um… In Asheville?'' she asked, trying to picture him as a stockbroker. It was not only annoyingly easy, but he looked damn good in her vision of him in a dark suit, white shirt, and red power tie.

"Wall Street," he said. "I take it from the way you're moving your nose again that that's worse?"

"I think it's worse," she said. "On the one hand, it means you must have been pretty good at what you did, which is good for you. On the other hand, it means if the things you did were ruthless, then you were good at being ruthless, which is bad."

He shook his head slightly, as if she had confused him. "How did we get to ruthless?"

"It goes without saying, doesn't it?"

"Just like it goes without saying that because I found you rummaging through my shelves, you're a burglar."

"That's totally different. I didn't…" No, that wouldn't work. It wouldn't do to tell him that not only was she not sure he lived there, but that she was hoping he didn't, that she was hoping for some little old lady who would tell her that the attic hadn't been cleaned out since Lucas Keller had lived there, and that she was welcome to take whatever old thing she found up there. Keller Lowry was no little old lady, though, and as glad as she was that the Keller place was still standing, and as happy as she was to see it, figuring out whether there was anything of value to her biography in this house was going to be very tricky business. Especially since she had no idea what Keller's motives for living there were.

"You were saying something?" Keller prompted. "Before it looked like a stray daydream came out of nowhere and took you away?"

She blinked. "Oh, I'm sorry. I lost my train of thought." She stopped, giving him time to make an inevitable punchline about missing a lot of trains, waiting at the station while the engine chugged down the tracks. Her friends and family constantly teased her about her daydreaming. It never hurt her feelings, at least until they'd refused to take seriously her plan to come to Ravens Gap.

"What?" Keller asked.

"Aren't you going to say something snide about my powers of concentration?"

He pointed at his dog under the table. "With Lord Cerberus down there just waiting for a chance to prove his devotion to you? I wouldn't dream of insulting you."

Only slightly comforted by his restraint, Maddie went on. "I was saying that it's totally different. I told you how I happened to be in your living room—circumstances. You had to mean to go to Wall Street, though, for one reason. To make money."

"You're right."

"But that's wrong."

"Money's wrong?"

"No, but it's wrong to pursue money for the sake of money."

"Okay." He stood up, and Ambrose barked. He stretched his arms above his head, as though he were getting ready for a run, and Maddie caught a glimpse of a flat, tan stomach. What she had said had made him angry, she could tell, and his cheeks grew a little brighter, a handsome contrast to his dark hair and eyes. As he started to pace around the small kitchen, Maddie shrank a little in her seat. She'd never dreamed he'd get so passionate about such a purely philosophical argument. It made her wonder what else he could get passionate about.

"Say I've got this goal in mind. There's something I want, but I'm going to have to have a certain amount of money to get it. Now, okay, I go along, take a job I love at a sacrifice wage, pinch every penny, dream about having what I want but mostly just trust in the universe to come through for me because I've been such a nice guy."

"Certainly, that's possible—"

"Or," Keller continued, "I could look around, decide what I could do to make the maximum amount of money in the shortest time possible to reach my goal. Does it make me a bad guy to get to my goal this way, instead of waiting for money to drop out of the sky?"

"I don't know," Maddie said. "I think it depends on what the goal was. What was it?"

"That's totally irrelevant."

"Not at all," she said. "It has everything to do with it. There are things worth the time and effort you're talking about, and things that aren't. So which was it?"

He seemed totally deflated by her question. He stopped pacing and stood with his hands on the straight-back kitchen chair. "I don't know. You tell me. I wanted to buy this house and land."

She responded wholeheartedly to that. All her life she had dreamed of a house like this, an old, eccentric house. It was a wonderful contrast to the flat ranch houses of her parents and grandparents. And knowing the history of the house, knowing that Lucas Keller had grown up in a nearby shack when this was some-one else's property, then built his dream home by

himself, made her love it even more. But why would
Keller Lowry want it? Feeling like a snake for not
telling him she knew whose house it was, she asked,
"Did your grandfather live here when he was
young?"

"He did live here when he was young. He helped
his dad build it. He told me about it all the time and
he drove me past it sometimes. When his dad died,
he tried to buy it back but he couldn't afford it, not
then and not ever. My mom could have helped him,
I think, but she thought it was unhealthy that he had
such an obsession about it."

"When did he pass away?" Maddie asked, almost
whispering, not wanting to break into Keller's reverie.

She had broken it anyway. He looked up at her
question, and then his face reddened slightly, as if he
were embarrassed to be caught in the middle of such
private thoughts. "He died about three years ago. I
could have bought it then, but the owners weren't sure
they wanted to sell. They wanted to develop the land,
but only if there was going to be an interstate near it,
and there isn't one. In the meantime, though, they just
let the house sit, let some feral cats battle it out with
mice in here."

"Was it empty?"

"Except for junk that was too hard to move, like
the huge shelves. No one ever wanted to move them.
And there's a ton of stuff in trunks and boxes in the
attic that no one's ever looked at."

She thought that the phrase "my heart hammered"
had never really been accurate until now. It felt like
five thousand little carpenters were in there, building
a house even bigger than this one. She forced herself

not to appear overeager. "What kind of stuff?" she asked.

"If I'd been through it, most of it would be gone by now."

"But there could be something really important up there," Maddie said. "Something of your grandfather's or something of Lucas Keller's."

"If there's anything up there of Lucas Keller's, the moths can have it. If there ever was anything of my grandfather's, I'm sure his father threw it away. I'm not betting on there being any valuable antiques up there, either, not after all these people have lived in the house."

"But what if there's an undiscovered manuscript?"

"Then leave it undiscovered," Keller said. "You said you liked his books, but, face it, most people have never heard of him. Let him die out."

Maddie sat up straight, appalled at what she was hearing. "How can you say that? It would be different if he were an inferior writer, but he wasn't. Just because he didn't get automatically transported into the literary canon doesn't mean that he wasn't important and good. You owe it to the scholarly community to preserve everything you can."

Until Ambrose barked, she hadn't realized that she had risen to emphasize her point, or that her own voice was getting higher and higher. More than a little embarrassed, she snapped out of it and took her seat again.

Keller was staring at her oddly. "For a painter, you know a lot about literary politics. Did you say you'd dated a professor?"

Damn, she had told him that, hadn't she? There was nothing like letting a little truth into a lie to screw it up, although she'd thought it was supposed to be the other way around. "Yeah, I did. I guess I picked up more than I knew." She wished he'd leave it at that—this falsehood stuff was all too much for someone as frank as she usually was, and she thought she needed at least a few minutes to regroup, contain her losses. But of course Keller went right on.

"I wouldn't have thought anyone would have been interested in Lucas Keller at all," he said. "But right after I moved here, a couple of people told me about a guy named Jeff Alvin who came around writing a book about him. I think he was from the university in Knoxville."

"Really. That's where I went to school," Maddie said, knowing that he would hear her hometown from Connie eventually. It wouldn't do to lie about things that could easily be found out.

"I wonder if you had any classes with this guy," Keller said. "Since you both have an interest in Lucas Keller."

"I may have. I don't remember. I took a few English classes, since I was an art student," Maddie explained, conscious that her nose was beginning to itch. It wasn't hard to imagine that it was growing like Pinocchio's. "You know how it is with professors. They never want to admit that the enjoyment of a book and the understanding of it can be the same thing." Oh, swell, now she sounded like some steel-haired lady on public television.

"So what happened to this guy?" Maddie pulled a napkin from a holder on the table and began shredding it idly.

"I don't know. He was kind of a pompous ass—"

Ha, Maddie thought. *Take that, Jeff Alvin.*

"So I don't think anyone talked to him. And I don't think he ever figured out where this place was. Connie said he asked him how to get here one day and he gave him directions that got him straight to the No-Tell Motel on the county line. A state trooper came into Connie's the next day and said he was going to arrest him for solicitation, because he was just sitting there in the parking lot, and then he found out that he was reading those directions over and over again. He couldn't figure out why they hadn't worked."

Maddie grinned, picturing Jeff Alvin in the parking lot, poring over a crumpled piece of paper by the light of the overhead dome. His image of himself as an authority was so total and complete that she knew that the concept of anyone lying to him would be totally foreign. He would be baffled, indignant, then simply have more fuel for his prejudices against rubes who couldn't even write directions, never understanding that in this case he was the rube.

"What's so funny?" Keller asked.

"Oh, that guy, you know, being made to look like a jerk."

"But he's a scholar. I thought you were on his side."

"I'm on Lucas Keller's side," Maddie corrected. "But you said this guy was pompous, so I immediately don't like him. Whoever he is," she added, aware that she was digging herself deeper into her lie. "Even if he were going to save Lucas for posterity, that doesn't mean he can be a bully. I'm not someone who believes that ends justify means."

You don't think so? she asked herself. Of course

she did. She was lying to this nice man and his noble
dog right now, all to justify her own ends.

For a brief second, she wanted to tell Keller everything, why she needed to be taken seriously and why
she wanted to do the book, and just ask him if she
could go up to his attic and look around. But they
were having such a pleasant time in the bright
kitchen, munching on their sandwiches. She knew
from her reading that heirs could be weird about their
literary ancestors. Good grief, even Jane Austen's relatives, who weren't her descendants, sometimes
mumbled that they ought to get something out of her
literary legacy, and she'd been dead for eons. For Keller's grandfather, she imagined that the wounds of
Lucas's betrayal had still been fresh, fresh enough for
them to have been passed onto Keller. It was better
to feel her way along about this, to try to find out—
maybe from Connie, maybe from Lucy—more about
who Lucas Keller had been in this town. That one of
his sons had grown to manhood—that was something
she hadn't even imagined, and she felt a pang of un-
certainty when she thought about how deeply she'd
been taken in by the story of his children's deaths.
There were things here she didn't understand, and until she did there was no need to involve Keller Lowry.

Then why was she sitting in his kitchen? Her manners could be sketchy at times, but she knew it was
bad form to eat someone's food before you put the
knife in his back. As to doing more than that, to having a flirtation with him, that was very bad manners
indeed. It occurred to her, looking across the table at
him, that the most enjoyable way of getting information about Lucas Keller would be to seduce his
great-grandson. But her confidence in her skills of

seduction was dangerously low, too low for her to risk making a fool of herself.

"What are you thinking about?" Keller asked.

You and me, taking a break from rummaging around the attic to soak in the white claw-footed tub, then twist around in the sun-dried sheets.

"Is your tub claw-footed?" If she were going to have these annoying fantasies, it would help to base them on some semblance of reality.

He blushed. He blushed? Maybe her fantasies weren't as far off as she thought. And what was he doing asking her what she was thinking? Wasn't that something that women were supposed to ask men to annoy them? Right now she'd love to know what was going on behind Keller Lowry's dark eyes. But she was too much of a coward to ask.

"Yeah, why? Would you like to see it?"

"I'd better go." She stood up, and as she did so, the pieces of the napkin she'd shredded fluttered to the floor. A friend had once told her to watch out for men who peeled the labels off their beer bottles—it meant they were sexually frustrated. Well, there was Keller, spic-and-span, and she was the one who looked like a case study for some amateur Freud.

"Yes, I've still got a ton of unpacking to do before I start work." That was a total lie—she'd moved with nothing but her books and some very basic changes of clothes.

"Did you get the job at Lucy's?" Keller asked as she walked out through the living room and onto the porch, Ambrose trotting along beside her.

She gathered up her shoes and slipped them on, wobbling a little as she did so. Keller moved to support her, and she edged away, tripping a bit.

"Got it," she said. "Yes, I'll be there tonight. You should come by." Like hell, she thought. The second he walked into the place, she'd imagine him in his claw-footed bathtub, and boom, someone's dinner would be at her feet. She was a good waitress, a surprisingly good waitress given her natural clumsiness, but she'd never before felt so, so…well, hormonally challenged.

They were at her car, and she was about to make a safe escape, when Keller said, "You never did tell me why you came out here."

"You never told me what you were going to do now that you're not a Wall Street maven anymore."

"Maven?" He grinned. What a cute grin he had. It was very hard to find a man who could have both a smoldering look and a boy-next-door look. Usually, the boy next door looked ridiculous when he smoldered, and the smoldering guy looked goofy when he grinned. But Keller carried off both looks. One side of her brain made this calm, level-headed analysis, and the other part, whatever part was making her knees weak, thought she could never get tired of looking at his constantly changing face.

"I was never a maven. I always planned to become a gentleman farmer, but it's not working out that way." He pointed in the direction of the garden. "If I can't do something with this, I may sell the house anyway and figure out what I really want to be when I grow up."

"Oh, no, you can't sell," Maddie said. Ambrose winced visibly, Keller less so, and Maddie was aware that her voice must have gone into the upper decibel levels again. "I mean, whatever you want to do. It just seems like such a waste to work so hard for something, then throw it away.''

"Sometimes you can work hard for the wrong thing. There's no shame in changing your dreams.''

Unless you've been the kind of person who's never held on to one dream long enough to see if it's what you really want, Maddie thought. *The kind of person she was.* Annoyed with Keller for making her think about this, Maddie snapped, ''Did you read that on a wall poster somewhere?''

To her surprise, he laughed. "Maybe I did. It was right there next to, If It Is To Be, It's Up To Me.''

She smiled back, and his eyes lingered on hers for a second. He looked so impossibly right, standing there next to his weathered white house, the land rolling off in the distance. He just needed a confidence boost, a little help. Maybe she could provide that, in a buddy-to-buddy kind of way, nothing in return. And then, of course, if he wanted to provide his friend with some research assistance, she wouldn't say no.

''Did the dream train catch you again?'' he asked.

''Yes, I guess it did,'' she said, ducking into her car. She retrieved the animal crackers for Ambrose, handed them to Keller and started the engine. Keller bent to close her door.

''So why were you here?''

''Why was I here?'' she repeated. "Oh, I wanted to apologize for the thing with the dog yesterday and see if I could help you get him to answer to Sport. But since you seem happy with Ambrose now, Ambrose I guess it is.''

She shifted into reverse, not giving him a chance to reply. He shut the door quickly, and she pulled away. She could hear Ambrose barking all the way down the drive.

"HER PIES. Oh, Lord, her pies. My wife couldn't force me to eat rhubarb, but Maddie makes this cherry-rhubarb that will just melt in your mouth. And her crust. God himself has a hand in that crust." Connie looked around, no doubt, Keller thought, to see if lightning would strike him. Either that or to see if the preacher was around.

He'd come to stock up on his usual ration of canned soup and bread, but he'd been waiting at the counter for an eternity while Connie went on about Maddie's magic in the kitchen. It seemed Lucy's was no longer somewhere you had to eat if you were a bachelor, or a widower, or if your wife wouldn't cook for you, but *the* place for the locals to go. Not only that, but Maddie had convinced Lucy to put a jukebox in, and sometimes long-married couples even got up and danced. Keller had heard the place was packed every night.

"And lasagna. You know how I feel about lasagna. Well, maybe you don't, but I'll tell you. Mixed. My feelings were mixed. But Maddie makes this lasagna with spinach. You know how I feel about spinach—"

"No, but I can guess."

Connie went on as though Keller hadn't spoken. "But she mixes it up with some kind of herb and ricotta—not cottage cheese, like Lucy used to get away with, but ricotta. Oh, what a meal."

Ambrose moaned. Keller felt decidedly deprived himself, though not so much of food as of the pleasure of seeing Maddie. Well, it wasn't all pleasure. Whenever he saw her, she did things he wasn't expecting, asked him questions he wasn't thinking he'd have to answer. She made him edgy, but it was an edginess he liked, the kind of secret thrill he used to get from walking in the city before the sun was up and knowing anything could happen that day. She promised surprises.

But there was no reason for him to see her, nothing that would keep them bumping into each other. He had reasons for not eating out. Everyone knew his stove didn't work, and every time he'd suggested having it repaired, the men in town had just laughed at him. It would have to be replaced, they said. Great, simple enough to drive to Asheville and buy a new one, except that no one would agree to install it. Something about incompatible wiring. And he could have the kitchen remodeled entirely, as he intended to, except that whenever he tried to hire men to help him work on the house, they were all busy with other projects and would call him when they got a spare minute, only they never seemed to get a spare minute. He could hire someone from Asheville to come help him with the house and the landscaping, of course, except that the one time he'd said something like that it had gotten back to the men at the feed store, who chided him for thinking their work wasn't good enough. So in the meantime, he defiantly ate at his own home, with only an occasional meal at Lucy's, because to do otherwise would remind everyone that even if he did move millions in Manhattan, he couldn't do something as simple as get a workman to his house.

He sighed.

"Making you hungry, am I?" Connie said, finally ringing up Keller's few purchases.

Hungry, but not hungry that way. He was hungry to see someone besides Ambrose and Connie, and he wasn't thinking of the men at the feed store. The day Maddie had sat in his kitchen was the best day he'd had in that house. The only thing worse than being alone was being with bad company, he knew that, but Maddie had been far from bad company. Odd, maybe; bad, no.

"So how's her painting?" he asked, more out of politeness than anything else.

Connie paused in bagging Keller's purchases and gave him a shrewd look.

"It's funny that you mention that. So far no one's seen her paint a thing. When she's not at Lucy's she's at the library. Mrs. Riddle said she sits there all day and reads old newspapers and goes through stuff in the local collection. She told her she wanted to understand the area before she painted it, but I asked her a question the other day about stretching a canvas, and she looked at me like she didn't have a clue in the world as to what I was talking about."

"Well." Keller didn't know why he was making excuses for her, but he was. "She's dreamy, you know."

"You got that right. But a dreamy woman who can tell the difference between salt and sugar when she's making a cake, now that's a rare one."

Uh-oh. There was matchmaking coming along. Keller could feel it. So far he had skillfully ducked all attempts at setting him up with anyone, mostly because the granddaughters and great-nieces he was supposed to date were safely out of town. And, of course, there was nothing wrong with being set up with Maddie Randall, in theory at least. But something told him this woman was too complicated to be led around by a bunch of old meddlers.

For one thing, he had gotten the feeling, while she was at his house, that there was something about her she wasn't telling him. She wasn't the kind who was used to keeping a secret, he could tell that, and the effort of it was almost visible on her face, in her every nervous gesture. When the guise slipped away occasionally, she became truly beautiful. He remembered how tight-lipped she'd been on the subject of the academic she'd dated. Was she running from a bad relationship? That's the last thing he needed, to be someone's rebound romance.

"Of course, she tells Lucy a lot more than she tells me," Connie was saying. "Only a little of which I'm able to worm out of Lucy. For instance, yesterday she went to Asheville and came back with a car full of gardening stuff. Now what's she doing with that? No one knows."

Keller grinned. He didn't know what Maddie was used to, but he knew that in New York, to admit that you were at all concerned with your neighbor's business was the best way of admitting you were a total provincial. Here, as he'd learned the hard way, it was the height of rudeness *not* to be concerned with how many peaches your neighbor had canned and whether the man next door wasn't watching a little too many football games on TV while his wife found excuses to go to Asheville twice a week.

"Maybe she's going to start a kitchen garden. You know, so she can pick stuff to cook at Lucy's." He thought of basil and sliced tomatoes, corn, grilled on the cob maybe, and dark green peppers. He pictured Maddie in Lucy's kitchen, her wild hair caught up at her neck, her dress swinging while she chopped peppers.

He shook his head slightly. This wasn't good. He was going home with a paper sack full of the blandest food imaginable, to a house that would have been empty except that there was surely something living in the closets he hadn't gotten around to cleaning yet. And ever since Maddie had stepped into that house, he'd had thoughts of her being there. Especially when he got into the claw-footed tub. It had been enough to make him start using the halfhearted attempt at a shower off the kitchen downstairs.

After saying goodbye to Connie, he drove past Mrs. Martin's, then past the library. Maddie's car wasn't at either place. Telling himself he had no reason to be disappointed that he hadn't seen her, he turned his car toward home. And there he found out why she hadn't been at the restaurant, the boarding house or the library. He also had the pleasure of knowing something before anyone else in Ravens Gap— namely, why Maddie Randall purchased so many yard tools. Because there, in his own sorry patch of land, stood Maddie, frantically batting bugs away from her face and frowning at a garden hoe.

4

"I THINK I'M STARTING to have heatstroke. Do I look as if I'm about to drop dead?" Maddie demanded as Ambrose bounded across the lawn to meet her. Keller moved a bit more slowly, taking in the sight of Maddie, her face flushed and her hair curling under the relentless heat. Did she look like she was about to have heatstroke? He considered. She looked... beautiful. And crazy as hell.

"I think I've been here an hour at least, which is more than enough time to be struck." She shook her head slightly. "Are those spots I see?"

"I haven't been gone an hour," Keller said, looking at his watch. "It's twelve-twenty. And those are more of those little bugs. They seem to like you."

"I'm surprised they could get past the cloud of mosquitoes around me. Every bloodsucker and his first cousin has been here."

"I don't think the mosquitoes really come out until dusk."

She shot him a look of pure poison. "Well, some enterprising bug must have advertised a midday madness sale on fresh human." She shook her head again, a little more irritably this time, and he backed away a little, thinking there was no telling what heat-inspired delusions could do to someone who already seemed more than a little delusional to begin with. But when she turned to him, her smile was bright.

"You meant one-twenty." It was a statement.

He looked at his watch again. "Twelve-twenty. I don't suppose you're in any hurry to tell me why you're in my garden with all these shiny tools."

He wasn't expecting her reaction.

"I've only been here twenty minutes," she wailed, plopping down cross-legged on the ground. Her jean shorts sent up little puffs of dirt as she sat, smudging her already-smudged T-shirt, apparently once white. Oh, damn, she was about to cry.

"I wasn't saying that you had to leave," he told her. She looked so forlorn that he had the strangest urge to sit down on the ground next to her and comfort her. Fortunately, he missed his chance, as Ambrose nuzzled close to her, then turned to Keller and pretended to bare his teeth. That is, he opened his mouth and made sure Keller saw his canine molars.

"You're welcome here, anytime, I swear. I was just asking."

"No, it's not that," she said, her face hidden and voice muffled by Ambrose's coat. "It's just that if I've been out here twenty minutes, do you realize how fast these mosquitoes must eat? I'm going to need a transfusion by the end of the summer."

He didn't know how they'd gotten from her in his yard with tools this afternoon all the way to "the end of the summer," but even someone as cut-to-the-chase as he usually was knew that this was not the right time to ask any questions. Instead, feeling like a million different kinds of fool, he sat down beside her.

"Well, you shouldn't be out here at this time of

day. That's how lunchtime came to be at noon,'' he said. He wanted to reach out for the unruly tendrils of red hair clouding around her head, but instead leaned over and patted Ambrose, who reluctantly deigned to be touched. "I mean, what says that we're always going to be hungry at this certain time every-day? It was so farmers would be out of the sun when it was at its most brutal.''

For a second he thought that he was making this up, then realized that he was repeating something his grandfather used to say. From here the old man used to launch into a tale about the huge midday meals he would eat as a boy, just so he could compare the chicken-and-biscuit-laden table of his childhood with the sliced bread and cold cuts Keller's mom offered him. Remembering how his mom used to nod and cluck her tongue sympathetically, all the while spreading mustard on those sandwiches, Keller smiled.

"What are you grinning about?" He looked at Maddie, who was watching him closely, her head propped up against a clearly ecstatic Ambrose.

"Nothing," he said, embarrassed to have been caught daydreaming. "Listen, I have some mosquito spray inside, and some of that lotion stuff. You would have seen it if you'd gone in.''

"I couldn't go in," she said. "I wasn't invited.''

"You weren't invited the other day." He thought he was just stating the obvious, but she plainly took it as an accusation.

"That's exactly what I mean," she said, sitting up straight. "You already think I'm the kind of person who bounces into people's homes with no invitation.

If I keep doing that, you're only going to keep thinking it.''

Slowly, carefully working back through her words, trying not to give offense, just in case Ambrose really meant his warning, Keller said, "Yes, but you already did it, which makes me think you probably are the kind of person who might, under the right circumstances, bounce into a friend's house uninvited. Am I wrong?" he asked quickly as Ambrose tilted up his jaw at him. Maddie shook her head, and he continued. "You either are that kind of person or you aren't, so if I already think you are, what do you have to lose by coming out of the hot sun?"

She was nodding, so he thought maybe he had gotten through this verbal minefield free and clear, when she said, "You can't go back to holding hands."

"What's that?"

"You know that saying."

He shook his head.

"You know, when the health teacher used to separate the boys and girls and give them different lectures. She would always use that slogan, You Can't Go Back to Holding Hands. Meaning, that once you decide you're going to have sex with someone, from then on, you're just destined to have sex with them all the time." She blushed. "It's just another one of those sayings I've picked up, and it seemed to apply to what you were talking about. I didn't think about it being about sex, per se, when I mentioned it. I mean, I don't want you to think I'm some kind of freak who just thinks about sex or talks about sex all the time." Finally, blessedly, she shut up.

What had he done to deserve this? His dog had turned against him, his plot of land was apparently cursed, and now the woman who'd been in his fantasies everyday since he'd met her was chatting blithely about sex and whether and how much she thought about it. And if he took advantage of the subject matter to reach across to her and kiss her, he was going to look like the worst kind of opportunistic cad. This was nothing but torture. The biblical Job thought he had it bad, but at least he didn't have to deal with Maddie.

"Well," he said cautiously. "I guess the guys didn't get that in their lecture."

"Once again, making the tempo of the relationship the woman's responsibility." That brittle, bright voice was back, making her sound more like the world's most efficient preschool teacher, instead of the woman whose free association babbling was getting them both into dangerous territory. He stopped himself from helping her up as she scrambled to her feet and wiped her hands briskly on her shorts. He noticed, but didn't mention, that her face was even redder than it had been when she was threatening to perish a few moments earlier.

"Now," she said, picking up a spade and looking it at experimentally. "Let's get started."

"You don't know anything about gardening, do you?"

"Well, I lived in an apartment, and there wasn't—"

"You don't, do you?"

"Well, my mother wasn't exactly a green thumb, so I didn't—"

"You don't."

She looked at him. "I've watched the Home and Garden network?"

He shook his head.

"I read the gardening section in *Southern Living*?"

He shook his head again.

She let out a short huff of breath. "Okay, I got a seed catalog in the mail once by mistake. How about you?"

"About as much as you do, I think." He picked up the hoe. "Let's get started."

"LITTLE TOM," Maddie heard the librarian, Mrs. Riddle, say. "I haven't seen you in here since you stopped reading Dr. Seuss."

Maddie glanced up to see Little Tom, his ball cap twisted in his hands, dwarfing the children's furniture around him. "I still know *Green Eggs and Ham* by heart. I say it for my boy while he looks at the pictures." Catching Maddie's eye, he waved at her. "I need to ask your patron something. I'll try to keep it low."

"I don't think there's anyone else in here to disturb," Maddie said as Tom pulled a chair out and sat down at her table. "There's Miss Miller in the genealogy room, but she's deaf."

Tom picked up the book she'd been reading and inspected the cover, and Maddie had a moment of terror when she couldn't remember what book she had brought to the table. She was used to being circumspect about what she was reading in the library, trying to hide even from Mrs. Riddle what exactly she was looking for in the archives. But today she had a gardening manual, and Tom snorted when he saw the title.

"Who needs a book to learn how to raise cucumbers?"

"Maybe people who can't get their good neighbors at the feed store to pass along any helpful advice," she said as he closed the cover.

He acted as though she hadn't spoken. Squirming a little in the uncomfortable wooden chair, he lowered his voice to a conspiratorial whisper and said, "I've got to talk to you about something."

She wasn't surprised he could find her so easily. In the short time she had been here, she had established a solid routine, and she thought everyone in town probably knew it by heart: coffee at seven with Connie, whose brew was infinitely better than Lucy's or her landlady's. On to Keller's, back to her room for a shower, then to the library, then to work at the diner. Her job had gotten easier now that the men at the feed store had finally exhausted their repertoire of jokes about city girls, especially once Lucy had made it clear that those who poked fun at Maddie couldn't partake of her cooking. She still caught a few frosty glances from their wives, though, when the men were a little too ready to compare their regulation mashed potatoes with Maddie's chili-and-garlic-enhanced ones. Nervously, Maddie wondered if Tom's wife knew he had come to the library to look for her. She was sure he was there for some innocent reason, but she also knew that his ninety-five-pound spouse was deceptively strong.

"It's about Cindi," he said of his wife. "She's a big fan of yours but she feels bad that she can't cook as well as you can."

"That's ridiculous," Maddie said. "I'm not even that great a cook. I just experiment a lot."

"Well, she has low self-esteem, she says," Little Tom confided. In response to Maddie's understanding nod, he said, "She's mentioned to me several times that she would like to get a couple of your recipes, but she'd die before she'd ask you herself."

I'll bet she would, Maddie thought.

"So if I could get them?" he said. "Maybe starting with that thing you make with the greens and the cornmeal?"

"Polenta with fresh spinach," Maddie said, nodding once more. She was ready to scribble down the recipe when something stopped her. She could hear the voice of the crafty Connie in her head, telling her you shouldn't get something for nothing in this world. It was almost like having her own little Jiminy Cricket, except, knowing Connie, she had to assume it was more of an anti-conscience, encouraging her to be shrewder and more devious than she was normally.

She might have ignored it, but then she thought of Keller, and how hard he had worked to live up to his picture of himself on his family's old land. Although he hadn't really come out and said so, she knew that the local men still thought teasing him was the height of hilarity. It was a shame, too, because she knew Keller would have paid them well to help him with some of the bigger landscaping and construction jobs.

Then she thought about the assistance she'd given him in the garden every day for the past week and a half. True, the time passed more quickly than it did that first day, mostly because she was so occupied trying not to babble or stare at Keller. But even with him there as a distraction, she couldn't forget that she was outside—in the outdoors—with the bugs and the beetles and, one unfortunate day, a mouse. She'd had to knock off an hour early just to lie on Keller's sofa and shake while he fixed lunch and Ambrose patted her head with his paw. No, even if she and Keller were making some progress in the garden, thanks in part to Maddie's reading about gardening and in part to some basic info she'd wormed out of Connie, it didn't make her feel any more charitable toward Tom.

"A good chef never gives up her recipes," she said primly.

He snorted again. "Chef? I wouldn't say Lucy's is swanky enough to employ a chef, would you?"

He had a point. "Chef, cook, whatever. If I give you my recipes, and you give them to your wife, she passes them around town, then no one has a reason to eat at Lucy's."

"No one had a reason to eat there before," Tom grumbled.

"She likes being successful," Maddie fibbed. Actually, Lucy liked the money, but Maddie knew that the hours were wearing her out. "She got to upgrade to a twenty-six-inch television for the counter, you know. So I can't just give you the recipes. It's not like your job, where, when you help someone, you guarantee that they return."

"Help?" he asked.

"Yes, you know, that thing that you give willingly and cheerfully in hopes that someday someone will give back to you?"

"Oh, yeah," he said, nodding slowly. "So if I were to help someone out with their garden, you might be more inclined to pass your recipes along to Cindi?"

"No." Maddie shook her head, hearing an inner Connie cheering her on. "Too little, too late in the agricultural department. But," she said, looking at him steadily, "I have heard a rumor that you do a little construction work in your spare time, and that you and your buddies might be free for a job pretty soon."

"Have you heard that, now?" Little Tom asked, rubbing his chin with one hand. "I think I understand. I wonder if there would be any other terms for this agreement?"

"Well, I'm sure when Cindi takes her special chocolate mocha sponge cake with rum sauce to the bake sale this year, she wouldn't want it to get out that it wasn't her original recipe."

She watched him process the message for a second, then he said, "You know what? I had something planned for the next couple of weeks, but I think it fell through. I wonder if I shouldn't tell Keller Lowry that I've decided now would be a good time for some of us to get started on his kitchen?"

"I'm sure he'd love to hear from you," Maddie said, as Little Tom rose from the chair. She watched him reach to tip his ball cap to her before realizing it wasn't on his head. As he walked out, with a nod to Mrs. Riddle, the librarian looked at Maddie quizzically. She gave the librarian an elaborate shrug before rising and heading into the tiny local history room.

Pamphlets, articles, photographs, playbills—if it had anything at all to do with Ravens Gap, it had wound up in one of the archive boxes housed in this room. In theory, there was some organization to the boxes, but Maddie had quickly figured out that she was better off just browsing through them. She'd come across several mentions of Lucas Keller in the papers of the 1920s and 1930s, but written in a tone that suggested the main reporter mentioned the author only when he had to, and only when it reflected badly on Lucas Keller. One gleefully reported town meeting in 1929 ended with Lucas bopping his infamous cane over the mayor's head. Great stuff for a biographer to find, but a disappointment to the part of her who still idolized him.

"Who were you, Lucas Keller, to write like an angel and act like such a son of a bitch?" Maddie said out loud as she lifted a box from the shelves. She'd gotten used to talking to herself whenever she was in this room, knowing that the other regular occupant, Miss Miller, wouldn't hear her. Unfortunately, nothing interfered with Maddie's ability to hear Miss Miller's incessant humming, so she carried the container back to the public reading area.

Plopping the box down on the table, Maddie wondered if this wasn't a futile effort. So far she had found one vague reference to a "gift" Lucas Keller's wife had given to the library when the old man died, a gift apparently received with all the enthusiasm of lumps of coal at Christmas. Maddie had brought the subject up to Mrs. Riddle one day, trying the old "he was my grandmother's favorite author" line again, but the librarian didn't have any idea what she was talking about, guessing that the librarians before her had simply dumped any such papers into the archives.

If I weren't such a coward, Maddie told herself, *I would just come out and tell Keller what I was doing here. Go up to his attic, give it a good search and be done with it. What other scholar decides the best way to get information is by taking a rake out into someone else's garden every morning?* There were people who spent years with dusty, yellowed clippings, but she was willing to bet that they hadn't gotten red clay dirt under their fingernails while doing it.

But as much as one part of her groaned at going

outside every day—with the bugs and the beetles and the mouse, who ought to know better than to show his ugly little mug again, after she had insisted that Ambrose spare his life—she knew she looked forward to it for one reason: Keller. Not because she enjoyed watching him, with his skin getting darker and his muscles more defined every day, although there was no doubt that it was one of the perks of this volunteer job. She enjoyed him, his calmly droll responses to her hyper chatter, his patience to her frustration. At first she thought she was trying to get him to talk so he could spill family secrets, then she decided she just wanted to make sure he filled the silence so she wouldn't have a chance to mouth off about sex education courses or claw-foot tubs. Then she calmed down enough to listen to him, and to find herself intrigued by what he had to say.

Like you've ever been attracted to the strong, silent type, Maddie chided herself. *You want the fast-talking urban Mr. Suave, remember, not the slow-talking boy from the sticks.* Well, not that Keller was the boy from the sticks, exactly. In fact, considering that he had lived in New York and she hadn't, she was actually more from the sticks than he was. Okay, she thought as she absently flipped through a stack of death notices and church bulletins. So she couldn't eliminate him for that reason. What about the fact that he had dedicated a portion of his life to the pursuit of money and she had practically taken a vow of poverty? How was that for incompatible values? Except that he had gotten the money and had gotten out, showing an amazing amount of focus and dedication, and she had never meant to live on Mother Teresa's salary, she just wasn't motivated enough to do anything else.

Okay, not only was there no reason not to be attracted to Keller, but he was perfect, too.

Maddie put down the stack of stuff she'd already looked at and peered into the rest of the box. More of the same. She had to go through it, though, because she knew that if she didn't, she'd start taking short-cuts with the next box and the next. Pretty soon she'd get so sloppy that she wouldn't bother to come to the library at all, or even pretend to herself that she was still researching a biography of Lucas Keller. She'd just spend more time dawdling over coffee with Connie, hang out at Keller's later, then go to Lucy's to cook in the evening. She paused and looked around the library, trying to remember why this was a bad thing. Oh yeah, because she was trying to prove something to herself.

When she looked back at the stack of stuff she'd put on the table, a letter she'd already shoved aside caught her eye again. The woman's spidery and faded handwriting was a pain, which was why she hadn't bothered, but now she paid attention to the carefully written signature. Mariah Keller.

Lucas's wife.

Five minutes later she'd copied the letter into her notebook, the copy machine a no-no for historical documents. She piled the rest of the stuff back into the box, Mariah's letter on top, and took it back into the archive room. Miss Miller, head down, was still poring through old census records.

"No more armed forces enrollments. No more wedding programs. No more wild goose chase," Maddie said, patting the box. "Mariah Keller, by shoving the juicy stuff in your attic, you may have just preserved it for life." Tempted to dance a little jig on the way out, she contented herself with tapping on Miss Miller's table and giving the older lady a joyous farewell wave. A bemused expression on her face, Miss Miller simply smiled and waved back, never once having paused in her humming.

"YOU GOING TO GARDEN in that?" Little Tom asked Keller. "It might have worked for Michael Jordan on the basketball court, but probably not for you in your yard."

"Chiggers," he heard a voice say.

"Briars," another chimed.

Keller blinked, feeling the water from his still-wet hair slowly dripping down the back of his neck. Ambrose looked at Keller in a dubious way, but remained polite in front of the crowd on the front porch. Little Tom was standing there, along with Mel and Sid from the regular crowd at the Feed and Seed. Tom's truck was backed up to Keller's yard, and there were actual implements of construction in the truck bed.

Before Keller could say anything in defense of his cut-off sweats and University of North Carolina T-shirt, Little Tom said, "We were in the neighborhood and thought we might drop by and check out that work you were talking about doing on your house."

In the neighborhood. Yeah, right, Keller thought as he let them in. He still hadn't gotten used to this dropping-in thing practiced by the citizens of Ravens Gap. And Maddie, Keller added to himself. She was one newcomer who seemed to get the hang of the local custom pretty quickly. In fact, he'd rushed out of the shower and down the stairs hoping it was her, but knowing it was probably one of the elderly widows who lived a couple of miles down the road. Somehow they had picked him as the man who could rescue cats from outbuilding roofs and open reluctant pickle and jelly jars. No matter how many times he had told them to call, they always drove over and got him, as though he wouldn't think it were an emergency if they used something as impersonal as the telephone.

Tom and company were looking around his kitchen in a very serious way. Conscious of how frivolous he must look in his bare feet and college clothes, compared to their work shirts and jeans, Keller tried to make himself sound tough as he said, "What do you think?"

"I can't seem to find your coffeepot," Little Tom said.

He should have known. "I don't have one. I don't drink the stuff."

"That's why Maddie stops at Connie's before she comes out here to help with the garden in the mornings," Mel said.

Keller tried not to look surprised. He didn't know that. If he had, he would have gotten a coffeepot and pretended to have a caffeine conversion. Of course, Connie would miss the time they spent together, but, then, he had more than enough reasons not to care what upset Connie, since it was no doubt his fault that everyone in Ravens Gap knew Maddie was helping him with his garden.

Of course, if they hadn't known before, they would today.

"I'm knocking," he heard through the screen. Ambrose trotted back over and nudged the door open with his nose.

"Don't stand on ceremony," Little Tom said. "Come on in."

Ambrose, apparently feeling that his own host duties had been called into question, sent an imperious bark in Tom's direction as Maddie crooned over him. Aware, yet again, of what a dork he must look like, Keller simply stood for a second and stared at Maddie like—no doubt about it—an infatuated idiot.

She looked gorgeous. Her skin was still pale—she wasn't the kind who tanned, not ever, but her cheeks were flushed, and her oddly colored eyes even more brightly lit than usual. She flashed him a gorgeous smile, one that he hoped didn't turn him visibly red in front of the crew.

"You look cute," she said. "But you aren't going to garden in that, are you?"

"I told him," Tom said.

"Chiggers," Mel said.

"Briars," Sid added.

"No, this is just the first thing I found when someone came over without calling ahead first and got me out of the shower," Keller said, trying to keep the annoyance out of his voice.

"If you weren't ready for us," Tom said, straightening out his posture, "we can come back another day."

Mel and Sid moved toward the door.

"No, no, stay," Keller said. He didn't know why the gods had decreed that he should finally have someone to help him with his house, but he wasn't about to let them go. They were going to make fun of him. Fine. The only way it could bother him was if he let it bother him. And if there's a beautiful and intelligent woman around whom you're trying to impress, he added to himself.

"I'll go change and we'll get started," Keller told Maddie.

"Actually, I've got an idea. Since these guys are here, maybe we should work on the inside of the house."

"That makes no sense," Keller said. "I think we would want to be outside while they're inside."

"Well," Maddie said, avoiding his gaze a little as she studiously patted Ambrose. "You know how it is when you do one room and all of a sudden the whole place just looks awful and you have to redo everything?"

Keller shook his head. Having never been involved in a renovation project until this morning, he could honestly say he didn't know.

"You're going to have to redo everything," Little Tom interrupted.

"Refinish the floors," Mel said.

"Repaint the ceilings," Sid added.

"Exactly," Maddie said, her face regaining that flushed look. "You and I can start with the easy stuff on the other side of the house, then when we—" she pointed to herself and Keller "—meet them—" she gestured to the others "—in the middle of the house, they'll have that much less to do, and you'll be happier with the results."

The imagined sunspots had been his first clue that Maddie wasn't exactly Nature Girl, a suspicion confirmed a little more every day. Why she continued to come and help him was still a mystery to him, but one he didn't try very hard to solve. Pity, boredom—he wasn't asking questions. Connie's theory, which he had graciously shared with Keller whether Keller wanted him to or not, was that Maddie had some sort of artist's block and that gardening was her way of avoiding painting. Keller didn't care. He was just glad she had chosen to come. Never mind that his eagerness to have her there was definitely uncool and that it put him in a spot where he was likely to agree to anything, just because he enjoyed being near her. Today, for instance, going from one small kitchen rewiring to a full-scale remodeling of his whole house.

"We'll stay inside today," he said, ignoring the smiles the men exchanged.

"Great," she said. "We'll start with the attic, since that's furthest away from the kitchen."

Keller did a little calculating in his head, decided she was wrong about the layout of the house, and decided not to mention it. "Sure, we can start with the attic. But there's no reason to go through all that stuff. We'll pile it up outside the door, then head to the dump with it later."

"No," Maddie said, sounding stricken at the prospect.

They all stared, and she said, "It's your attic, of course, and your junk to do whatever you want with, but it's just that when I was growing up, I read all these books about girls who had hideaways there, or secret rooms. I grew up—well, we had basement ranchers, and a basement is just not the same. I've never actually been in an attic and I have all these ideas about what might be in there. Old costumes, forgotten books—"

"Moths," Tom said.

"Silverfish," Mel added.

"Mice," Sid finished.

That last one got her. Keller watched Maddie's

cream-colored skin blanch all the way to the shade of wallpaper paste. "Mice?" she whispered.

Ambrose barked. A reminder, Keller knew, that Maddie hadn't let him take out that garden mouse last week.

"There aren't mice," he said, putting his hand on Maddie's arm. My, she felt good. And what a show he was making for the town's male gossips. But he couldn't seem to remove his hand. "If there were mice, we could hear them down here. I don't think there are silverfish, either, because I think it's pretty dry up there."

"Moths?"

He couldn't lie to her. "Moths are possible."

"Likely," he heard Tom say.

Keller watched her swallow hard, then seem to make up her mind. "That's okay. They're just uglier butterflies."

"Until they get in your hair," Tom said.

"That's bats, isn't it?"

"Moths, too," Mel agreed.

He had to get her away from these guys before she went screaming out the door. Going through the junk in the attic was probably one of his lowest priorities, but it had to be done someday, and at least if he were in the house he could stay in communication with Tom, smooth out any problems before they happened. For some reason, he was pretty sure there were going to be problems.

He decided to solve one of those right away. "When you go out next time, get a coffeemaker and some coffee, and I'll reimburse you for it."

"How sweet," Maddie said, looking genuinely pleased. He would have been pleased with himself for making her look so pleased, had he not been under the watchful smirks of the other men. This was ridiculous. He and Maddie were nothing more than buddies, he reminded himself, taking his hand off her arm. The last time he'd even remotely felt as if she knew he was an eligible member of the opposite sex was when she'd given him that impromptu sex education lecture the first day in the garden. Since then, those vibes had been totally shut down. She wasn't interested in him. He was a pal, a buddy, probably indistinguishable in her mind from Connie or Ambrose. Given that the townspeople were already starting to see visions of matchmaking dancing in their heads, he couldn't afford for these guys to think he was besotted over her. Taking cracks about his handyman skills was one thing. Teasing him about Maddie was another.

Turning away from her to grab some lawn bags out of the closet, Keller said, "We'll be in the attic if you need us."

"Okeydokey," Tom said, passing the tape measure to Sid. "Although the attic isn't the room furthest from the kitchen."

"That would be the room where Mariah Keller herself died," Mel said conversationally, and Keller watched Maddie hesitate. Knowing Maddie, she was probably thinking about ghosts, although whether in fear or excitement was anybody's guess. Then Sid said, "The room with the oak four poster and the chenille bedspread, and the picture of Grandfather Mountain on the wall. That's the room furthest from here."

"That's my bedroom," Keller said. Instantly, he knew he left himself, and Maddie, wide open for jokes. "But we're not going there to work. Actually, we're not going there at all." He'd never defended someone's honor before, and he wasn't exactly sure how it was playing. "We're going straight to the attic."

"But aren't you going to change clothes first?" Sid asked.

"Why must you critique what Keller has on?" Maddie asked.

"You're right," Mel said. He turned to Keller. "The mice won't care if you're dressed like Michael Jordan."

"All the better to bat the moths out of Maddie's hair with," Tom said, stretching the tape measure out again and giving one end to Sid. "Unless you're thinking of Michael Jordan the baseball player instead of the basketball player."

"Then you're going to have problems," Sid agreed.

"Then you're going to have moths in your hair," Mel added.

Keller looked at Maddie, who wore an expression he and Ambrose had seen only once or twice in the course of their adventures with her. It could only be described as murderous. Telling himself he was the worst kind of coward, he headed past Maddie and up the stairs. As he topped the stairway, he heard her fierce whisper to the men. "I have two words to say to you—plumber's butt."

He stopped, stood and grinned. Why had he ever thought he needed to defend her honor when she did such a bang-up job of defending both of theirs?

5

BLUSHING AS SHE CAUGHT up with him on the stairs, Maddie realized Keller must have heard her comment to Little Tom. Of course, when the restaurant where she'd worked had undergone its renovation, one of the workers had told her that a crew's talent could almost always be judged by the way they wore their pants. When the waistband was down to the hips, you knew you'd hired the best. She considered sharing this with Keller, then thought better of it.

She'd shown up a little bit early this morning, eager to figure out a way to get into the attic. She never dreamed that Tom and company were going to get started right away. That woman must be desperate for my recipes, Maddie thought, flattered. On her way over, she had told herself that the hardest thing was going to be keeping her mouth shut about her discovery yesterday. Mariah Keller's letter had plainly stated that significant papers and manuscripts, while not destroyed, hadn't been donated to the library either. Instead, she had stored them away for safekeeping in the family home, along with the rest of Lucas's things.

She should just be straight with him, Maddie thought, looking over at Keller. But today, with a houseful of people banging away downstairs, and her own nerves rattled, and Keller looking really, really good in those shorts and T-shirt...well, today just didn't seem like a good day.

"I think I am going to grab my shoes," Keller said, touching her on the back.

She kicked herself for getting such a charge out of those times when Keller touched her. It was ridiculous. She'd really gone around the celibacy bend when a man's friendly punch in the arm could send her swooning. But it was more than that, she thought. She had noticed that he wasn't a casual toucher. He wasn't one of those guys who slapped other men on the back or put his arm around every waitress in town. Okay, so she *was* every waitress in town. Still.

This attraction was making it very difficult for her to treat him like a buddy, although she was trying. In desperation, she had fallen back on that old public-speaking trick: when someone makes you nervous, imagine him in his underwear. Of course, the first time she tried it, it backfired within seconds, since the picture of Keller in his underwear (briefs, she was sure) had exactly the opposite effect. It was more swoon-inducing than a whole horde of garden mice. Instead, when they were alone together, she decided to pretend she was looking at someone to whom she couldn't possibly be attracted. Her octogenarian dentist back in Knoxville. Her hairy-eared junior-high-school music teacher.

Just now, as Keller came out of his room with his tennis shoes on, she tried to superimpose over his lean and lovely body the three-piece suit of her least favorite childhood minister. Instead of Keller's soft black hair, curling up in the back as it dried, she tried to picture the preacher's bad toupee.

"What are you grinning about?" Keller asked, looking ready to share the joke.

Some other time, Maddie thought. "I'm just excited. Eager to see what's up here."

Keller opened a door off the hallway, revealing a narrow and badly lit staircase. He flipped a switch on the wall, and she saw light fill the attic above.

"Hope you aren't disappointed," he said. "Watch your step."

"Disappointed?" Maddie asked, heading up the short flight. "Why on earth would I be disappointed? I'm sure it's lovely. It's probably absolutely—" The words caught in her throat.

"Charming, you were going to say?"

"Charming," she finished weakly. Stunned, she looked around.

She couldn't have said what she had expected. Well, yes, she could. Some storybook setting, with a rocker pulled next to the window and the uneven wood flooring polished to a warm glow. Picturesque trunks with wearable vintage wedding dresses spread out over them, costume jewelry spilling out of hatboxes. Instead, she was staring at a ripped cardboard box full of rusty screws and nails, and another box torn open to reveal an assortment of mildewed grain sacks. She couldn't see the floor, and as for the window, it was only a tiny square of warped glass, completely covered in dirt.

"You change your mind?" Keller asked.

"No, no. This is manageable. Just a little bit of hard work, right?" And just a matter of finding the oldest junk in the room, she thought, because, logically, that should be where any papers are.

She heard a whine from the bottom of the steps, as

Keller said, "No, Ambrose, you can't come up." He addressed Maddie again. "That's the last thing we need, Ambrose chasing something up here."

"Provided there's something to chase," she said, gulping.

"Of course," he said, smiling at her reassuringly as she heard Ambrose sigh, then the click of his toenails as he walked away from the stairway door. Keller took her hand. "Believe it or not, it's not as bad as it looks. Come on."

Feeling his strong hand on hers, trying not to think of whether her palms were going to sweat all over his, Maddie obediently followed Keller up the remaining steps and onto the floor of the attic. He dropped her hand to squeeze past one of the boxes, and she followed, still feeling the pressure of his hand on hers.

"A little breathing room," he said.

"Oh, this is perfect," she said. They were in an empty space in the middle of the boxes, enclosed by heaps of junk, but free to move around. "It's like when you were a little kid and you hid in the clothes racks while your mom shopped. I loved that."

She looked at Keller, who was staring at her. "You never hid in the clothes rack?" she asked him.

"No."

"You never get that feeling, even now, when you're in a department store, that you want to get under the sports jackets and khakis and sit cross-legged?"

"Never," he admitted.

She sat down on the floor, then tugged him down with her. The stacks reached well above her head, but the floor was warm—if it hadn't been for the fan going, she guessed the room would have been unbearable. The floor wasn't that dirty, and it was smooth, no doubt worn down by all the boxes pushed across it through the years.

Keller sat next to her, obviously uncomfortable at sitting in this unorthodox place. "I've noticed something odd about you," she said, stretching out her legs and leaning back on her elbows. "You never sit when there's something else you think you could be doing."

"Maddie, I think that's normal."

She shook her head. "Not for me. And not for Lucy or Connie or Little Tom."

He leaned back a little bit, too. She allowed herself one glance at his muscled and suntanned thighs before she made herself look away.

"You're extrapolating from a self-selected sample of admittedly lazy people. Mrs. Martin's always busy."

"But is she happy?" Maddie asked.

"I don't know. Is she?"

"She's too busy for me to ask her," Maddie admitted. "But I can tell you that I would have preferred a landlady who would watch *Jeopardy* with me after work at night."

Keller was grinning. "Is that what you do at night?"

"I know, I know," she said. "You don't have a TV, and you think it's the tool of the government to numb people into not making decisions for themselves. Or you think it's time you could spend picking out mutual funds or whatever. But I can't give up *Jeopardy*. And sometimes *Oprah*, if it's not too depressing or too uplifting. And the occasional *Be-*

witched, if it's one where Darrin gets humiliated at the end. There, are you satisfied?''

He was grinning. ''I don't have a TV because I can't get reception out here. It's not for philosophical reasons. It's just that that's been the only part of your schedule unaccounted for in town. They all ask each other, what does she do when she gets home at night?''

''Would it make you feel better if I told you that during commercial breaks I go outside and sacrifice mice to the goddess of agriculture?''

''I know you, remember? You can't get anywhere near a mouse.''

Maddie knew she ought to be relieved that with all the town gossips knew about her, they didn't know the real reason she was here. Instead, feeling lower than low, she turned the conversation back to Keller.

''So my life is an open book, but what about you? If you find it so hard to take it easy, what do you do? Besides garden?''

He stretched out all the way, his head gently hitting the floor, his arms at his sides. ''Can't tell you.''

''What do you mean you can't tell me? You know everything about me,'' she said. *Except the real reason I want to rummage through your attic,* she added silently.

''Well, when I moved here, I thought I'd find enough to do. But I was used to working sixty and seventy hours a week at the brokerage and there was nothing that was going to keep me that busy. So I started goofing around on the computer.''

''You play video games?'' She tried to keep the dismay out of her voice.

''No, no,'' he said. ''I've been working on this

software for small businesses." He sounded genuinely excited.

"That's it? That's your big secret?" She didn't know what she had expected him to say he did—write sonnets under the moonlight, throw clay pots, stage interpretive dances on the lawn?

"Is there something wrong with that?" He leaned up a little.

"No, not at all. It's just that you're so..." She tried to say it as nicely as she could. "...type A."

"As opposed to you, you're what, Type Z?"

"Type Slug," she said. She leaned back all the way. "I could lie here and daydream all day and never notice that time was passing. Could you do that?"

"Would I want to do that? That's the question."

"Come on," she said, tapping him on the arm. "Lean back all the way again. Shut your eyes. Okay, clear your mind."

"How do you clear your mind?"

She sighed impatiently. "I don't know. Just do it."

"You'd make a great counselor, Maddie. Shape up. Snap out of it."

"Okay, being sluggish and being patient aren't the same thing. Very clever of you to have figured that out. But you're not supposed to talk."

"Okay, I'm not talking," he said.

She leaned up on one elbow and looked at him to make sure he had his eyes closed. His eyelashes were to die for. She could buy tube after tube of guaranteed-plump mascara and never achieve anything like that. His lids fluttered open.

"I knew you were staring at me."

"I was coveting your eyelashes," she said.

"You know, there are other parts of me to covet."

"None that I need right now," she said briskly. "Shut your eyes."

She was starting to sweat, despite the hum and whirl of the fan. Pulling her shirt away where it was stuck to her chest, she said, "Now, it's Saturday morning. You wake up, walk outside, stretch and look around. The sky is blue with just a hint of white in the background, the air is fresh and clean, and you can smell the morning glories, thick with dew."

"What time is it?"

"I don't have a watch," she said.

"No, I mean in this fantasy. Because the morning glories would be closed up unless it was right at dawn."

"Okay, they're closed," she said.

"I don't think they smell either," he said. "I think that's honeysuckle."

She counted to ten. "Whatever."

"Is this leading up to a trip to the garden? Because I don't think an imaginary trip to the garden is going to do anything to help me relax."

"Will you be quiet?" she said. "How are you ever going to relax if you keep talking?" She placed a finger over his lips and started to go on.

"Like this?" He opened his eyes and looked at her, and she almost felt an actual slip in time, as the mood of the room changed from one of lighthearted chatter to serious attraction. Keller lifted his arms and laced them around her head, pulling her close to him. As she bent closer toward him, she told herself she was merely seeing exactly how black those eyes were. Since she was so close, she told herself, moving her hand from his mouth to the nape of his neck, she should satisfy her curiosity about whether his shock of black hair was really as soft as she supposed. It was. Then his lips touched hers.

She was not shy. Remembering, vaguely, how tentative she'd been with Jeff Alvin, she was surprised to find herself kissing Keller Lowry with an intensity she'd forgotten she could possess. Her rediscovered sensuality wasn't putting him off, though, and soon all thoughts of ever kissing anyone else evaporated. He tasted of peanut butter and sweetness, but there was a richness and a power behind the kiss, and she met it.

He groaned a little and pulled her all the way on top of him. She slipped a hand under his shirt, tracing her fingertips along his stomach.

Those shorts showed off his legs to his advantage, but they left nothing to the imagination, and as she stretched her body along his, she could feel all of him pressing against her. Knowing she shouldn't, she pressed back.

He sat up halfway, still kissing her, and she felt him fumble with trying to find a front clasp to her bra before he reached around her, kissing her cheek as he did.

She sniffed the shampoo scent of his hair, felt the dampness of the morning's shower and marveled at the shape of his ear. How far gone must she be, that she could find a man's ear attractive? Don't think about it, she told herself, moving her mouth down his neck as she felt his warm hands on her chest.

There's no reason to think this will ever happen again, the sane part of Maddie's mind told her. This was just because of the heat and the crazy morning and being so close to each other in this magic little space. And if it never happened again, this was her last chance to see if she could make him tremble the way he was making her tremble.

As Keller moved his mouth to hers again, his hand circling her breast, she stroked him through the fabric of his shorts.

It made him shake with hunger, and that, in turn, made her wild and flushed, emboldened by the power of her touch. Sitting up, straddling him, she motioned him up, pulling his shirt off as he sat up, too. She marveled at how beautiful he was as she ran a hand over his stomach again.

He rubbed his hand along her thigh, and she shivered. She reached for his hand and turned it over, palm up, drawing a pattern on the calluses he'd gotten gardening. Because of me, she told herself, although she was pretty sure her help had been wanted. Because she was having too much fun to come out and say why she wanted to be here. And because now, sometimes, she thought she wanted to be here for reasons that had nothing to do with career or scholarship. She drew his palm to her mouth and kissed it gently.

"Maddie, I've never wanted anyone more in my life than I want you right now," Keller said. His arms circled her, holding her tightly, and his breath was audible even over the loud buzzing in her own ears. "I don't have—I don't have anything."

Tomorrow she would be grateful, she told herself. Tomorrow she would be glad that they had this reason not to finish what they had started. But instead of accepting it gracefully, rearranging her clothes and going on, she heard herself say, "So can we make out some more?"

He moaned, pulling her down with him again. This

time his body was stretched out over hers. He said, "I have the feeling this is how teenagers get in trouble."

She did, too. But there was something about this moment that was urging her on, as if she knew that if she relinquished it once, she would never recapture it. "You don't feel like a teenager," she whispered, breaking her mouth away from his and bringing it to his ear. "Ask me to touch you again."

She knew what it cost, what it meant, for him to ask, and she thrilled again at her power. "Please," he said, as she slipped her hand inside his shorts.

"Briefs," she said. "I was wondering," she gasped as he moved his own hands to her shorts and unsnapped them, beginning to pull them down her hips. "Wait, I don't know—"

"How far can we go? Without going too far? Let's find out," Keller said, moving his mouth to her stomach and tracing his tongue down to her hipbone. Pushing her shirt back up and out of his way, he kissed her breast gently before taking her nipple in his mouth. Crying out slightly at the unfamiliar sensation, she moved her hands up to his hair, clutching fistfuls of the soft black stuff. He had a hand clasped around her thigh, and she felt the warmth and the strength of it as a counterbalance to the dizziness engulfing her. She wanted to be here, wide awake, an equal participant.

"You ask me," he said, leaning over her, his dark eyes close to hers.

"Will you touch me?" she asked.

His hands reached to tug her shorts down further as she arched her back a little. He scooted down, bent his head close to her body and kissed the inside of her thigh, his breath tickling her there.

His hands moved slowly, languorously upward along her thighs, and just as she thought she'd scream if he didn't reach for her now, she heard a crash and a yell and a string of curse words from far away in the house.

Keller pulled away from her slightly, and she arched back toward him, bringing his lips to hers.

"It's nothing," she whispered.

"Okay," he said, burying his face in her hair, stroking her teasingly along her stomach.

There was another crash, more curse words and the mad and frenetic barking of Ambrose, clearly audible. They paused and listened, then heard the dog, still barking, run up the stairs and stop at the door to the attic stairwell.

"Don't you think they can get along without us?" Maddie asked. As if hearing her, Ambrose gave another commanding bark.

Keller sighed. "I am being paged."

"I guess so," Maddie said, pushing a lock of his hair off his forehead.

"It is my house," he said, reaching for his shirt.

"And you should know if something's happened to it, or to them," Maddie agreed, scooting away from him a little, untangling her limbs from his. Suddenly self-conscious, she tugged her shorts back on and re-snapped them, then folded her arms over her chest.

"Do you need any help?" he asked.

Psychiatric, she thought. Advice to the lustlorn. "Getting myself together? No, I'll be fine. If there's a fire, let me know. Otherwise, I may just sit here for a few minutes."

He gave her one more sweet brush on the lips before he stood up and started to squeeze past one of the surrounding boxes.

"Keller?" she asked.

He turned around immediately.

"Yeah?"

She didn't know where the vixen of a few minutes ago had gone. To the convent, she hoped. And good riddance. She could hear the embarrassment in her tone as she said, "I think you need to maybe change into jeans before you meet the guys?"

He looked down, and she saw that he was blushing, too. "Consider it done."

He got past the box, and she heard him race down the stairs as she let her head fall back again, hard, against the attic floor.

"You can't go back to holding hands," she said out loud. Trouble was, she didn't want to.

"HEARD YOU LOST your kitchen," Lucy said to Keller as soon as he walked into the diner.

"I don't like that word, *lost*," he said to her, taking a seat at the counter and trying to not look around for Maddie. "That implies that it somehow got away from me, and I could find it again if I looked hard enough. I prefer demolished."

"Little Tom likes the phrase *act of God*," Maddie said, coming from the main kitchen area. She carried a large casserole dish, steam slipping from it as she set it on the small work space. "I thought I recognized your voice." She looked around for a second before asking him, puzzled, "What have you done with my boyfriend?"

For just a second his heart stopped long enough for

it to fill with a corny rush of sentiment, a chest—and maybe khakis—bursting pride that she was actually referring to him in public as her boyfriend. Then, stricken, he wondered what he had done to make her fear that he was not the man he was yesterday. Finally, it dawned on him that she was talking about Ambrose.

"He's fine. He's at Connie's right now." He saw that Maddie was blushing and knew that they were being obvious as hell. He cleared his throat and peeled one of the napkins from the countertop dispenser and began shredding it. "It's been so long since I've eaten here, I couldn't remember if dogs were allowed or not."

"Sure they are," Maddie said, taking a cloth and viciously scrubbing the countertop two seats down from him. It already sparkled. "So why don't you go over there and get him?"

"I'll go in a minute." It was nothing he could admit to her, but now that he had sat here looking at her, remembering the day before, he was going to find it very uncomfortable to stand up again any time in the next few minutes.

"No, go get him," Maddie persisted. "He's sort of our chaperon," she said to Lucy. "Not chaperon, exactly—"

"Mascot," Keller said quickly. "Mascot."

"Y'all forming your own baseball team or what?" Lucy asked, bringing Keller a glass of tap water with a few smallish ice cubes in it, and a basket of crackers. "You want iced tea? Sweet or unsweet?"

She poured his unsweetened iced tea out of a pitcher behind the counter and shot Maddie a flinty-eyed glance. "Were you going to offer the gentleman supper?"

"Oh, yeah," she said. "It's just so early for the dinner rush to start. Did you get in the garden today?"

"It didn't seem the same without you there," he said, watching the color flood her cheeks, afraid it was flooding his own. For two people who'd had so few inhibitions yesterday, they were pretty easily embarrassed.

She pursed her lips slightly and began chewing on her pen cap, falling back into waitress mode. "Well, the special is moussaka. It has eggplant—"

He thought he must have made a face, because Lucy jumped in quickly to say, "But you don't even know the eggplant is in there."

"Then why put it in at all?" he asked. Maddie's head shot up and she narrowed her eyes at him. It was a familiarly frosty look, the expression she always got when he disagreed with her, and he was relieved to see it. If she could look at him like that, he still had hope that whatever this mysterious thing they had started yesterday was, it would include their easy friendship.

Lucy, heading off whatever Maddie was about to say, interrupted. "Now tell me straight what happened to your kitchen."

Briefly, he went through Tom's tale of woe while Maddie tossed a salad, her back to him. He explained to Lucy about retaining walls and popping bricks, the upshot of it being that there was now a pretty large hole in his kitchen and Little Tom and company looked to be permanent residents. He omitted the story of how difficult it had been to keep his composure around the men yesterday when all he wanted to do was go back up to the attic and be with Maddie. So he didn't have a kitchen? So what? What was that compared to having missed his chance with this woman?

His not having a kitchen was the main reason he was at Lucy's, or so he had told himself—and Ambrose, who wasn't fooled—but he knew he was really there to see Maddie. He hadn't expected her this morning—not with the all-new chaos, as opposed to the old familiar chaos, not if she might be feeling shy about what happened yesterday. But her not being there felt like a real loss. As he watched her finish the salad, he saw her lick a drop of blue-cheese dressing off her finger. The unconscious gesture made him glad he was sitting down or he thought his knees might have buckled.

She caught him staring. "You didn't see that," she said, waving the salad tongs at him.

He shook his head, nearly unable to speak. This was ridiculous.

What had happened the day before had been the most erotic experience of his life. Nothing about being with other women had been remotely like being with Maddie. Never had his whole self been so closely attuned to someone else. He had to wonder what it would be like to possess the rest of that moment, to follow through on what they had started. Was it even possible that there could be passion more intense than what they'd already experienced?

Belatedly, he noticed that there were tiny piles of shredded napkin around him. He scooped them up, rearranging them into smaller stacks while he watched Maddie finish icing a layered cream cake. Lucy had given up asking him about his plans for fixing his kitchen, either writing him off as hysterically mute or understanding that he had his mind on other things.

In fact, his mind was so busy with those other things that he had actually gotten up an hour early and driven to Bryson City, where he didn't know a soul, to buy condoms. He was prepared for a sullen and probably pimply teenager who would snicker at his purchase; instead, he got a pinched-faced matron his mother's age, who blatantly checked his left hand for a wedding ring, then made a distinct clucking sound under her breath when she didn't see one.

He knew he didn't know Maddie as well as he wanted to. He also knew that she was probably a closer friend to him than any woman he'd ever pursued. The relationship he'd had with women before her now seemed superficial. Wanting her might be separate from enjoying her company, but he didn't think so. He wanted her as a friend and as a lover. But he also wanted to know her secrets, to understand everything about her.

Other people were filing in for dinner, and if they were surprised to see him, they didn't let on. Everyone knew the story of his kitchen catastrophe, although they, at least, pretended to be more confident than he was that Little Tom could actually fix it. Although Connie had told him several times, he hadn't really understood how popular Maddie was with Lucy's customers. Was it really possible that she was going to be gone after the summer? Although he'd brought the subject up, she'd never really talked about what her home was like or, beyond waiting tables, what she did in Knoxville. He guessed he hadn't been very forthcoming, either.

It was hard to explain why he'd felt this self-imposed pressure to move here, to prove he could fulfill something he'd said he'd do. But now that he was here, he was ready to admit that he needed something else out of life besides enough money to live on, a dog who worshipped him and the occasional elderly neighbor knocking on his door. The software he'd been fiddling with was giving him some new ideas about what else he could do as far as a life's work went, but he'd always just assumed his love life would magically fall into place. Someday he'd be introduced to a friend of a friend's wife, some slim and pleasant-faced preppy blonde in upscale catalog clothes, and that would be that. He'd call her. She'd call him. She'd take off early on Friday from her office in Raleigh or Charlotte or Atlanta to drive up to Ravens Gap for the weekend. A few months later, she'd ask her firm if she could telecommute three days a week, and because she was such a wonderful creative director/corporate executive/top producer, they'd have to let her. They'd have a big wedding at her parents' church in the suburbs of Raleigh or Charlotte or Atlanta, and there would be at least six perfectly made-up sorority sisters and one homely cousin in the bridal party. This was the way it had happened for all of his fraternity brothers, and there was no reason to think it wouldn't happen that way for him.

He looked up at Maddie again, in some kind of swishy white dress with red flowers all over it. The red should have clashed with her hair, but he decided it didn't. She was leaning over the counter, talking into the hearing aid of one of Connie's friends. He'd never even guessed that a face could have as many expressions as he saw on hers. She looked nothing like that bland, blond woman he'd assumed he would marry. Watching her now, he saw her eyes widen and her face light up as the door swung open, and he wondered, jealously, who could be getting that kind of greeting.

Who else?

6

"HEY, BUDDY, I missed you today." Keller watched as Maddie blew Ambrose a kiss across the counter. "The Board of Health won't let me hug you right now, but I owe you one, okay?"

It obviously didn't escape Ambrose's attention that Maddie had made him sort of a minor celebrity in town. Tilting his nose up slightly, he trotted over to sit under Keller's feet, making it clear that his owner was lucky to share his distinguished company.

A disgruntled Connie followed the dog in and took the counter stool next to Keller.

"What's up?" Keller asked, accepting another re-fill on his iced tea.

"You never told me he howled," Connie said.

"You've heard him howl."

"No," Connie said. "I've heard him bark, woof, growl and make all kinds of other dog noises, but this wasn't a dog noise. This was just unearthly."

"Samoyeds do that. They howl like that," Maddie said, bringing Connie a glass of iced tea without being asked. "It has something to do with being stuck in the Arctic with only the polar bears to hear them."

He'd never thought of Ambrose as anything but a mutt with a Park Avenue coat. He'd gone to a shelter in Manhattan hoping to pick up an apartment-size dog, but instead had ended up with Ambrose. Having the dog only made him more determined to get to the country. "What makes you think he's a Samoyed?" Keller asked.

"Well, I found this dog book at the library, with different pictures, and I started flipping around it, looking for someone who looks like him. I thought husky, obviously, or Akita, but then I saw Samoyed and I knew that was it."

"Now why were you looking at Ambrose's picture?" Connie asked.

"You were going to paint him, maybe?" Keller suggested.

"Oh, no," she said, rearranging the salt shakers in front of them, avoiding his eyes. "I'm not that great at animal portraits yet. I just wanted to make sure, you know, that we were following all the rules, doing all the things he likes. Like he likes to roam, but he's loyal to one person. That would be you," she said quickly.

"Well, you know, I'm sure he wouldn't mind you practicing your painting skills on him."

Below the seat, Ambrose spoke slightly in assent. Before Maddie could reply, though, someone at another table called her name and she skittered away.

Connie jerked a thumb over toward where Lucy was sitting down, taking a break. "I don't know what Lucy's going to do when Maddie goes."

"She did just fine without her," Keller said.

"But that was before people knew the difference between her food and other food. She doesn't like being in the restaurant business, never has. I bet she'll close." He looked at Keller meaningfully. "No, Lucy's won't be the same when she leaves."

He'd be damned if he were going to cry on Connie's shoulder. "I just hope my kitchen's fixed by then."

"That's all you're hoping for, huh?"

Keller was saved from answering as Maddie passed a plate of the eggplant dish down to Connie. He took a bite and chewed thoughtfully.

"Nutmeg," he said.

"Well, obviously," she answered. "And?"

"And? Hmm." He took another bite. "Aha... cumin."

She grinned and gave him a thumbs-up sign before moving on to other customers.

"Hell of a cook," Connie said. He pointed to Keller's now-clean plate. "You're gobbling it without even savoring it first, like it's one of those peanut butter sandwiches you eat everyday."

Was there no limit on what was worthy of gossip in this town? Were all his habits dissected in this way? "How do you know what I eat every day?" Keller asked.

"Keller," Connie said, plainly disgusted. "You buy your groceries from me. I swear, for one of those uptight city types, you're getting to be downright moony."

It was true, Keller thought, that the taste of the spices Connie had so easily identified had completely eluded him. No wonder people lost weight when they were in love, he thought.

In love. Now where had that thought come from? He was attracted to her. He liked her. He lusted after her. He'd give up any number of things just to be with her. But he didn't know her well enough to be in love.

Keller became aware that Connie was talking to

him. "Why do you think she's researching your dog?"

"To paint him, don't you think?" Keller said, looking down at Ambrose, who managed to strike a noble portrait-ready pose while lying down. No small feat, that. Lucy, on her feet again, walked by Keller and took his plate, and he reached for another napkin and began folding it compulsively.

"I think she's looking to take him with her," Connie said. "When she goes. You know how attached he is to her."

"That doesn't mean he's going with her," Keller said, wanting to say that he couldn't believe she was going at all.

"I don't know what you'll do when they leave you," Connie continued solemnly.

"The dog is not going anywhere," Keller snapped, beginning to shred the folded napkin over the countertop. Ambrose wiggled out from between their stools, stood, stretched, walked over to the end of the counter and settled down again.

"See, he's already distancing himself from you," Connie said. He pointed to Keller's stack of napkin bits. "You know, I read something once about people who compulsively peel beer labels off bottles."

"So you like the dish?" Maddie said brightly, suddenly before them, sweeping his little heap of paper off the counter and into the palm of her hand.

"Perfect," Connie said. He leaned his elbows on the countertop and said, "Listen, I've been thinking. I was reading this article about towns that paint murals on their older buildings, and I was thinking I could do that to the store. I could have a scene with this street, only with horses and carriages in it. Since you're an artist, you could help me out with it.''

Keller watched as Maddie turned away, busying herself with collecting dishes. ''I'm not sure I'm up to that, yet,'' she said. ''I think you'll probably want to look for someone a little more experienced.''

''Oh, hell, it doesn't have to be perfect,'' Connie said. ''I'll lend a hand. I paint a little myself, you know,'' he told Keller.

''I remember you saying something about canvases.''

''Oh, yeah,'' Connie said. ''I'm always trying to get Maddie to talk painting techniques with me, but she won't.''

''Because people who talk too much about their art never practice it,'' Maddie said, walking away from them and stealing a quick pat on Ambrose's head as she went to clear a table on the other side of the room.

''And people who don't practice art don't know what to talk about,'' Connie said, so quietly that Keller almost didn't hear him. He knew Connie was trying to tell him something, but as mixed up as he already was about Maddie, he'd be damned if he was going to listen.

''SO TELL ME what you're really doing here.''

Maddie looked at Connie, coffee cup in hand, leaning back in his ubiquitous rocker on the front porch of his store. It was another beautiful day, sort of like the day she had conjured up for Keller's relaxation fantasy. *Not that we were noticing the pretend scenery after a while*, she thought ruefully.

She looked across the street to the restaurant, where Lucy would have the morning programs blaring. She was lucky that she had gotten this far with her fib to Connie, especially since he had been eager to talk painting with her when she first started meeting him for coffee, confiding to her that many of the paintings in his store were his own. He had gone from the amateurish painting she'd seen on the wall on her first visit there to some really good landscapes. She wanted to be annoyed with him for putting her on the spot about the mural last night, but she knew she had no right to indignation and that he might have called her on her lie a long time ago.

She took a sip of her own coffee, then met his cagey stare. "What do you think I'm doing here?"

"I've been puzzling over it. You're not a painter."

"No," she admitted. "Can't draw, hate to get my hands dirty in clay, and if I'm not color-blind, I'm most definitely color-ignorant. So, no, I'm not a painter."

"I thought you were one of those rainbow people," he said, referring to a band of well-known modern nomads who regularly camped out in the woods of Appalachia. "But you bathe too regularly for that."

"Thanks for noticing," she said. He went on.

"If this were a movie, you'd be running some kind of con, but I've tried and tried to see what you're going to gain by helping a tired woman with her restaurant, planting someone else's garden and keeping an old man company. I just don't get it.

"Then I started thinking about all the time you've spent in the library," he continued, as Maddie's pulse quickened. "You could be filching ephemera," he said. She squirmed with unexpected guilt as his guess got colder, not warmer. "But I've been to my share of antique malls, and despite what they might tell you in magazines, I've seen that junk is still mostly junk. I figure you'd be making about a dime an hour.''

"So I'm not a library vandal," she said.

"No. Then I look at how much attention you've paid to Keller and his dog.''

"Have I?" she said, setting her coffee cup down beside her chair.

He shot her an exasperated look. "My body has gone decrepit with age, not my brain.''

She didn't say anything. She knew that if she tried to defend herself for spending so much time with Keller, she'd end up hinting at what happened between them the other day and how she felt about him. Before she branded herself as the loosest and most amoral woman to hit Ravens Gap in a century, she wanted to hear what other Mata Hari roles Connie had envisioned for her.

"So then, noticing how much attention you pay to our handsome young rich fellow, I wonder if you're some kind of black widow.''

That one puzzled her. "A what?''

"A black widow. You know, those women who marry millionaires, then inherit everything when they die mysterious deaths. First they always do away with the man's pet.''

"What?" She was genuinely outraged. "I would never, never let anything happen to Keller or Ambrose.''

"Aha," he said.

"Are you through playing Hercule Poirot?" She was getting impatient. "Because I'll just tell you.''

"Is he the French guy with the mustache?" Connie asked.

"Belgian.''

"Right, right. No, I'm not. Give me a few more minutes. I notice when you talk about Keller, you sound like you care about him. Now, if you were going to off him, it wouldn't be in your best interests to care, would it?"

"Off him? Where do you get this vocabulary? Late night detective movies on cable TV?"

"Satellite dish," he clarified, continuing. "And all that's provided you could even get him to marry you, because as much as I think he's gone dippy over you, I'm not sure he's the marrying type yet."

Great. She was being accused of murder and having her ego slashed all at the same time.

"And if you could go to a bigger city, it wouldn't make sense for you to come to Ravens Gap to find a man with money, would it, with the whole town watching you two make eyes at each other."

"We are not."

"*Please,*" Connie said. "The man doesn't even taste his food when he's around you."

"I'm not conceding this point to you, but go on."

"Then I think back to when you met Keller. Your surprise wasn't faked. You couldn't believe how much he looked like Lucas Keller."

"Is this the part of the movie where you gather all of us into a room and say, 'I know you're wondering why I called you here, but one of you is a killer'?"

"Only if this is the part of the movie where you pull a gun out of your purse and wave it around until somebody knocks it out of your hand."

"My purse is in the car," she said. "Your lucky day."

"So then I think about Lucas Keller. And then I think about the library. Then I remember that you're not the first person to be asking around after the old coot. And you're not even the first person from Knoxville.''

He paused, and she took it as her cue to jump in, speaking more slowly than usual. ''So then you wonder if I'm the spurned ex-girlfriend of the jerk who was here last year. And then you wonder if I'm here to finish what he started, so I can show him up academically? And,'' she added hesitantly and a bit sheepishly, ''you think I probably didn't mean to lead any of you on about any of this, because I never expected to get so involved with any of you?''

''No,'' he said, putting his own cup down and looking at her. ''I hadn't gotten to that particular plot twist yet. Why don't you tell me about it?''

A little less than an hour later, she'd driven up to Keller's, then sat looking at the house. Connie had only encouraged her to do what she had already known she must: tell Keller the truth. She had never meant for this to get so out of hand, and if it had been just about poking through the attic, it wouldn't have. She never meant to care about Keller, to treat him as anything more than a friend for the summer. That day she saw him in Connie's store, if she could have guessed the way he would make her feel, how important he would become to her, she would have either spilled the beans then or turned right around and headed back to Knoxville. She'd never guessed there was so much potential danger in what she was doing. Poking around town, asking questions, trying to be circumspect about what she was doing—that was a lark. Falling in love wasn't.

It was a bad idea to mix romance with those things that gave you your sense of self. She'd learned that the hard way with Jeff Alvin. He'd left her feeling not only foolish about romance but foolish about her life in general. As she'd been reminded this morning, trying to explain it to Connie, this whole Lucas Keller obsession had gotten tied up with her own emotional issues, like proving she was smart, proving she deserved to be taken seriously.

Add all that to the fact that it was almost impossible for her to explain anything in twenty words or less. By the time she got to the part about what a pathetic, flighty creature she had always been, Keller would have zero interest in being around her. Her need for approval was a dangerous mix with her southern belle-like chattiness, especially since she had seen how the combination worked in her mother. If Maddie's mother bumped into a neighbor at the grocery store, she immediately had to justify what was in her cart. "I wouldn't buy these artichoke hearts, because you know how expensive they are, but Maddie made that artichoke-and-parmesan soufflé that's so popular now, and I had to try it myself. You haven't had it? Oh, you have to have it." It was in her genes.

But even once she explained to Keller all about the hows and whys of how she had come to Ravens Gap, and why she needed to get up to his attic, there was still the other thing that had happened there last week, and whether she thought she wanted something like it to happen again soon. She had always been the original instant-gratification girl, but she was trying to change that part of herself, not encourage it. She still planned to finish her research here and go back to Knoxville, where her family was, where she still had friends, albeit friends who thought she was crazy.

There was simply no reason for her to stay here, she told herself, trying not to think about Keller as one of those reasons.

She wished could turn off her romantic side. She wished she was the kind of woman who could sleep with someone without trying to delude herself into thinking it was more than it was. Just one kiss—well, a lot of kisses, and what would have been much more than that, had Little Tom and the act of God not intervened—anyway, just one *interlude* and she was getting all hearts and flowers about it. The only thing more ridiculous would be for her to do what she had done with Jeff Alvin—jump from situational attraction straight into visions of their future together.

Jeff had told her one day her conversation was fascinating. Then he'd kissed her, and boom, she was seeing the two of them together in a book-lined study somewhere. Although now that she knew Jeff, she knew he'd never deign to share his study with anyone. The closest she'd get was bringing fresh pots of coffee in there while he snapped at her about how harshly she was grinding the beans.

She knew better than to leap from kisses to reveries, but she had already started to do that with Keller, like when she looked at that book to see what kind of dog Ambrose was. She was curious, yes, but when had natural curiosity passed into picturing the three of them on the front porch at dusk, iced tea and citronella candles and mosquito lotion at hand?

Her experience with Jeff Alvin should have left her wary of this routine, but she still knew it by heart. Next she'd be arguing with herself over whether to keep her maiden name or hyphenate. Or worse yet, thinking about which room could be turned into a nursery.

A loud crash ensued from the house. Okay, until the construction crew shaped up a little, they weren't coming anywhere near the nursery.

She heard the screen door slam and saw Keller step out onto the front porch. She could tell from his wired stance and the way he was pacing slightly that he must be trying not to lose his temper with Little Tom and company. She watched him as he turned and saw her, and she felt a rush of happiness mixed with guilt and apprehension when his face lit up. If she couldn't stop herself from these sugary daydreams, the least she could do was be completely honest with him.

"Hey. I was hoping you'd show up. Things aren't going very well here today, to say the least."

"What's wrong?" she asked, as the dog raced to meet her.

"The house is still falling down, there's still a hole in my kitchen, and when I went out to the garden this morning, bugs had eaten all the pepper plants, even though Little Tom says bugs hate peppers."

Okay, so maybe she should cheer him up before she brought him down again.

"I've actually been thinking about the peppers," she said, walking toward the house as she spoke. She talked fast, trying to drown out the niggling part of her brain that reminded her she had something to say to him. "I read this tip last night in one of the books I checked out. It says you should pour dirty dishwater on them, something about the nutrients that are in the water, although I know that's not the kind of thing you usually want to think about when you're putting your hand in the sink to pull the drain. And it comes right out and says they could get fairly stinky after a while, so you want to have water, you know, that was used maybe to wash dishes after a little midday snack, not the water you used to clean up after a whole Sunday dinner. What do you think?''

He looked at her oddly. ''I barely have dishes. I don't even have a kitchen sink, thanks to these guys. I don't guess bathwater would do?''

Oh, great. Now he had to bring up that tub. She was still having fantasies about him in it, although now they'd been enhanced by her having actually experienced his kisses, his touch, his taste. She stumbled a little on the path.

''Careful,'' he said.

''No, I think it definitely needs to be dishwater,'' she said. ''Well, if we can't do the peppers, I was thinking we could thin out some of the basil. I know you don't really have any use for it right now, but I thought maybe I could make pesto. The basil might be hard to keep fresh once it's picked, so that would mean that I'd need to go into work a little early this afternoon, but I wasn't going to the library today, so that shouldn't be a problem. I'll still have plenty of time here.'' He and Ambrose were both staring at her, Ambrose's head cocked quizzically, Keller with an amused expression on his face.

''A little too much coffee,'' she said hastily. A little too much coffee, a little too much truth, a little too much honesty, a little too much promising both Connie and herself that she would spill her guts to Keller today. ''A little honest work will get that right out of my system.''

''Great,'' he said. ''Attic or garden? Your pick.''

Her pick. Nothing like having to take a little upfront responsibility for your actions. Let's see, should she go to the garden, with its broiling sun and plague of insects, and toil in the dirt, which would make her feel better about what a liar she'd been but which she could probably also use as a penance for her actions, temporarily absolving her from her duty to confess? Or should she go to the attic, where she could look for papers by Lucas Keller under the deluded eyes of this wonderful man, and where she might also compound her sins by seducing him, again? Really, it was no contest.

She was going to tell him. And maybe the attic, where its closeness and its coziness had worked its spell before, would be an easier place to pour her heart out. Then after she told him, he would tell her to have at the boxes and they would be great friends. Or more than friends. The chance that she might again get to steal another of his kisses was reason enough for her to go there.

She knew she should resist temptation, just like Eve should have told the snake to go wrap himself around a limb somewhere. Snow White should have told the witch that she was all full up on Wheaties, no room for a poisoned apple, sorry. Goldilocks should have been a little more modest in her needs—

"Goldilocks," she said. "I just figured out the moral. Remember? We had this discussion?"

"You were breaking into my house. How could I forget?"

She ignored that. "Well, the moral is, don't be greedy. See," she said, proud of herself. "I told you it didn't have anything to do with breaking and entering."

"I'm not so sure that the two aren't loosely related,'' Keller said. ''Can I ask you what made you think of Goldilocks all of a sudden?''

''No, you can't,'' Maddie said, stepping up to the front porch and opening the door. ''It would take too long to explain. But I choose the attic.'' Where did some stupid fairy tale from a male-dominated society get off telling her not to be greedy? Why couldn't she have a romance with Keller and prove something to Jeff Alvin? Why shouldn't she have the papers and Keller's kisses? As for what would happen after the summer, she just wouldn't think about that right now. Southern lady lesson number two, she thought to herself. And say what you might about Scarlet O'Hara, she didn't get where she was by being any Goldilocks.

LOOK, A KISS WAS one thing. But there were kisses and then there was what had happened between them the other day, which was obviously something that was not going to stop at one kiss. It was something that was only going to lead to One Thing.

Which was fine. Not just fine. Desirable. Wanted. An occurrence that was both hoped for, planned for (thanks to his trip to Bryson City) and looked forward to, although if she could now make him forget to breathe just by looking at him, he wasn't sure he wanted to know what would happen to him if they went any further.

''Keller.'' Maddie touched him on the arm, and he was startled to realize they'd reached the stairwell. She put her hand on the doorknob and said, ''Are you ready?''

Probably he was going to just sit in the attic and stare at her like a half-wit all day. That would guarantee that she would forget whatever attraction was between them. Besides, both of them knew better than to start something here, this afternoon, not with workers hammering away below, a dog salivating to get upstairs and tear up the attic, and a whole town already gossiping about them. When he made love to Maddie, he wanted to be far from potential distractions. He wanted to give her his full attention. He was no sexual virgin, but maybe he was a romantic one. Nothing in his past had prepared him for the way that making this woman happy had become of such paramount importance.

"Let's go," he said, reaching to hold Ambrose's collar so he wouldn't follow her up the stairs. Just as she switched the attic light on, Ambrose slipped away and bounded the couple of short steps into Keller's room.

"He had a funny expression on his face," Maddie said, turning around.

"Because he's a dog."

"Whatever you say. You know him best." She topped the stairs as Keller started to follow, then ducked back out. That had been kind of a weird grin, sort of like the one he had worn that Easter they were visiting Keller's parents and the Honey Baked ham disappeared.

"I'll be right up," he called. He walked into the room just in time to see Ambrose snatch the condom box out of the open drawer and run to the door with it.

"Give it back," he said.

The dog shook his head, the red box bobbing in his jaws.

"Now," Keller said.

Ambrose trotted into the hallway.

"Look," Keller said, trying to keep his voice as quiet as possible, although there was probably no way for the men to hear him over the music from the kitchen's small CD and tape player and the groan of the new coffeepot as it brewed. "I know we haven't been paying as much attention to you and I know that you're clever enough to figure out that it probably has something to do with what you're holding there, but I swear, if you will give it back I will make it up to you."

He heard Maddie's footsteps above him in the attic, and Ambrose listened to them for a second before veering toward the stairs.

Keller raced down after him, lunging after his collar as he neared the kitchen. Ambrose stopped and stood absolutely still as Keller skidded past him and partly into the kitchen doorway.

"You okay, there?" It was normally hard to miss Little Tom, but it took Keller a moment to find him, camouflaged in a coating of plaster, standing next to plywood boards twice his height.

"Fine," Keller said, pushing Ambrose's head, with its telltale box, out of the doorway. "Just checking to see if you needed anything."

"We're making some progress here, aren't we?" Sid asked, gazing around with obvious pride.

Damned if Keller knew. If it were at all possible, the kitchen looked worse than it had immediately after the accident. But he wouldn't dare tell the guys that, not on a day when he wanted to keep them occupied.

He edged back out of their line of vision, still keeping Ambrose's head out of the door. There was no way the dog was going to relinquish the box, not without losing quite a bit of face, but he pretended not to notice as Keller pulled the cardboard flaps open and removed the first packet. They were linked together, like carnival tickets, and as he pulled one the whole line came spilling out.

"You know what?" he whispered harshly, trying to stuff them all in one pocket, giving up and breaking the line in two. "You're going to look like some kind of pervert carrying a condom box around for the rest of your life."

"What did you say?" Little Tom hollered.

"I asked if you still liked the Braves."

There was silence, then he heard the disgust in Tom's tone as he said, "I hate the Braves. Yuppie whiners."

"I must be thinking of someone else," Keller called back. He checked his pockets, making sure they weren't visible. He'd go back to his room and find a good hiding place before he went up to the attic. But he couldn't leave Ambrose down here with the rest of the evidence. "Listen, Ambrose," he whispered. "It's not too late for this to have a peaceful ending." He tugged at the box.

"That's Frank at the hardware store who likes the Braves," Little Tom said. "His wife went to high school in Atlanta and he thinks everything that came out of there is by God's own design."

"No more steak. No more chicken. No more car rides. No more sleeping in my bed," Keller said as Ambrose stretched out on the living room floor and began gnawing on the cardboard.

"Dry dog food," he said, more loudly than he'd intended.

"What did you say?" someone yelled from the kitchen.

"I said that's really romantic of Frank," Keller yelled back without thinking.

There was an extended silence from the kitchen, then a few audible snickers. "Boy, has he got it bad," he heard one of them say, and he was just deciding whether to protest or play deaf when he heard a shriek from somewhere above his head.

Ambrose dropped the box and tore upstairs, and Keller heard the men throw down their tools. They raced past him as he grabbed the slobber-covered box, looked around for a second, then stuffed it under the sofa cushions. He caught up with the men at the top of the second-floor landing.

Maddie was standing in the hall next to the attic stairwell, a sheaf of papers in her hand.

"A mouse?" Tom asked.

"A bat?" That from Sid.

"A ghost?" Mel asked. Whether he was hopeful or fearful, Keller couldn't say. His own relief at finding Maddie safe was replaced by an odd tightness in his stomach as he watched her gloat over whatever she was holding.

"No, look, it's a set of letters written by Lucas Keller to his publisher," she said.

"But it's not the old coot's ghost?" Tom asked.

"It's better than his ghost," Maddie said. "It's proof that he wrote another manuscript."

The three other men and Ambrose nodded, pretending, Keller saw, to understand what she was talking about. He didn't understand, so he didn't nod. Instead, he heard himself say, "I guess I don't know why you would be all that excited about this. I know you said you thought he should be better known, but I didn't know it was this important.''

"You've read his books?" Tom sounded surprised, and no wonder, Keller thought. Who else under eighty had?

"You said you read them all at your grandmother's, right?" Keller asked. He felt the sarcasm rising in his throat, but he couldn't keep it out of his voice. "When you weren't going outside to play in the fresh air, of course."

What a bad liar she was. Even now, the excitement in her face gave way to nervousness, and as she started stammering, it was clear that he had caught her at something, although he wasn't yet sure exactly what, only that it had something to do with the ancestor he so resembled.

The other men looked, as one, from Maddie's flustered face to Keller's. In one movement, they began backing toward the stairs.

"Got to check on that order of Sheetrock," Little Tom said.

"As long as you're safe," Sid added, fleeing down the steps.

"Glad it wasn't a ghost," Mel said. "It's a fear of mine."

Keller didn't acknowledge them as they left, although Maddie gave them a weak wave before launching into a rapid monologue.

"I was definitely going to talk to you about this today but you said you were in a rotten mood so I thought you could cheer up a little first. I was going to tell you before today, but it was so nothing, it wasn't even worth mentioning. Well, that's not it, it's just that you know how descendants can be, and Jeff

Alvin had already been here poking around, although he hadn't found you. But at first I thought if you knew someone was looking for stuff about Lucas in your attic, you—'' She paused for breath. "That is, the generic you, the generic descendant, might want something for it, and Jeff Alvin probably has some kind of grant or something, and I'm operating all on my own in my research, and of course, all that thought about you wanting something was before I knew you—''

"Jeff Alvin?" He interrupted. "That's the professor guy, right?" His tone must have been harsher than he meant, because Ambrose, who had been listening intently, moved in front of Maddie. He was in no mood to deal with the beast equation of beauty and the beast.

"Back off, Sport. You're on my nerves anyway."

Maddie and Ambrose looked at each other, both pairs of eyes wide. The dog took little mincing steps backward into Keller's bedroom doorway and lay down, watching them.

"Keller, please don't be so upset. I did fib about why I wanted in your attic. You really are going to need to clean it out, eventually, but it's true that I wanted to see if I could find anything about Lucas Keller.''

"Seducing me was just an added bonus?" he asked.

That brought a hurt glare from her. "This outraged Victorian maiden act doesn't look good on you," she said.

"Neither does that hippy, dippy, granola girl, I'm-just-in-town-to-paint-the-scenery act you've been trying.''

"Okay, so I'm not a painter." Her words had slowed. "What I wanted to tell you, what I was going to tell you, only it's so hard to explain, is that for me, the hippy-dippy-granola-girl-in-space act is for real. It's a lot more real than I ever wanted it to be. But if that hippy-dippy act were on Lucas Keller's biographer instead of on someone who can't decide what to do with her life, I think I would feel a little better about myself. And I can write a biography of him. I'm a good writer and a good researcher. I just needed a chance to get ahead of Jeff Alvin."

"That's why you're here? To write a biography of Lucas Keller? That's why you were interested in me, because of my connection to him?"

"That's not all of it—" she began, but he stopped her.

"Let me tell you, all that was made really obvious by the way you befriended my dog and helped me in the garden. You know, there were more direct ways to get what you wanted."

"I know," she said, with such obvious misery that for a second he didn't want to fully understand why he was mad at her. "Those were things I did because I wanted to. If I could spend the rest of my life goofing around the way I have this summer, I'd be happy. But I've goofed around long enough. I need to be taken seriously."

"Taken seriously by Jeff Alvin?" So much of what she was telling him still hadn't registered completely, but one thing he was sure of was that this had something to do with that oafish guy Connie had told him about.

"You don't have to make it about Jeff."

"So it is about Jeff Alvin," he said.

She managed to look both heartbroken and annoyed. "I just said it wasn't."

"He's the ex-boyfriend you were talking about, the academic," he said, remembering how she had clammed up after she mentioned him that first day she came to his house.

"He's a professor. He has the all-important higher degree," she said. Her face became animated again. "But Lucas Keller was *my* discovery. His book fell on *my* head that day in the library."

7

AMBROSE LOOKED at Keller, who looked at Maddie. She started blushing, and he tried not to remember that he had seen that same blush on more pleasant occasions.

"Did you just say his book fell on your head? That's how this whole obsession started?"

"How I discovered him isn't the issue. Pretend I found one of his books at a rummage sale, if it makes it sound more respectable."

He wanted to outline what he understood so far. "A book fell on your head while you were at the library looking for something else. Before you put it back on the shelf, you started reading it and just went crazy over it. You read all his others. You told Jeff Alvin about these great old out-of-print books you had discovered." He hated to even say the man's name.

"And he wasn't even interested," she rushed in to say. "He laughed at me. He laughed at Lucas Keller, but I kept collecting what I could find about him. Then this whole interest in Appalachian writers kind of exploded, and after we broke up he said that since I was going to be a waitress all my life, he might as well use my research for his own book." She was back to talking fast. "He wasn't even that into modern American lit—he was trying to prove that Percy

Shelley wrote Mary Shelley's novels, including *Frankenstein,* although his idea was sort of going nowhere considering that Mr. Shelley was dead for most of his wife's career—''

''Stop,'' he said, so loudly that he got a warning bark from Ambrose. If he let her go on, pretty soon he'd be so confused he'd have forgotten what they were arguing about. And wasn't that exactly what she must want?

''In the final analysis, you're only here to impress Jeff Alvin.''

''No, I'm not here to impress Jeff Alvin. I don't even want Jeff Alvin to know I'm here. I'm here to prove to myself I can follow through on something I start.''

''But even though Lucas Keller chose you to rediscover him.''

She jumped a little. ''That's so weird that you said that,'' she said. ''That's exactly how it felt, but I've never told anyone else.''

Her eyes were bright with excitement, and he felt guilty about teasing her, then annoyed with himself for falling again for that dreamy act.

''Damn it, Maddie, I don't believe Lucas Keller knocked that book on your head and you don't either. The fact is, if you wanted to come here and study Lucas Keller, that's one thing. It's just that you didn't have to do it by taking all of us in.''

''You're right, and I'm sorry.''

He waited for what she'd said to soothe him, and then realized it didn't.

''Look, let me say what I want to say. You discovered my great-grandfather. Fine. But you wouldn't be doing anything about your discovery if you didn't want to get even with Jeff Alvin.''

"I don't know. Maybe." Her green eyes were serious, and he knew she was being honest with him. "That's a fair question, but I don't know."

"And you wouldn't want to get even with him if you didn't still care about him." Whatever all this had to do with old papers and his junk-filled attic, and whether any scholar in his or her right mind would care what some self-absorbed old coot wrote, he couldn't stop coming to this one inescapable conclusion.

It wasn't as though what he said ought to be any great shock to her. He didn't expect her to say, "By golly, Keller, I never thought about it that way." He knew her well enough to expect a token protest. But he didn't expect her to be so convincingly, sincerely ticked off.

"Make it about romance. Of course. That is so male." Her voice suddenly dripped with contempt for his gender, and even the dog squirmed a little at the indictment. Rather than being insulted, as she'd apparently intended, he just felt confused.

"It's typically male to think about nothing but romance? I've been living on the farm way longer than I should have. My sex needs me."

"Crack jokes," she said. "You know what I mean. It's just like a man to think that women do nothing except those things that will get them a man."

"I don't think I ever said that."

"Oh, you most certainly did," she said, pointing her finger at him for emphasis. "You think I packed up and moved all the way across the mountain because of Jeff Alvin. You think that just because I'm a woman, I can't have ambitions related to career. I can't have ambitions related to something that's just about me. Nobody asked you if you went to Wall Street because of a woman.''

"No, the truth is much less glamorous," he said. "I went so I could buy a house my grandfather wanted kept in the family, even though his father, the son-of-a-bitch, wouldn't even let him cross the doorstep when he was alive.''

He saw from her face that he'd hit a guilty spot, but his victory was bittersweet, because her face went blank and dull and stony then. "Okay, you win. I'm in the wrong, and I knew that when I came here this morning. Your family had a history with your great-grandfather that I know nothing about. Burn his papers if it makes you feel better.'' She handed them to him. "I won't trouble you anymore.''

"Why do you always do this?" He'd gotten an admission of guilt, and it just made him miserable. She'd twisted everything around again. "How do you always make me feel guilty when you are so clearly, blatantly in the wrong? You did this when you broke into my house.''

She sighed. "So you're the kind of guy who brings up past misdeeds in current arguments. I'm glad I found out about that. All the self-help books say that's a big no-no in relationships, by the way.''

"And pretending to care about some guy because you're trying to gold-dig his ancestor and make your old boyfriend jealous, I assume that's within acceptable boundaries, right?''

She started to speak, then stopped. Finally she said, "I'd better go.''

He felt like ten million different kinds of fool as

he felt the bulge of the condom packets in his jeans. He felt even more ridiculous as the sound of hammers suddenly rose in symphony from below, and he realized the men had fallen silent during his and Maddie's argument. The crowning humiliation came when his dog got up slowly and followed Maddie down the stairs. Damned if he would call out to either one of them

"Maddie?"

"Yeah?" He couldn't read her tone.

"I'm not lying about this. Lucas Keller really was an incredible SOB."

As soon as he said it, he couldn't believe he'd given her such an easy setup.

"You know what, Keller? Maybe it runs in the family."

"YOU KNOW, I would have stolen the man's dog or called him a son of a bitch, but I wouldn't have done both."

Maddie took out the pan of bread, half of the rolls burned to a crisp, and slammed it down on top of the grill.

"You know what, Connie? I didn't do either of those things. The dog followed me down the road, and I tried to take him back, but he kept jumping into my car. Believe me, I'm not happy about it. Mrs. Martin made us sleep on the sleeping porch last night." She picked up one of the hot rolls and dropped it as it burned her fingers, cursing as she did so. She saw Lucy and Connie exchange glances.

"Well, I told Little Tom that I found it hard to believe the word SOB was in your vocabulary, but now..." Connie let his voice trail off.

"You tell Little Tom if he's going to eavesdrop, he might as well do it right. Keller called Lucas an SOB, so I suggested that particular gene had been passed on."

She stomped back to the bigger kitchen and got some more bread dough, returning to the counter with it and shaping more rolls. Connie was silent, and she thought she might have finally shut him up. But then he said, "You know, Lucas Keller really was a son of a bitch."

She took a deep breath. "I am prepared to admit he was complicated."

He stuck a spoon in his iced tea, swirling it around idly. "No, there wasn't anything particularly complicated about him. He was just an SOB."

She stuck the new batch of rolls in and slammed the oven door closed. "I know, I know. He chased you with his cane when he caught you out of school, then when you got there they made you carve your own pencils."

"She's in a really bad mood, isn't she?" Connie asked Lucy.

"I've never seen her like this," Lucy confided.

"I hate being talked about in the third person," Maddie said, her voice rousing Ambrose, over by the door. He barked, but his heart obviously wasn't in it, and he soon went straight back to sleep.

She ignored Connie in favor of stomping around the kitchen, but she turned around when she heard a more serious tone in his voice.

"How do you think Keller feels, that you never asked what the feud between his grandfather and Lucas was about?"

"He didn't really give me a chance to ask," Maddie said, but she knew that wasn't true. She'd just been so determined that Keller see her side of things that she'd been irritated, not interested, when he'd mentioned his grandfather, even though it was obvious that he had strong feelings about the injustice he said his grandfather had suffered. She waited for Connie to continue.

"Let me give you some background," Connie said. "Lucas Keller grew up poor. Poorer than most. His parents couldn't afford shoes, much less for him to go to school. But he was a genius, I'll admit that much. He read everything he got his hands on, then he started writing. His books sold well, but they didn't bring him respect in the town."

Lucy had been sitting silently beside Connie during his chat, but now she glanced up at the clock and said, "We'd better get him married with children before the lunch crowd comes in."

"Never rush a man telling a story," Connie grumbled, but said, "Well, anyway, he married, and they had Michael."

"Your Keller's grandfather," Lucy said.

"Not my Keller," Maddie corrected. But Connie kept talking.

"They built that big old house that Keller's living in now, but then Lucas and Michael started fighting over whether Michael should go to college. Lucas wanted him to, but Michael wanted to marry a girl named Sarah Miller."

Lucy interrupted. "You know, crazy Mrs. Miller at the library, the one who pretends she's deaf? Sarah was her aunt."

"Pretends she's deaf?" Maddie asked. "She's not deaf?"

"Am I going to get through my story before Little Tom's crew comes beating the door down for the lunch special?" Connie asked. The women fell silent, and Lucy made a lip-zipping motion.

"Lucas hated the Miller family. Hated them," Connie said. "And just as his son announced he was going to marry Sarah Miller, Lucas was just finishing a novel that was plainly based on the Millers. It was awful, apparently. Cruel and mean, and not very well written besides. So Michael told his father he'd burned it."

"He'd burned it?" Maddie asked.

Lucy sniffed the air, then said, "Oh heavens, the rolls again."

Maddie ran to the oven and took out the pan of now-black bread. They all stared at it.

"We're having pasta anyway," Lucy said. "The man on the morning program said not to serve more than one starch at a meal."

Connie got up and propped open the door to let the smoke out. "Michael didn't burn the manuscript," he said. "He was trying to stall while his father calmed down. Then, he thought, maybe grandkids would soften him up a little. Well, Lucas was furious. Cut Michael off without a cent. Then wrote a doozy of a story about how he was killed in a logging accident."

"I read it," Maddie said.

"Brought tears to your eyes, didn't it?" Connie asked. At her nod, he went on. "From then on, Lucas didn't budge on his story that Michael was dead. And Michael was too proud to expose his father. By the time Michael earned enough money to support Sarah Miller, of course, she'd married someone else."

Maddie considered all that Connie had told her. "What happened to the awful book?"

"Michael sent it on a few years later, and Lucas sent it off to the publishers. By then, he had this sentimental reputation to uphold, and they wouldn't publish it. He blamed Michael for that."

"I wonder if it was really that bad," Maddie said, leaning against the counter.

"I guess you'll never find out, now that you've insulted Keller Lowry. I guess you're never going to get in his attic again."

Maddie looked at him sharply, wondering if the gossips knew more than she thought they did, but Connie was poker-faced. He probably just meant that she wasn't going to get to search for the manuscript. He didn't know about her other disappointment, that she wasn't going to get to see where her relationship with Keller might have gone. She sighed deeply, and Ambrose woke up and let out a little warble of sympathy.

"I believe both of you got up on the wrong side of the sleeping porch this morning," Connie said. "Harriet Martin ought to be at the church right now, bossing around the women's auxiliary. Sneak the dog up to your room."

Maddie winced, remembering the mini scene that had ensued when she'd brought him back to the boarding house last night.

"No, that's okay," she said. "I guess we'll just go walk around town like the friendless souls that we are."

Connie and Lucy traded alarmed looks. "You're taking this way too hard," Lucy said. "Are you sure you don't want to just sit with us a while? I'll make a strawberry pie.''

Connie snorted. "Food poisoning. That's going to take her mind off things.''

"No, I'll be all right,'' Maddie told her. "If I don't make it for dinner, do you think you could do without me for one night?''

"You're going to let her cook?'' Connie squawked.

"I did it for years before Maddie got here and I can do it again,'' Lucy said. "You go home and take a bubble bath and some Tylenol, honey. I have everything under control.''

"No bread. No bread anywhere in the building,'' Little Tom said, pounding a nail into the wall for emphasis. It went in crooked, and he popped it back out again.

"Salad as wilted as a beauty queen at a Fourth of July parade,'' Mel added.

"And when the fettucine Alfredo came out...oh.'' Sid stopped, apparently unable to go on.

"Keller,'' Tom said solemnly, pausing at his task. "There wasn't any Alfredo about it. It was pure Elmer. Elmer's glue.''

Keller smiled a little, but his heart wasn't in it. He knew they were trying to cheer him up, but all they were doing was reminding him that thanks to their scene yesterday, Maddie had been too upset to work. Little Tom said Lucy and Connie told him she had taken the day off because she didn't feel well. They also said she was taking good care of his dog. Some comfort that was.

"We waited on you, but you didn't show,'' Little

Tom said. He looked around the kitchen. "I know you didn't cook for yourself."

"I wasn't very hungry," Keller said, ignoring the men as they all looked at each other and nodded knowingly. "I had a peanut butter sandwich. Anyway, it doesn't sound as if I missed much."

"Au contraire, mon frère," Mel said, and they all stared at him.

"Mel, you get a little bit more out there every day," Tom said. Turning back to Keller, he continued, "We hadn't gotten to the best part yet. Just as everyone is whining and moaning, about to start banging their iced tea spoons on their glasses like a bunch of convicts banging cups on the bars of their cells, Connie jumps up, puts on Maddie's apron, goes back to the kitchen and starts whipping stuff up. He makes Lucy sit down, and pretty soon the whole place is filled with the smell of garlic and Parmesan cheese and something else...."

"Rosemary," Mel said. "He dusted the bread with it."

They stared at him again. "Mel, you have depths none of us ever knew about," Little Tom said.

He grinned shyly and went back to measuring something.

Keller sighed. Connie's triumph was proof that life in Ravens Gap would go on without Maddie. But what would he do? A life in this house by himself no longer seemed like what he wanted. He had settled his grandfather's score with the old man. He had enough money. He had gotten everything he wanted. Everything but the one thing he wouldn't allow himself to want.

"Look, I'm going to head into town for a little while. Don't bother locking up."

"I may have to get out of here a little early today anyway," Tom said, sounding genuinely apologetic. "Somehow Daddy and I have screwed up the quarterly sales tax big-time again."

"What software program do you use for your inventory and accounting?"

Little Tom gave him a look that said, *Yeah, right.* "We use a ledger and a shoebox full of receipts. I think it's the same shoebox my grandfather used."

"Cardboard was sturdier back then," Mel said. They all looked at him. "What?"

"Daddy actually wants to get a computer, but then he goes to one of those big stores in Asheville and they start talking ninety miles an hour and selling him stuff he doesn't need, and he gets disgusted and comes back."

"I've got an extra PC," Keller said. "From the last time I upgraded. Do you think your dad would let me give it to him?"

Little Tom thought about it for a moment. "He'd have to do something for you."

"Next spring, he could give Maddie and me lessons on the right way to garden. I'll see you guys later," he added, before they could notice that he had misspoken. Next spring, of course, Maddie wouldn't be here.

CONNIE CAUGHT MADDIE tossing suitcases into the back of her car in front of Mrs. Martin's boarding house, her other possessions in boxes on the stoop.

"I can't believe you're such a coward that you would leave without saying goodbye."

"I'm not leaving town," Maddie said. "Although, believe me, that sounds tempting right now. I'm just moving out of this place." She shoved another box into her car. "What takes you away from the coffee-pot this morning anyway? Do you have a sixth sense for trouble?"

"No, I think that's you. I have an ear for it, though, and the town is buzzing. I ought to be mad at you, because before they started yakking about the wild party that got you thrown out of Harriet Martin's, they were all talking about my wonderful cooking."

She leaned her head against the car for a second, sure that the ache in it wasn't going to be helped by Connie's tale. After she left Lucy's yesterday, she had picked up a few things in Bryson City, then headed back to her room for an evening of self-pity and self-disgust. She'd started reading a new paperback, just before sunset, Ambrose napping beside her, and the next thing she knew it was dawn. Ambrose was licking her in the face, whining to be let out, and Mrs. Martin was standing over her still-made bed, yelling about mad dogs and crazy young women.

"Wanton and reckless destruction of property by a wild animal."

"Oh, please," Maddie said, lifting her head from the car. "He dribbled ice cream and smooshed potato chips on the carpet. I cleaned it up before I left."

She looked at Ambrose, patiently lying across the sidewalk, panting. He didn't look any crazier for the pint of designer mint chocolate chip he had scarfed while she slept. She didn't even like ice cream that much—she only bought it because that's what people in the movies always ate when they were miserable. At least Ambrose hadn't gotten the economy bag of

M&M's she'd bought to jazz up the ice cream, since she had eaten all those right away. Maybe that was why her head hurt. Sugar on an empty stomach and broken heart. She groaned.

"Boozing with abandon," Connie said.

She deserved all this. She deserved all this because she was a bad person. Once she had been merely a flighty person. Now she was both flighty and dishonest. A bad combination in anyone's eyes.

"I had wine in my room, yes. And even though I don't remember Mrs. Martin saying she didn't allow boarders to bring alcoholic beverages into the home, I accept that the subject just never came up. But did she tell everybody that the bottle was unopened?"

"No corkscrew?" Connie guessed.

"And even if I had a corkscrew, no glasses. Not even a Dixie cup in the bathroom."

He wasn't even trying to hide a smile. "And the sinister literature scattered around the room?"

"The what? Oh. I was reading a mystery with a skull on the front." She picked up another box.

"It's for the best, I think," Connie said. "She never really appreciated you anyway."

"You're right," Maddie said. "Whereas the staff at the No-Tell Motel are really going to take me into their bosom."

"Is that where you're going?"

"I am either going there or I am going to sit in some abandoned field in my car. I haven't decided yet. It depends on which one bills itself as being more insect- and rodent-free."

"And which one takes dogs?"

"No," she said, shaking her head vigorously. "No, no. The dog is not mine. The dog is going back to live with his owner this afternoon, if I have to tie him to the front porch and let him pull the house down trying to catch me.''

Ambrose howled.

''I wouldn't have given him that suggestion about pulling the house down,'' Connie said.

''Speaking of suggestions, Connie Turner—''

''I'm glad you don't know my middle name. You sound like you're in a middle name kind of mood,'' he interrupted.

''Speaking of suggestions,'' she went on. ''I believe you are the one who said, 'Oh, Maddie, Harriet Martin will never find out about the dog. You don't have to sleep on the sleeping porch with the mosquitoes. Take him to your room.''' She shook her head. ''You pretend like you know everything, and somehow I started believing your hype. You tell me Harriet Martin will never find him? It must be true then.''

''I do know something you don't.''

''What, that Mrs. Martin would really enjoy it if Ambrose rampaged through her formal living room and left a bunch of his hair as a treasure to remember him by?''

''Want to hear it or not?''

She thought it might be about Keller, and her heart jumped a little, but then Connie said, ''I know the real story behind why Harriet threw you out.''

''I hope the real story doesn't get any wilder than the made-up one.''

''She's giving your room to somebody else. Someone who offered her a lot more for it.''

She sat down on the step. ''Who is it?''

''I don't know.''

She gave him an annoyed look, and he shrugged.

"Believe me, the only person who knows is Harriet Martin. She hasn't told a soul who it is or even if it's a man or a woman, although she's not so secretive that she can't drop around the figure this person is paying her."

He mentioned a sum, and Maddie's jaw dropped. "So she was going to toss me out anyway?"

"Right. The dog just made sure she wasn't going to have to look bad doing it."

Maddie sat in silence a moment. "I shouldn't mind about leaving."

"You're going to finish your research here, though, right?"

"No," she said. "I don't think so. I think the words *Cut your losses* would apply in this situation."

"Why are you staying at all then?"

"I want to find someone to take my place at Lucy's." She looked up at him. "Did you say you cooked last night?"

"Yep. If you were more tuned into the grapevine, you'd have heard about my rosemary loaves and fettucine tossed with garlic."

"You're going to do it then."

"Take over the cooking? I have my own store to run."

"Please. You spend most of your time at Lucy's anyway. Someone else can run your store for you. Not everybody can cook." She sighed. "Goodness knows Lucy can't. Little Tom's wife is coming along, though. I gave her all my recipes last week."

He nodded, having already known it, of course. "And Mel's been studying them, too," he said. "It turns out he has a deep appreciation of spices."

She stood up, put the last box in and surveyed her

work. "Well, there you go," she said to Connie. "He can be your assistant. Maybe you can help Lucy out with some plans for expansion."

"You ever think of opening a restaurant?" Connie asked.

She shook her head. "I'd love to, but it has to do with more than being a good cook. You have to be a lot more together than I am."

He looked at her with a seriousness she'd never seen. "You underestimate yourself, Maddie."

"I don't know that it's actually possible to underestimate someone who now has her whole life crammed into an oil-burning four-door sedan whose air-conditioning doesn't work."

"There's an apartment in back of the store," Connie said. "Back when my wife was alive, I used to put her relatives up there. Then, while they were in town, I'd do something or say something to them that would put me in there as soon as they left."

"Connie, if anyone has imposed too much on this town, it's me."

"I don't want to think what the rest of your friends here would do to me if they caught you having to pay your rent by the hour at the No-Tell Motel or sleeping in your car. Come look at it and see what you think."

She followed him, and Ambrose got up and fell into step beside them. She realized that he almost never mentioned his wife to her. For someone used to being glib about most things, it had to hurt to have one thing that was almost past joking about.

"You and your wife were happy?" she asked.

He stopped as they rounded the corner near the library. "It's not hard to be happy with the person you love. The trick is to forget all that stuff that tells you you can't be.'' He paused as they stood in front of the library, and Ambrose took the opportunity to plop down on the sidewalk. ''And if you ever tell anybody I said such a sentimental thing, I'll have all your secret recipes copied and circulated so fast you'll be meeting your pesto coming and going.''

''They won't hear it from me,'' she said, motioning for Ambrose to come along. He stayed where he was, then put a paw over his eyes as she sighed. ''Go on,'' she told Connie. ''We'll either be over there in a minute, or I'll try to take him back to Keller's.''

''Be careful when you return that dog. Careful you don't break his heart again.''

''The dog's heart?'' she asked, deliberately misunderstanding.

Connie shook his head before crossing the street toward his store. ''Don't play dumb or cold with me, Madelaine Elizabeth Randall. I know better.''

He'd gotten her again, and he knew it. He grinned. ''Keller's middle name is Michael, by the way. Just don't say it in anger.''

8

"IT'S NICE TO SEE you here. I don't believe you've ever been in here before."

"No, I haven't," Keller said. The librarian, Mrs. Riddle, was using a regular voice, so he did, too, although there was one patron, an elderly woman he vaguely recognized from around town, seated at a computer terminal. "I brought a lot of books down from New York with me," he said half apologetically. Still, that was no excuse for not coming here and he knew it. The building dated from his grandfather's childhood, but the inside of it had been renovated and opened up to light and space. He felt good being there, and even though it was no longer a secret what Maddie was looking for or why she spent so much time here, he knew it would be the sort of place she liked anyway. When he'd left the house to come check out Lucas Keller's books, he'd been pretty sure he wouldn't find her here today, but he glanced around anyway.

"You looking for Maddie?" Mrs. Riddle asked. "She's not here."

"No," he said, trying to tell himself he wasn't disappointed. "I wanted to see the place. I don't get out as much as I should."

That was an understatement. He had heard so much from his grandfather about the pleasures of owning land and being master of all you surveyed. He hadn't known it was going to get pretty damn old pretty damn quick. As he'd learned from sitting around with Tom and from eating at Lucy's, it wasn't even that Ravens Gap was boring. Face it, he was boring. Growing a garden and living off the food there, being as self-sufficient as possible, wasn't going to make him less boring. If anything, it was going to make him more of a misanthrope.

He pointed to the computer terminal. "Your catalog's on-line?"

She sighed a little. "I wish. No, I just put a computer in for Internet connections for the community, although they're mostly still hesitant about it. Miss Miller uses it to e-mail her relatives out of the county. She can't use the phone as long as she's pretending she's deaf."

Keller looked at the woman, who certainly didn't seem to know they were talking about her.

"She pretends to be deaf?" he whispered.

"Yes, and talk all you want. I'm hoping some day she'll get irritated enough to admit she can hear." Mrs. Riddle gave Keller a mischievous smile. "We spend so much time together it would be a relief to have someone to talk to."

"It must have been nice to have Maddie around," he said before he could stop himself.

"It was, wasn't it?" the librarian said, smiling sympathetically. Her look told him she knew all about their fight—the whole town must. And even though he was in the right, he'd never felt so unhappy about it before.

"I'm going to look around," he told her. He didn't want to ask her where Lucas's books were kept, since it did seem a little odd that he didn't have any at home. He'd never thrown a book away before he moved to Ravens Gap, always given them away somewhere, or piled them into the box of free books that sat outside every used bookstore. But he hadn't even thought twice about pitching Lucas Keller's works. He'd taken a look at the spines, thought about what the man did to his grandfather and shoved them into the trash. If Maddie was so determined to see something in them, though, maybe there was something to see.

Several shelves into the general fiction section, he found the *K*s. Kale, Keane. He had just raised his head to the upper shelves when an older looking dark-green volume tumbled off and brained him between the eyes.

He cursed, then looked at Miss Miller by the terminal. She didn't seem to have noticed.

"Sorry, Mrs. Riddle," he called out.

"This old building settles," she said. "I should make people wear hard hats."

He reached for the book, doing a quick alphabetical calculation, telling himself it couldn't, could not possibly be, what he was afraid it was.

Whistling Past Dark. By Lucas Keller.

Under no circumstances was he ever going to tell Maddie about this. If he let go of being mad about her lying to him, and if she let go of her hurt and whatever feelings she still had for this Alvin person, and if they ever had a civil conversation again, he still wasn't going to tell her about this. That was all he needed, to get caught up in her crazy scheme, to reinforce her idea that Lucas needed to be rediscovered. To allow that arrogant old man to make the world the way he wanted it even from beyond the grave.

"Damn you, Lucas Keller," he said, louder than he meant to. Miss Miller looked up—he saw her raise her head at his grandfather's name. But just as quickly she ducked back to her computer, as if she had never responded to his outburst at all.

You faker, he thought, amused and surprised. He had begun to be fascinated by the idea that there could be such secrets in Ravens Gap. What had he imagined? A town where no one was complicated, no one three-dimensional? Where the jovial Connie wouldn't be aching so much for the late Ruby Turner that he could barely talk about her? Where Little Tom would be all bluster all the time, instead of feeling insecure about the financial makeup of the store? Had he made the same kind of blanket assumptions about the townspeople that they had made about his great-grandfather?

He opened the book and began to read. He was dubious, then interested, then so caught up in the words that he forgot about everything but the book. Until today, he would have said his ancestor was a scam and a fake, but the man who wrote this hadn't become fake yet. He remembered that there had been pride mixed with his grandfather's anger when he spoke about Lucas Keller. This must have been why.

He might have stood there all day, but a low, keening howl started sneaking in around the edges of what he was reading. It wasn't a sound he heard very often, thank goodness, but it was terrible enough to make sure he remembered the occasions he had. Connie was right. It was unearthly.

He walked out of the stacks, still holding the book.

The howling was louder out here. He looked at Miss Miller, typing into an e-mail program, seemingly oblivious to the noise.

"Is he outside?" Keller asked Mrs. Riddle over the din.

"I think he's on the sidewalk," she semi-shouted.

He handed her the book, no longer caring if she knew what he was reading. "Could you hold this for me while I take care of this?" He raced out the door to find Ambrose—oh, hell, he'd gotten used to the name, so why not call him that?—lying down on the sidewalk, keeping up the eerie wail.

Maddie was bent down over him, her back to Keller, talking to him loudly, holding his paw. "I know. I've caused you misery and unhappiness, and it's my fault that you're now as rootless as I am in the world. I may not be able to change things for me but I can change things for you, Ambrose. Walk back to my car, and I'll take you to Keller's." Ambrose saw Keller, who put a finger over his lips indicating for the dog not to let Maddie know he was there. He was interested in this little monologue. "He's a great guy, and I'm a rat. I'm a rat as big and as ugly and as sharp-toothed as any of the ones that I won't let you kill. I didn't deserve to know someone as special as Keller and I don't deserve you. I know, you're swayed by the idea that I cook and he doesn't, and you like the fact that I gave you a cool name instead of a plain one, but all that is surface, Ambrose. He is a hard-working and kind and special guy who doesn't need to name his dog something goofy to prove to the world that he's more than what he is. So you have a choice. The honest good life with him or shabby pretension with me?"

Barely had she finished speaking when Ambrose hopped up, gave her a good lick in the face, and waddled over to Keller, who let his dog jump up on him as he rubbed his thick fur.

"I know the decision must have been a difficult one for you," Maddie said, smiling ruefully at Keller before sitting all the way down on the sidewalk. "I'm so glad he's okay. I read about that howl, but reading about it isn't the same as hearing it, is it?"

"No," Keller said. "Speaking of which, I heard all the kind things you said about me. I felt like that kid in that story, the one who goes to his own funeral?"

"Tom Sawyer and Huck Finn," she said, crossing her arms over her knees. "And you knew that. You're humoring me, and I don't deserve to be humored. I owe you a million different apologies."

"I'll take one," he said. "And then you can stop beating yourself up."

"I'm really sorry," she said. He reached to help her up, and she took his hands, dropping them as she got her balance.

"I'm sorry, too," he said. "I'm sorry that I said you were only doing this because you were still in love with Jeff Alvin. I don't know if you are," he said, holding up his hand as she started to speak. "And you know what? It's none of my business. Even if I have heard that he's a jerk. Even if I do think you're probably too good for him."

"I'm not in love with Jeff Alvin," she said. "But to say I'm too good for anybody is a real stretch."

"Whatever you say. But I didn't want to talk to you about that. I wanted to tell you that I started reading Lucas's first book. I'm intrigued. I'm intrigued enough to want to help you with your project."

To his dismay, she was shaking her head. "I don't have a project anymore. I'm not fooling myself that I'm going to be Lucas Keller's biographer. I'm just going to be someone who liked his books."

"Someone who got a little obsessed with him."

"Well, he was a handsome guy when he was young," she said, smiling. "I still think he was a great writer. I still think you would be doing the world a favor by salvaging anything of his that you find. But I'm only going to be here another week or so. Just long enough to teach Connie, and maybe—don't laugh—Mel some of my recipes."

"I wouldn't dare laugh at Mel," he said. "But I don't think I'll tell him that the long-dead Lucas Keller pushed a book off the shelves on to my head today, either." So much for not telling Maddie about the book. But he wanted to say something that would make her happy and he also wanted her to know that he didn't always have to be the sanctimonious, practical guy he sometimes feared he was becoming.

It worked. She smiled and said, "Now I'm sure you're humoring me. Let me move my car to Connie's, then you can continue to embellish your story."

"Wait until you see the bruise I'm going to develop on the bridge of my nose."

"He has great aim, doesn't he?" Maddie called as she started walking back toward the boarding house. "But I just got a gentle rap on the head. Probably he has a few issues with you."

No doubt, Keller thought. *No doubt.*

"SOMETHING JUST OCCURRED to me," Maddie said, wiping her face with the end of her pink T-shirt.

Keller looked up, caught a tantalizing glimpse of

her stomach as she lifted her shirt, and quickly glanced back down again into the last box he'd opened. Fishing tackles. Old vinyl tablecloths. There was nothing any more worth saving in this box than there had been in any of the others so far. He looked at Maddie warily, hoping she hadn't caught him gawking at her like a lust-filled idiot. When he spoke, his tone was light.

"Is this one of those things that's going to make less sense after you explain it to me than it did before?"

"Probably," she said. "You know, I was just thinking, maybe this is what Lucas Keller wanted all along. This whole thing, hitting me over the head with the book, having you come to Ravens Gap to live, maybe it was all orchestrated just so he could get his attic cleaned out. It would have made a lot more sense for him to have haunted a Merry Maids franchise."

Only Maddie. "Could you please not talk about him as though he's still around?" he asked. "You're going to slip up and do it in front of Mel, and I'll never get my kitchen finished."

"Blame it on Mel. You're the one who gets uncomfortable."

He shoved the box into the pile meant for the dump and pulled another one toward him. "I'm not afraid of ghosts."

"I didn't say you were afraid of ghosts," she said, popping open a carton of stuff. "You just don't like the idea of someone else knowing your business twenty-four hours a day. I'll bet when you were a little kid you resented Santa for the same reason."

He stared at her. How did she know that?

"I knew it," she said, gleeful. She reached into the

box in front of her and pulled out an arrangement of plastic fruit and a set of fondue pots.

"Fondue! You had a childhood in the suburbs. I know you remember fondue. Maybe I'll do a theme night at Lucy's before I leave." Keller watched her as she set the cookware aside and put the rest in the pile for the dump, then reconsidered and pulled the plastic fruit out. He shut his mouth before he could ask her why, but she got his message.

"Seventies artifacts are still a favorite. You don't know what I'd pay for these in a trendy thrift store."

"Why would you want to pay for those anywhere? Is your place in Knoxville big enough for all the stuff you're taking back?"

He hoped that asking her questions about Knoxville would help him get used to the idea that she was leaving, that she had a life somewhere else, an apartment somewhere else, one she was subletting for the summer. It was amazing how quickly his own landscape had been whittled to Ravens Gap, but he had to remember that hers hadn't been.

She'd been an incredible help in the past few days as they'd tackled the attic in earnest. Keller had hauled stuff away and cleaned up the few valuable things they'd found. Maddie had grabbed anything remotely interesting to her, which had added up to quite a pile. They'd first attacked the trunks and boxes near where Lucy had found the cache of Lucas's letters, but nothing else seemed to be from that same time. He'd gotten interested in his great-grandfather just as Maddie's project, and her time here, had come to an end.

Lucy and Connie were still in denial about her leaving, but Keller knew he couldn't expect her to stay when the reasons she had come here were no longer valid ones. And he didn't think that having the chance to hang out with him and Ambrose was a good enough reason not to go, not to someone who was itching for something big to do. Ravens Gap was too small and too comfortable for someone who was as bright and adventurous as she was. He had gotten used to her, but he couldn't expect her to stay.

Still, he owed her a lot. She had won the town over on his behalf as well as her own, and instead of being the grumpy recluse he once was, he now had a whole social circle. The men at the feed store had called a truce in their teasing, since, according to Little Tom, the computer he had given them and the small business software he was writing were going to benefit the seed company tremendously. Or as Little Tom put it, save their butts.

He had a real place here, not just a place to live, and he knew that he owed that to Maddie. She had blown into town, fixed things and blown back out again. He looked over at her, hoping she wouldn't catch him. He was going to miss looking at her.

"I guess your car is pretty much packed, still?" Keller asked. Asking these questions was like poking the classic sore tooth. He wished he could stop himself.

"Yeah, it's got a lot more junk in it than I ever wanted it to have. I wish I were like Mary Poppins, with just the hat stand and the bag and the talking umbrella. Actually, there are a lot of ways I wish I were like Mary Poppins, 'practically perfect in every way.' Did you know that *Mary Poppins* is basically the same story as *Shane,* which is also the same story as *The Lone Ranger?* Can't remember the archetype right now. I'm rusty on my psychology." She frowned. "Maybe I should become a nanny."

He shook his head, trying clear it. "Are you good with kids?" he finally asked.

"Haven't the slightest idea. I've never been around one. I've heard they have an inner ability to detect BS, and I probably need people like that in my life, don't you think?"

"Don't I think? Hmm, somehow you've gotten me into the attic looking for something I swore I didn't care about, my dog is downstairs wearing a collar with his new name, you have the whole town comparing cilantro and basil, and you're asking me if it would be helpful if somebody stopped you before you struck again? Got to reserve judgment on that one."

She blushed, of course. "Probably I need you to keep me in line."

"Probably I need you." He let her comment hang in the air for a second before busying himself with the trunk he'd just opened. If she were being honest with herself, she'd know she didn't need him. Not to make her way in the world, not for anything. He worked so hard at making himself secure that he had forgotten that security wasn't what everyone craved. He grabbed a stack of *Ladies' Home Journal* magazines from the box he'd opened and looked underneath them. Just papers.

The handwriting looked familiar. Then he placed it. Although it was harder, angrier, blacker than that on the papers Maddie had shown him last week, this was Lucas Keller's script. The famous missing manuscript. Rather than being excited about his discovery, he realized, with regret, that now there was certainly nothing to keep her here. His throat tight, he turned to Maddie and lifted the stack of pages out of the box.

"This is it."

He held out the pages, as if holding out an offering, and she walked the few steps toward him. He tried to hand it to her, and to his surprise, she backed away.

"No," she said. "You should read it first. It's yours."

Now was not the time for her to go all meek and timid on him. She had found what she was looking for, so why not just take it and get out? "Maddie, don't be ridiculous. I want you to read it first. Condense it for me. Take it back to Connie's with you, please."

"Are you sure?" she asked. When he nodded, she accepted the pages from him, almost cradling them in her arms. She looked down at the manuscript, then frowned slightly. "Let's finish up here first. We're almost done. I'll read it after work tonight."

She tried to hand the bundle back to Keller, but he refused. The last thing he needed was her feeling as though she were obligated to stay.

"Maddie, I've got the rest of my life to finish this attic. Go on." He pushed the stack of old magazines toward the pile meant for the dump as she took her treasure and slipped away.

"HEARD YOU GOT the book. Is it everything I said it was?" Connie asked her as she walked into his store.

"Little Tom ought to own stock in the telephone company," she said. "Anyway, I haven't read any of it yet." She set the manuscript down on the counter, and both she and Connie stared at it for a moment.

"An odd feeling about it, isn't there?" he asked, peeling the first page off the stack.

"Like what?" she asked. She didn't wait for his answer because she knew what he meant. "Books don't have auras. They're inanimate objects. You've been spending too much time with Mel, obviously."

"Suit yourself. You're the one who said 'aura.' I don't think that word's even in my simple vocabulary. Speaking of Mel, I talked to him a few minutes ago when Tom called. We decided we're going to cook tonight so that you can explore your discovery in peace."

"Oh," she said, a little deflated. "Oh, no, that's okay. I was planning on reading it after work."

"Don't be ridiculous. Everyone knows how long you've looked for this."

Everyone knows how I cheated and lied to find it, she filled in silently.

"And it just makes sense that we do a test run tonight, since if you're so determined to leave, we're going to take it over anyway. At least Lucy's not mumbling about closing anymore."

"But I was going to make black bean chili."

"And we're going to make spinach enchiladas. So we're keeping your Mexican theme. If I didn't know any better, I'd say you don't want to be alone with that book."

Or she didn't want to be alone with her thoughts. "Well, it sounds as if you've got it all planned out. I'm sure you'll fill me in on anything I miss." Never mind that she was going to be missing it forever, after this week.

"I'll give you a little gossip to start you off with. Someone saw a cream-colored import car at Mrs.

Martin's, suitcases on the curb. Matching suitcases, like from a set.''

"Well, no wonder she preferred whoever it was to me.''

"That's not the kicker. No one has seen this person, but Edith Miller from the library was seen outside, having a conversation—actual talking and listening—with Harriet Martin. This must be someone important, to get her to stop playing deaf.''

"I can't believe I was fooled into thinking she couldn't hear me,'' Maddie said, annoyed. "It would have been nice to have had a conversation every once in a while.'' Not, she thought ruefully, that she'd made a habit of letting any of her new friends get a word in edgewise.

"I'm sure we'll all dissect her behavior to death tonight at the diner. I'll give you reports.''

"Thanks,'' she said, heading toward the back of the store. *Thanks for not needing me anymore. Thanks for giving me carte blanche to sit alone in a dark room and read a book that, yes, thank you so much for mentioning it, does have a kind of funny feeling about it.*

Truthfully, the small apartment in back was anything but dark. It was brightly decorated, short on windows but filled with whimsical lamps in all shapes and sizes. An inviting crocheted throw in 1970's gold and avocado hung along the back of the comfy sofa. As soon as she had showered and changed clothes, she kicked off her shoes, sat down and started to read.

A few hours later she put the manuscript down and walked out into Connie's empty store. It was nearing dusk, and he had already gone over to Lucy's. A sign on the door told people that if they needed something, they could come to the café and get him. She looked out the front window to Lucy's, lighting up the night. She imagined she could hear the laughter and chatter.

Did Lucas Keller drive by the inns and the private homes where people were gathered and hate them because he wasn't there? Did he write to impress them, only to find them less than impressed, or worse, disbelieving? Did he get tired of fighting Ravens Gap?

What else could explain the angry rant she had just read? She knew that the work of the great humorists—Mark Twain, Ambrose's namesake Ambrose Bierce—was sometimes mean, but it was never so mean that it forgot to be well-written or funny. This book was just horrible. It was almost as though Lucas were trying to live up to all the awful things that people said about him. *You think I'm nothing but a grumpy and horrid old man? You ain't seen nothing yet.*

She couldn't believe he would have wanted this discovered. She needed to talk to Keller about the book.

Maddie, you've intruded on his life enough, she told herself. Still, she peeked out at the line of cars parked along the curb in front of Lucy's, and her heart did a little double take when she thought she saw Keller's sedan. A second later, she made out the slight dent along the right side and realized it was hers. He wasn't there.

You've given up being impulsive, she argued silently, but she was heading toward the back for her keys anyway. *Leave that poor man alone,* she told herself, but she knew she had the rest of her life, post-Ravens Gap, to leave him alone. She started to pick up the manuscript, then thought better of it. The drive to Keller's would let her put some space between her and it. And she would be able to talk to Keller more clearly about it if it weren't staring her in the face.

It was completely dark by the time she reached Keller's. Once she topped the driveway, though, the lights in the house were a warm invitation. The summer night was chilly, and she wished she'd tossed a sweater on before she came.

Keller opened the door right away. He was surprised to see her, obviously, but was he also pleased? She couldn't tell. "Hey. I thought you'd thrown me over for a night of Lucas Keller," he said. "Come on in."

She followed him into the living room and sat down. She was still shivering a little and she hoped her teeth weren't chattering too much for him to understand what she was saying. "A night is way more than I'd want to spend with Lucas Keller at this point. I have to be honest with you. This is hard for me to say, but I think that your grandfather might have done the right thing by taking this away from Lucas."

"That's what you came out here to tell me?" She couldn't read his expression, but she went on.

"I think he would have done a better thing if he had gotten rid of it completely, but I think he trusted that his father would come to his senses. I'm just sick that he never did. The things he said about that girl's family were awful. He had no right to be so angry with your grandfather for so long. I didn't bring it tonight but I'll bring it back tomorrow. Then you can do what you want with it."

Keller's expression had gone from unreadable to slightly amused. She wanted in on the joke. "What?" she asked defensively.

"I wonder if our conversations will always start out this way."

"What do you mean?" She told herself there was no reason why her palms should start to sweat and her throat should constrict just because he used the future tense when talking about the two of them. It was a warning that was borne out a few seconds later, when he said, "I mean, if I bump into you on the street twenty years from now, you'll probably start right off in the middle of some sentence about peppers or Lucas or the dog."

"I didn't know I was so predictable, or such an open book."

There was that amused look again.

She let out a sigh of impatience. "Okay, so maybe I did know. Anyway, I'm not sure where we'd meet in twenty years."

He got up and went to the kitchen and came back with two glasses and a bottle of red wine. "Think this will make you feel a little warmer?" She watched his hands as he uncorked the wine, the easy grace of his movements as he poured. Even in jeans and a sweatshirt, he was the most stunning man she'd ever seen.

"Much warmer," she said, swallowing hard. Trying to distract herself from the sight of him, she said, "Twenty years. Let's see, you're driving through Knoxville on your way to Atlanta."

"Knoxville's not on the way to Atlanta."

"You're taking the scenic route. Anyway, you're with your wife. Her hair is smooth and blond and bobbed, and her clothes are all crisp and coordinated. I'm in some thrift store ensemble, heavy on the scarves, pushing a stolen grocery cart full of torn and water-damaged books. The cops don't have the heart to take it away from me. You try to speak, but I keep muttering to my invisible companion.''

"Lucas," he said.

"Of course. So, am I close?"

"Close," he said, settling down next to her on the couch. She gave him a wary glance, but he was poker-faced. "Although I doubt I'm ever going to turn into the kind of guy who takes the scenic route."

She opened her mouth to say something, but he jumped ahead of her.

"Let me try. This might be easier than it looks. Let's see. My kitchen never got finished, and the roof caved in, and the bathtub fell through the upstairs, but I had to send the workmen home because I was broke. They didn't mind, though, because they all bought stock in the Feed and Seed and, thanks to my software, it's booming."

"So you should be doing well."

"No, no," he said, shaking his head. "I'm too Type A to let go of my design, so I obsessively re-work it, night and day. I'm at Connie's, making my weekly trip for Cheetos and soup-in-a-cup. You stop with your husband on your way through the mountains. He's a professor type, with a cardigan tied around his shoulders."

"Let me swear to you that I would *never* marry a man who tied a cardigan around his shoulders."

"This is my story, so let me tell it. By this time I've lost all social skills and I'm too inept to speak to you, but finally you pull your sunglasses down and say, 'Keller, is that you?'" He surprised her with a flawless imitation of her voice.

"You're good at this. That was very good." Telling herself they were just buddies, just friends, she patted him on the leg, shocking herself with the little sizzle she felt when she did so. "And I'd always recognize you. Provided you were wearing the North Carolina sweatshirt."

"I'll remember that. In case I'm lost somewhere, you'll know how to find me. Hey, you're still shivering." He took off his sweatshirt, revealing a T-shirt underneath, and handed it to her. She slipped it on, breathing in the smell of him.

She'd never been so totally and completely aware of someone else's physical presence. Her relationship with Jeff had always been a lot more intellectual than physical, and she'd grown to think of herself as someone who was not very sensual. Now, with the soft cotton of the sweatshirt against her skin, and the taste of the wine still in her mouth, and Keller next to her, she felt like one big bundle of senses. Before she had a chance to humiliate herself by attacking him, she tried to wrench their conversation away from their futures and back to safer ground.

"About your grandfather, Michael, he got over this woman, right?" Great. Like love and romance were safer topics.

"Oh, yeah," Keller said. "He was really happy with my grandmother. But I think the whole thing left him a little cynical. He used to tell me, family is fickle, true loves are a dime a dozen, but land is forever."

She sat up straight. "He said that?"

Keller grinned. "You're offended?"

"You know I am, down to the very core of my soul. Did your mother know he was feeding you these crazy ideas?"

Clearly a little self-conscious about talking so

much about himself, Keller shrugged and said, "You know, I guess he kind of warped me by talking about what I'd have to do to get this place, how I needed to go earn my money out in the world, then buy it, because if I didn't have to depend on the land I'd love it. I guess he started that kind of talk when I was still a baby. But what was my mom going to say? Sorry, we don't want you to be so focused and directed?"

"Why can't you go smoke behind the woodshop building like the other kids?"

"Exactly," he said, smiling. She realized again how much she loved to see him smile.

They fell into companionable silence, then she said, "I wished I'd known you then. I liked serious boys. I guess I was a little bit of a geek. I went through my childhood feeling like someone I knew very well was missing."

As soon as she said it, she berated herself for how spacy she sounded, but he was nodding as though he understood. "That must be an only-child thing, don't you think?"

"I don't know," she said. "I just wanted so badly to have someone who would listen to me when I talked, get the gist of what I was saying."

"Don't you think everybody wants that?" he asked. "And don't you think it's sometimes hard for someone as special as you to find it?"

"As special as I am? What do you mean?"

An impatient look flitted across his face. "Maddie, please don't play modest. Nothing about you ever irritates me except when you switch into your 'Am I okay?' mode."

"But you do think I'm okay?" She was trying to

get to the heart of what he was saying. It sounded like a compliment, yes, but was it a random kind of general compliment or was he saying something deeper than that? Instead of elaborating, he turned to her and kissed her, his lips touching hers sweetly, softly.

"Maddie," he said. "And I mean this in the nicest possible way. Shut up."

9

"I'M SHUTTING UP," she said. "I'm definitely becoming quieter, although it occurs to me that as a feminist I ought to be outraged on behalf of my sex, since men have been trying to silence women since time immemorial." She couldn't stop babbling, because the minute she did he was going to kiss her again and she knew what that would lead to, and she wanted the thing it would lead to so badly that she was afraid she would only be disappointed by the having of it.

Then he kissed her again, and there was nothing soft or sweet about it. She met him with a hungry, greedy kiss of her own, and he pulled her body closer to his on the couch as his mouth moved to her ear and he whispered, "I'd like to meet the guy who could silence you."

"Keep trying," she gasped as his muscular hands strayed under her shirt, his fingertips tracing little patterns all over her stomach. She slid down underneath him, sinking into the sofa cushions.

"Why haven't we been doing this all summer?" he asked.

"I know you don't want to get me started on a rhetorical question." She moved her own hands under his T-shirt, in awe of the feel of the fine muscle of him against her palms. This man had a marvelous body. She moved her hand toward his rib cage, feeling the pounding of his heart, thrilled with the idea that she had made it race that way. She squirmed a little, trying to press her body closer to his, and as she did she felt an object under the seat cushions.

"Wait a minute," she breathed. "There's something—"

"It can wait, can't it?" He had pushed both of her shirts up and was caressing her skin along the outside edge of her bra. He bent his head to kiss her along the border of the lace, and she shivered with the feel of it. Distracted, she forgot about whatever it was until she felt the lump under her back again.

"Hang on. I think Ambrose must have buried a bone in here, although it feels more like—" She latched onto the object and held it up. "A condom box." She looked at it again. Color fading, letters bleeding, tooth marks all over it, and…empty. Most definitely empty. Ambrose, who had been lying on the other side of the room, suddenly bolted for the kitchen.

"It's a long story," Keller said, looking a little sheepish.

She made a decision. "I don't have time for a long story," she said. "Do you have any left?"

He kissed her again, then stood, taking her by the hand and pulling her up with him. "All of them."

She followed his lead up the stairs, then bumped into him as he hesitated on the landing. "I'm trying to decide between the bed and the bathtub," he said.

"I had no idea that you had that fantasy, too," she said. She leaned against the wall next to the bedroom, pulling him close to her. His hands encircled her waist, and then his mouth was on hers, needy and starved. She bit at his lips slightly as he moved to pull her two shirts off.

"I've had that fantasy since the minute you asked me if I had a claw-foot tub," he said. He moved to unsnap her khaki shorts, and she popped open the button on his jeans, wanting to touch him, wanting to be as close as possible. When he tugged her shorts off, brushing her slightly with his hand, she sank down on the hardwood floor, pulling him with her.

He stripped his T-shirt off, and her hands went immediately to his chest, stroking the line of muscle down his stomach. She pushed him back on the floor a little, and moved her face along his chest, her mouth caressing his nipple, then his stomach, down to the top of his unbuttoned jeans.

"Maddie," he gasped, as she tugged his jeans from his hips and he yanked them off the rest of the way.

She stretched out on top of him as he moved quickly to unfasten her bra. She watched his face fill with need and want as he took in the sight of her. As his hand cupped her breast, and he raised up to take her nipple in his mouth, she reached to touch him and felt him move beneath her hand.

"Okay," he said, his voice ragged. "This is definitely how teenagers get into trouble."

"Are they in your bedroom or the bathroom?" She raised up and as she did, she straddled him, rocking a little against him.

"The bedroom," he said. "They're in the bedroom."

"I don't think we're going to make it to the tub this time," she said, standing and walking the few steps through the bedroom doorway. She sat down on the bed, enjoying the sight of him as he fumbled in a bedside drawer. She slipped her underwear off, kicking it to the floor. As he turned to her, she scooted up on the bed, then pulled off his briefs.

He pulled her toward him, and his hand moved between them, touching her. She cried out slightly, and she moved under his hand as he lowered his mouth to her neck and her breast. He took his hand away, and she arched against him, looking for him. Then she felt him fumble with the condom, and suddenly he really was inside her, filling her beyond belief. He moved so that she was on top of him and he was rocking with her, the two of them in a rhythm that was as natural as it was uncontrollable. Just as she felt as though she simply couldn't bear this much pleasure, she exploded in fulfillment, then felt him shudder and grow still inside her.

They lay there together for a few moments, as she sank her face into his chest and he stroked her sweat-damp hair.

"I wish you could stay," he whispered.

Did he mean tonight? Did he mean forever? She didn't want to spoil this moment by asking. Instead, she said, "Well, now that I'm here, there's no way I'm going to miss out on the tub." She kissed him. "You never did tell me your fantasies about that."

"You first," he said.

"Okay." She disentangled herself from him, then stretched out on the still-made bed. Moving her hand to his chest bone, she said, "I think about running the tub full of hot water. You lower yourself into the water, then I step in, too. I lean back against you, and I feel you grow hard under me." She stroked his thigh as she spoke. "I turn around, move on top of you, then you slip inside me."

"That's it. Come on." He rolled toward the edge of the bed, stood up and motioned for her to follow.

"Where are we going?"

"The tub," he said, grabbing a packet from his bedside drawer. She caught up with him and he kissed her, his hands pulling through the tangles of her hair. "Maddie, I've never appreciated this talent of yours the way I should have, but never, never stop talking again."

She kissed him, savoring the softness of his lips and the tangy taste of him. "I thought you'd never ask."

"It's GONE," Maddie said.

"What are you talking about? What's gone?" Maddie had left the bed, and the house, just before dawn. Keller had tried to talk her into staying, but she said she didn't want to run into the work crew. It was almost ten, though, and Little Tom and the other men hadn't shown up yet. Keller paced around the kitchen, cordless phone in hand, feeling oddly unsettled at hearing Maddie's voice but not having her close to him.

"You've never called me before," he said suddenly.

"No, normally I just walk into your house uninvited. Keller, listen to me. The manuscript is gone. I left it in my room last night but when I woke up this morning, it was missing."

He walked into the living room, unable to settle down, and began idly opening and closing drawers in the battered corner desk. "Did you see it when you got in?"

"I didn't look. I didn't want to turn the light on so I just tripped over the cat and crawled into bed."

"I wish you'd stayed," he said. "I would have liked to have woken up with you."

There was a silence on the line. Maddie? Silence? Finally she said, "I hope Little Tom and company aren't hanging on your every word."

"They're not here yet. I don't know what happened to them. Why don't you come over? We can have a picnic. An indoor picnic, so there won't be any ants or bugs or odd species of afternoon mosquitoes."

"I can't," she said, sounding a little bit distant. "I've got some packing to do here."

They said goodbye, but the phone trilled again within a couple of minutes, and Keller snatched it up. "Maddie?"

"It was in my car," she said dully. "I glanced into it on my way into Lucy's and it was just sitting there in the front seat."

"So you left it in the car last night?"

"No, I didn't leave it in the car," she snapped. "I didn't have it in the car. I know I didn't take it with me to your house or back again this morning—don't you think I would have noticed it?"

"How did things go last night?" he asked her.

"Oh, I don't know. How about, the whole town's sick to their stomachs today? That's where your work crew is. I appreciate that Connie wants me to stay, but I don't think he had to resort to biological warfare."

"Other than that, Mrs. Lincoln, how was the play?" he heard Connie shout from a distance, and he realized that Maddie must not be alone.

"Look, if I don't see you today, I'll see you tonight at Lucy's for sure, right?"

"If government agents don't swoop down and close the place, I guess so." She paused. "You're avoiding the whole issue of how this manuscript got in my car, aren't you?"

"Maddie, I just don't see why someone would break into your apartment, steal an old manuscript, then bring it back."

"Yeah, I know. If they wanted something to read that badly, they could have just gone to the library, where John Grisham would have been a more likely choice than Lucas Keller. I've already heard it from Connie. I'll talk to you later."

He needed to see her. He needed to show her that last night wasn't a fluke or a mistake. He didn't know what he would say when he got into town, but he was filled with an almost physical ache to be near her. But she sounded like she had enough going on this morning without being bothered by his insecurity and his selfish needs. So should he go or not go? He took another aimless walk through the house, trying to decide. Ambrose tired of watching him and went to hide under the bed.

Why did Keller feel so restless here today? Out of all the spirits who ought to be haunting this house, he knew there was only one that he was ever going to truly notice. Maddie. She belonged to this house and she always would. He was trying to figure out how to tell her that when Ambrose came running down the stairs, barking wildly.

"The ghost of Lucas Keller get you?" Keller asked him, but then he heard a knock on the door. He'd been so preoccupied with thoughts of Maddie that he hadn't even heard anyone drive up. He knew it wouldn't be Maddie but hoped that by some miracle it was.

It wasn't. Keller stared at the man on his porch. His blond hair was thinning a little on top—blond men always went bald, but tell that to the women who fawned over them—and his eyes were kind of a flat noncolor. He wore the same thing Keller had on—khakis and a polo, his minus the bleach stains, but his outfit was topped off by a blue sweater tied around his shoulders. Keller knew his type instantly—the broker who slapped everyone else too hard on the back when he lost his clients' money, the frat brother who was only in the house because his legacy went back to the pilgrims. The kind of guy you would feel sorry for if he weren't such a jerk.

"Jeff Alvin," the man said, extending his hand.

"Of course you are," Keller said, grasping it only so he could judge the shake. Fishy, of course. Why hadn't he figured out that Maddie, who had turned belittling herself into an art form, would be involved with one of these Mr. Superior types?

"May I come in?" Jeff said, stepping through the door. "I don't know if you've heard of me. I'm a professor at the university in Knoxville, and your great-grandfather is one of my specialties. I didn't realize he had any descendants, but one of the town's residents got in touch with me and told me you might have some of his letters and other odds and ends. Maybe a manuscript?"

"What resident?" He knew in his heart that it couldn't be Maddie.

"I wouldn't like to say."

He wanted to wipe that smug little smile right off

the man's face. "If it brought you to my doorstep, I'd like to know."

"Edith Miller," he said, sighing impatiently. "She was here when I was in Ravens Gap previously, but I didn't get to know her. She contacted me by e-mail recently. I'm operating under a limited grant so I can only offer you a token amount of money for the documents, but I'm sure your interest is in having them in a safe place."

"How did you get interested in Lucas?" Keller asked. "He's kind of a has-been, isn't he?"

Hands in his pockets, struggling visibly for an answer, Jeff Alvin looked completely out of place in the old farmhouse. He wouldn't understand anything about Lucas, Keller realized. Not the sensitive mountain poet or the bitter old man who was too proud to make up with his son.

"Well, I've always had an interest in Appalachian work," he began. "And then someone—Madelaine Randall, I believe you know her—brought him to my attention."

"She did all the upfront research on him, didn't she? Or am I not remembering this right?"

He pursed his lips a little. "I'm not sure what she's told you, but Maddie is a wonderful, imaginative thinker. Not a very disciplined scholar, though, and not someone who always understands the nuances of this work."

"Like why it's necessary to sneak into someone's apartment and 'borrow' a manuscript for the night?" Maddie, waving a large stack of papers, slammed the door behind her, and both Jeff and Keller started at the sound. Her pale skin was glowing with a reddish, angry cast, and her hair was on fire from the light filtering in through the window. Keller thought she had never looked more beautiful, more vibrant or more fascinating to him.

"Don't you knock?" Jeff dropped the smooth professional manner for a peevish whine.

"She doesn't have to knock," Keller said. "She's free to come and go as she pleases here."

"It's a photocopy," she said, handing it to Keller. He held the uncreased pages and flipped through them, seeing that she was right. "I found it in his room at Mrs. Martin's." She turned to Jeff and widened her eyes at him. "You know, she really ought to have better security during the day, when she's never home."

"Don't be ridiculous," Jeff said, but he paled, and there were tight lines around his mouth. "You didn't find a photocopy of a manuscript in my room." He spoke to Keller. "She's so delusional she probably had it copied herself."

"She is not delusional," Keller said, but both Maddie and Ambrose looked at him with something like pity.

"Keller, you're sweet," Maddie said. "But Jeff knows me and he definitely thinks I'm delusional. That's not an argument you're going to win."

Keller, sullenly stuck on the implications of "Jeff knows me," didn't say anything. Maddie continued, "However, anyone who knows me also knows how unlikely it is that I would get out in the middle of the night and drive to a copy shop in Asheville just to prove a point. I'm lazier than I am vengeful, don't you think?"

She seemed to expect some sort of response from

Keller, who thought carefully before saying, "You're not that lazy."

Damn. Wrong answer. In response to her look, he said, "But you're definitely too lazy to drive to Asheville in the middle of the night and have that copied."

"Thank you," Maddie said. "But Jeff was not only enterprising enough to head for the copy shop in Asheville, he had enough energy left to be incredibly rude to the clerk who was working there." She turned to Jeff. "She remembers you very well and she described you exactly, right down to every little wisp on your wispy head."

Keller watched Jeff struggle not to raise his hand to smooth the hair on his balding head, and for a second he almost felt sorry for the guy. But then Jeff turned to Maddie and said, "I hope your twisted fantasy life affords you some measure of fun, because your life is going to be one dismal slide downhill. You're flighty, and you're careless, and you're undisciplined."

Keller hadn't been in a fistfight in years, but he was ready to yank the guy up by his collar. Before he could come to Maddie's defense, though, she said simply, "But I'm free. And you're not."

Jeff dug a card out of his pocket and tried to hand it to Keller. "Call me if you change your mind about letting me see the manuscript."

"Oh, you went to so much trouble to have it copied that, if it's okay with Keller, I think you should take it."

Keller, not sure what she was up to, refused Jeff's business card and turned to Maddie. "You don't think you should be credited with this discovery?"

"No. If Lucas had asked me—which he didn't."

She said that last part a little loudly, looking toward the ceiling as she spoke. No doubt Jeff didn't know what she was talking about, but Keller grinned. "I would have said not to publish this book, but he submitted it to his publisher more than once, so obviously he thought differently. But as far as being credited with the rediscovery of Lucas Keller, my ego isn't invested in it the way Jeff's is, and I'm glad. I love his other books and I appreciate the things that happened in my life because I went looking for him." She handed the stack of papers to Jeff. "To me, that's much better than having to pretend I like him because I have a fancy condo and a big car and a sense of overimportance to worry about."

"Yes, being a waitress is definitely better than all those things," Jeff said. He was holding the manuscript tentatively. No doubt he had a hard time believing that Maddie was really going to let him walk out of here with it.

"That's not what I'm saying. I know there's nothing more noble about waitressing than there is about what you do, as long as you're doing what you do for the right reasons. But you're not. To you, Lucas Keller is still a hillbilly, although now he's one you have to pretend to like. You're a fake and a phony, and because you are, I know things won't work out for you in the long run."

Those tight lines were still on Jeff Alvin's face. "I had forgotten how annoying your New Age drivel could be," he said. He turned back to Keller. "Thank you for the opportunity to review the manuscript. I'll be in touch with you."

Hope not, Keller was about to say, but as Jeff turned, Ambrose growled and lunged past him. He didn't try to bite the man, didn't even come anywhere near him, but it startled Jeff so much that he skidded into the desk, knocking a drawer out with his knee and spilling the contents.

"Are you okay?" Maddie said. She moved quickly to his side, too quickly for Keller's taste, but then passed him by to collect the drawer's contents while Jeff struggled up by himself. She stared at one envelope for a long time before picking it up and tucking it into her skirt pocket. With a curt nod to Keller, Jeff started out the door.

"I should sue you over your mutt, but Maddie is right. I admit that I did take that manuscript and copy it. So perhaps there is a little karmic justice after all, Maddie."

She looked at him blankly. "If you think a bumped knee cancels out all the damage you've done in this world, then you have a lot to learn about karma." She unceremoniously slammed the door after him, then took out the letter she'd tucked into her skirt. She handed it to Keller.

"And I think you have something to learn about your great-grandfather." She grinned. "I imagine he's working pretty hard on his karma right now, too."

He turned the envelope over in his hands—yellowed, stiff but graced with Lucas Keller's now-familiar handwriting. It was addressed to Michael Keller, Keller's grandfather and Lucas's son. The envelope was sealed, but the address was incomplete, and there was no stamp. He was hedging his bets, Keller thought, turning it over in his hands again.

"I'd better head back to work," Maddie said. "I want to leave you alone with that, and things are still in a bit of disarray at Lucy's. Plus, I was rolling pie crust when all this hit me.''

"All this?'' He still hadn't opened the letter.

"The cream-colored sedan, the fact that no one had seen Mrs. Martin's new boarder and that it was Miss Miller's family Lucas trashed, so she wouldn't mind helping someone with a biography if she thought it might throw a little dirt on Lucas. I left what I was doing and ran over there.''

"And he wasn't there, so you just went in?''

"I know you think I have a breaking-and-entering habit, but I swear to you, once I leave Ravens Gap I'll be a model citizen.''

Once she left Ravens Gap. He couldn't think about it. "What are you going to do?'' Keller asked. "You aren't still in love with Jeff Alvin.'' It wasn't a question. He knew Maddie well enough to be able to read her feelings, and that hadn't been love she felt for Jeff Alvin.

"That was never an issue,'' she said. "You only thought it was.'' She smiled a little sadly. "At the risk of tempting the universe, I think I'm walking out of town a lot smarter than I came into it. Although somewhere down the road I'm sure I'll have to pay for that sanctimonious speech I laid on Jeff. I sounded like Dorothy when she wakes up from her coma in Kansas.'' She squinted a little at Keller. "Have you noticed how when she comes back from Oz she suddenly has all the answers, but what she learns is pretty mundane? Don't look out of your backyard for happiness. Don't wish for the rainbow when you've got a sweet little setup right here? I'm not sure that's supposed to be the moral, and I've only just touched on the formal criticism— What?''

He realized he was smiling. "I've missed that side of you."

"Babbling Maddie?"

"Babbling Maddie," he said. "Maybe she'll make an appearance at Lucy's tonight."

"Using her talents to explain to the angry mob how the pie crust wound up with the consistency of cement? I'm sure it will be quite a show."

He wanted to touch her, to hold her, but before he could reach out for her, she had slipped through the door and was down the porch. He listened to the car start, then slowly opened the letter, taking himself decades back to what was probably the first and last time his great-grandfather had ever admitted he had been wrong.

When he had finished, he sat there for a long time, then picked up the phone to call Lucy, counting on Maddie being too busy to answer. "Lucy? Keller. Can you meet me at the Hardees in Bryson City? I've got something I want to talk to you about."

"EVERY SMALL TOWN has a woman who's pined away all her life for some man, but in the meantime she keeps busy with the church and her business and other people's kids, and before she knows it, fifty years have passed and the whole town turns out for her funeral. It's an honorable life."

Maddie pulled the bourbon pecan pie out of the oven. "I take it this is a recommendation?" she asked Connie.

"No, that's just your worst case scenario. I was trying to demonstrate that even in your worst case scenario, you get some perks."

"And you were so convincing," Maddie said. "I

don't know why the Spinsters' Union hasn't just snatched you right up as their spokesperson.''

Connie frowned but continued. ''Now, you also have your best case scenario. You sit around waiting for the man to come to his senses, and one day that old marriage clock goes off, and he wanders around trying to find somebody to marry. He sees you, and there you are.''

''What's the marriage clock?'' As long as she kept talking to Connie, Maddie thought she might stay so annoyed and argumentative that she could forget that tonight was her last night here. She looked around the diner. Lucy had run out to do some errands, but Connie was there, testing out tonight's pie. Little Tom and his dad were eating early, along with Mel and Sid. Their color was a little off, but Maddie had fixed them some chicken noodle soup and they swore they were feeling better already. There were a few other brave souls who had come in, seen Maddie and put the word out that she was back. It was going to be a busy night, Maddie thought. All the better.

''The marriage clock,'' Connie began, but Little Tom looked up from his soup and gestured for him to keep his voice down.

''Cindi's back there in the kitchen practicing pie crusts. Try to keep her from hearing about it.''

''The marriage clock,'' Connie began again, this time more quietly, ''goes off at some point in a man's life, whether he's eighteen or forty—mileage varies— and says, I've taken care of other things. I guess I should find a mate.''

She looked at him suspiciously, then leaned against the counter. ''Taken care of other things? What do you mean?''

"Well, a man can't concentrate on two things at once. Not like a woman. So if he's too concerned with career or money—"

"Or playoff season," Little Tom interjected. "The Bulls were losing once when Cindi and I were dating. Almost didn't notice she'd left me till they had the championship sewn up."

"Your transmission might be having trouble," Sid said.

"Or you could be having one of those where-am-I, who-am-I, why-marry-when-we-all-return-to-dust kind of moments," Mel said. They all looked at him. Finally Maddie spoke.

"An existential crisis?" she suggested.

"That's it," Mel said, nodding. "That's what Keller's having."

"I don't have time for him to have an existential crisis," she said, knowing she was telling them more than she wanted to, but also knowing it was no secret how she felt about Keller. "I can't wait around for someone who might one day look at me and love me, or who might just as easily be at the supermarket the day his marriage clock goes off. He could fall in love with some blonde in the avocados, and I would still be here, in his town, parading my broken heart around. This is his home. It's not mine. It would be presumptuous of me to stay."

"I've never known you to mind being presumptuous. That's one of the things I love about you. That you drag people into your plans whether they're ready or not." At the sound of Keller's voice, Maddie looked up to see him walking through the doorway. Behind him came two deliverymen carrying a tall, round, department store clothes rack, crammed with plaid and polyester jackets. Lucy, trailing behind them, tipped them as they left.

Maddie gaped at Keller.

"This is what you were talking about, right?" At her nod, he said, "I know it's a little big for the restaurant, but I couldn't really see fitting it into the house, either. When we expand here, we'll use it as a coat check."

"When we expand?"

"I've sold the place to Keller," Lucy said. "Connie told him I was unhappy running it, and he called me today to tell me life's too short not to do what you love. I'm going to Asheville to start college. I think I want to be a high school journalism teacher."

"I bought it because I figured I'm never going to have a kitchen," Keller told her, as Little Tom and company conspicuously looked the other way. "You can run the restaurant if you want, but if you don't, you don't." She stood, still gawking at him, while he seemed to notice that the whole restaurant was staring at him. "Do you want to try this?" He extended his hand to her, and she took it, as they ducked beneath the coats into the darkness, sitting down cross-legged on the floor.

"He bought up every coat in the Goodwill, then made them sell him the rack," she heard Lucy tell the crowd at large. Ambrose nuzzled his way into the cocoon with them, and Keller pushed him back out gently.

"You don't have to be the chef if you don't want to. I don't care what you do, as long as it makes you happy. I just want you to stay. Will you marry me?"

"Somebody's clock just went off in a big way," Connie muttered, but Keller and Maddie ignored him.

Keller rushed on before Maddie could answer. "I read the letter, and you were right, it was a huge apology from Lucas to my grandfather. The thing is, it was dated five years before he died, so he had time to make up, but maybe it didn't fit some timetable of his own. I don't want to be like that. I don't want to be so scheduled and organized and by-the-book that I miss out on something wonderful, just because it was unexpected."

She started to speak, but he kept on. "And I came to tell you that I've been thinking about this Dorothy thing, and whether the lesson was really so simple as you thought. I don't think it's about being satisfied with what you have. I think it's about finding the magic in the ordinary. Like all the stuff I love about you that would never have been on my top-ten list of qualities to look for in a wife."

He paused, and in the cozy darkness Maddie could sense him looking at her expectantly. "Like what?" she asked.

"Like the way you chop a pepper or roll out a pie crust, or take ten minutes to sit down and have a serious conversation with a dog and actually expect him to notice, or the way you get me wondering what it's like to sit under some used coats somewhere—"

"Keller Michael Lowry," Maddie said. "And believe me when I say I mean this in the nicest possible way. Shut up. I love you more than I ever thought anyone could love anyone else. Of course I'll marry you." She kissed him there in the darkness, as they heard a collective "aw" from the restaurant.

"My middle name is Elizabeth," she said when they stopped kissing. "Just so we don't start off on unequal ground."

"I think we'll always be on unequal ground," Keller said. "But I'm going to do my damndest to keep up."

"I know you hate to hear this, but I owe your great-grandfather a big one."

"He owed my grandfather," Keller said. "I think he tried to make it up to him by sending you to me." Before she could respond, he continued, "That's the last time you'll hear any of that kind of thing from me. At least one partner needs to be the skeptical type."

As he finished saying it, the jukebox came to life, and the café was suddenly filled with the sounds of Elvis singing "Blue Christmas." They stared at each other, then crawled out from under the coat rack, hand in hand.

"This is our song," Maddie told everyone assembled.

"But you didn't meet at Christmas," Lucy said, as Keller took Maddie in his arms and they began, slowly, to dance.

"We just wanted to nail down a song before the holidays were upon us," Maddie said.

Little Tom retrieved Cindi from the kitchen and took the tiny woman in his arms. Lucy was dancing with Connie. Maddie looked over at Sid and Mel, Sid looking fretful, Mel white-faced.

"I'm not dancing with him," Sid said.

"I don't think he's in any shape to dance," Keller said. "What's wrong?"

"No one put a quarter in that jukebox."

"Power surge," Connie said, humming.

"But," Mel lowered his voice ominously. "That song has never been on the jukebox."

"I had it slipped on there," Keller said. "A couple of days ago."

"Thank goodness," Mel said, color filling his face again. He got up and helped himself to some pie. "It's—"

"A fear of yours," Keller and Maddie finished as Mel nodded. When he turned back to the pie, Maddie whispered, "Did you?"

"No," Keller said. "Did you?"

"No. You're going to need to tell your great-grandfather not to mess with Mel. He's going to be a great cook, and I can't afford to have the family ghost scaring off the help."

"You'd better talk to him," Keller said. "I think he likes you best."

She held him tightly as the song wound down, then kicked on again. Ambrose growled, and Maddie watched, her head on Keller's shoulder, as the wind caught the screen door, opening it, then closing it again.

Epilogue

Books of the Season
Alvin's Lucas Keller Bio Disappoints

Traveling Home, Madelaine Randall Lowry's whimsical story of how a long-forgotten novelist helped her find true love and true happiness is still a runaway bestseller in hardcover. Thanks to interest generated by the book, publishers have rushed Lucas Keller's work back into print, and the time seems right for a biography of the author. *Hillbilly Bard,* by Dr. Jeffrey Alvin, disappoints on every level. There is no indication that Alvin has ever really read the author, much less understood his works. As if to make up for his lack of insight, Alvin claims to have once had access to an unknown manuscript by Lucas Keller, one he refers to often in the bio. Where is this manuscript? It seems it mysteriously flew out his car window while he was driving across the North Carolina-Tennessee border. It may be the first time "a ghost stole my homework" has been used as an excuse for poor scholarship. Let's hope it's the last.

Asheville Happenings
Author/Chef and Family Celebrate Success

Is Lucy's Diner worth the twisty, winding drive to out-of-the-way Ravens Gap? Do you have to ask? Co-owner Keller Lowry proudly confided to us that tourists from as far away as Vancouver, that's the *other* side of Canada, folks, have hit Lucy's to sample the to-die-for cooking of his wife, co-owner Madelaine Randall Lowry, her executive chef (Mr.) Connie Turner, and assistant chef Melvin Bird. Of course cooking isn't the only thing Maddie and Connie do well—Maddie's book, *Traveling Home,* has spent fifty-two weeks on the *New York Times* bestseller list. Connie Turner's charming watercolor illustrations add to the appeal of this wonderful story.

If you go to Lucy's, Maddie and Connie will sign copies of the book, but only, Maddie warns, if there's nothing burning in the kitchen. When they aren't at Lucy's, Maddie and Keller (founder of a software venture) are at Keller's family home in Ravens Gap with their twin toddlers, Michael and Constance, their dog, Ambrose, and an infrequently seen black barn cat named Luke.

HARLEQUIN
Duets ™

Fabulous Fall Fiesta!

Harlequin Duets™ has got something
really special planned this fall to thank
you for trying our new series!
You won't want to miss it!
Beep beep!

Watch for details in all
Harlequin Duets™ books,
starting next month.

HARLEQUIN®
Makes any time special.™

If you enjoyed what you just read,
then we've got an offer you can't resist!

Take 2 bestselling
love stories FREE!
Plus get a FREE surprise gift!

Do the Harlequin Duets™ Dating Quiz!

1) My ideal date would be:
a) a candlelight dinner at the most exclusive restaurant in town
b) dinner made by him even if it is burnt macaroni and cheese
c) a dinner made lovingly by me—to which he brings his mother and two ex-wives

2) If a woman came on to my ideal man, he would:
a) flirt back a little, but make it clear he's already taken
b) tell her to go away
c) bail me out of jail

3) The ideal setting for the perfect date would be:
a) a luxurious ocean resort with white sand, palm trees, picture-perfect sunsets
b) a desert island with just him and a few million mosquitoes
c) a stateroom on the *Titanic*

4) In his free time, my ideal man would most often choose to:
a) Watch sports on TV
b) Watch sports on TV
c) Watch sports on TV *(let's not kid ourselves, even ideal men will be men!)*

If you chose A most often: You are wonderful, talented and sexy. A near goddess, in fact, who will make beautiful music with just about any man you want. The only thing that could make you more perfect is reading Harlequin Duets™.

If you chose B most often: Others are jealous of your charm, wit, intelligence, good fashion sense and ability to eat whatever you want without gaining a pound. The only workout you need is a good evening with Harlequin Duets™.

If you chose C most often: Don't worry. Harlequin Duets™ to the rescue!

Experience the lighter side of love with Harlequin Duets™!

HARLEQUIN®
Makes any time special.™